Daughter of
the Northern Fields

Pamela Haines was born in Yorkshire. She was educated at a convent in the Midlands, and then read English at Cambridge. As a child she wrote prolifically but she did not take up writing as an adult until her late thirties, by which time she was married with five children. In 1971 she won the *Spectator* New Writing Prize with a short story and in 1973 completed her first novel, *Tea at Gunter's*. Acclaimed by the critics, it was joint winner of the first Yorkshire Arts Association Award for Young Writers. It was followed by *A Kind of War* in 1976, *Men On White Horses* in 1978, *The Kissing Gate* in 1981, *The Diamond Waterfall* in 1984 and *The Golden Lion* in 1986.

PAMELA HAINES

Daughter of
the Northern Fields

This edition published 1995 by
Diamond Books
77–85 Fulham Palace Road
Hammersmith, London W6 8JB

First published by HarperCollins*Publishers* Ltd 1987
First issued in Fontana Paperbacks 1988

Copyright © Bluestar Productions Ltd 1987

The Author asserts the moral right
to be identified as the author of this work

ISBN 0 261 66718 1

Printed in Great Britain

For Lucy, as promised

CONTENTS

ACKNOWLEDGEMENTS

Thank you to the many people who helped me with this book, especially Elizabeth Armstrong (née Ogden), whose grandmother was taught by Charlotte Brontë, for her family memories; Dr Juliet Barker, curator and librarian, and Sally Johnson, assistant librarian, Brontë Parsonage Museum; Dr Alan Betteridge, district archivist, Derek Bridge, reference librarian, and Dorothy Nutter, assistant reference librarian, Calderdale Libraries; Helen Gledhill, senior assistant, Sowerby Bridge branch library; Hector Pagan, formerly of Wooler and Co., solicitors, Leeds; and, as always, Tony Haines.

FOREWORD

1948 was the centenary of Branwell Brontë's death. In the September of that year my father took me to a meeting of the Brontë Society. I was about to take Cambridge Entrance in English Literature and the Brontë works were one of my special subjects.

At that time my father, Harry Burrows, was senior partner in Wooler and Co., a Leeds firm of solicitors with an office in Park Square. He had taken over from my grandfather, Benjamin Burrows, whose partnership with Ernest Wooler had been dissolved in the early 1930s. Ernest Wooler was a collateral descendant of the Miss Wooler whose school at Roe Head Charlotte Brontë attended, and at which she later taught. Miss Wooler became a close friend of Charlotte's and it was she who gave Charlotte away at her wedding to Arthur Nicholls.

The talk was: 'Branwell Brontë and the authorship of *Wuthering Heights*'. There was a good sized audience. Seated two rows ahead of us was a very small, white-haired man who, as soon as the talk began, pulled a sheaf of blank papers from each of his jacket pockets. He immediately began shuffling them noisily, so that several people looked over at him. Then he brought out a fountain pen, but had trouble with it. The ink wouldn't flow. In the end I saw a large blob go on to the knee of his trousers. All in all he caused great distraction and, although he settled down after a while, he kept sighing and muttering to himself.

He did not stay for the tea and biscuits after, but left immediately the talk had finished and before question time, cramming the papers back into his pockets with as much rustling as he'd taken them out. There was a general feeling of relief when he had gone. I did not think of him again. Then one evening that December my father returned home and asked me, did I remember 'that old chap who was such a nuisance at the Brontë Society talk'? It appeared he had turned up in Park Square that afternoon, carrying a large sealed brown-paper parcel.

'It was definitely the same chap,' my father said. 'He asked me if it was true that Wooler and Co. had connections with the Miss Wooler of Roe Head, and when I told him yes, he asked me if the firm would look after his parcel. It wasn't to be opened till 1986, which would be the centenary of his mother's death.'

And that was all. We discussed the mystery a bit, but since the old man had said so little we did not get far. The box went into the strongroom of Wooler and Co., then later when that room became too full, into the vaults of Barclays Bank in Park Row. Over the years I forgot about the incident. Meanwhile, in 1969 Wooler and Co. amalgamated with the much larger Leeds firm of Dibb Lupton. My father stayed there till his retirement in 1975. He died in 1978.

A few months ago I was surprised to hear from Dibb Lupton that Barclays had been in touch with them *re* a certain package, to be opened in 1986. The instructions inside the first wrapping were that the contents were to go, unopened, to the senior partner of Wooler and Co., or if deceased, to his eldest child.

And so I acquired the package. Inside were three exercise books, a small oilskin packet and a manuscript. The exercise books contain about thirty thousand words; the manuscript, very much larger, is an autobiography. They are written in different hands.

These items, unaltered (except for the dividing up of the autobiography into parts and chapters), form the contents of this book.

London, August 1986   Pamela Haines

PART ONE

Luddenden

1

The doll sat up by the hearth, parcels stacked all around her. Feet in silver slippers peeped from beneath her silk and lace frock; her wax hands were outspread, her rosebud mouth slightly parted. Long flaxen hair, so unlike my own (hated) thick red, curled to her shoulders.

And she was mine. Mine, mine, mine. All mine that Christmas of 1848. A birthday gift too, for my sixth birthday was on Christmas Eve. I had had to wait all through yesterday. It was the same each year: that my birthday must run into Christmas. A joint celebration, with special attention to me: extra presents, a cake iced with my name. And how I hated it, how I resented having no day of my own.

It was not so for my brothers and sisters . . . And here they come – to receive *their* presents. They don't seem to have any the less. Halliwell, who is almost five and very sturdy, has a box of toy soldiers. Then little Agnes, three in October, with my mother's dark colouring and the Woodward shaped head, for her there is a stack of picture bricks. When she sees the bright colours she gives a squeal of delight, pulling away at once from Betty, the nurse's, restraining hand.

And lastly Joshua, little Josh, held in Betty's other arm. Twenty-two months and so plump – already larger than Agnes (just as Halliwell is already taller than me). From the sleeves of his smocked, tartan Christmas frock, ten fat fingers reach out to grab at a wooden duck, painted blue.

So many people here today. The Woodward family, and Papa's sister, Aunt Martha Lumsden, widow of Uncle Eli, come over for the day from Halifax. His mother, stout fearsome Grandma Woodward, who has taken a chill, but not so severe she cannot leave her room.

And then my aunt and uncle Armstrong, on my mother's side: Uncle Sutcliffe and Aunt Flora (I do not like Aunt Flora). Their children, Theophilus – or Phil as we know him – and little Meg.

We children are all busy with our gifts. Phil and Meg had theirs first because they are guests. Already they are squabbling over

15

a picture book, Meg turning the pages too quickly. The grown-ups talk amongst themselves. Beside me, Papa talks to Uncle Sutcliffe.

'You saw in yesterday's *Guardian*? Another death at the Parsonage.'

'Who'll that be? The old man?'

'No,' Papa says, 'another of the young ones. Emily.'

'Followed soon on Branwell, didn't she, eh?'

Papa says, 'She never came this way, didn't Emily. Never came visiting her brother . . .'

'Well, they say deaths often come in pairs . . . Do you mind when old Ackroyd went? And then his lad – drowned the next week.'

The other side of the room, my mother has Joshua on her knee now. She plays with his fingers, while Grandma Woodward speaks to her. I think Grandma is criticizing her.

Grandma Woodward is very large and very square. Her face is like a box which I do not wish to open. Square chin, square nose and eyebrows in a straight line. She has a grey moustache and pouchy cheeks. Her lips are permanently pursed. I do not like her, but I am not afraid of her, as some people are. My mother perhaps?

But today I have eyes only for the wax doll. She is to be called Victoria. I decided that some months ago. Victoria, our Queen. And the name too of her little daughter. *Victoria.*

Beside me, Uncle Sutcliffe and Papa are talking. Mama's brother, Sutcliffe, with his great tall frame, his drooping whiskers and down-turned eyebrows. Shaggy and gentle, he does whatever Aunt Flora directs.

Now there are squeals of excitement from Joshua. Halliwell marching his soldiers, and imitating the boom of cannon fire. Phil shrieking. Aunt Martha looking disapproving. Grandma Woodward tut-tutting. My father, who is not afraid of his mother, lifts a warning finger and then laughs. My mother declares that of course the noise is fearful. She apologizes to Grandma Woodward.

But now suddenly it is I, Christabel, making the noise. Because Agnes, who has tired of her bricks, snatches Victoria, thrusting up her skirts rudely, pulling her flaxen hair. So I hit Agnes on the head, very hard. She gives a shriek, and I hit her again. Not because I wish to hurt, but because she is hurting Victoria. And then suddenly I feel a blow on my cheek, stinging.

16

'No, you don't, little lass,' says my father.

And then the sharp voice of Aunt Martha: 'Why, the little firebrand! Whatever . . .'

Then Papa again: 'Let that be a lesson to you, little lass . . . Nay, Christabel, Christabel. Give over.'

I am crying with pain and indignity. They are all looking at me. My cheek hurts and my head hurts. I shall run from the room, not because I have done wrong, but because Papa who gave me Victoria, Papa whom I love so dearly (and Mama, how I love Mama too), Papa is angry with me.

I was a seven months' child – and my father's darling. Did I know that, or did someone tell me? Did I overhear? I was always eavesdropping . . . I was his darling, just as he was mine. There I would be, sitting on his knee, my arms round his neck, as he jogged me perhaps, or as I played with his hair, pulled at his ears. There I would be, in his snug, while standing opposite might be Benjamin Mason perhaps, overlooker at our mill, or Uncle Sutcliffe. Yes, I would be allowed there while they talked business. Talk of the mill. That language was as everyday to me as household talk, the talk of the servants, of Betty the nurse, of my mother.

I was the first born, you see. That was why. The first born of James and Caroline Woodward (formerly Armstrong).

Sitting on his knee in the parlour, I looked at picture books. He kept some for me in the glass-fronted bookcase, locked, to the right of the fireplace. It was only he might bring them out – only I who might look at them . . . 'And what is that, eh, little lass?' And then when I had said that it was a tiger, or a man with a beard, or a gigantic castle, he would encourage me to make a story.

'Make out about it,' he'd say, and then I'd come out with the wildest fancies. Once I'd started I couldn't stop, and then he would say, 'But that's a sorry tale. Let's have a merry one . . . Now this picture here, isn't it maybe a sailor coming back to his family –'

And indeed there would be the jolly tar, head flung back, arms wide in greeting, wife and children gathered round. But only *I* knew: one month hence he would sail again, and die in a terrible storm at sea. Only I knew he would drown in the wild seas.

And then there it would be, in confirmation, perhaps a few pages on: a ship tossing on the waves, almost submerged beneath them. I would know it was death and loss.

'Oh yes, he's dead,' I would say, 'he's certainly dead *soon*, Papa.' Then my father would become serious for a few moments, smoothing my forehead:

'What a little worrier,' he'd say. 'What a little fretter.' Then he would marvel at the size of my forehead. 'There's maybe too *much* in there . . .'

Such a high forehead. Auburn hair, small body. But then Mama was small. And although she was black-headed as was my father, there was Cousin Millie Oldroyd from Colne, formerly Wainwright, who had been a bridesmaid at my parents' wedding but not seen since. Her hair was clearly remembered as a flaming red.

'A right throwback to the Wainwrights, is Christabel. Fancy seeing that colour again . . .'

But Cousin Millie, they said, was tall and hawklike. Unlike me. 'Christabel's very small . . .' (How often I heard people say that of me. *'She's very small . . .'*)

My father was quite a reader, uncommon perhaps for someone of his background at that time. Both he and Uncle Sutcliffe were keen members of the Luddenden Reading Society, whose home, with its panelled library and many many books, was in an upstairs room of the Lord Nelson Inn. They borrowed books regularly.

'It's very interesting, what I have here,' he would say. 'It says that in Africa . . .' Or, 'This writer thinks that when Napoleon was first in Russia . . .'

Mama read too. Poetry. And tales in magazines. But she loved poetry best. She had a tooled leather notebook into which she would copy any verse that took her fancy. And another, of blue leather.

Perhaps that was why I was named after a poem. For she named me after *Christabel*, by Samuel Taylor Coleridge . . .

We were a mill-owning family. The Woodwards. As had been my mother's family, the Armstrongs; as was still my Uncle Sutcliffe. Owners of one of the many-windowed, grim and dark gritstone buildings, with their tall smoky chimneys, to be seen high up and low down in the valley, where not so long before cottagers had worked their looms in small stone cottages.

We lived in the West Riding of Yorkshire, in the small village of Luddenden, not far from the Lancashire border, and some two miles from the town of Sowerby Bridge and four miles from the larger town of Halifax: a centre of the Yorkshire wool trade.

18

A little further away were the still larger centres of Leeds and Bradford.

No dark satanic mills, these in Luddenden. They merged easily into the landscape. They did not spoil a green and pleasant land, for this was a dark, wind-scoured, russet and brown and grey vista. Surrounded by moors and fells, vast expanses which the rough-coated sheep cropped short. Below us were dark, lush, wooded valleys, damp and dripping. For me the mills had always been there.

Horsfield Mill, down in Luddenden Foot, had belonged to my maternal grandfather, Samuel Armstrong, and now was run by Uncle Sutcliffe. Their home nearby was called Buckley House. Appleyard Mill was ours. It stood on the hill above Luddenden, within easy sight of our home, Wade House, built only twenty-five years ago by my now dead grandfather, Joshua Woodward.

It was not far down into the village of Luddenden itself. Luddenden, with its twisting narrow streets. Buried in a glen, surrounded by fells. Up in those hills were traces of Roman camps, signs that the Romans had been before us. Small cobbled ways amongst the stone cottages. A steep hill leading out, up by the church. From the bottom of Luddenden, the village seemed to wind up and up, layer upon layer, houses piled crazily up behind the church, the roofs at different levels.

And almost opposite the church, an L-shaped building: the inn, once the White Swan but known since Trafalgar as the Lord Nelson. Branwell Brontë, friend of my father and Uncle Sutcliffe, had drunk there with them, borrowed books, gone out with them, visited their homes. Seven years ago now, when he had been for a while clerk-in-charge at the small railway station down at Luddenden Foot.

From our house in Stocks Lane, from the nursery window, I could see the vicarage, the other side of the road. And beyond that, looking downhill, the church. St Mary's, Luddenden, in the parish of Halifax. In the ravine between vicarage and church a stream tumbled, foaming as it rushed by to join the river Calder. Dark peaty water. That dark dank churchyard, with its poplars, its yew trees.

The churchyard frightened me. It was not just the grey lichen-covered flat tombs, or the dark aspect – but rather my fancy that it was haunted. The ghost who walked it was The Reverend Grimshaw, famous Methodist preacher and former parson of Haworth, buried eighty-five years ago now. St Mary's had been

19

rebuilt. His grave was now inside the church. But it was outside that his ghost walked. Betty, our nurse, had told me so.

I was full of fears. And who should wonder, I think now, when I remember the tales Betty told us? Tales of the 'fairishes' down in the hollow – or 'bottom' as we called it – or sightings of the gytrash: a terrifying black dog of bad portent. But worst of all to me seemed her tales of the graveyard – and William Grimshaw.

St Mary's. We were there every Sunday in the Woodward pew. Three rows behind was the Armstrong pew. Our parson had been old and white-haired. Mr Bickerstaffe – very bent, with a shuffling gait and a shaking hand. His voice had grown faint. This winter, with the coming of the cold weather, he had died. Now we had a new parson: The Reverend Francis Hume. It was said that he was quite rich – or rather, that his wife was. Also, that he was a great scholar. Greek and Latin. 'An Oxford man,' Papa told Uncle Sutcliffe. 'They say he's fully the equal in learning of Mr Brontë over at Haworth.' Mr Brontë, Papa told me, had published several books. Poems, moral tales.

Mr Hume was quite other than Mr Bickerstaffe. His hair was dark to Mr Bickerstaffe's white, his manner vigorous and lively. His wife, on the other hand, was not at all lively. She was rumoured to be in very poor health, and certainly looked it. Unlike her husband she had little colour. Her head drooped on a long neck. She looked almost too fragile to walk.

His first Sunday, when he waited to meet us coming out of church, Mr Hume had noticed me. Greeting Mama and Papa, he asked:

'Is this the eldest Woodward?' Then bending down, so that he was my height:

'And what are you called, little one?'

When I told him, boldly – for I was seldom afraid of people, even those as big as Mr Hume:

'What a lovely name,' he said. 'Christ – and the bells of heaven. *And* a beautiful poem . . .'

Then he smiled at me, and Mama smiled too, and took my hand.

When he preached, Mr Hume had a ringing voice. But I noticed that just as no one had listened to Mr Bickerstaffe's sermons, neither did they listen now. From inside our box pew, I would watch my father struggling against sleep, giving sudden starts, whilst my mother looked straight ahead of her, her thoughts somewhere else. Turning my head to gaze at her, I imagined sometimes I could see, reflected in her eyes, other people, other places. What they called a 'faraway look'.

If I turned round, I would see Uncle Sutcliffe leaning back, Aunt Flora sitting very upright. Aunt Flora was very dainty and very precise. She drew and painted with pastel crayons and, Mama said, fancied herself as an artist. I did not want to look into her head. I knew that I would not like the furniture there. Whereas with Mama I would try and try . . .

Papa's sister, Aunt Martha, said to me on another occasion: 'You should not stare at your Mother so, Christabel.'

I said cheekily, 'But I wasn't staring. *Mama* was. *I* was just looking . . .'

'Sharp,' Aunt Martha said. 'So sharp you'll cut yourself one of these days.'

There were others to watch in church. Not just the Woodwards and the Armstrongs, but also the people of the village. Some of them worked in Appleyard and Horsfield Mills. The Irish, though, were not in church. Emigrant workers from Liverpool, employed by Uncle Sutcliffe and his father before him, and who lived in shacks down by the canal, in Luddenden Foot, they were Romanists and worshipped the Mother of God instead of God himself. Betty explained it all to me.

The Mason family, the Holroyds, the Turners, Greenwoods. The Ogdens. Kit Ogden, already at twelve as tall as a grown man, with his long spindly arms and legs, his awkward walk that was almost a run, his profusion of brown curly hair which only added to his height. I had always noticed Kit in church.

Then this September, coming out of church one Sunday, I tripped him up. How it came about was this: He and his mother would usually go from the door to his father's year-old grave (Mr Ogden had been a wool sorter at Appleyard Mill), Kit running ahead always in his awkward manner. That day I broke away from the family, and running straight in front of him, tripped him up. I had not meant to do it. He fell awkwardly on his ankle. He winced when he tried to rise. I was up by this time, and bawling. We had fallen in a tangled heap. His leg had caught mine, but I was not hurt.

Mama and Papa were on the scene quite soon. Papa said, 'What's up with the lad? On your feet, Master Ogden.' Meantime he was shaking me, yet pulling me to him roughly and affectionately the while. 'Get up, lad.'

Mrs Ogden, a small, worried woman, apologized to Papa, over

and over. 'The clumsy lad . . .' Then reaching out to me: 'The little lass – is she badly?'

Secure in my father's clasp, welded to his side, I shook my head. Other folk had gathered round. Kit, although standing up now, could not walk.

And then my mother insisting ('After all, it's Christabel's fault . . .') that Kit come up to our house to be cared for. Papa looking at her as if she were mad. 'The lad'll be fine, the lad'll be fine.' But Mama stood firm.

So Kit came up. He was to stay with us at least that day, or until he could walk on his ankle. In the event he stayed two weeks. The weather turned to rain, then a high wind. It was the September equinox: even as his ankle improved and he was able to hobble about, it was not really possible to go outdoors.

Mr Rushworth, the surgeon, called, and found nothing broken, although to help matters along, he bled Kit from the arm. For the first few days Kit must have a low diet, with only broths and tea and a little bread. More bread, warmed and wet with water, as a poultice for his ankle.

'I'm not used to be laying down all day,' he said.

I asked him: 'What's it like being Kit Ogden?'

He told me: 'That's a daft question and all . . .'

But I'd meant, what was it like to be a millhand, instead of a mill owner's daughter. To live in a weaver's cottage, with almost no books. He said there were only the Bible and something called *Pilgrim's Progress* that he could make neither head nor tail of. When I read, for I was just becoming fluent, he marvelled. I read to him from *Sinbad's Tales*, and we looked at the pictures together. He could scarcely read at all, and that only slowly and painfully. Yet he'd been to school, if only for a little while.

After the first few days he stayed with us, he ate so much that Betty said he'd be out of his trousers by the time he left. She said she'd wager they were a full inch shorter in the leg, and all without him moving hardly at all from the sofa. He joined us for nursery meals – Betty shaking her head ('Don't take your manners from Master Ogden. *I* seed you blowing on your broth, Kit Ogden').

I think Papa forgot about him, because when we went downstairs to be with Papa, we had not Kit with us – although occasionally I spoke of him. 'I read *that* book to Kit today,' I would say, as we turned the pages, and 'Kit?' he'd say. 'Kit? Oh, aye – the Ogden lad. He's never still about is he?' Then he'd call to Mama:

'Lina, have you not sent home the Ogden lad yet?'

I overheard my mother reminding him that money must be paid to Mrs Ogden for the loss of Kit's earnings, *through my fault*. And my father answering impatiently that it had been seen to.

Halliwell was too young for Kit and grew bored in his company. Agnes and Joshua stared at him in wonder. It was I who spent the most time with him. (Miss Walton, our governess, must have been glad to be spared my company.)

Kit had been to school. School, school. I wanted to know all about it.

'Oh aye, school,' he said, moulding wax (his hands were wonderful to watch), fashioning a lamb or duck for Joshua. 'School – it were nowt.'

They had leave from the mill, for one month in the mornings, for the next in the afternoons. 'I can give you twice times four, only I don't cypher and I can't make t'letters missen.'

I told him I'd show him, for I had just begun and wrote already quite respectably, although I could not yet join my letters. I wrote out for him the alphabet, and two rhymes for him to copy. I fancied myself as a teacher. He was pleased with his efforts and I was pleased for him. He sat on the nursery window seat, tongue curled on his upper lip, pen held almost vertical, pressing into the paper. 'I'll mak it yet,' he said.

And what else had he done at school? I asked him, avid for the life I didn't know. He told me of the teacher, Miss Wheelwright: 'She'd this girt basin of bread and milk, kept allus on t'side. Sugared, it were. And if we'd the right answers then she'd dip in t'spoon and we'd a sup of it. T'lads got more than lasses – But that were Miss Wheelwright . . .'

His uncle's farm near Midgley, with its lambs and hens and ducks, I could not hear enough of that. It was a wonderment to me. But he thought nothing of any of this. It was the railway fascinated him. Leeds to Manchester, a branch line of which ran through Luddenden Foot. I had often seen the station with its small stone house amid dark dank trees and slippery cliff side, and thought it a gloomy place. My parents' friend, Branwell, had worked there. The railway ran behind and above the canal and the river Calder. When visiting Uncle Sutcliffe and Aunt Flora at Buckley House, we would stop to watch the engine puff and steam its way along the high embankment. I shared Kit's enthusiasm at the notion of travelling by railroad.

But he wanted more. He wanted to be if not clerk in charge, or stationmaster, then the one to wave on the trains. 'I'd fetch Mam to stay wi' me, we'd live in that little house, and she'd not have to labour and she'd watch for trains all t'day . . .'

I was puzzled. I thought his cottage in our village far prettier. And who would not want to work in Papa's mill?

Betty grew tired of his presence. Now when he shared our nursery meals she would serve him last. Once she lectured him, saying, 'Ye munnot fancy because they've had you up here . . . There's to be no coming round the house asking for the childer. You ken your place, and mun go back to it.' Betty could be hard. She wore her hard face then, and had the hard voice to go with it.

I couldn't remember a time when Betty hadn't been there. Swarthy, with a sharp face and a large mole on her cheek with a hair growing from it, she came from Haworth – twelve miles away – and as a young girl had been Mama's nurse. Then when I was born, she had come to be ours too. Her sister, Mercy, who lived still in Haworth, came over to see her regularly. Mercy had the same face but with a redder complexion and no mole.

Kit's mother came to take him home. She wept over him. But had she not lost her husband last year? Mama reminded me of how precious her son, her only son, must be to her.

'*As are you to me*, Christabel.' I knew to what she referred – for I had once almost died. She thought I remembered little of it. But it was not so. My memories were vivid. And strange.

I was bled with leeches and dosed with a foul-tasting ammoniac-flavoured mixture. Tartar emetic ointment burned and blistered my chest. Vapour, smelling of ether, rose from a boiling kettle. I inhaled it several times a day.

Three years old. I knew only that I was ill. Very ill. My small body racked with coughing. I vomited: the pain was in my stomach, my belly. I didn't eat. I coughed, coughed, coughed.

The kink-cough, as they called it, took over my body, and me. The cough was Christabel. Christabel was the cough. And every paroxysm ended in sickness. That unmistakable whoop signalling the close of a spasm. Small lungs are not strong enough, small systems cannot withstand this disease. Nor is there any cure for it. Even now, mothers pray that it will pass their children by – or that it will at least wait till the frame is strong enough.

I was dying. Although I knew nothing much about it, it seemed

24

I was likely to die. That very night, there might be one paroxysm too many for my weakened constitution.

The man who stood at the end of the bed and then came nearer, standing beside me now – he was dressed in black. His face was very high-coloured. He spoke with an odd slurred accent.

My mother spoke in hushed tones. She called this man 'Father'.

'Father,' she said, 'it must be now. Quickly. Mr Woodward is at the mill but may soon return. My mother-in-law . . . I expect visitors later . . .' She was drawing the curtains at the head of my bed. 'The servants suspect nothing . . .'

I heard, or thought I remembered hearing, tears in her voice:

'. . . It would mean so much to me. If I am to lose . . . I cannot tell you any more. This child, my *first* . . . Father, you say you come from a large family, that seven of you died – if you remember your own mother's agony, Father, then I implore you. Use the powers God has given you . . .'

And then, in a calmer voice: 'What do you need? Water, oil?'

'*Domine exaudi orationem meam, et clamor meus . . .*'

Words in a foreign language. My mother weeping over me.

Devils – cast out? But it was the cough cast out. Soon after, not many days after, and I was cured.

Christmas of 1848 now, and I ran out from the parlour and into the stone-flagged passage. Still crying, still smarting from the blow my father gave me. I lifted the skirt of my dress and rubbed my eyes – and waited for someone to come after me.

Then I heard my name called. My mother came slowly to where I stood. She opened her arms to me. I saw that she was crying.

'Oh, Christabel,' she said. 'You must not be so bad. Of what use is it to hate and be angry –' she took my head in her hands '– when the end of it all is death? When those we love best, but scarcely know we love, are taken from us? Death, dead,' she said, her fingers in my hair, smoothing it back now from my high, too high, forehead. 'A second death. No wonder there was a second death at Haworth – following on that first one. The waste of it all, Christabel. The waste. And *perhaps it has not ended yet.*'

I buried my angry head in the softness of her best silk, and wept too.

*

The family gathered once more the first Sunday of the New Year. Uncle Sutcliffe and Papa stood talking in the parlour. As so often I picked up fragments and tried to make sense of them. It was like the conversations when I sat with Papa in his snug. Visitors, and talk of the mill – and all the while Papa would be cuddling me on his knee. Today though I sat on a footstool, where I could see his legs straddled before the fire.

'Railways,' Uncle Sutcliffe was saying. 'Our money, we've had it in the York and Midland nigh on two years now. You're late, James. There's not much to buy that isn't a heavy price. Flora says –'

'But he's not one who *builds*, isn't Hudson – for all they call him Railway King. I'd rather one who builds them. *Brassey* now . . .'

'Nay, James – he's got it right, has Hudson, with his "Mak all t'railways come to York". And what's more, he's a millionaire. Twice Lord Mayor of York. He didn't get there from sitting on his backside –'

'That's as maybe. But who's to say that's not where he'll end up? Woodward brass – best put in the mill. You don't think me right, eh, then, Sutcliffe?'

It was cold in January, very cold. Thin sheets of glass on the road, where Halliwell and I could slide. Molehills thrown up, covered with ice. Halliwell kicked at them. Lone bleak hips, coral-coloured, left on bushes. Hazel bushes stripped bare. We went out with Betty, wrapped up to our very eyes. She was a chilly body and supposed us to be too, but in those days I scarcely in my excitement felt the cold at all.

Victoria went on all the walks. She was my precious darling and I persuaded Betty to begin sewing her a new outfit. This beautiful creature, all my own. I could decide when she should rise in the morning or go to bed. I could sing her lullabies and tell her stories. When she was praised for her beauty, *I* was praised. Sometimes in the night I had to spring out of bed just to see that she was all right.

Josh was mine too. When I spoke or thought the words 'my brother', it was of little Josh I spoke or thought. Halliwell, I took for granted: when I had first become aware I existed – he was there. But Josh was different. 'Would you like to see your little brother?' they had said, and there he was in the nurse's arms, mewling – but so dear, so dear. Then as he began to walk, to talk – it was my hand he held for his first steps, my words he tried to imitate. When Trissie, my King Charles spaniel, had puppies last spring, it was he and I who sat in the basket with them.

'Cisty, Cisty!' he would cry. A mixture of 'sister' and 'Christabel', for he could not say my name. Joshua was mine: 'Where's my Josh?' I would say. And, '*Your* Joshua . . .' Mama or Papa would say. (Oh, fortunate small girl: my father's darling, *and* with a darling of my own.)

Betty had different moods. It was not worth trying to please her early in the morning, since her temper was always short and she would strike out for no reason at all. She was always best later in the day. Sometimes, before tucking us in for the night, she would tell us a tale or two. And all of them true. She swore to their truth: 'May God strike me, if I fib.'

Halliwell laughed out loud at them. Sometimes an excited laugh, sometimes nervous. He told Betty, 'Your face is funny when you talk.' But lying there in my cot, or sitting round the nursery fire, with the clothes drying on the wooden horse and Josh perhaps on Betty's knee, and just the light of two candles on the washstand, I did not want to look at her face.

'. . . And then, when it's past midnight, a girt black dog – the gytrash they call him, he howls summat terrible. Like the wind that wuthers out yonder . . .'

While the wind moaned outside in the snow-filled sky, or even when it did not, Betty told her tales. And most frightening of all, yet surely not meant to be, were her tales of The Reverend Grimshaw, parson many years ago at Haworth, but buried here in Luddenden, carried the twelve miles over the moors on his bier. Of his frightening sermons. Of his holiness. Of his son Johnny, who was not holy, and who drank himself into an early grave. She told us how he had whipped his father's horse into a foam as he galloped him over the moors.

'And what did he cry?' said Betty. 'Being mindful of his father, what did he cry but, "Once you carried an angel, and now you carry a devil . . ."'

And of his daughter Jane, who had also been an angel, but who had died at Charles Wesley's own boarding school – of homesickness, Betty said.

Grimshaw. Grim by name, grim by nature. Although there were other, happy stories of him. And after all had he not been transported to the seventh heaven?

When Mercy came over to visit her sister, then I would lie in bed and listen as they talked on the other side of the half-open door. Their voices were alike, but Mercy's was harder and certainly louder. Sometimes I heard her answers to questions of Betty's I had not caught.

I learned of many people in Haworth village. Not just Mr Brontë's family, with its now two remaining daughters, but of Mr Greenwood, the stationer, Mr Brown, the sexton, of the Sunday school that Betty and Mercy's nieces attended and where the Misses Brontë taught.

I would drift in and out of sleep. Their voices which began low would rise, especially Mercy's, as she warmed to a tale. Then maybe Joshua would cry and Betty would start up and Mercy would realize the time and they would send down for a tray of tea before settling for the night. They shared Betty's bed – I had seen them once in identical night caps when I crept in there one light, summer morning, holding a hand to my bleeding nose. Early next day she would return the twelve miles with the carrier.

Oh, Betty's tales, for whose truth she vouched – how could they not be true since Mercy, or Tom, or Andrew O'Dick's, or some such utterly reliable person had seen – or heard or felt? (Which was worse, to see, or to hear?) What sudden chill of blood when the wind moaned outside the nursery, and Betty spoke of 'the girt black dog. A gytrash it were . . . that's a spirit dog. Nay, child, it's never real.'

Although not real, yet it seemed so – padding over the moors, the size of Uncle Sutcliffe's brindled mastiff, his baying, so like the wind (*was* it after all the wind?), was a baying for blood.

This apparition never came by day. Betty was of the opinion that it was a soul, a *lost* soul. 'Who has lost it?' I asked. But she and I, we confused each other. Had not a visiting preacher, only this Advent, thundered out, 'For what shall it profit a man if he gain the whole world and *lose his own soul*?'

She did not answer me but left me in this confusion. Except that I knew. That dire threat when we were out: '*Don't get lost.*' The soul in the gytrash was of someone lost who could not find his way home. And home, Betty said with grim satisfaction, was Heaven. 'It'll be they can't find their way there, and mun go to hell . . .'

But I begged her not to speak of that. I stopped up my ears, and Halliwell stopped up his in sympathy, though he was laughing, nervously, also.

*

On the feast of the Epiphany, the new vicar, Mr Hume, gave a party for the Sunday school. Mama and I came in to hand out the gift of an apple and an orange each – a custom Grandma Woodward had begun in Mr Bickerstaffe's early days. This year Mr Hume had arranged for a truly large Christmas fir. When we arrived the children were sat at a trestle table, putting away mutton pies and hot plum puddings. Mr Hume was playing with and amusing the children as Mr Bickerstaffe never had. He told Mama that he meant to be much more zealous than his predecessor in visiting both the sick *and* the well.

'But then I have the advantage of excellent health – although Mrs Hume alas, has not . . . You see, it is my great belief that "a house-going parson makes a church-going people".'

His voice was very deep and he looked at Mama from beneath heavy brows – and then at me.

'And here is Christabel,' he said. He caressed my head, rumpling my curls. Then he smiled at me, very slowly. I knew that smile was especially for me.

'Are you a good girl, Christabel?'

'Yes,' I said.

'And shall you always be?'

'Oh yes,' I said. I wanted so much to please him. 'I mean *always* to be good.'

One week into February and Victoria had a sad accident. Agnes sat her close to the fire, the wrong side of the fireguard. Her clothes did not catch fire, but her poor face . . . She ceased to be Victoria, and became a distorted lump of wax. Agnes, who had not done it on purpose, wept almost as much as I did. But I continued to love Victoria. For it had not been her fault either.

2

'There's to be no coming round the house asking for the childer. You ken your place, and mun go back to it,' Betty had told Kit.

He had gone back to it. But she had not taken account of my missing him. Two weeks was a long time for us to have been together in the nursery, sharing porridge, talking, and playing school. Although I thought of him in some ways as grown – after all he was already so tall, and had earned his living for several years – I had been in the position of teacher. It was from me that he had learned to form his letters properly. And then when he had gone, the lessons had ended. With Betty's words in his ears he had said nothing about coming back again.

I saw him at church every Sunday. He smiled at me always. Sometimes we exchanged a few words, and he would ask after Trissie, or perhaps whether I had finished the drawing I had been making of Sinbad the Sailor. But most Sundays, after the service, he and his mother went straight to Mr Ogden's grave. I did not like to run over there to speak to him.

When the worst of the icy weather was over, I asked one Sunday if I might walk up to visit Kit? Betty spoke to Mama, who thought it a good and kind idea.

His home was a weaver's cottage right inside the village. Its upstairs rooms, formerly a workshop, had many small mullioned windows, to give as much light as possible in the days when weaving had been done there.

Mrs Ogden came to the door. She looked flustered, and surprised, and began chattering immediately. But almost at once, Kit came up behind her:

'Miss Woodward! Aye . . . but you're welcome. Come in then. Take a seat – I never thought . . .'

He seemed more surprised even than his mother, although not nearly so embarrassed.

'I'll ask Mam if she's got milk in – you'll take a sup?'

Then he broke off for a heavy bout of coughing. When it had eased, his mother said:

30

'He's been poorly – else he'd have been up at t'farm. His uncle's. He's there oftentimes Sundays . . .'

'I know,' I said. 'He told me about it. Didn't you, Kit?'

We were shy with each other. Or rather, he was shy and I did not know what to do about it. I was cross about the 'Miss Woodward'. When they had sat me down with a cup of milk and a crackney, I said:

'You've to call me Christabel, Kit. And I'll call you Kit – like we did before . . .'

But before he could say anything, Mrs Ogden said, 'He's been practising his letters, isn't that right, Kit?'

'Then I'll expect to see them,' I said, very pleased. I was the teacher again.

'And he says too, as how you can read anything – even words that go right across t'page –'

'I don't know,' I said. I saw she thought me wonderfully clever. Finishing up my milk and accepting another crackney, I asked:

'Were you practising reading, Kit?'

'Aye,' said Mrs Ogden, 'he's had his nose in that –' and she pointed to a large book with leather binding, lying on the edge of the dresser.

Kit said laughing, not so shy any more, 'I've a tongue in my head, Mam – I'd liefer talk to Christabel missen . . .'

That made his mother more flustered still. She could not stop talking. I said to Kit:

'You've to read to me then.'

'Now? Have I to do it now?'

'When else?' I said. 'That's why I've come – to see how you're getting on.'

'Aye, right then,' he said. 'If I give you two pages and they're not ill done – will you come up to me Uncle Thomas's – to t'farm?'

'Kit!' his mother said. 'You're never telling Miss Woodward what to do . . .'

But I could not think of anything more lovely.

He took the book down from the dresser. It was the one he had spoken of, *Pilgrim's Progress*. I opened it at random. I knew I would be able to make any of it out, but I was not at all sure about pronouncing the words – if I had never heard them spoken. But then perhaps Kit and Mrs Ogden had not either.

'I shall read first,' I said, 'and then you must follow after with the same passage. Look, here –'

He came and sat beside me on a stool before the fire.

I read: '"*Though with great difficulty I am got hither, yet now I do not repent me of all the trouble I have been at to arrive where I am. My sword, I give to him that shall succeed me in my pilgrimage, and my courage and skill to him that can get it . . .*"'

Before I left I had arranged to go the very next Sunday to his uncle's farm.

'I wish I could trust you, Caroline. Caroline, you never look me full in the face, and yet you're not a lass who . . .'

Grandma Woodward's voice fell away as my mother shut the parlour door behind them both. I was lying on my stomach, reading a book behind the sofa. I was an eavesdropper, avid, untiring – success bred success.

Mama said, her irritation scarcely disguised:

'Don't follow me about. I wish –'

'This was once my *own* house, Caroline. I think you forget. I watched it go up brick by brick. And it came before, I'll remind you, Buckley House – for all its fine looks and air. The levelling, the path reclaimed from the hillside, the foundations laid. I saw it all. I can assure you, this place is fully the equal of Laurel Bank next door.'

My mother was silent. She must have taken up some sewing for I heard the sound of her scissors snipping.

'I want to speak to you, Caroline. That is why I have followed you in here. I may be an old woman, Caroline, but I've a tingling of my fingertips. Something tells me –'

'Tingling of your fingers! Pricking of your thumbs, more likely,' my mother said angrily. I loved to hear her angry. 'Are you a witch then?' she muttered under her breath.

'Are you a good wife to my son? I think you are not a good wife to my son . . .'

'What constitutes a *good* wife?'

'You shouldn't have call to ask that. Your own mother . . . But Bessie Armstrong – always weak, that one. I don't doubt she never told you of your duties.'

'Duties!' my mother said. 'Perhaps you could leave me in peace – *both* of us in peace – to conduct our own marriage.'

'You think I'm blind, and deaf perhaps?'

'James has spoken to you?' Her voice trembled a little. 'I can't think what his complaint can be – unless it's that you're forever finding fault with me.'

'Well, if you can't, you can't. You'd never wish me to spell it out, Caroline. To *speak* of such matters –'

'I don't wish you to talk to me of any matters . . . And now, please, I have sewing to do.'

'James said –'

'I don't care to hear what James said. I cannot think he'd speak to you, unless he'd over-indulged. And when he's drunk . . .'

'Don't become tearful with me. I know what *I* know. And *James does not*.'

'Let me be.'

'It is only a suspicion. The tingling of my fingers. I think –'

'Have you been prying?'

'Have you something to hide?'

'I have secrets. As has everyone. I have the same rights to privacy as anyone else.'

'I'd not pry, I don't need to pry, Caroline. But there is something you've not told me. *Or James* . . .'

My mother did not answer.

'I have my suspicions. But the enormity of it, the unlikelihood – and my own son after all. That you would . . .'

'There is *nothing*. You must let me alone!'

'You think me a daft old woman, because I've maybe seen the truth. If it *is* true, then my son –'

'For pity's sake, if you love your son at all, in common humanity, *let me alone*!'

There was silence. Then I heard my mother catch her breath in a sob. And the creaking of Grandma's stays as she rose from the sofa.

'I know when I'm not wanted, Caroline. I'll be away.' Her voice was for a moment placatory. 'I'm sure I never meant to upset . . .'

The door closed behind her. I wanted to rush up and throw my arms about my mother. But – how to confess I had been there all the while? And what of next time, when I hoped to hear, not something sad (and mysterious) like this, but gossip about the mill, or some choice item from the *Halifax Guardian*?

But before I could make the decision to go to her or not, the door had closed behind her too.

As for what I had just overheard, I knew only that Grandma disliked Mama. It was no wonder Mama called her a witch sometimes, when she invented such wicked stories. I was at once

33

completely and utterly on Mama's side. And how to imagine that Papa was angry with her, when *I* had never seen any such thing? I imagined Grandma prying in Mama's bedroom, reading the poems in Mama's bold copperplate. I was allowed to look at them, I was allowed to read them, if I wished. But that Grandma, in her clicking pattens, and her musty smelling dress, should go spying . . . It was not to be borne. And what secrets were there anyway?

That spring I went several times up to the farm with Kit. The farm was off the Midgley Road before Hebden Bridge, and his uncle would send the cart to fetch us. At bedtime I would be brought back directly to Wade House. Betty did not care for my going and shook her head at Mama for allowing it.

'There are farm lads eat at the table,' she said, 'and I don't doubt you'll be picking up their rough ways . . .'

Indeed there were farm lads, for Kit had five boy cousins, all older than him – though none so tall. Fred, who usually came over to collect us, was the tallest. There were three girls as well. With all their family, we were fourteen round the table. I scarcely noticed how they ate, only what they ate – because it was so good.

They all made a great fuss of me – I could do no wrong, but must always be spoilt and fed as much as I could eat. I think now that they may have wanted to make me grow, yet no one ever used the dreaded words 'She's very small . . .' Rather it was, when they heard about Kit and the reading: 'What a big clever lass, eh, Kit?'

And poor Kit, before the cart came to collect us, had always to read two pages of Bunyan, as nearly perfectly as I knew how. After the third time, though, I brought him a book from home. And we read together *Sinbad's Travels*.

In the summer, a disaster happened to Uncle Sutcliffe and Aunt Flora. Not to us, though. When the bubble of railway prosperity burst, we were spared, because of my father's scorn and refusal to invest.

He gloated now as we sat over Sunday dinner.

'Right, wasn't I, eh? Poor sackless Sutcliffe . . . all that fine talk. He knows nowt, and that's the truth on it. And that woman of his –'

'Hush,' my mother said. 'That's enough of the matter. It's sad for them, but we don't need to speak of it at table.'

But he would not be stopped, even though his own mother raised a warning finger. George Hudson, the Railway King, whom Sutcliffe had praised so, and whom *he* had distrusted, proved now to be nothing but a common criminal.

'Twice Lord Mayor of York – daft that looks now, eh? They'll be changing the name "Hudson Street" soon enough . . . I reckon he'll be clapped in gaol as like as not. Divvies paid out of capital. And that's not the end of it. They say there's nigh on eighty million pound gone. It'll be the workhouse for some.'

I spoke up: 'Uncle and Aunt – have they to go to the Bastille?' (For that was what the workhouse in Halifax was called. Aunt Martha, when I stayed with her in Wentworth Terrace, had shown it to me.)

'Hush now, it's none of your concern, little lass,' my father said.

'What will happen to poor Uncle Sutcliffe?' I persisted. I did not care about Aunt Flora (or Phil or Meg).

'They'll have learned a short sharp lesson, I don't doubt. It was good they'd not all their eggs in the one basket. Too many eggs – aye. But not all.'

Grandma Woodward made mention of Aunt Flora's portrait painting. 'Sutcliffe – he ought to send that woman out to addle her living . . .'

'Oh I don't know,' my mother said, knowing the dig was at her family. 'She doesn't paint so very well. I think *Christabel* draws better . . .'

My father would have none of this. He closed the subject with:

'It's the turn of the dice. It's happened. And that's all about it. But – and I'll tell you now – you'll never catch *me* doing owt so sackless . . .'

When we children went out in the dog cart with Betty, up Stocks Lane towards Luddenden Dean and Mount Tabor, spilling out to run towards the woods, I shuddered always as we crossed the meadow. It was known as the Grave Field. There was a footpath running through it, and coming back I would hurry always, hurry hurry. And if we had Joshua with us, I would pull him along faster than his little fat legs could go, so that he stumbled or was dragged, crying, mud on the hem of his frock.

Betty would be cross at my impatience: 'What's up with you?'

And I'd tell her: 'It's the *Grave* Field, we've not to linger –'

'What if it is?' she'd say. 'The bodies'll have long since gone to dust. It's just a field. You'd walk through a graveyard without making a fuss . . .'

'Hurry on,' I'd say, just the same. 'Hurry *home*.'

Who had told me? I couldn't remember now. Couldn't remember when I hadn't known. The Plague, when it came not to Luddenden, but to this village nearby. The terrifying plague, when strong men rose up fit and healthy and were dead by sundown. Everyone in that village died – except one man. And he dug his own grave. He knew his turn would soon come.

I had nightmares about that field. That it was dark winter, and I was alone. There was always this grave which would yawn before me suddenly, lying open, *waiting*. I screamed and screamed, and woke up. Betty was out of patience with me, saying I screamed, and had nightmares on purpose. It was only Mama, dear kind gentle Mama – only she understood . . .

But now today, here we were, happy, oh so happy this sunny afternoon in May, off to pick primroses. What matter that we must go through, and come back by, the Grave Field? I had three-year-old Joshua by the hand, Agnes running on in front. Halliwell, just recovered from a low fever, had been left at home.

Just before we left, we had run into the kitchen. Sarah, our cook, was baking oatcake on the backstone. I can smell it now, fragrant, hot, a little crumbly – and spread with treacle. Betty told us off. We were sticky but happy, licking our fingers as we climbed into the dog cart. At the top of Stocks Lane we had to wait to let a waggon pass. It was one of ours, dark red, and painted on the side: *Joshua Woodward and Son, Worsted Spinners and Manufacturers, Appleyard Mill, Luddenden*. How proud I always felt. It rumbled and creaked by, weighed down today with stones.

'What are all those stones for?'

Betty said they were for an engine bed up at our mill. But already I was thinking of the primroses I would pick. And in no time it seemed we had left the cart, and walked through the Grave Field and into the woods. Arms full of primroses. A basket full of them. The pockets of my pinny bulging. Josh sat down in the leaves, and drummed his heels, and asked suddenly to go home. 'I'm hungry, Josh is hungry, I'm hungry, Nursie . . .' He still had the marks of treacle on his face. Betty spat on her handkerchief and cleaned him up.

But I was happy still. I scarcely minded that day, hurrying through, dancing back through the Grave Field.

We came then out of it, and onto the road. A simple road, fields either side. Joshua was the first out. Betty was closing the gate. I was watching her.

A cry. A splash. And I looked back. Josh, who a second before had been there, was not. Agnes screamed:

'He's gone, he's in the water –'

I looked down, I screamed too. I glimpsed – small fat hands clinging to the stone. Broken stone, the cover of the conduit.

There was a conduit under the road. Water ran from it to a dam in the Grave Field.

'Oh, help, help!' I yelled. And then – oh but I couldn't even see his face, just the fat hands clinging, grappling with the stone.

And then he was gone.

Betty was kneeling down in the road, muttering, 'Dear God, God help . . .'

I screamed again and she slapped me.

'Don't move,' she cried, getting up, 'don't move while somebody's fetched!'

I tried to go after her, but could only run around and around in little despairing circles.

'Don't move!' she called out. She'd swept up Agnes under her arm and was running with her to the dog cart.

She was gone minutes only, because a little way further on, where the road turned, she ran into Benjamin Mason. There were two men with him.

There they all were, staring dumbfounded at the hole. Benjamin saying, 'There'll be no other way into the conduit. And the current . . . I reckon it'll take him up by the dam.'

Giving commands:

'The water's to be turned – so as to let the dam off. Then if current carries him up, there's mebbe a chance . . . Only we've to make haste.'

'Make haste, make haste,' he said over and over. He told Betty off to take Agnes and me home:

'And fetch the bairn's dad here, fetch Mr Woodward up.'

But I wouldn't move. I was hysterical. Frozen to the spot. Betty, now almost hysterical herself, slapped me again. Then she was gone. The men scarcely noticed me. I called down the hole:

'Josh,' I called. 'Josh, *come back* . . .'

Then, 'Let me down, let me down!' I thought I could maybe

go after him. But Benjamin took hold of me, saying in calm tones, 'Leave be. Leave be . . .'

They talked amongst themselves. I followed them up towards the dam. Some women had joined us from the cottages nearby. Then two other men. A carrier's cart came by with a driver – and Kit.

I was never so glad to see Kit. I ran to him, crying and calling.

'What's up, what's up?' he asked and I sobbed out the story.

But now the water had been turned. Would the current bring Josh up? *Would he be all right?*

Ah yes, one of the men told us. The Outhwaite lad, twenty years since, he'd been carried near on half a mile, and none the worse for it.

The dam was let off. There was no Josh.

'He's mebbe caught fast in the conduit,' one of the men said. I didn't know if that meant he might still be all right. I was confused, shaking. My teeth chattered with panic.

Kit volunteered to crawl up the drain. Long arms, skinny frame, he'd be the best person. Of the next hour, I remember little. It was as if some black cloud enveloped my head. I recall Papa arriving – and my legs which would not carry me towards him . . .

When at last Kit came out, he had found Josh. Dead. About halfway along the drain, he had come upon a broken cover. Forming a V shape, and standing up, it had trapped Josh. That was where he had stuck. And drowned.

And now the Grave Field had a real grave . . . They reckoned afterwards that some time that day, a waggon (and had we not seen our own mill one?) heavily, perhaps too heavily laden, passing over had crushed or broken the stone covering. And so Josh, running out, stepping on it, had . . . But I did not want to remember.

Josh was not the only Woodward son. But he had been especially mine. Many people lost brothers, and sisters. But with Joshua that day –

I think, you see, it was because the ground had opened up, and swallowed him.

A week or two later, Kit and his mother called at our home. Kit brought me a baby lamb from Uncle Thomas's farm. It had been orphaned in the sudden sharp spell. They were rearing two of them in their kitchen. Did I want one?

Mrs Ogden, small and red-faced and agitated. So unlike him. All that he had in common with her were his large red hands. They were always red, winter and summer. Redder still when they dangled by his side. And yet, they were *kind* hands.

Standing there, holding the white bundle which nuzzled his arm, he said:

'I ken it'll not make up for Master Joshua. Only, it's a little small thing and . . . Any road, I reckon it needs you . . .'

I was not allowed to keep it though.

Perhaps I had caught Halliwell's fever – although it was too late really for that. I know only that for two weeks after the funeral I lay in bed, at first tossing and turning with heat, then as time passed, feeling weak and lightheaded and chilled. Food nauseated me. Unappetizing toast water and beef tea grew cold on the table beside me. I wept weakly for Josh, and thought once that I saw the lamb, Kit's gift, gambolling before the fire.

The weather had turned cold and wet. At night rain lashed the windows of the night nursery. Betty and Mercy sat over their tea and talked. Out on the landing the clock had already struck ten.

'I'll swear it,' Betty said. 'I saw him.'

'It's him, you think it's *him*?' Mercy said. 'I never . . . It makes your blood run cold. I'd not walk there night time. A kirkyard's not the place . . .'

'I'd not the choice. It'd grown dark so sudden. I'd not meant to be there, that place. But then when I looked behind – oh, I tell you, Mercy, I all but screamed – it's like you *ken* someone's there. Even when there's nowt to be seen.'

'Aye. But Grimshaw, of all folk. How would you know him when you never saw him?'

'True enow,' said Betty.

'Though I will say, there are folk at home, folk in Haworth, that can still tell of him. His sermons on hell fire . . . They say if you'd never been scared before . . .' Her voice grew louder: 'He could put fear into the strongest man, could Grimshaw . . . I heard, folk drinking in the Black Bull, if they seed him coming, they were like to jump out of the back windows and make off. *That* scared they were . . .'

She paused. They were both silent. Then, 'But the worst was, Samuel told me of this fellow . . . He were stood in a shop, and in comes Parson Grimshaw. And he sees the fellow. "The devil's been very busy in this neighbourhood," Parson says. "I can touch the man with my stick who lay with another man's wife last night –"'

'He said that?'

'Aye, them very words. And then he says, "The end of these things will be death . . ." Really feared of him they were. He'd seen Christ. That were the trouble no doubt. He were never the same again. It were that made him the way he was – fierce against any wrongdoing . . . And then to have that lad for a son. It's maybe for *that* he's turning in his grave . . .'

'He's turning for summat. And he's about . . . Never again after dark, Mercy. Even in daylight, I'm not *easy* . . .'

The peaty stream rushed by the church on its way to the Calder. I used to think it wanted as quickly as possible to be past, to leave behind the tombstones in that sunken churchyard with its grey-green flagstones and its great tall trees. Poplars, dripping after the rain. Gloom – and ghosts.

If I had been frightened those early days in the Grave Field, in the days before little Josh's drowning, it was as nothing to my fear of the graveyard now. *And Josh was buried there*. I would have to, I *wished* to visit his grave. But not always with the family. I wanted sometimes to be alone with him. To take flowers from the garden, and sit beside the newly engraved stone ('In Memory of Joshua Woodward, beloved son of James and Caroline Woodward, died 15th May 1950, aged 3 years and 3 months, *All flesh is as grass*'). There I could speak to him, and even believe, perhaps, that he could hear me.

Of what was I afraid? Only that I, like Betty – and how many others? – would be the chosen one to see the avenging spirit of Parson Grimshaw. How could he lie peacefully with the present-day wickednesses all about him? Even my own wrongdoings . . . Just as he had known of the man in the shop who had done nothing more than lie down with another man's wife (and what could be the wickedness of *that*?), might he not, sleeping in his grave, *know* that I had stolen peppercake meant for Agnes?

One July afternoon we went all together to Josh's grave: Betty, Halliwell, Agnes and I. I asked for some pink button roses from the garden and carried them myself to lay on the stone.

And there we were in the kirkyard. After a little while, Halliwell grew restless, and began chasing Agnes amongst the tombs. Betty said that we should go back home.

'Aren't you coming on then?' she said to me.

'No,' I told her. 'I want to sit with Josh.'

'Quaint bairn,' she said. 'Joshua – he's up with the angels, not down there.'

'No,' I said, 'he's there. I saw him buried. He's down there . . .'

'What talk,' she said, pulling Agnes by the hand. Halliwell following her a few paces behind, in marching step, an imaginary rifle over his shoulder.

When they had gone I sat down on the stone, for my legs felt weak. My head was full of sadness, my eyes full of tears, ready to be shed.

'*All flesh is as grass*', I read on the stone. Oh, my bonny Josh. I called down to him, leaning my head on the stone. 'Are you lonely, Josh?'

I heard the water rush by below the church. A blackbird sang in a thorn bush just beyond the grave. All was still. I scarcely noticed, so habitually shaded was it in the churchyard, that the sky had darkened. Presently some fat drops of rain hit my bonnet, and splashed on to the newly carved stone.

All was still again. Only black clouds. In the distance, a sudden rumble of thunder. I turned and saw the church, grey and shadowed. The squat Norman tower.

Then behind me, I heard a sigh. Long drawn out. No, it was not the sighing of the wind. The air was too still for that. I had my back now to the church. Josh's roses lay on the stone; one of the buds had broken off and hung limp.

I could not turn round. I could not move. Betty's voice spoke in my head. I knew then certainly that behind me stood Parson Grimshaw. Waiting.

If others had seen him, why not me? For them he had appeared in the hours of darkness. But had it not grown as black as night now?

And I was alone – except for him, who stood waiting.

I thought I heard a sound. Was certain I heard footsteps. I screamed. The high pitch of my own voice frightened me further. The wildest of terrors – I could not, dare not, turn my head. Instead I would lie on Josh's stone. Yes, yes . . . But then everything, all the world went black as my head spun, and my mouth pressed the cold stone.

A hand touched my shoulder. Two hands. I was awake, conscious again. My forehead just above the stone. I screamed.

'Christabel, Christabel,' said a voice. 'It *is* little Christabel? Whatever has frightened you?'

And then I felt myself lifted up, and held tight. My eyes squeezed shut, I squirmed with terror, even as slowly I recognized the voice.

No, not Parson Grimshaw.

'Christabel. It is Mr Hume. I was in the vestry when I heard you. I could not think . . . Whatever has frightened you, little one?'

'Parson Grimshaw,' I stammered, feeling foolish even as I said it.

As he stood there holding me, there were more claps of thunder. Then the rain began in earnest.

He carried me through the vestry door at the side of the church, and then into the church itself. I buried my head on his shoulder.

'Here we shall be dry, and perhaps not too dark . . .'

And then as we were sat down together: 'Whatever is this about Parson Grimshaw, Christabel?'

I told him of Betty's tales, and of Mercy's. And then I sobbed the story of Johnny Grimshaw, and little Jane who had died of homesickness.

'But Christabel,' he said, 'Christabel, William Grimshaw was not always an *angry* man – he was also, very often, a kind man. And a good preacher. He brought God to many people. So, why should he not sleep in peace? Come, little one –' And he showed me the brass by the communion table. 'He and his wife rest quietly here. He does not walk the churchyard, Christabel. You must never, never listen to such nonsense –'

'But ghosts –' I began.

'Ah, ghosts,' he said, 'if there be such things – *he* is not one of them . . . And then,' as he spoke he stroked my head gently, 'why were you all alone, Christabel? Where is your nurse?' I explained, but he said, 'You should not be alone –'

'I am accustomed. I *like* to. And besides, I wanted to be with – my brother.' I wept as I spoke. 'He *needs* me.'

He took my hand. 'Christabel. You must believe, little one, that he is in Christ's loving arms. So how can he not be happy? He has only gone ahead . . .' He lifted me up by my hand: 'And now, dry your tears, and let us walk up together to your home.'

As we went up the path, he made me promise that whenever I should miss Josh too badly, or become frightened – of anything:

'You will come to me. I should like to be your friend, Christabel. Mrs Hume and I, you see . . . God has sent us no children. So, will you think of me as your friend, Christabel? And when you have fears again – tell me of them?'

3

The bells of St John Baptist, Halifax, were pealing as I hurried down Kirkgate with Aunt Martha Lumsden. Eight bells. Over five thousand changes. Aunt Martha knew all about them, for when Uncle Eli was not being a schoolmaster, he had rung the changes.

'And as a young lad, your uncle – he pealed them for Waterloo. Did you learn about Waterloo, child?'

Yes, a little. Although Halliwell knew more about it than I did. Halliwell these days frequently deployed his ever growing lead army. Certainly they had fought at Waterloo.

On the outside of each bell, there was a legend. The eighth bell read: 'All ye who hear my mournful sound, Repent before you lie in ground.'

'They've a sweet ring, have these present bells. Although I daresay they miss your uncle's touch.'

To me they were very sweet. And exciting. For as they pealed, they sang. Over and over, cascading: '*Daughter of the northern fields, daughter of the northern fields*.' No one else heard. Aunt Martha did not, the rest of Halifax did not. For it was only to me they sang.

Why should they sing that? I thought of the answer only a few weeks later, as my mother and I leafed through her blue leather volume of transcribed poems. Although she allowed me to look at both books, it was from this one she would sometimes beg me to read to her.

'Never mind Christabel – if the words . . . a stumble or two, I shall not mind. Just that it should be *your* voice . . .'

> 'Lord of the Northern fields of heaven, [I read]
> May light like thine to me be given . . .
> . . . And while the tempests round me fly,
> Howling across a midnight sky . . .
> Then, then how droops the sailor's soul . . .
> . . . For tossing on an unknown sea
> How may he hope to look on thee?'

Mama said: 'Don't you think that fine, for a young lad? He wasn't above thirteen when he wrote that – so you see what he had of promise, Christabel. It is of course Branwell Brontë I speak of.'

By now I knew that his sisters had all written novels under the names of Currer, Ellis and Acton Bell. The disguise had been penetrated locally some time before. I do not remember now if I learned through Mercy's excited talk, or whether Papa brought the news home from Halifax.

I was spending a week with Aunt Martha, in her house in Wentworth Terrace. I did not mind staying with her, even though she talked so much, and pushed me about, and was stern. She had no children of her own and I was sent, I think, because she wished that she had. She was lonely in spite of a busy life of public protest. For she had been a widow over three years now. I remembered clearly Uncle Eli's death because it was the same week that I discovered I could, miraculously, read the newspaper. And there in the *Halifax Guardian* had come upon a paragraph, ringed in black I suppose, by Papa. I spelled it out with difficulty and triumph:

AWFULLY SUDDEN DEATH – On Saturday evening last, Mr Lumsden (the respected headmaster of the National School in Harrison Road), while walking towards his residence in Wentworth Terrace, suddenly dropped down dead. This awful visitation created a deep and painful sensation in the town. Mr Lumsden, from his mild and gentlemanly conduct, having gained the esteem of many influential classes of the community. He was in the 57th year of his age. An inquest was held upon the body on Tuesday last, before G. Dyson, Esq., when a verdict of 'Died by the visitation of God from natural causes' was returned.

Today we were visiting his grave. The bells of St John Baptist were pealing still as we entered the churchyard. There were no railings and the gates were always unfastened. To Aunt Martha's scandal, children were using it as a playground: sliding over the gravestones, jumping over tombs. In a far corner, some lads were throwing stones. Leaving me, she rushed forward with her umbrella.

I was not afraid in this graveyard. While Aunt Martha shooed and shouted, I read the tombstone of soldier John Logan, who had lived one hundred and five years, through five kings. Three wives and thirty-two children later, here he lay. 'Respect the soldier's dust,' I read.

Although she was my father's sister, Aunt Martha was not at all like him, either in manner or appearance – except perhaps for her nose. They had both the same fleshy nose. Her ears were rather large and stood away from her head, but I did not see them often since she was seldom without a cap – a widow's one now – or bonnet. She was older than my father, in her early forties.

'Child, child!' she would say, tut-tutting over my questions. My behaviour. The way I was brought up. 'James never was anything but soft in the wrong way. You need more discipline. Your Uncle Elias, *he* was soft. Never cared for beating the lads. I'd tell him, "How ever are they to fetch up bonny men?" Many's the time your dad had the stick, when he was a lad. He'd do well to mind that now . . .'

'Oh, look at that now,' she said as, coming out of the church, we crossed the bottom of Horton Street. 'No, *don't* look, child . . . I must write to the paper to complain yet again of *nuisances*.'

What she referred to as 'nuisances', my nose and eyes told me was no more than the overflow of night soil from inadequate drains. Halifax was crowded, too crowded, especially in the area north of the church. When my grandfather had been a boy, there had been no mill chimneys. Now, there were thirty-one.

I never stayed with her in the warm weather, or indeed in the summer at all. The first whisper of fever, I was whisked home. Two years ago there had been a bad outbreak of cholera. We had not seen Aunt Martha, nor she us, for the duration of it.

She spoke of Edward Akroyd, who was doing good work: building cottages for his operatives, with allotment gardens, a recreation ground, and a 'convenience' as she called it for each house, emptying into the river. For all her talk, and we seldom went out without her holding forth on the evils and wrongs of present-day Halifax, she cared about the poor and disadvantaged, the slum dwellers and the undernourished. Those she helped had also to listen to her opinions (but then so did I):

'. . . I'll own there's evils, but some they're of their own making. This passion for railroads and cheap tickets on Sundays. Folk that've been six days in the steam and heat of the factory, spending the Lord's Day rushing through the countryside, gallivanting in cold draughty carriages. It's no wonder they sicken and die . . .'

Her voice hammered on. On and on.

'Too much dirt here . . . I place a lot of it at the door of the Irish. They should have stayed in Liverpool. Wasn't that haven enough after eternal hungers? Potatoes – putting all their trust in an ill-looked vegetable like that . . . And if you'd seen ever in their houses, child. None of God's air can get in. Windows fixed shut, and any road, so small there's little light. And how many to a room. You'd be shocked.'

But her worst scorn was reserved for their religion.

It was the last day of my stay. A cutting March wind blew round the corners of the streets, lifting dust and refuse. I walked with her down Gibbet Lane, where she wished to visit a draper's. Gibbet Lane was named after the Halifax gibbet, a guillotine which had cut off felons' heads at a later date than anywhere else in England. (One of the parish church gargoyles played a bagpipe, just as a bagpipe had used to be played on the gibbet platform.)

There was a church here too in Gibbet Lane, also with gargoyles outside. The Roman Catholic church, and not much older than I was. 'That Popish Mass House,' Aunt Martha called it. Today, as we walked past there came from its walls the sound of singing. More of a wailing than singing.

'What –' I began.

'Stop your ears,' Aunt Martha said. 'It's a pagan sound.'

'What's a pagan sound, what sound is a pagan, Aunt?'

'Hurry in,' she said, turning the door handle of Mr Cox the draper's, pushing me before her. 'Well away from the dirty things. Well away from them all, please, miss.'

Inside she took off her gloves, to feel between finger and thumb the dimity unrolled before her on the counter. 'A lighter weave,' she said, 'with spring coming on – a lighter weave. Do you have no . . . Shall I be forced then to wait till I can visit Leeds?'

I grew restless. I watched, through the shop window, a two-horse waggon loading up in the timber yard opposite. Then as I gazed, I saw: coming surely from the church – no, spilling out – such a collection of people. More women than men, a few children, all with shawls covering their heads, like millhands. But all of them worn and grubby, trailing dirty skirts, the men with long hair, the children without clogs.

Quietly I opened the shop door, to see them more closely. I knew who they were. They were the Liverpool Irish. Like the

Irish who lived down by our canal and whom Uncle Sutcliffe employed at Horsfield Mill.

And then the man came out, and stood in the doorway of the church. Dressed in a white robe with a girdle, and big feet in black boots. A face I knew.

Or thought I did. Surely it was the face that had bent over me, five years ago now? Muttering words in a language I didn't understand. The kink-cough. And near death.

A hand on my arm, the door pulled to, and the rest of me jerked back into the shop. Aunt Martha slapped me.

'Mischievous bairn,' she said to Mr Cox, 'the minute one's back is turned.' She pushed me on to a chair. 'Stay there.'

From my seat I could see nothing outside now. I began to fiddle with a packet of pins lying on the counter. She slapped my fingers. Above the fusty smell of the materials, cloths and buckram and braids, I thought I could catch the other scent, the heady smell that wafted out from the church door. Would it still be there when we came out?

It was. Aunt wrinkled her nose in disgust. The congregation had almost dispersed now. The priest stood talking to some children by the schoolrooms in Clarence Street.

'Disgusting,' she said, in a cross voice. She was angry with me still, holding my hand in a vice-like grip. 'What a stench . . . *Incense* they call it . . . When they used the old Assembly Room, before their church was built, they say it took all of Monday to be rid of it . . . Today must be one of their *Holy*days as they call them.' She was talking to herself now. 'Holy, indeed. Antichrist, that's what. Antichrist.'

It was pronounced the same as 'Aunt'. I could not understand. I exasperated her yet again: 'Whose auntie is Christ then?'

'Child, child! I can't be doing with your nonsense. What *is* the child talking of?' She gave my hand a shake. 'The Irish of course. They're Roman Catholics. They're disgusting with their dirty ways . . . Your uncle said –'

I never heard what Uncle Eli said because just then the priest began to walk in our direction.

'Come along,' she said. 'That's near enough. Hurry on, child . . . It was a bad day's work, giving them bishops again. I don't know what the government was about. Romanist bishop this and Romanist bishop that. As if the Chartists and the revolution weren't enough to worry about . . .'

*

I still went sometimes with Kit to Trough Edge Farm, to his Uncle Thomas. Perhaps once every five or six weeks. Betty had given up remarking on it. But she always scrubbed me very thoroughly on my return. 'Were you in with the calves again then? You never know what's in those cowsheds – and happen you won't till you're taken poorly . . .'

How happy I was with Kit. When I thought about the time we spent together, either on the farm or perhaps out walking – for sometimes on a Sunday we would just go out walking, until my legs tired – then in my memory it was always sunlight. Sunlight, although time and again the north wind had blown, or the piercing east wind. Once we had been caught in summer hail, with stones the size of pigeon's eggs.

One Sunday soon after I came back from Aunt Martha's, we walked in the direction of Luddenden Foot. We ended up at the railway station. I was not surprised, for Kit, although not so keen as once he was, still hankered after working there.

I reminded him then that we had known – no, my parents had – the Miss Brontës' brother, when he had worked there ten years ago. And now the sisters had become famous writers.

'Uncle Sutcliffe says he and Papa went on the razzle with Branwell Brontë.'

'On the *razzle*? Did they now?' Kit said, laughing.

We arrived just in time to see the half past twelve train for Liverpool. Together we watched it steam out. Kit then went into the office and talked to the stationmaster, while I was allowed to sit on a high stool and look at the ledger. Although he appeared shy, Kit had no difficulty in such situations.

As we walked back, 'I'd not mind that,' he said. 'And Mam'd like it – me on t'railways. Any road, I've still t'notion.'

'Why don't you?'

'We've our home, that goes with mill work. And so . . . Then well – it's mebbe best kept as a fancy. I'd mebbe not like it when I were doing it. That's often t'way wi' notions . . .' And then he grinned and laughed. Kit laughing was a lovely sight, for his long arms went everywhere, waving about as if they belonged to someone else. Then he said more seriously:

'But I reckon what I need is to tak care of Mam . . . you don't know your fortune, Christabel, that you've a dad –'

'I do, I do!' I said, thinking just then, for that moment, that I must be the luckiest child in the world – with a father like Papa, and a family such as ours. And a friend like Kit.

I asked Mama: 'Can I read – do you have Miss Brontë's book?'

'Which one?' Mama looked alarmed and distracted at the same time.

'*Jane Eyre*, it's called – they call it, don't they?'

'Ah, that one. Well . . . Why do you ask, pet?'

'I want to read it.'

'Oh, we don't have it,' she said hurriedly. 'I've misplaced my copy. I don't know where it's to be got.'

'The Lord Nelson Library?' I said.

'I wouldn't know. Papa will know. But it is certain to be out. And . . . also, it is not a book for children, you know.'

'I am not a child.'

'Not a child? At eight. Oh, Christabel . . .'

'Tell me the story then,' I said, 'if I am not to read it. Tell me *what happens* . . .'

On Easter Sunday Aunt Flora and Uncle Sutcliffe came over to dinner at Wade House. We ate late, at two o'clock. Aunt Flora had painted some eggs for us: a delicate design of spring flowers. We were required to thank her at once. But by this time, Halliwell had already cracked his and was extracting the meat. Papa cuffed him.

Today they had brought with them Aunt Flora's brother. Alexander Gilbert was a solicitor down in London. I did not like him at all. He was very smartly dressed, with a smooth manner and a habit of inclining his head when he spoke, which was with a very affected voice and an accent I had not heard before. He seemed also an odd shape. He moved with difficulty, stiffly. His cheeks were unnaturally red.

Phil and Meg thought him wonderful. They spoke of him all the time. 'Uncle Alexander means to invite *us* to the Great Exhibition!'

'My first journey north –' Alexander was saying.

'And I don't doubt you fancied us all savages,' said Papa. 'Well, we'll not confound your expectations. Do they please you, our rough ways? You should have seen Sutcliffe's bonny behaviour before he reformed. Before your sister tamed and ruined a good lad . . .'

He was meant to be cutting up the Yorkshire pudding. Halliwell pulled at his sleeve now and he stopped good naturedly enough, and began to serve the batter.

Aunt Flora said, 'Alexander has promised to make us rich.'

'What's all this about money?' Grandma Woodward said, pouring rich onion gravy over her pudding and then slopping a dribble over mine.

'After our disaster,' Uncle Sutcliffe said. 'The railway collapse . . . Alexander has promised to make us rich.'

'Oh aye,' my father said. 'That's right, is it?'

'Our disaster. We've to see it like an Act of God,' Uncle Sutcliffe said.

'I thought it was George Hudson, not the Almighty . . . Any road, it's worsteds – *they're* what'll make us rich. Put your brass in the mill, Sutcliffe.'

Alexander tittered. Then head inclined, he said:

'Profit, loss, *trade* – you've a safe little world here. Safe and deuced dull . . . The secret of the universe is not here, among these dark chimneys –'

'Alexander has seen Halifax,' Aunt Flora said. 'He was quite horrified. Bradford and Leeds he will not even approach.'

'I think I would need a *mask*. One must grow up with the effluvia to become accustomed to it.'

'The daft lad, what's he on about?' Grandma Woodward asked.

'*Wise* investment,' Alexander was saying, 'that is the answer. Put your money in the hands of someone who knows. And best of all, someone in the family –'

'Not *my* family,' Papa said.

He had been growing increasingly short with our visitor. When later on, Alexander went for a tour of the garden with Aunt Flora, he said:

'Well, that brother-in-law of yours – he's not one of those can say nowt in a long time . . . And what an elegant shape, eh, Sutcliffe?'

'That Mr Gilbert, that kin of Mrs Sutcliffe's,' Betty told Mercy, 'they do say he's corseted. Laced in like a woman, and not a bonny one at that. And you should have seen his rosy cheeks. Old Mrs Woodward was muttering . . . I heard the mistress say too. He *rouges*, they reckon.'

'It were a bad match, any road. Mr Sutcliffe, he ought to have found one of his own kind.'

'Aye. Rosy cheeks, indeed . . .'

Kit was not my only friend. I had also Mr Hume. I was never afraid now in the churchyard, only sad because Josh was buried there. But if any idea of a ghost, a Grimshaw ghost, had come into my head, I knew to whom I could run. When I remembered our meeting it seemed to me that, if he had not come, I might have died. I had heard stories of people who *died of fright*.

And indeed three or four times since, I had had a fearful nightmare about Josh's death. Because it was so dreadful and haunted me long after Betty had given us breakfast, I had each time escaped my governess and made my way up to the Vicarage.

Mr Hume had time for me. I saw that he was busy, because the table in front of him was full of papers. But each time he said:

'Ah, Christabel – you remembered my promise! You are going to let me be your friend.'

And then, sitting me down beside him, he listened to my tale of horrors.

Early in May, Grandma Woodward had an apoplectic stroke. Although she survived it, her brain had been affected. She ceased to be the Grandma Woodward we had known. For years she had kept indoors, especially on Sundays, seldom feeling well enough to attend church. But now she was more or less confined to her room, where we would visit her at least once daily. Sometimes she spoke nonsense, but mostly her mind wandered, stuck in the days when Joshua Woodward had founded the mill. I wondered if it was not some of it a blessing for Mama, who could now no longer be criticized.

The second half of June brought bright sunny weather. Papa and Uncle Sutcliffe travelled to London for four days, to visit the Crystal Palace in Hyde Park. The Great Exhibition had opened the month before. Appleyard and Horsfield Mills had on show: furniture damasks, crimson and green durant for lining damasks, royal-blue wool damasks, green and gold silk and worsted damask, Coburg and Orleans cloths, and much much more. We had seen their brilliant colours (and no doubt also had our river Calder).

How I would have loved to join them, to visit London. In Papa's snug, where I so often sat with him, amongst the smell of cigar smoke, and samples, a poster hung on the wall opposite his desk. *The Globe in miniature, or the World at one view*. There were all the kingdoms: their length and breadth in miles, their chief cities . . . their military strength, their rulers, arts, religions. All the railways of the world. With most of this I could not be bothered. But London. Ah, the excitement of London. There was reckoned, how many tea gardens, how many hospitals . . . how many child criminals, drunkards, prostitutes (I asked what these were and Papa explained they were women gin-drinkers). Facts upon facts. The print was so small that I had to peer close up to take it all in. London. How dearly I would have loved to join Papa and Uncle Sutcliffe.

But in the event, I was to go on a quite different visit.

On the Friday of that same week, before we had even dressed, my mother came into the nursery. She spoke quietly to Betty then, after kissing Halliwell and Agnes, she said:

'We are going out together, Christabel. Just you and I. I would like you to wear –' and she picked from the cupboard a dress in tartan silk, which had been made for me just this spring.

As I sat beside her in the carriage, she was visibly nervous. I asked twice, 'Where are we going then? Where are we going?'

'To Haworth,' she said at last. 'Over the moors to Haworth.'

It was a journey of some twelve miles. We did not of course go over the moors, but by road. She did not talk much. But I kept up a flow of chatter most of the way.

'Haworth – it's where Mercy lives. But there's the Brontës too –'

'Those that are left,' she said.

'Well then, Miss Brontë that wrote *Jane Eyre*. And your and Papa's friend, Branwell. The one who . . . the poems. Is that who we are going to see?'

'Where he lies buried, yes. He is dead, remember Christabel.'

It was warm in the carriage. The sun came up higher even as we drove. Unaccustomed heat. Vivid blue sky. The leaves were dappled in sunlight as we drove past the turning for Ewood. And the estates that Johnny Grimshaw had inherited at the age of twelve.

Haworth came into view. When we reached the foot of the steep hill leading up into the village, Mama said:

'It's best perhaps when Papa and Uncle Sutcliffe return, that you don't say exactly where we have been. Unless of course you should be asked . . . Papa was sad too at Branwell's death. He would not wish to be reminded.'

She said we should leave the carriage at the bottom, for the road was too steep. She told John, the coachman, 'We shall be some time.'

53

The road was indeed steep, and narrow. Cobbled, with its stone setts laid endways so as to grip the horses' hooves. As we trudged slowly up, a cart passed us, the horses straining. On either side of us, tall houses, of familiar millstone grit, with today, the vigorous sunlight softening the stone. At the head of the village, we came to a public house, the Black Bull Inn.

There were not many people about. It was the hour for most of them to be at the mills. One or two persons looked at us oddly. We were not particularly smartly dressed (my tartan was only my second best). But we were strangers.

Behind and above the church was the graveyard. How unlike the green and russet, the rushing water, the ivy of my Luddenden churchyard. Bare of trees, and so crowded: how many must have died. Tombs tilting, one on to the other. And glimpsed behind – for it was still only June – the dun-coloured moors.

My mother had tight hold of my hand. We went through the tall iron gate, and into the church. St Michael and all Angels. My eyes adjusted to the light. The pews were very dark, black almost. As with ours, names were written on their sides in white letters.

The pulpit had three decks, with a stair. My mother told me, 'Go up it. Yes, you may . . .' The top deck had a sounding board. Upon its underside I read: 'For me to live is Christ, and to die is gain.' Ph 1.21. William Grimshaw A.B. Minister 1742 . . .

'Mr Grimshaw,' I said, climbing down.

'Yes, pet.' Her voice was low because we were in church. She was sitting quietly in one of the pews.

Then, 'I think it is here,' she said, rising up. 'Come Christabel.' She went over to the communion table. A wall tablet on the right side of it had written on it: 'Here lie the remains of MARIA BRONTË . . . Here also lie the remains of MARIA BRONTË DAUGHTER OF THE AFORESAID . . .'

And on and on, more and more. The first inscriptions widely spaced, with biblical quotes. The last, for Anne Brontë (a record only for she had died two years ago at Scarborough), had used up all the space.

I saw then what she wished me to look at, what it was she had come to see. 'Here also lie the remains of PATRICK BRANWELL BRONTË, who died Sept. 24th, 1848, aged 31 years . . .'

She sat for a while in the pew before it, her head bowed. Then she buried her face in her hands.

'Mama, are you all right, Mama?' I tapped her on the shoulder. 'You're not poorly?'

She lifted her face. I saw she had been crying.

'No, I am not poorly, Christabel.' She stood up. 'Now there is something else we have to do.'

The church clock struck midday as we walked again through the tall iron gate. Two children, carrying a bundle of laundry, stopped and frankly stared. I put my tongue out at them.

We went up the lane now, past the schoolhouse on our right, towards the greystone building standing above the churchyard. It was square, two storeyed. As we walked I saw that my mother trembled. A stone wall separated the house from the graves. In front grew a lilac bush or two, the blooms dead. Our feet crunched over the gravel as we came up to the door. Some small pink flowers were in bloom in the strip of earth before the house. Mama pulled the bell.

At first no one answered. To either side of us, the sun glittered against the small, shining windows.

Then a woman servant opened the door. From the hall behind her came the sound of a dog barking. Deep. As we stood there an aged large yellow dog, grey about the muzzle, padded up behind her. There was a smell of dinner cooking.

Mama asked, 'Is Miss Brontë at home?'

The servant looked doubtful.

'Are you Martha?' Mama said.

'I might be –'

'Can I see your mistress then? We –'

'Miss Charlotte's gone to Manchester.'

I thought she was about to shut the door. Another dog appeared, a King Charles this time. Like Trissie. I wanted to run up and stroke it, but I was afraid of the big dog.

'*Mr* Brontë then?' Mama said. 'If he's at home? I was – we were friends of his son . . .'

'I mun see –' the woman began. But at that moment an old man came out from the room at the front.

He was tall with very white hair, and the bristly beginnings of a beard. There was a green shade over his eyes. He wore a very high, very full white neckcloth – it seemed as large as the face above it.

'Can I help now, Martha?' His voice was courteous. He spoke with an accent I half-recognized. The servant muttered something. He put his hand behind his ear, to hear better. Then he turned in our direction:

'Well, what can we do for you?'

A tall man, a very tall man. And I was so small. My mother

too. I was frightened and put the small reticule I carried up before my face, so that only my eyes showed.

'. . . a Mrs Woodward,' Mama was saying. 'My husband . . . Mr Woodward and I, and my brother . . .' Her pretty voice faltered. 'Friends of your son –'

'Where? Where was this?'

'At Luddenden. Luddenden Foot. The railway –'

And then he was muttering something – to himself? To us? I caught the words 'false friends' . . . He seemed distressed or enraged, or both. His face quivery. I kept my face hidden still.

My mother was upset too. Her mouth shaking. I thought she was about to weep again. She had taken my hand to lead me away. We walked back past the schoolhouse with its small belfry, and into the village again.

'If he had but seen you,' she said. 'He cannot have *seen* you, Christabel . . . But then, his sight. There was trouble, of course.'

She expressed surprise that I had been so shy. 'Hiding like that, pet. What made you so shame-faced? A child that's never shame-faced – what made you so today?'

I said, 'I didn't *want* that cross gentleman to see me.'

'He had much to be angry, and sad, about, Christabel.'

She said then after a few moments, as we passed the church again and came to the Black Bull, 'I can scarcely move for cramp in my head. The muscles of my face . . .'

It was not like her to complain. I had never in my life heard her complain. Although sometimes unhappy, she was always well and strong. And because of this, I grew concerned, and frightened.

She went into the chemist's shop in the square, where she bought some laudanum. As we walked slowly down the hill, she lectured me on the evils of opium, and opium derivatives. 'It is only for pain, Christabel pet. But alas, many begin that way, and then cannot control it . . . It is a wonderful crutch if you are temporarily lame. But, how easy to become lame *without* it, so that you are always in need of your crutch.'

Kirkgate, the steep hill down from the village, had become more crowded now. Many millhands had come out for their dinner.

I had become hungry and asked if we might not buy something to eat. I felt a sudden sick emptiness. But she said that John the coachman had food for us, and that we would stop and eat somewhere on the moorland road.

4

Three years now since little Josh was drowned. He had not been painted or drawn during his lifetime, except for a pen and ink drawing at nine or ten months. Now Aunt Flora had drawn him from memory for Mama. I did not like the drawing. It did not resemble him although it was correct in detail. The shape of the head, square, the button eyes, the curls, the full lips – she had all that, but she did not have Joshua. Mama was very polite about it and told her it was 'a vivid likeness, a true likeness'. It was framed and placed in the dining-room.

'What a dear little lad,' some visitor said, and Mama explained that it was her youngest and that 'we lost him, three years since'. But I knew that it was not Joshua. Aunt Flora had not captured him and I was angry with her for that. The dimpled cheeks were easy to portray, but what of the look on his face when he pulled at my skirts, shouting, 'Cisty, Cisty!' or when he romped with Trissie, or just before he began to cry? I never wanted Josh to cry. But his happy face, that was not there either. And Mama knew that surely?

I determined to draw him myself. I knew I could do better. No Woodward or Armstrong had any talent with a pen or paintbrush, but my father had always been impressed with everything I drew, from my first infant scribbles to the elaborate copies I was now making of drawings in *Fraser's Magazine*. It was a real gift, he said. And unlike my red hair it could not be attributed to Cousin Millie, who had been the clumsiest creature alive – heavy with her pastry, and not one to wield a pencil with skill. (Music was different. Mama had a pretty voice, low and true, and Papa a fine baritone, to be heard in church each Sunday. I was expected to sing well.)

I knew I could do better than Aunt Flora. Yet when I took up my pencil, and tried, it would not come right. The Josh in my head and the one on the paper, they were not the same. I wept over this drawing – I had wanted so much to present it to Mama, to see her face as she smiled and cried, 'But that is Josh exactly! Let's move Aunt's drawing at once. Oh Christabel, you are so *clever*!'

My last governess had praised my likeness of Trissie. But though I rubbed and redrew, and licked and chewed my pencil, there appeared only the crudest, wooden-faced and dull-eyed child. *And yet I remembered him.* I realized then that he would live now only in my head – and in Mama's and Papa's and Halliwell's and Agnes's and Betty's. Whenever he should leave our heads, he would be gone for ever. Until we met again in Heaven.

My last governess . . . Yes. I was ten, but I had already had six governesses since the first Miss Walton, when I was five. I think of those governesses now and feel pity for them. It could not have been an easy life in charge of Christabel Woodward – nor later, Halliwell and Agnes. Halliwell was already proving a governess baiter, but in a sly manner. Mysterious tappings on her bedroom wall, letting a mouse out of a box-trap to run beneath her skirts, tying lengths of cotton to trip her up.

With me, it was quite other. I answered back continually, questioned everything. There was not a fact of history or geography or botany which I was not prepared to argue. But mostly I was simply rude.

This summer we had yet another, new at Easter: a Miss Dutton. Her reign had lasted four months now. But already she was showing signs of unhappiness, dissatisfaction.

Mama had tried talking to me: little lectures on the difficulties of a governess's life. She always took the side of the governess of the moment, however hateful that governess might be. Other people's mothers did not. Cousin Phil told us haughtily that:

'Mama believes *us*, whatever we say . . . My word, we have fun! Rattling good tales we tell of them. They don't dare to say we're fibbing – they might lose their places. Governesses starve if they can't find places.'

But we had a stout one that summer. I thought a spell of starvation wouldn't hurt her. I was very hateful (I blush to write some of it now). Miss Dutton was stout, and by far the oldest we had had. She had been many years with a previous family – she told us she had taught nine of them and would have liked I think to be engaged for one of *their* children. She was to accompany us to Filey where we spent three weeks that July.

From the white house in the crescent on the hill top, our pony and trap clattered down the wide curving road to the sands. Long afternoons – Trissie running barking into the sea – watching the bathing machines, playing in the rock pools. On really warm days a picnic table would be set up. Or if the tide was right, we might walk along the Brig, that great length of rock stretching out to sea for over a mile. A natural pier. It was important to turn back in time. At the end of the Brig was a cave. But could one shelter there? No. For once the tide was up, the sea would come in and dash us against the cave walls. I was mesmerized, frightened, daring – I dreamed of being trapped there. I dawdled as we walked back, dawdled at the turn, took risks. Halliwell ignored us all, marching resolutely on before – he was at the head of his army. But Agnes clung timidly to Miss Dutton, who refused to be frightened on my behalf. Her phlegm forced me to extremes of foolhardiness.

'Look *down* at this rock pool, Miss Dutton. If you get down like this, if you're careful – look what I can see.'

'Stop her, look at Christabel!' Agnes screamed. She had become an anxious child, easily agitated. Her agitation (caused so often by me) irritated my mother, who would grow impatient and tell her to be less of a baby.

'Stop it, stop her!' Agnes screamed now. But Miss Dutton, although Agnes plucked at her skirt (I could see this from the corner of my eye, as I swayed at the water's edge – I saw too Agnes's screwed-up, panic-stricken face), Miss Dutton said only, slowly, calmly, 'Foolish child,' ignoring the pulling at her skirts. 'Foolish child.' And it was not me she meant.

On summer evenings that August, back home now, when we had been put to bed, far too early, I would get out and, threatening Agnes if she should so much as murmur or call out, would draw back a little the heavy curtains. It was still light now until after eight o'clock. I would trace the outline of the church below, fancy I heard the creamy fall of the mill stream, watch the slight movement of the tops of the churchyard poplars, the elms. Soon, too soon, their leaves would fade.

If I watched long enough I might perhaps see dear Mr Hume leave the Vicarage, to make his way down to the church or to pay an evening visit to a parishioner. My friend, Mr Hume. Just as Kit was *my friend*. Two people I loved – and yet both so different.

I needed them that summer. I was so difficult – a worry, I knew, to Mama, exasperating Papa. I was still his darling, of course, but more and more often instead of cuddling me, he would have to reprimand me. As yet another governess left, or as there was yet another report from Betty of my disobedience, my impudence, obstinacy, lies (yes, I told fibs too), he would sigh and pull at his hair, and say:

'What's to be done, eh? What's to be done with you?'

And then when I had had a severe telling off, there in his snug, often I did not feel so like sitting with him, in that room in which I had spent so many happy hours. Smarting from his tongue, I did not want to climb on his knee – and perhaps too I was growing too old for that?

How fortunate then I was in my friends. Yes, I needed both my friends. And how good it was that Mr Hume knew nothing of the hot water in which I lived almost constantly, and that Kit knew but thought nothing of it.

The month of August was sultry. The days long, and often overcast. How did I spend them? For it was only on Sundays that I could go with Kit to the farm.

Sewing. There was a missionary basket for which I had to sew. My picked, pricked efforts, often blood-stained, were in the end of little use. Mama would curb a smile and then say, a little distractedly, 'You must learn to sew better. Miss Dutton, please go over with Christabel. The size of the stitches. I know she is only a child but . . .' I held the sewing up to my face, the better to see it (my sight varied, altering from day to day. Crinkling up my eyes, on a clear day it was surprising how far I saw. But with sewing, which I hated – perhaps that was why – I could not see those stitches, unless right before my face).

A Thursday afternoon. Papa had ridden over to Halifax and Mama had left that morning with Halliwell, to take the train from Luddenden Foot. They were to stay three nights with his godmother in Leeds. A sleepiness lay over the house like a great yawn. We had earlier walked up to the village with Miss Dutton. Agnes, after dinner, had to go to bed. She was sick – returning the cooked plums she had just eaten. She lay in the night nursery, looking peaky. She cried for Mama. Betty was afraid it might be the beginnings of what they called summer cholera – there were three cases in the village. I had heard that Mrs Hume was one of them. I could not bear to think of the pale head-hanging Mrs Hume with burning, liquid innards. I thought that her husband would not let her suffer.

Betty was to go out. Ellen, one of the maids, would look after Agnes. And meanwhile, what to do with the afternoon? The sky darkened, then grew light again: I felt at the same time restless and yet tired, fractious. Perhaps it was this mood caused me to pick a quarrel with Miss Dutton.

She required me to read to her: 'It is no use to walk out again. I can tell you from the sky that we shall soon be soaked . . . Here is a chance now your brother is absent and your little sister in bed. We shall read –'

But reading was a private joy. I hated to read aloud to her. It was not just that I mispronounced the words – for often I did so, words whose meaning I had known for years, but which I had never said aloud – they were *my* words. It was ugly perhaps, the way I would not share them.

'Well,' she said, picking up *The One Hundred Wonders of the World.*

'No,' I said, 'I shan't.'

She paid no attention, saying only, 'Begin on page fourteen. I will take up my sewing and you may read to me that chapter. It will be practice in reading aloud *and* a gathering of information.'

'I shan't. Why should I do schoolwork?'

'This is a book I have frequently seen you reading on your own. And you are on your own as often as you can.'

'I like to be,' I said hotly. 'I like to be alone. And that book, it is my book. I shan't read aloud –'

She said nothing.

'I like to be alone,' I repeated.

Her curious flat face and pale fish eyes stared back at me.

'Shan't!' I shouted, my behaviour like that of a child half my age. Because she paid no attention, I shouted the louder, 'Shan't! I want to be alone, I like to be alone.'

Now she stared back, in that curious manner she had, staring at some place past me, *as if I weren't there.*

'All right,' I threatened, 'I shall go out by myself. I'm going for a walk. By myself.' For a moment there flitted across her face a weary, exasperated look.

'I have had enough,' she said suddenly. 'Enough.' To no one in particular. Not to me. 'Enough.'

'And I've had enough of you,' I blustered. 'Always telling me this, always . . . I want to be free. To go off. To go *anywhere* . . .'

It wasn't a very brave cry. For after all I was free enough. I did quite often walk out by myself, provided I said always where I was going.

I do not know now how long I meant to stay out. I did not take a cloak or wrap against the possible rain. But I remember that I took off my slippers and put on my boots, and that wearing them, I went back into the room, where Miss Dutton sat, as before, staring. Her sewing, which she was to have done while I read, lay untouched on her lap. I did not speak.

Outside the air was closer, heavier than indoors. I did not go far at first, wandering around the garden, that part near the drive. On a thorn bush, a ladybird, 'ladyclock' as we called them, crawled from a leaf onto my hand. Fly away, fly away home. And as suddenly she flew. The heavy air was full of little mites, thunder bugs. I felt as I walked down Stocks Lane as if the sky would fall in on me. Down towards the church the stream ran low, the fall feeble. The trees were menacing in the murky light. I wished that Mr Hume might come out of the Vicarage at this moment, and ask me to walk with him. We would talk together as we went and I would at once feel better.

But I saw no one as I walked down the lane. I did not turn towards the village. A two-horse waggon rattled behind and then past me, laden with beer barrels.

What did I do with myself? I passed that afternoon wandering. I went into a field up behind our house, where cows were grazing. I sat near a small pond. There the flies bothered me. I brushed them away. Then for a while I slept, half-propped on the grass.

I dreamed that my boots hurt, that I sat looking at a red raw patch which throbbed. When I woke suddenly, my boots did hurt. As I stood up, they felt heavy, my feet swollen inside them. My bonnet stuck to my hair with sweat. It seemed hotter, more oppressive than ever. I had no desire to go home, or indeed anywhere. I had no idea what time it was, or how long I had been asleep. No desire, except for a drink. But the pond was stagnant, green-filmed and fly-covered.

Back on the road, after a while I saw I was not far from Luddenden Foot. The railway station – I would stop there, beg a glass of water. I hoped now that Miss Dutton would have begun to worry about me. Let her worry, I thought. Let her get into trouble with Mama . . .

I did not go as far as the station. I turned instead towards the river. Beneath the lowering sky, it ran greasy and scum-covered, effluent and dyes marring the clear water. Above were the high banks of the railway, and beyond that, the hills, pastureland, dotted with farmhouses. Below the river ran the canal, its near bank dotted with the shacks, tin-roofed, tumbledown, in which the Irish workers and their families lived. Once Grandpa Armstrong's, now Uncle Sutcliffe's workers. Time would not be up at the mill yet. There would only be a few mothers of very young children at home perhaps, or the very old and the sick.

I wandered along, kicking the ground with my aching feet. There was a smell of jack-by-the-hedge, wild garlic, which grew just back from the water's edge. Smoke was coming from some of the shacks. I approached nearer. I was frightened – and curious.

A dog came running towards me, a squirming little dog like a small pig, even down to the curly tail. One eye was sore and encrusted. I stroked and played with it. It lay on its back to be tickled. A small barefooted child wandered out, dragging a bad leg. Then stopped before me, staring.

'What do they call you?' I asked. He or she – I couldn't tell which, for it was still in skirts and torn ones at that – did not answer. I asked again.

But by then a woman had come out from the first of the shacks. 'Noreen,' she called, 'Noreen.' Coming up and snatching the child. Hair almost covered her face: 'What is it, what do you want?' The dog had run to her and she made as if to kick it. She pushed the long hair back from her eyes. The little dog ran back to me.

'Can I see your home?' I asked. She gazed at me as if I were mad. Some other women had gathered round now and were looking at me curiously but not unkindly.

'I'm thirsty,' I said, 'and need a drink of water.' I followed her and the child into the shack. Inside the light was poor, and the air smelled. Something was boiling on a stove at the back. An old woman was bent over it, her dress ripped at the back, a clump of white material showing through. Her thin wispy hair fell to her shoulders. A pail stood on the floor by the door. The woman reached for a tin mug, dipped it in and handed it to me. As I drank – it tasted warm from the stove, and brackish – I could feel others crowding round me, pressed against my skirt. The shack was suddenly full. The little dog, or another little dog, nipped my ankles.

On a three-legged stool there was a small white statue of a woman in a long blue veil, with bright red eyes. Her feet were missing. On the dirt floor just beneath her lay a bunch of wild flowers.

The woman who had given me the drink said,

'You're from where now? Little lady, aren't you, aren't you the little lady?' She poked a finger at the old woman, who turned from the stove: the face looking towards me was hairy, straggling on the chin. The eyes dark and down-slanted. I did not know what to say. I could not answer their questions. And indeed they did not seem to need answers, for they were squabbling amongst themselves, pushing and shoving, so that I nearly fell.

The old woman spoke rapidly to the younger one. Weird, wonderful, never-heard-before language. Jabber, jabber, jabber . . . Then pointing at me. Finally, the younger woman took my arm, and then, with small children dragging at my heels, and the little dog too, she led me outside and into another and much larger shack. She said to me, 'They're all but back, did you not see them? The children, the fellas . . .'

As I stepped outside, I saw coming towards us, tiredly, a thin column of older children, men, women, on their way back from the mill. It must be later than I thought. I had no idea now of time.

Inside this second shack, in a makeshift cradle, two babies lay end to end. One asleep, the other mewling. After a moment a woman standing there picked the mewling one up roughly and pushed it against her breasts. I had never seen such a thing.

'Who's the little lady?' There they were, asking again.

I wanted to say then, 'Don't you know me? You don't recognize me?' But why should they? It was not like those millhands, not like the Ogdens, who saw our family weekly in St Mary's church. And when was I ever at Horsfield Mill?

Yet how often, passing by, I had looked across at that gathering on the canal bank. Part of the landscape, my landscape, those shacks, rambling, cluttered, messy, there by the canal. Now suddenly I was part of it: it was almost as if I had long gazed at a picture – they had after all in some ways not been real – and now had walked inside that picture.

One of the men, they called him Fergus, came up and stared at me. 'She's the little lady indeed, a fine lady, look at that now . . .' (Stained skirt, wrinkled stockings, hair full of grass – but of course I looked fine. And rich.) 'And you're after paying us a visit then? Where's she from, won't she say now?'

But they none of them wanted an answer to their questions. They wanted only to ask them. To crowd round me, press upon me. Their voices caressed me, just as their hands did.

And so it was that in a little while I found myself so much a part, so firmly settled in, that I was eating with them. I had not known I was hungry. But it was of course many hours since the meal eaten in the nursery with Miss Dutton – in that other world.

I was in the larger shack again, the babies were back in the cradle – but now there were seven eight nine people or more. It was not a meat meal. And there was no table at which to sit. There were turnips, those same I had smelled cooking, mixed with oatmeal into a sort of porridge. And the potatoes in a basket. A bowl of salty water stood by – they thrust their potatoes in before eating, and I did the same. 'Have a dab then, have a dab,' the man Fergus urged.

The children were never still when they ate. No one hindered their running in and out. How unlike my staid nursery meals with Halliwell and Agnes and Miss Dutton. The little dog, and then two others appearing from nowhere, fought for the scraps the children dropped. Everyone ate with their fingers. And then a mug of tea: not the tea-kettle tea I drank at home – pale, milky, tasteless – but a brew which dried my mouth.

There was the sound of a mouth organ. It set the dogs barking. The children left their meal and wandered out, food squashed in their hands. On the grass a small man with a red kerchief, showing almost black in the dying light, was dancing. Another sitting cross-legged played the mouth organ.

A fire had been lit. Further along, another was being started. The crowd grew. Three men were dancing now. And then some children with them. The music was fast, whirling.

My feet began to tap. One man put his arms round me, then pulled me into the circle. I scarcely knew what my legs did, my feet, my head. Someone held me up, pushed me here and there. Left, right. Up, down. Up, down. Wilder and wilder. Perhaps it was only for minutes – I remember it as hours.

They were drinking all the while. 'Fetch a jug, fetch a jug . . .'

For a moment I was afraid. The sky, evening sky now, dark, and then a low rumbling over the hills, distant thunder, growing closer.

But then I was swept up again – around me people drinking, shouting, singing. In the distance all was darkness, purple-black. Far away a light – was it the Weaver's Arms? I was swept up into a dance. Another man now held me by the hands, then by the waist, a moment later throwing me to another. I was hot, tired, at the same time excited, wildly – by the music, the warmth, the rhythm. Clapping hands, swaying.

They were making a fuss of me.

'Och the dear little pet, will you look at her now? Look at the dear . . . And hair as red as Maire's here. Maire . . . Here, Michael now . . .' And I was pushed into the arms of a boy only a little taller than me. 'Hasn't she the hair of Maire?' I could not distinguish the heat of their breath from the heat of the evening air. Electric. I was held up in the air, my bare feet waving wildly. Twirling in the dance . . .

The first drops of rain fell. And then with a rush, more and more. There was a flurry, laughing and shouting, no more music suddenly as we ran for shelter. And then above the laughing, chattering, the cries of a child, great claps of thunder. Lifted through a door, I was at once outside again, to see the great forks of lightning flashing across the hill tops.

'Away in,' said a voice, the man they called Fergus. 'Come away in, pet.' The steamy heat inside: I was hot, too hot, even though while dancing I'd shed my cloth jacket, had left my boots and had been dancing in bare feet.

'Jesus Mary Joseph,' said the mother. I was in the place now where I'd eaten. Fergus had his arm about me: 'Are you afraid, pet? Little one. Are you ever afraid?'

The rain lashed the tin roof. Then more enormous claps of thunder. All of heaven, the heavens opened, booming. I broke away, put my head round the poorly fastened door. I saw the sky, the hills below suddenly illumined, green, yellow. More flashes of lightning. The sky came towards me. I had never been afraid of a storm before, had always loved them. I would not be afraid now. No, in spite of the crying children around me, I would not. For I, who so often at home felt alone now, was excited, warm, loved, still part of the dance. The storm was part of the dance.

Someone, the mother or the grandmother, had thrust some rag over the window. The little dog whimpered and ran about.

'Hush now, will they all sleep, why don't they sleep?'

Fergus said to me, 'This little one, she who was dancing – what do they call you?'

'Belle,' I said, 'Belle.'

'Well now, Belle, you can't ever go home in this, can she, can you? Belle, is it? Belle, Holy Mother of God – listen a while, *listen* to it –'

The grandmother muttered something from the corner. She had lain down, covered by some old rags.

'Jesus,' Fergus yelled, as the thunder crashed. *'Jesus!'* He smelled of beer as he put his arm about me again. 'Jesus – will we pray now?'

'Light a candle, have you another candle now?'

Another man came in, banging through the doorway. 'It's Conal. Will I sleep here?'

'He can't stand. Look at the way he's wet.' Then they gabbled with the old granny in that language I could make nothing of.

'What do you speak?' I asked.

'The Gaelic of course. Isn't it our language?' And Fergus pointed to the granny, and then to two others.

He explained to me that the granny had come over in the Hunger, six or seven years ago now. Different people answered my questions, but I couldn't always understand what they said, so broad was their brogue, voices thick with it, thick and distorted with drink.

'Wouldn't you live with us?' Fergus asked now. 'Wouldn't she ever? Would you like that, Belle?'

'I could light candles to the Virgin,' I said.

'Would you ever? Would you do that? You could be our own little . . .' They all joined in, it seemed voices from everywhere: 'Little love . . . look at her hair now, did you ever, and the stuff of her frock . . . how she danced . . . you could live with us now . . . Fergus, Maire, Terry, listen to that now . . .' The smell, the strangeness, which was at the same time familiar. I could slip easily into this smelly warmth, this overflow of easy effortless affection, blanketing thought. For a second I saw myself, starting a new life . . .

'Did Belle never say where she lived? Fine clothes she has . . .'

'Hush, wisht. Oughtn't they all to sleep? There's no going out the way the storm is.'

One of the women handed me a bundle of rags. She wrapped them round me. 'Lay there, lay still.' She pointed to a place on the floor where a child lay whimpering, its arm round a dog.

'Hush, wisht. Sleep now. Just listen to that storm, will you? Jesus Mary Joseph, Holy Mary Mother of God.'

They all kissed me. Fergus said again, 'Would you ever live with us, Belle? Isn't she the dear one? Little pet, come and live with us.' His breath smelled. He smelled.

Everyone seemed to be lying down now. When I thought of

the ritual at home. Betty. Hot water jug, teeth, scrubbing of the face, nails examined, turning inside out of clothes. And here I was, half my attire missing, huddled with a weeping child and a small dog beneath two rags, on some sacking lightly stuffed with straw. It smelled. They smelled.

So I lay there listening while the skies rained down outside, and the very walls shook. And the prayers in both languages flowed on. Reminiscence blurred with prayer. Talk, exclamations.

And yet I felt strangely safe, and happy. Excited. An adventure. I knew of course that their God, but most especially their Virgin, His Mother, would look after me as so evidently they were looked after.

For a little while more the storm raged. Then died down. The voices grew silent. A heavy snoring from the men, who were sprawled, half-sitting, one near the shrine, another by the door. The last candles guttering.

I dreamed. I must have slept a while, for I dreamed.

The banging, the shouting, awoke me. Invaded my dream. I woke with a start. The noise outside. Voices.

Banging next door. 'No, here, here . . .'

'Open up, open up!' The door flung open. Lanterns. Two men. Benjamin Mason from the mill.

And then . . .

'Here, in here. The little lass – she's here. God be thanked. Praise be to God. She's safe.' Then calling out,

'Mr Woodward, sir, she's here, sir . . .'

It was all confusion. In the half-light, the sudden rush of night air. Damp air. The swinging light of the lanterns. Papa's voice. And then his arm round me. He suddenly filled the room – his voice harsh, anxious. Shouting now, and waving one arm. The other about me. Two men held up lanterns. We were stood now just outside the shack entrance. I caught sight of Fergus, bewildered, shambling to the door. Children cried and whined. Dogs barked.

Shadowed in the light of the lanterns, the hills and the railway line, up behind the river and canal, seemed full of menace.

'Away from her,' Papa was saying, 'you've done enough – away, get back. I'll have the law –'

I shook with fright. Rudely awoken, not sure what was happening.

'Away from her,' he kept shouting, 'away! Don't one of you try now . . .'

I sobbed. I told him, 'They've been kind, I had my tea with them, I was asleep for the night . . .' I tried to say, 'It was only for the night, it was only for . . .' For what? The adventure would have been over in the morning surely? I would have said my thank yous and taken the road home.

Even as, accompanied by the men with lanterns, he was taking me away, Papa was shouting imprecations, warnings to them all, to my friends, to those I had thought my friends.

'Don't think you've heard the last of this – don't think your employment's safe . . . Thieves,' he shouted, 'thieves, robbers of children . . .'

I don't want to remember the journey back. I sat in front of my father on his grey horse. As we jogged our way home, I shivered and sobbed. I knew that he was angry with me because he did not speak. His left arm held me in a vice-like grip. Benjamin Mason rode alongside on the bay mare, carrying a lantern. The other men went their ways.

As we came up Stocks Lane, a solitary light burned in the upstairs window of the Vicarage. In our house, downstairs, lamps were lit everywhere. Servants stood in the hall.

'Where's Mama?' I began, forgetting she was away, then starting to cry all over again.

No, I don't want to remember the roughness, the feeling, the mood of that homecoming. Handed over to Betty. 'A good scrubbing,' my father said, '*at once.*' I did not even go up to our quarters, to the nursery. It was to be done in the kitchen. Standing there in the scullery, waiting while the water was heated, shivering and sobbing still. Dawn creeping up outside. Birds singing. And being scrubbed and scrubbed . . .

'What mun we have next,' Betty said, rubbing viciously. 'What mun we have next?' The cloth was rough, the soap strong. It burned my skin. She poured water over my head, rubbed my hair, her fingers working into my scalp. 'The master's beside himself. And the mistress – when *she* hears the dance you've led us . . .'

My skin raw, smarting, my eyes soap-filled and red, shivering with fatigue and fright I was sent to bed in the guest wing. To stay there all day – or until such time as I was allowed up. In the night nursery, while Betty collected my things and I stood in the doorway, Agnes regarded me with frightened eyes.

I took the almost faceless Victoria into the bed with me. I was left alone. I cried for Josh, as always when unhappy. I fancied that had he been alive I would never have left on such a journey – to go so wildly wrong.

I cried for Mama and wondered how soon she and Halliwell would be home. I cried because I knew I must surely have hurt her. What had I done? My body ached, my skin hurt. And I had been too proud, too bewildered to ask Betty – why the scrubbing?

I left my breakfast untouched. At one o'clock, with the sun blazing outside, the little maid Ellen brought up my dinner. Stewed beef and parsnips and boiled potatoes.

'Aren't you going to eat up?' she said. 'You'll not leave that too?'

I asked her, 'Are they going to let me out? When –'

'I ken nowt, miss. I ken nowt.' She stood beside the bed. Then her curiosity got the better of her. 'Miss, whatever did you want to run off for? That Miss Dutton –'

'Where is she?' I asked, realizing suddenly that I had not seen her. She had not been sent to reprimand me. Only Betty, who had locked me in, according to Papa's dictates.

'Gone. Dismissed she was. I heard the master say she mun go. She's packed her bags and good riddance . . . She never said nowt yesternight, and it were for that the master were vexed – he were in a right plisky, for she never said nowt till gone bed time . . . And then there's Betty come looking for you, for she were out hersen while after tea . . . But she's just sat, that Miss Dutton, just sat, daft like. Then she says how she's not seen you sin dinner time. So Betty's downstairs calling for t'lads, and they're off to find the master . . . and there's a din that'd wake t'dead . . .'

But what had happened? What had they been saying? What were their fears? I learned only gradually, and then from Mama. Their fears of disease and dirt and fever. For there had been fever in the shacks only last month. It might lurk there still. And there might be other unknown dangers. It was for all these I had been scrubbed raw.

Betty stood beside my bed. The sun had moved round, so it must have been late afternoon.

'You're to get dressed.' She held out a yellow dimity dress, and my blue kid slippers, newly polished. 'The master says you've to come down.' I protested that I'd rather stay up here with her. I would dress, yes. But I wanted to stay with her. I asked, 'When is Mama coming back?'

'Well may you ask. She'll not be happy when she hears. That

70

were a wicked thing . . . Why ever did you do it? Why ever? What was up wi' ye?' she said over and over as she did my hair. I had been lying in bed unkempt. Now with the comb she tugged at the knots whilst the tears smarted in my eyes and my head grew sore. '*What got into you?* Don't you care to live with us any more?'

'I only wanted to see,' I muttered. 'Betty, I never meant to *run away*. I only wanted . . .' Because Mama, whom I needed so much, was still away, I wanted then to bury my head, a small child again, in Betty's black-aproned bosom. I felt worn with the disgrace of it all . . .

It was only when she'd finished my hair and rubbed again with a flannel my scrubbed raw face ('I can do that,' I told her, 'let me wash my own face'), only when I was quite tidied up that she said:

'You're to go down now. The master wants to see you. Your dad wants you . . .'

'Well,' Papa said, in the hall, his voice grim. 'I've nowt to say to you, lass. For I've decided against a hiding. I reckoned . . . We don't know what to do with you. *Nay*,' he said, as I smirked nervously, 'don't look at me that way, lass. Christabel –'

He was standing with his back to the dining-room door:

'I've given the task to someone else.' He flung open the door and giving me a push, said, 'In there with you –'

And inside. There, seated at the table, a book open before him, was my very own Mr Hume.

He looked at me as I walked in. His eyes, piercing eyes, fixed on me.

'Oh, Christabel,' was all he said. But his voice was low, and sad. 'Oh, Christabel . . .' He told me then to sit down, patting the chair next to his at the table. Then he closed his book, and put it to one side of him.

'I am so disappointed in you, Christabel. I thought you were to be such a good girl. And *now* . . . That you should have run away, deliberately. That you should have caused your father such dreadful anxiety . . .'

'But Mama,' I began, 'she doesn't even *know* –'

'God knows, though, Christabel.' His deep voice was so solemn, so sad, it pierced me. I moved uneasily in my chair. Where was my friend? Looking at me now with such a face.

'And anyway, Miss Dutton –'

71

'Don't try to blame your governess – she was not without fault, certainly she should have reported your absence – but, Christabel dear, it was you, was it not, who ran away? Who left loving parents to become demented with worry –'

'What about Jesus?' I said, my voice, my manner, impudent – while I tried to curb my fear. 'What about Jesus in the Temple? *He* went off and left his parents. *He* let them worry.'

'Yes, Christabel, yes. But what was Jesus's answer to his distracted parents? Do you remember?'

Eyes lowered, I murmured, '"Wist ye not that I must be about my father's business?"'

'Yes, Christabel dear. His Father *in Heaven*. He was *God's Son*. Do you really mean that you see yourself the equal of Christ?' I lowered my eyes. 'That is not what you mean, is it?'

'No.' I spoke from a full heart. A throat choked with tears. I did not want to be in the right, I did not want *not* to be found fault with (yes, I had done wrong). What I did want, and oh how I wanted it, was to be *right* with dear Mr Hume again.

'Well,' I said, 'I was going to come home. I always meant to. I had not run away – for ever. I only wanted –'

'But to your family, to your Mama and Papa, Christabel – how could it have seemed otherwise?'

Trissie yapped. I heard her breathing, snorting under the door, then scrabbling at the keyhole. It felt curiously reassuring, as if someone wished to rescue me.

I repeated stubbornly, 'I was going to come home . . .'

'Your father was not to know that,' he said sadly. 'How could he?'

Silence. A short sharp yap from Trissie. I wondered if now I might leave. But without his blessing? I sat on. And it seemed he expected me to, for he said next:

'But that is not all, Christabel.' He spoke still, more in sorrow than in anger. 'It seems . . . Did you not wonder that it was I who was asked to speak to you?'

'No,' I said valiantly. 'Not really. You are my friend, aren't you?'

'Indeed. Oh, indeed.' And leaning forward, he placed both his hands over mine. Pressing them hard on to the table: 'You see, Christabel, it is not only this escapade, distressing as that is. It is everything. Your whole manner. Your disrespect for your elders, your disregard for the truth. In other words, you are out of control.'

'Can I go, may I go now?' I said, feeling the tears about to rush. He would never now think well of me again. And yet, I had not *meant* to be bad. Oh, why could we not all be happy and love one another?

'*May I go?*'

'But Christabel, I have not finished. Look at me. No, *look* at me . . . Your father felt that it might be better, that I should be the one to tell you. He thinks, and knows your mother will agree. The answer to your being so out of control, the best thing to happen, is that you should go away to school.'

It was like a blow. Thump. As if someone struck me in the chest.

'Away? To school? Where?'

'Ah, that is not decided. But it seems it had been spoken of earlier, as a possibility. And now, after this escapade –'

'But Mama and Papa and Halliwell and Agnes. And Betty. And Trissie. And *you*!' I cried, bursting into noisy tears. 'Without all of you . . . I shan't. I won't.' I twisted and pulled my hands free from his.

But he took them again, holding them very gently in his cupped palms.

'You will,' he said. 'You will, Christabel dear.'

5

———◈———

'Christabel Woodward, what is the metropolis of Turkey, and what is its latitude? *Christabel*, I am speaking to you.'

Sarah Mullen, in the desk to my left, stood up, eager, breathless, correct.

'Constantinople,' she prattled, 'finely situated in forty-one degrees north latitude, between the sea of Marmora and the Black Sea. The inhabitants are computed at four hundred thousand. Of these two hundred thousand are Turks, one hundred thousand Greeks . . .'

'That will do. Very good, Sarah.'

Miss Pagan, our geography teacher, standing ramrod stiff beside the great globe on its stand. Soon she would force me to go up there and point before all the class. To find the latitude, I must turn the globe and bring the place to the graduated edge of the brazen meridian, when the degree on the meridian would be the latitude north or south . . . And so on and so on, ad boredom and infinitum. I was not good at geography.

'Christabel Woodward, what is it that interests you so outside? If the wind turns, then your neck I fear may stay at a latitude of – how many degrees, young ladies?'

There was a polite tittering. A ripple of it. I was not one of those who tittered. I never tittered these days. Or laughed at all.

Gazing out of the window in that classroom at The Beeches, I saw only a great stretch of lawn, sad drifts of leaves blowing across it. A gardener – no, two gardeners now – attacking them with besoms. The autumn wind sending more scurrying down from the reddened beeches which stood at the far edge of the grass.

'Constantinople forms an unequal triangle, resembling a harp, being about twelve or fourteen English miles in circumference, enclosed by walls, and on two sides by the sea and the harbour called the Golden Horn . . .'

As I stared outside, I remembered that this was a foreign country. And winter coming on – although today there was a clear blue sky with white clouds driven by the west wind.

A foreign country. The girls' school known as The Beeches was in Yorkshire, but such a different Yorkshire. Except for a short visit to Leeds, I had never before been further than Halifax. It was not that I missed the smell of the mills – how could I? It was not the house itself, for that was not so very unlike ours, built perhaps fifty or sixty years earlier when the Georges were on the throne. But much larger, in its own spacious grounds – a park almost. Walled around, with an avenue of beeches. An orchard behind the house. When I had arrived three weeks ago, the trees were still bowed with fruit, red apples, pale gold pears. There had been days still warm enough to sit under the branches, to reach up and fill our pockets with the fruit.

The countryside around was strange to me. This gentle landscape. When we walked out in crocodile three afternoons a week (and twice to church on Sundays), I would wonder where I was, how I had come here. I would stare at the gentle stretches of green meadow – flowing oh, so smoothly towards the horizon. No drystone walls between the fields. Poplars divided them here. Even the cows seemed different, placid in their lowlands beside the river. Ah yes, the river. The Ouse. How lazily it wound through the lush meadows, a broad smooth ribbon, green and willow banked.

This was the Vale of York. Luddenden was also in a valley, but its very name meant, did it not, the Valley of the Loud Noise? Craggy, wooded, birch and sycamore, and looking down from a height to the becks where the water rushed over stones. How different. And how I longed . . .

But here I must stay until Christmas. The Beeches had been Aunt Flora's school. In her time, it had been only recently opened, having been before the home of a man who had made, and later lost, a fortune in the West Indies. The two Misses Baldwin had bought the house from him some twenty years ago. Aunt Flora had been one of the first pupils. She had been happy there even though her home had been far away.

When the decision was made that I must go to school, it was she who suggested The Beeches, since my mother's old school was now no more. There were two schools at least in Halifax, and several others within easy distance – perhaps I would have been happy there, who knows? But Aunt Flora spoke to Uncle Sutcliffe, who spoke to Mama, who was at her wits' end, not wishing me to go away at all (she said so, she wept so, I believed her), and to Papa. And well, the general opinion was that if Sutcliffe and Flora said so, it must be so. (Forget the railway share disaster. This was a different sort of matter altogether.)

It seemed to me that it was all arranged within days. Weeks only certainly. A simple exchange of letters. Aunt Flora's assurances that I would be happy. And then, behind her mouth (I heard her): 'They know well how to curb an unruly temperament. We shall hear no more . . .'

The first Sunday after the visit to the Irish, I went up to see Kit. I had seen him already in church with his mother and imagined even then that he knew of my disgrace. So ashamed and distressed (and self-important) was I, that I fully expected Mr Hume to mention something of it in the pulpit. I sat alternately blushing and shaking, imagining all eyes on me. I could not believe it when the service came to an end and there had been no public shaming.

Although was not the private shame as bad, if not worse? The loss of Mr Hume . . . For as we came out of the church he greeted us just as usual, and yet I knew, from his sorrowing voice when he said my name, that everything, everything, was wrong between us . . .

So I did not try to run after Kit, but went instead up to his cottage. Mrs Ogden was there of course. I could say nothing.

'Are you poorly?' she asked, almost at once. 'You're very fevered like about t'face . . .' She appealed to Kit: 'We'd best sit her down, eh?'

No, no, I was quite all right, I told them. Heated only from the walk up. And indeed the weather, clear for a little after the thunderstorm, had grown sultry again.

I became certain they knew something. I did not want to sit there making polite conversation – saying that yes, Halliwell had been away to Leeds, and Agnes had been sick but was well again. Pretending a great thirst, I drank greedily two cups of water, and wondered if I could not just go away.

Then Kit suggested a walk. 'If you reckon you're not poorly . . .'

I said as soon as we were out of the cottage:

'Did you know I'm in trouble, Kit?'

'Aye,' he said, 'I ken there were summat . . . Only –' He said no more.

'I ran away,' I said. And then I told him the story.

76

At first he did not say very much. I thought perhaps I had shocked him, but then after a while he said:

'Poor lass –'

'They're very angry,' I said, beginning to cry.

'Nay, don't weep, Christabel –'

'I'm to go to school. Away from Luddenden –'

He smiled then: 'Hadn't you always t'notion to go to school? Mind how you asked me over and over – about Miss Wheelwright's?'

'But that was different – that was in Luddenden,' and I began to cry again.

I would not be comforted. Kit put his arm about me – it was so long an arm that I thought it would go right round again. And I laughed and said so.

'I ken there were summat that night,' he said now. 'On account of your dad and Mr Mason – they came up t'cottage . . .'

But I had not thought of that.

'. . . Asking if we'd his little lass hid with us –'

'Oh, Kit, you weren't accused?'

He laughed, 'Nay. But they were right vexed – and worrit. And no wonder. If it'd been my mam, I wouldn't rightly say how she'd be . . .'

It seemed to me then so obvious, that they should have thought first of Kit. My friend. Whose home I visited on my own.

He asked me now: 'How did they find you then?'

'Oh,' I said, 'I think it was some persons at the Weaver's Arms. When Papa kept asking – there were some who remembered noticing a little girl dancing – but dressed differently, they said. And so . . . But it was a long time before he found anything – before they told him . . .'

'I reckon like, being worrit made your dad more vexed?'

'Yes.' We sat together on a grassy knoll. In the sweltering heat, the view before us was hazy. The midday light shimmered. Ahead of us was nothing but moor – wave upon wave of purple heather, meeting a blue-grey sky.

'Will you still be my friend?' I asked.

'As if I'd not,' he said. 'A friend is a friend.' He laughed at me. 'Why ever am I to stop then?'

'I thought you might think . . . I'd been very bad.'

He laughed again. 'Happen you have the daftest notions . . . if that's *bad* . . .'

'We have nearly the same name, you and me,' I said. I had

77

only just thought of it. 'You're really Christopher, aren't you?'

'I reckon so –'

'That's two of us named after Christ . . .'

He did not seem too impressed. 'You could ask Mr Hume,' he said, 't'meaning of *Christopher* and *Christabel*. He's a scholar . . .'

But I did not want just then to think of Mr Hume. I broke off the conversation. We played catch instead amongst the heather. Kit never ran as fast as he might – I knew that – for with his long legs he would have had me at once. But we had a good enough game.

When I got home, Aunt Flora was there, with news of The Beeches.

And so it was that I went to school.

We were arranged in class according to the year of our birth. All of the ten girls in mine were already eleven. It was my misfortune to be born in late December.

And I was small. Small for my age. Small. 'She's very *small*,' I overheard. The first day in class I was seated three rows back and in such a way that I could not see the board except by craning my head. A tall, lanky girl, sat in front of me. When I should have been copying, I pushed my head from side to side (also I could not see well: I needed with my short sight to be placed nearer). 'Ah, you're very small,' the teacher said, bringing me now to the front row.

The other girls had looked at me incuriously, and then returned to their books. It was as if for most of them – with one exception – I was not there at all. And indeed I had not been for the first six weeks of term. Everyone already knew everyone else, and even those who had been new, now had friends.

'Carrot top' they called me. I'd been used all those years to being the only one in the family with red hair (other than Cousin Millie from Colne). But that there should be anything strange about it or worth mocking, I had never thought . . . 'Carrot top,' they said, 'look at little carrot top.' I wept into my pillow, as I thought of Mama who loved my hair. Who loved me.

Not only was I the youngest in class – I was also the most ignorant on almost every subject except perhaps literature, and of course drawing, for which I was occasionally praised. Again and again in those first weeks the depths of my ignorance were plumbed. Geography – but we have seen that already; French –

not one word; history – here I was all anecdotes and no facts. Or not those that Mangnall's *Questions and Answers* required of me. Charles the Second had hidden in an oak tree, but when? And who came before Henry the Eighth? Charlotte Corday assassinating Marat bloodily in his bath – when? Facts, facts. And I did not have them.

I was not sure of whom I stood most in awe: the teachers, my contemporaries, or the great girls. Those amazing beings, goddesses almost some of them, fifteen, sixteen years of age. Confident, tall – they all seemed tall though it could not have been so. And privileged. Going up to bed a full hour and a half later, allowed to linger in the dining-room over cups of tea, to walk anywhere in the grounds unsupervised. Some, the most privileged of all I thought, could even take classes. (I knew nothing then of apprenticed pupils, and thought that surely everyone must envy them their right to stand in front of the board, to correct, to reprimand, above all to pass on knowledge.)

These were the great girls. Apart from envying them their privileges, I wanted them to notice me. But some looked down on me – often literally from their great height. Others laughed at me, which was worse.

What caused the laughter? I never discovered. Once as I scurried past on some errand, I saw one turn to another as they sat over their mugs of steaming coffee, point to me, and then whisper something to her neighbour. A peal of laughter – the hateful sound echoing in my ears, even when I had left the room.

There were those who were kind to me. For instance one Elizabeth Musgrove. But it was an uninterested kindness. Even as she said, 'How is the world with you, little child?' I saw her mind go bounding ahead of her body, telling her it was time to join her friends gathered around the fireplace (for had they not always first place before the fire in the big sitting-room?).

On Sundays we went twice to church, in crocodile. Oh how I hated that. All our walks were in crocodile. Yet for most of my life I had roamed wild, on the moors beyond Luddenden, on the hills behind our house. (It was that very licence that had allowed me to run away to the Irish.) To be tied, lovingly to my mother, or unwillingly to an aunt – that was all right. But never this. And then, the agony of choosing a partner – or of not being chosen. The numbers were often uneven, and I might end up with a great girl, or worse, a teacher.

Prayerbooks in our gloved hands, forbidden to chatter, we

walked slowly down the leafy lane that led to the church; no drystone walls here, only green hedgerow.

Too much time to think. Mama, Papa, why could I not be with them? Kit, when should I ever see Kit again? Only a few weeks since our walk on the moors, but already it had happened in another life. Nothing was certain now. Kit would forget. Every Sunday at the farm without me . . .

As we walked, the solitary bell ringing in the distance, I thought too of Mr Hume, and of how I had lost his approval, perhaps even his friendship. And then a great desolation swept over me – an empty waste stretched before me, my life as bare as the trees outside from which the last leaves would soon fall.

Church. How I longed to sit in our pew – black wood, white letters, high sides. WOODWARD it would say. And to look up and see my friend (once my friend), standing there in the pulpit. What matter what he spoke of – just that he should speak. Here the parson was called Mr Dibb, a small and tubby figure with a high eager voice and a fussy manner. To me he seemed almost ridiculous. And indeed the other girls laughed at him, calling him Mr Dibstones.

It was not a warm church. Late autumn now and the weather had turned bitterly cold. It was so cold I wanted always to pass water. Within five minutes of morning service beginning, the cold, the misery . . . all I could think of was when we would be back and I could rush to the water closet: a hot stream and – relief. I tried everything. Foregoing the hot coffee before we left, taking nothing, not even water. But then my body found it from somewhere. And I would sit there with the knife-like pain distracting me from the pain in my heart.

The rain splashed against the classroom window. It had rained for a whole week now. Icy rain, blown by the cutting east wind. It was already the middle of November.

Geography again. London this time. Even before Sarah Mullen could trill her answer, I had stood up.

'In London,' I said, 'there are thirty-six thousand children trained to crime, two hundred and thirty thousand drunkards, thirty thousand prostitutes and others, making a total of four hundred and seventy-one thousand persons steeped and living in crime and wickedness.'

I sat down in triumph. Silence. My words brought silence.

Miss Pagan spoke.

'Christabel Woodward, you will come to see me after class.'

All heads turned towards me. The colour rushed to my face.

Miss Pagan fixed her gaze on the globe. 'Girls, we did *not* hear what Christabel said . . . And now, who among you can answer the question – What features is London most famous for?'

I went up afterwards. The others filed out.

'Where,' she asked me, '*where* did you learn such vileness? An oasis of depraved knowledge standing out in the desert of your ignorance. You should be ashamed.'

'It's just some – facts I know,' I told her.

'Where?' she persisted. '*Where?*'

I thought suddenly of my father, the warm little snug, the smell of tobacco, his cigars, the lamp. That poster, *The Globe in Miniature, or the World at one View*. I thought of all the books of my childhood. Of what I knew that was important. And of my home, and how I loved it.

'They are *facts*,' I said angrily. 'Facts about the sad way some people have to live. Something should be done about it, indeed it should . . . Meanwhile I don't care about the foolish facts *you* try to make me learn –'

'Ah,' she said, 'you put me quite out of patience. Go. Leave the classroom. You will be punished for this.'

And I was. But for half a day or so, I was regarded with something like awe. A girl called Julia told me, 'I don't know how you *dare* talk about such things.' Another, Maria, said smugly, 'I was sure you would be – and now you are in hot water.'

Amongst the girls, the only one I really feared was Maria. Pug-faced Maria, afraid of nobody, and fond of very few unless possibly herself – Maria was very pleased with Maria. Her family was nothing to do with trade and they were very rich. They visited her frequently, bringing her extravagant presents. She had privileges. She told us, 'I could have a room of my own if I wished – only I don't.'

She had many excitements in her life. One week in early November, during recreation time, as several of us were walking about the grounds, one of the great girls called us over. 'Come to the gate –'

Maria stood there already. 'Yes, you may look,' she said to us all. 'I expect them any moment.'

The clip-clop of hooves, and round the corner came a smartly dressed party. Her father, two of her brothers, a cousin and an older sister. All of them riding to hounds, on their way to the meet at Boroughbridge. I think she had hoped they might open the gates and come through and show off. But there was merely a raising of top hats from the men, and then the last to go by, her cousin, throwing over a small packet which, red-faced, she rushed to collect. 'It's a billy do,' she said proudly, stuffing it in her pinafore pocket. She pronounced it with great confidence. '*Billy do*.' As an afterthought, she told us, 'My cousin's name is William, and he will be Lord Iredale one day.'

('I don't suppose you know what a billy do is,' Sarah Mullen said to me afterwards. 'Anyway, it's something she shouldn't receive.')

From then on the pattern continued of their coming by every week or ten days, if the meet was anywhere nearby. It filled me with envy, for anyone whose life and family should be so exciting. The dazzling pink of their coats, the glossy chestnut or black flanks of their mounts, the saucy hat and veil of Maria's sister who was as pretty as Maria was ugly.

It should have consoled me that Maria was ugly. But her ugliness seemed neither to worry her nor to be an impediment. She quizzed. How she quizzed. The first day, she had reduced me almost to tears with her:

'Tell me, tell me now, who is your father, how many brothers and sisters have you and what are their ages, where do you live? Luddenden – I have never heard of it. And a mill, who wants to see a mill from their window? I *am* sorry for you . . .'

The person with whom, after the first few weeks, I was most often paired off was Julia. We shared in the dormitory too. I hated it that we were so much together. I hated it because she was kind to me and I was unkind to her. She could not breathe through her nose. Her thick-lipped mouth was permanently open. And she believed anything and everything I told her. I wanted only to tell her the most enormous fibs. As we walked together I would test her to see how enormous a fib she would believe.

'I ran away,' I told her, 'that's why I've been sent to school. I ran away to go and live with the Irish down by the canal . . .' I told her I wanted to be a Papist, a Roman Catholic. My father was one. My *real* father. He was a Jesuit priest. 'But this is a *deathly* secret.' She quaked with terror as I told her of what would happen if she were to reveal it. We had learned earlier that week about Jesuits. 'Did you not notice,' I said, 'how quiet I kept when that subject came up?'

But she irritated me by her lack of curiosity. I wanted her to ask, 'What sort of Jesuit, in what country, when, what, *how*?' But she did not. Poor Julia. And yet I envied her too, for Maria seldom bothered with her.

I was not the only one Maria quizzed. There was Camille too. She slept in the same dormitory as Julia and I and had been at The Beeches the longest of everybody, coming when she was only five. Camille. Oh, how I would have loved to look like Camille! She was indeed the prettiest girl in the school. Her hair, her beautiful curls, were natural. Each morning when her nightcap came off there would be this tangle which the touch of a comb turned easily into the neatest of golden ringlets. She had shell-pink nails which she would sit in the dormitory and buff with a piece of chamois leather. Her complexion was pink and white, her eyes large and china-blue. And she had rosebud lips, shaped like a bow. I wanted to look like her, but inside myself still to be Christabel. I would not have liked to be Camille.

A spoilt darling she was. Her voice was perhaps her only bad feature: the hint of a squeak and quite an affected lisp. It could be heard answering in history class all the questions on the French Revolution, for although Camille's father was from Yorkshire (and what name more Yorkshire than Boothroyd?), her mother was French. And in French class she sat smugly, occasionally pursing her lips to a point and saying for us, '*Confitu . . . ure . . .*'

There was about her an aura of romantic tragedy, for her maternal great-grandfather had gone to the guillotine. (Where now were my tall stories, my whoppers, beside this truly stirring past?) Her grandfather, a child at the time, had escaped to England. Camille told us with her lisp:

'You see Grandpère was smuggled out in a basket of clothes . . .' I wanted to know more details. I could picture the scene. I saw myself as the coach galloped through the night: the smell of the clothes (were they clean or dirty?), the feel of them against my face, the promise to be quiet . . . 'You see he was *petit, petit, petit.*'

It was I then who quizzed her: 'But what did he remember? What did he remember?'

'Oh nothing,' she said, 'nothing. They gave him cognac to drink, you see. He slept all the while. He was four years old . . . He was the youngest son of the Comte de Freycinet.'

'Maman is French,' she told us again later, 'they were brought up so. We speak it at home, *toujours*, Maman and I. I am an only child . . . I expect to make a very good marriage. I would like to go back, I think, to live in France. I would not need to fear the guillotine. Although of course they still have revolutions . . .'

Maria thought little of her. 'Camille indeed,' she declared, both to us, and to Camille's face. 'What a silly name. Tell me,' she said, staring at Camille, 'why not Camilla?'

'Because I am *française*,' Camille lisped.

'You're in England now,' Maria said. '*And* in Yorkshire. Anyway,' she said, 'they don't go together – Camille and Boothroyd. They don't mix.'

No, I was not the only victim of her quizzing. But perhaps I minded the most. Was it not she who had said, the first day, 'You're very small, why are you so small? I'm waiting for an answer.'

'I was born small,' I said angrily, but near to tears.

She burst into mocking laughter.

It rained heavily, beating against the wide sash windows of the dormitory. I heard the wind get up as, face buried in the pillow, I tried to stop the nightly sobs which I knew would come however I fought. (And yet how much worse were the mornings. Oh really I do not care to remember the mornings.)

I heard my name: 'Cisty, Cisty,' in a small voice. I was awake, I was certain I was awake. And Josh was calling me. How could I mistake Josh's voice?

'Cisty, Cisty!' And then a knocking at the window. I ran from the bed. A face was pressed against the glass – I could make out only the eyes. Distorted, they stared back.

Shivering with fear, I lifted the sash. It came up only with difficulty. And there, waiting to be let in was – such a creature. Such a bloated and bedraggled . . . And what was that which trailed from its hair?

'No, no!' I cried. 'Who are you? Go away! Go away, get back!'

'Cisty, Cisty, it's Josh!' the creature wailed. 'It's Josh – let me in, *let me in* . . .'

I screamed and screamed. I heard him wail again, despairingly, 'Cisty, Cisty!' But in my terror I only screamed the louder.

And then I woke.

A housekeeper was bending over me, holding a lamp. 'The whole dormitory is awake with your cries. Have you night terrors?'

It was a lesson with Miss Pagan first thing that morning. I hated her now. She seemed like an avenging witch with her pointed nose that she thrust forward – at me. Her eyes were set close together in her narrow face. When she became excited they ran in towards her nose. Cross face, cross eyes.

Those teachers . . . There was our music teacher – like a cushion, or was she perhaps a pale bun, with currants for eyes? Dreamy, exhausted: 'My dears,' she would say in her vague voice, 'what shall we sing today?' She kept order by proxy. When there was any trouble, another gentle sigh: 'Oh dear, I think we need Miss Baldwin.' Once only, she walked tiredly from the room while the noise raged on, and brought in the younger Miss Baldwin, Miss Amelia, who immediately rapped the knuckles of all the girls in the front row. (*'Never* let me be sent for again . . .')

Calisthenics. Deportment. Miss Joyce could frighten us all. She rapped out the commands with a voice as sharp as the raps she gave to erring knuckles. Ridicule was her weapon, Camille her pet. Camille moved with easy grace. It seemed that even when she tossed the golden ringlets, the book on her head remained in place. Mine did not. And it was only by poking forward with my bottom thrust out, and my fists clenched tight, that I could keep the volume of Barrow's *Five Hundred Questions on the Old Testament* from crashing down to bang the heels of my neighbour.

French – that was an unhappy experience. But English . . . If I was ever happy at The Beeches, it was at Miss Church's lessons. She did not appear till November was half gone. Her predecessor, a dry and rather surly person, leaving hurriedly to nurse a sick father.

Miss Church was a being apart. And would have been so if only because of her kindness to me. Hers was the only lesson I cared about, the only lesson in which I could hope to shine at all. ('Recite me a poem,' she had said, the first day, and joyfully, I did, not stumbling once.) How I envied and admired her tall calm presence. The black hair, sheen of a blackbird's wing, coiled round her head. Her long white expressive hands, her low sweet voice which for all its quietness commanded authority in the classroom.

Wordsworth's lines on the French Revolution (*'Bliss was it in that dawn to be alive, But to be young was very Heaven!'*). She read this to us. But Camille was excused learning it. Gravely, Miss Church explained, while Camille preened herself:

'Camille can hardly be expected to echo Mr Wordsworth's

sentiments. It would be unfair to expect her to . . . And yet, and yet we must remember that a love of literature rises above all such opinions. Poets do not make good politicians.'

And to me, what was her first remark?

'Ah,' she said, '"*the lovely lady Christabel, her father loves so well, what makes her in the woods so late, a furlong from the castle gate?*" Christabel,' she had said. 'Christabel. Samuel Taylor Coleridge. You must read the poem,' she said, 'you must read this story of your namesake.' But I was too shy to tell her that indeed I had been named after that very Christabel.

How happy The Beeches would have been, had Miss Church been its headmistress, its matron, teacher of geography . . . And, I thought to myself afterwards, had she been my governess there would have been no more stories of dismissals and insubordination. She was not at all like Mama – I didn't want her for a mother. Perhaps for an aunt. Or yes, yes, for an older sister. But most of all for a friend. I dreamed of how she might become my friend.

I had not expected to receive letters from my father, but my mother wrote every week. How I lived and longed for those letters. When one arrived I would not read it at once, but slip it into the pocket of my pinafore to read quietly when I should be alone. And all that day, it would be as if a light shone, glowed there in my pocket. The very paper, when I broke the seal and opened it, would smell of her, and it would smell too of home. I could picture her writing it – the flurry of her bold use of the pen, the bitten lip. How often had I seen her, pen flying over the paper, and then how she would blot, and lean back and look, correcting.

The last week of November, and the cold today had turned to an icy sleet. The letter had been delivered in the morning: it sat now in my pinafore, as it had sat all through geography, history, music. It was afternoon now, and free time. Everyone was gathered in the sitting-room. There was talk amongst the great girls of roasting chestnuts before the fire.

I escaped. My refuge – the library. I loved that library, where no one ever came. How easy it was to steal in there, on these gloomy winter afternoons. Once there, I had only to choose a book and hurry with it to the window seat, then close the curtains around me.

But today first, I would read my mother's letter. And so I sat, knees drawn up, curtains drawn, while outside the sleet hit and ran down the pane.

'Kit Ogden spoke to me after church, asking for news of you and if you were well. He attends evening class here, with Mr Hume, and I think truly wishes to better himself . . . Trissie still sleeps on your bed, in spite of Betty's punishments. Yesterday she stole Agnes's dinner! Betty threatens to ban her from the nursery.' A tear rolled down my cheek. My cheek was as wet as the window pane. And then I turned to my book, and consoled myself with the exciting tale of *Eugene Aram*. I was almost half-way through.

An hour or more passed. The light, never very good, began to go. And then, suddenly, I heard the door open. And footsteps. The voice of one of the housekeepers:

'Please to sit there, and wait. Someone will come to you presently.' There was a soft murmured answer. Then the door shutting. Footsteps receding.

I was not sure what to do: I wanted to peek quickly from behind the curtain, but if I were to frighten whoever it was? I imagined someone running screaming from the room, as indeed I might have done. I sat very quiet, not even rustling the pages. I heard the creaking of a chair, then a heavy sigh. Moments passed and then, another sigh. And again. Two sneezes. A stomach rumble. I thought then *I* might be going to sneeze. I dreaded the arrival of a teacher, perhaps even Miss Baldwin.

The sleet had ceased now. Snow was falling. And the light was scarcely enough to read by. Then a voice, not it seemed to me very adult, said twice, 'Oh dear . . . oh *dear* . . .' and then something between a sob and a hiccup, followed by quiet but unmistakable weeping. Heartbroken, convulsive. On and on. I *could* not stay for that.

I parted the curtains and jumped down. A young girl was hunched in one of the two brocade chairs before the fireplace.

A sharp intake of breath: 'A-ah,' was all she said. 'A-ah.'

'Don't be frightened,' I said, 'I'm only me. Christabel. Christabel Woodward.'

She looked up. I saw that she was about my age but, unlike me, was tall and slender. Her thick brown hair was smoothed back. Her features were small and regular, her eyes deep blue. She had composed herself now. Apart from a wetness about the eyes, a glistening, there was no sign she had been weeping. She said, with a brave half-smile:

87

'My name is Paulina Liddington. But I am always known as Polly . . . I have just arrived at the school. They told me to wait here until my luggage was sent up, or someone came to fetch me . . .'

'Your parents – did they not bring you?'

'They left at once. My father had to –' Tears filled her eyes again. 'I have never been from home before. I have come because my mother is very seriously ill, she has a tubercular consumption. She has been sent away for a cure . . . and also my governess has just left, under a cloud, because she drank hollands and would not wake in the mornings, and so it was thought better I remained away . . . until Mother is better – *if* she . . . They wish me to become used to school, at once. Only, it is not very pleasant to come so late, when there are perhaps only three or four weeks remaining.'

I too had come late, I told her.

But by now the tears were falling again. She said in a small voice, 'You heard me weeping, I think?' I nodded.

'Usually,' she said, 'I am a very happy person.'

She asked me no questions. I liked that. And because of that I volunteered information.

'If you were wondering,' I began, 'what I was doing behind the curtain –' But just then the small clock above the fireplace chimed four o'clock. Clearly, down the corridor, I heard the gong ring for tea. I told her:

'There is no need to sit here and wait. I think they have forgotten you . . . Come with me. I will look after you.'

'Thank you,' she said. 'You are very kind, Christabel.'

Then I put my arm about her waist, and we walked out together towards the dining-room.

I took her inside. 'This is Polly,' I said. 'She has just arrived.'

I had found a friend.

6

Home at last on a darkening afternoon. Ten days to Christmas, ten days to my birthday when I would be eleven. I had a sore throat, a blocked nose and an aching head, it hurt me to cough, but nothing and nobody could dampen my excitement. As we jolted into the village and up Stocks Lane, along the drive – gloomy laurels, trees stripped bare – the lamps shone a welcome outside. And at once Mama was on the doorstep.

And then I had tumbled out and run up the steps and into her arms.

'My little darling – oh, how we've longed for this day, Christabel!'

For a second only, grey ghost of Joshua, glimpsed behind her skirts. Should not my little Josh have been there to greet me? But then there was Trissie leaping and twisting in the air, covering me with kisses.

Agnes, who had not been well, came up now and took Mama's hand. Halliwell had grown – a few inches surely. He stood very straight, and stared. 'You're very plump,' he said.

'No, I'm not,' I said.

'You haven't grown at all. Mama,' he said, *'she's very small.'*

There was an air already of Christmas. Holly stood banked in the hall. All that last week at school had been touched with happiness, all the joys of anticipation. I looked with different and already removed eyes on Camille's posturings, Julia's open-mouthed wonder (I did not even bother with new whoppers) and above all at Maria's boasting ('What *I* shall do at Christmas, what *we* shall have . . . larger than, louder than . . .') With our music teacher we sang 'While shepherds watched . . .' And I knew Christmas, and home, were near.

Betty was amongst those to greet me. And there was the governess. Miss Dutton had been succeeded by a Miss Milner. She was young and fair with a pale skin which easily flushed. Mama was kind to her. I was not under her jurisdiction, but I wanted to be kind too – so happy was I to be back.

I learned that Agnes was very good with Miss Milner, but

Halliwell still a tease. He had turned nine in October, and in a year or two would share a tutor with Phil. But Miss Milner stood no nonsense from him. It seemed she was firmer than one would expect from her milky-white easily flushed skin, her timid manner. I told her the next day:

'I can teach Agnes for you if you wish.'

She smiled at me. 'Who knows but I shall accept? You are after all, a *school*girl . . .'

I had five weeks, five whole weeks. Not until the end of January did I need to return. It stretched far out into the distance. Perhaps it would never come. And did I not have before then a treat, about which as yet my parents knew nothing? For what had made those last few weeks at The Beeches all right had been Polly. Indeed, I had a friend. And that friend had invited me to her home. A letter would come from Mr Liddington to Mama, suggesting that in the New Year I should spend ten days with them.

But meanwhile there was Christmas. And Mr Hume.

Next morning early, I was round at the Vicarage. He was down at the church, the housekeeper told me. I was afraid suddenly but as I walked through and along the path, there he was, among the graves, just about to begin the walk back up.

The churchyard was dank with dead leaves squelched underfoot, rimed with frost. A grey sky above threatened snow.

'Ah,' he said, 'welcome home, Christabel. We meet again amongst the tombstones.' He caressed my head gently. 'But we are not afraid these days, are we?'

'No, no,' I said, glad enough to speak of Grimshaw's ghost. I had been dreading he would make reference to our last meeting. I wanted it to be all forgotten. I wanted it to be all fresh and new as if it had never been. I thought in some way, it was as if by going to The Beeches, by suffering, it had been some sort of punishment, the sin purged. That now I was cleansed of it all.

He said, 'I am so very glad to see you again, Christabel dear. You are happy to be home?' When I nodded, he said, 'I think you would not run away now?' And gave a delighted laugh.

But as we walked up the path, 'Mrs Hume has not been well,' he said. 'I must ask for your prayers . . . She works so hard, too hard, for me, you see.'

I thought of her as I had last seen her, in church: her head drooping on its long neck like a snowdrop, her pale skin all lumps and bumps, her hand shaking as she turned the pages of her hymnal.

'She likes to help me with my Greek, my Aeschylus – I am annotating a new edition of the *Oresteia*, you see – as well as to visit the sick. There is so much visiting, of the sound in health also. I believe strongly in the dictum that "A house-going parson makes a church-going people." So I am out much and cannot be with her. And then there is my own writing . . . But you see, I have energy for all this –'

As he walked beside me, it seemed to come from him, the energy. I imagined them sitting together and wondered what they spoke of. I thought of him so full of life and she so drained, and wondered that he could not give her some.

'You are still fond of reading? And of music, and drawing?'

'Oh yes, yes,' I cried, and I began to tell him of the books in the library. 'But except for English, the lessons are not to my liking. It is all knowledge for which I can see no use.'

'Ah,' he said, 'and what is the *use* of Aeschylus, and Virgil, and Horace – and yet every moment I can spare from my parish is spent in their company . . .'

I wanted to say then that surely they had beauty, whilst Mangnall's *Questions and Answers* had not. I cried angrily, 'Why oh why should I learn the latitude of Morocco or Calcutta?' At that moment hating Miss Pagan.

'Oh, Christabel . . .' And he laughed.

We had arrived almost at the Vicarage. 'And do you have some friends?' he asked.

'Ah yes,' I said, for that was my triumph. 'I have a friend.'

But I was not sure if it was he I meant, or Polly.

Carol singers from the village stood beneath our windows. There was a fiddle too, a trumpet, a flute. They sang 'O come all ye faithful', and then drank hot punch in the hall, with Betty and Miss Milner, and Halliwell and Agnes in night clothes.

The day before, I had been up to see Kit. At first we were awkward together. It was not like the easy reunion with Mr Hume. I wondered if he thought I had become rather grand, after leaving Luddenden, and meeting so many other people.

'Well, you've not changed, Christabel,' he said.

'Did you think I would?'

'Happen I did –'

'Well, I shan't,' I said. For I thought then that I was able to decide such matters.

'I've done well,' he said, 'at Mr Hume's school. I reckon t'reading – it's come on a lot. Mam says –'

'You won't need lessons from me any more then –'

'A teacher that's away at school hersen –' he laughed. 'What were I to do, eh?'

We continued talking. It grew a little easier. But we made no plans for going out together. Nor did we make any arrangements about reading, or writing. Those days were over.

On Christmas Day, Uncle Sutcliffe and Aunt Flora came over as usual to spend the day with us. Phil had a tutor now, and it was suggested that next year Halliwell share with him. Meg giggled often, maliciously when possible, and did not get on well with Agnes.

Uncle Sutcliffe told my father:

'Alexander's really made our brass work for us –'

Aunt Flora began to sing her brother's praises. 'Alexander is quite extraordinarily able with money. He can make it grow on trees, I think.'

'He'll be up this way, happen next month or so,' Uncle Sutcliffe said. 'If you've a mind to give him some Woodward brass –'

'Over my dead body,' my father said, only half-humorously.

'There's no call to speak of dead bodies,' Aunt Flora said indignantly.

'Well,' said Uncle Sutcliffe, 'well, James. I reckon you'll look foolish when he's made our pile for us. I've thought nothing of putting in all the spare profit. And more besides.'

'If James were to invest the money the landlord takes from him at the Lord Nelson –' Aunt Flora began acidly.

'Thank you,' my father said, 'I'd rather have it in liquid.' And he laughed – at Aunt Flora.

The carriage drove up a long tree-arched avenue. All around was park land. At the end of the drive stood Liddington Hall – grey, enormous, with turrets and battlements. Polly's home.

For now it was time for my long-awaited visit, for which my parents had so readily given permission. I had not wanted Aunt Flora to know – I never wanted her to know anything. But Papa had let it slip. 'How very grand,' was all she said. Yet we had known she was impressed. My father reminded me: 'It's nowt to be ashamed of – a millmaster's daughter.' I had not thought it was.

Liddington Hall. Of course it was large, and grand. Beside Wade House, which in Luddenden was of such remark, it was a veritable castle. Our home would go three times into it. And so old: two hundred and fifty years. The family itself was older still, with their own arms and crest carved in the oak panelling of all the rooms. They went back, Polly said, to the time of Richard Crouchback who had murdered the little princes in the tower. It was her mother's family, however, not her father's. Descent was allowed through the female line, and her mother was heiress. Mr Liddington had taken her name. He had been a physician in Leeds, a much respected one, and then for many years a Poor Law Commissioner. Now that he owned Liddington Hall, he no longer worked.

As the carriage drew up that first afternoon, I remembered Polly saying, 'I am a happy person.' I wondered if they would be a happy family.

The first thing to remark was that it was a house without a mother (although there were housekeepers, and an aunt, who sat in Mrs Liddington's place at table). Her family had thought my companionship would be good for Polly, and . . .

Because of her illness, I had imagined her mother as frail and pale, wasting with her disease, but in the portrait hanging in the hall ('Here is my mama,' said Polly proudly) she was seen to be high-coloured, with black and determined eyes.

They did not have tea at six, but dinner at eight, to which I was allowed down. Often there would be visitors. Once it was another medical man, and he and Mr Liddington took over the conversation, debating the merits of different seasides.

'. . . And you have sent Mrs Liddington to Penzance? I cannot but agree – in climate it is a full four and a half degrees higher than London . . . What advantage Italy when the accommodations are so universally bad? As for Madeira – deaths from consumption are as frequent there. Both Gourlay and Heineker are *adamant* in discouraging . . .'

Polly was the youngest child. An elder sister and brother had both died of a low fever while visiting away from home, seven years ago.

'I like to tell myself I remember them,' Polly said, 'but in truth I can't. Although I have dreamt of them.' And I told her then of how I had dreamt of Joshua. It was between us a bond.

She had two elder brothers, Henry and Edmund. She said of Edmund:

'My brother is rather a medical person. He wishes to be a physician and will go to Edinburgh to study under the same person as Papa.'

Of Henry, who had his seventeenth birthday while we were there, his father said fondly, 'He is our little agitator, our little Radical.' Certainly he was little. Although almost two years Edmund's senior, he stood well below his brother. Thick brown hair, a narrow nose, and brown eyes which would suddenly come to life, fire, as he began to speak.

I could not be bothered with Edmund. He was too earnest. But Henry I followed about like a little dog, worrying at his heels. Polly did much the same. He shook her off as he shook me off. Polly didn't mind.

She said, 'I can see that sometimes he is an angry person. He would like to right the world.'

But his father said, 'I trust he will not do it, nor plan to do it, from Pembroke . . .' Next year Henry was to go to Oxford, to Pembroke College, where an uncle was dean.

I piped up. For once I had something to say. 'My friend, Mr Hume,' I said, 'that is where he has studied. He is editing an edition of . . .' but I could not remember the name.

The cold weather continued. We visited neighbours with an ornamental lake, frozen hard, for a skating party. Another day we drove the five miles into Harrogate, where after a morning's shopping with Aunt and a visit to the Pump Room, Edmund began a long discussion with his father on the merits of the different waters.

'The Moffat waters, not so strongly impregnated as . . . Harrogate, the sulphur waters, milder and better than the best mercurial alteratives . . . Yes, indeed they often increase the desire for food. Exercise is *essential*.'

Discussions such as these often led to the topic of Mrs Liddington's consumption. Edmund was happy to talk dispassionately, medically of it, at any time. Henry became agitated by mention of it.

On the last but one day of my visit, Mr Liddington left for Cornwall to visit his wife. He took Edmund with him, although Henry was the older. They travelled by train. Polly was promised that if all was well, she might visit in the spring.

We were left in the charge of Aunt Mary Liddington, a person with whom I had barely exchanged more than a few words since my arrival. She seemed to regard us all, humorously, from a distance. 'You do as you like,' she would say to us all. 'But meanwhile, *I* shall . . .' Polly, obviously puzzled and wanting to sum her up, told me:

'I think she is a contented person, don't you? She pleases herself. And is pleased *with* herself.'

How I loved to be with Polly, for whom the world made such sense. The sun shone, the clouds came, it rained – but all was natural and in order. Night followed day, day followed night. And God over all. She was my calm centre, in the storm which was my soul. I knew that I must never lose her.

Back to school, and because I was Polly's friend, it was not so bad after all. She was simply a shield against everyone. I told no more whoppers to Julia, and could ignore Maria's quizzing.

But the person who most lightened my days was Miss Church. I thought her the most beautiful person I had ever seen. She it was this term who escorted us to morning service. No hardship now to go. When Polly was ill with a sore throat I walked with Geraldine (yes, Geraldine. I had seen her name in the volume of Coleridge she lent me. 'Geraldine Church', in a small neat hand).

Winter still. How cold it was as we sat in the school pews. And Mr Dibbs as foolish and fussy as ever. But when he waited outside to greet us afterwards, Miss Church would stay a while speaking to him: calm, kind, gracious. She reprimanded me for complaining of him and mocking his ways.

'He is not married, Christabel. They are the ways of someone who has lived alone too long. It is not good for people to live alone.'

I wondered sometimes if she cared for living amongst all of us – at the Misses Baldwin's beck and call. I imagined how happy she would be in a home of her own. '*I have no family*,' she told me once. She never spoke of relations. Perhaps she could start a school of her own, and I could go to live with her and help?

I spent much time in the library still, with permission now. Miss Church showed me books there which brought my history lessons to life. One day I found a book, *Daphnis and Chloe*, by Longus. Latin on one page and French translation on the other. My French was still poor, and I puzzled for many afternoons over this text, worrying at the words I knew, and trying to match them on the Latin page, of which I could understand nothing (but ah, the music of it).

Miss Church came upon me. 'What is this, Christabel?' She shook her head and said that it was not at all suitable. 'There must be other texts . . .'

'I don't care about the French. It's the Latin. Do *you* know Latin?'

'Indeed. Should you like me to teach you?'

Ah, but *yes*.

'Next term then. We shall arrange something. I shall speak to Miss Baldwin. I have no Greek – but you shall have my Latin.'

I wrote to Mr Hume. I told him everything (almost) of what I did. And told him that I was trying to be good. I could think of little news to give him. I spoke of Mr Dibbs and the content of his last sermon, which had been about the labourers in the vineyard. He wrote back to me, two full pages, and told me that I might write again. So afraid was I to lose this letter that I carried it about with me everywhere, rolled up into a small hard scroll.

Christabel. When did that poem begin to haunt me? What did I not understand? I was always one for nightmares. That poem brought me many.

This tale of Christabel, her father's darling, who sees out at night a strange lady, making moan. ('A voice faint and sweet: "My sire is of noble line, And my name is Geraldine" . . .') Kidnapped by warriors and abandoned. How Christabel comforted her, and took her to her ailing father . . . Geraldine would not pray with her ('And will your mother pity me?'), acting strangely, shooing away the spirit of Christabel's dead mother. She has a viper in her bosom, which Christabel sees ('a snake's small eye . . .'). And finally, she betrays Christabel – turning her father against her.

I did not think I really understood the poem. But I dreamed of it again and again.

I told Miss Church – *Geraldine* – who gave me poems by Dryden to read. Polly consoled me when I woke shaken or weeping. She herself wept sometimes. Never, though, like that first afternoon.

'I have *never* felt a stranger here,' she told me, 'because I met you at once.'

She and I prayed together nightly for Mrs Liddington, that she might be spared, that the soft climate and gentle breezes of Penzance might cure her.

Easter came and went. The days grew lighter, and longer. There was an expedition to pick bluebells – not in crocodile. In mid-June we went home again.

I saw Kit – and it was not the same. I could not think what it was – except that it was not the same. He was as kind as ever, wanting to hear everything I had been doing. His mother, used to my visits, fussed over me. She told me how clever Kit had grown. She too wanted to hear about school – though she was seldom still long enough to take heed.

No, I did not know what it was – the awkwardness. For he felt it too. Neither of us said anything. It was as if, I thought (later, much later), we had walked over the moors together and then, at the crossroads, taken each a different turning.

Uncle Sutcliffe, in the snug with Papa and me. It is a warm summer evening so there is no fire, only a smell of cigar smoke. A carafe of water and a decanter of whisky stand on the desk. I was sitting with Papa when Uncle Sutcliffe arrived. They don't mind that I stay . . .

Uncle Sutcliffe has a sample in his hand, which he has taken from a large envelope. Papa takes it from him, rubbing it between finger and thumb:

'No bad thing, a government contract. If you can get it. Overcoating – the troops. Fighting the Russkies, it'll be a cold cold winter . . . What weight?'

'Twenty-five, twenty-six ounce.'

'How much?'

'Four thousand yard maybe . . .'

'It's an ill war that doesn't make us addle more. Callous it may sound, but if the Russkies aren't beaten by winter . . .' He passes the sample back, then pours them both a whisky. He stretches out his legs.

'Know what I heard, Sutcliffe? It seems Miss Brontë's wed. Taken everyone by surprise –'

'Publishing folk?'

'Nay. Her dad's curate. Nicholls. They say he's been after her a great while – but the old man made difficulties.'

'Well,' Uncle Sutcliffe says, 'no more Brontës now. It's gone with Branwell, has the name.'

'Aye, and he was in a bad way when he went. By all accounts they'd a terrible time with him at the Parsonage.'

'That Thorp Green tale?'

'Best not to speak of that now. Not here –'

'Any road, we've our memories,' Uncle Sutcliffe says. 'Seeing his name down at the library, you get reminded.'

'Caroline, when she's about – it's best still to say nowt. She'd grown very fond. Mothered him, we used to say. She took his death hardly . . . I've often thought, after the railway upset, if we'd maybe kept in touch. But we were wild in those days. Wild. And he, with us . . . But it was always my contention the fellow could write. Remember that long poem about Nelson? A grand future lost somewhere on the way . . . instead it's those mousey girls. Tales of passion. You mind *Jane Eyre*?'

'I've not read *Villette*, but they say that's strong too. Perhaps not one for the ladies, even if written by one . . .'

'And married now, eh? To a curate. There's your grand pretensions for you. With those looks, though, and her age – she's fortunate to be wanted at all, fame or not . . .'

'Let's keep our memories, eh?' Uncle Sutcliffe says. 'You've that drawing he made of us. The one sitting back to back, and a pint pot each . . .'

'In the wild days –'

'Reformed characters, aren't we?'

'*You* may be,' Papa says. He laughs. Then he looks over at me and winks.

'Any road, this contract, Sutcliffe. I'll ask Thompson to let me have samples. We're not rivals in this, eh? Your success is mine . . .'

A week later I went to stay with Polly. She greeted me with eyes shining.

'Mama is better,' she cried. 'God has answered our prayers. She is cured, she is a well person. And can come to live with us again. She comes home in three weeks' time.' And then: 'Oh Christabel, I shall miss you *so much*. For I am not to go back to school. I may stay at home, now that Mama is to be with us. I have a new governess arriving next month . . .'

We parted after a fortnight. Tears, promises. We would write to each other *every* week, and at Christmas we would meet again. And next summer, could I join them at Scarborough?

The Beeches. Without Polly.

I did not want to go back. I asked that like Polly I might leave school, and have a governess again. Mama weakened – I knew that she wanted me to live with them again. But Papa was firm. Although I was his darling once more, with my misdeeds never mentioned, I knew they were there at the back of his mind always. More than that – he scoffed at the notion that I might be pliant, might behave well with the gentle milk-and-water Miss Milner. 'The poor lass – she'd be threatened out of existence.'

I spent a week with Aunt Martha. I asked her to intercede for me. But 'Where'd be the sense of it,' she said, 'when you've the chance of a fine education in beautiful clean surroundings?' She was busy teaching evening classes at the Mechanics' Institute, and lectured me on being grateful, to God and to my parents, for opportunities denied to others.

And so I left Mr Hume, and Kit, and went back.

The Beeches, without Polly. But there was worse to come. Where was Miss Church? Geraldine. Where was Geraldine?

She was in Wales it appeared, and would not be back in Yorkshire for a further month. She was touring in the company of Mr Dibbs. Indeed they were on their honeymoon, having been married two weeks ago. Miss Baldwin sent for me on my second day back and handed me a letter which had been left behind for me. In it Geraldine explained that she was to wed, and so would no longer teach:

'But naturally I shall keep my ties with The Beeches. And of course I shall see you all on Sundays. Perhaps, Christabel, you will be allowed to come and take tea with Mr Dibbs and myself . . .'

Geraldine Dibbs. Geraldine Dibstones. I was disgusted. And my Latin lessons? She had not even mentioned those . . .

Nearly five months to go. And everything – lessons, girls, crocodile walks – was the same. Miss Pagan stood before the globe, and chastised me. As before, I did not know the answers, and did not listen.

'On the south-west of Greece lies the confederacy of the Seven Islands, consisting of Corfu, Leucadia, Cephalonia, Ithaca, and others, having an independent government, but under the military protection of Great Britain . . .'

'Christabel Woodward, for what is the island of Cyprus famous? Christabel . . . *Christabel* . . .'

At church we had a locum until Mr Dibbs (and Geraldine)

should return. Polly wrote to me. She was happy, her new governess was 'a very placid person – and we work pleasantly together'. But her greatest happiness was her mama, at home again. She hoped I would write soon and tell her everything.

But there was nothing to tell, save unhappiness. When I did write, I wept on the page. For I had become very homesick.

However had I managed in cold January? Now it was mid-August and warm, damp weather. In January I had had Polly, and Geraldine. Now I could only long for home. Mama, Papa, Halliwell, Agnes, Betty. Trissie. And the moors round Lud-denden. The canal, the river, the sound of the blacksmith's forge before the church. The church itself. Mr Hume. Kit, even though it seemed we were growing apart, Kit . . .

The food. I could not bear the food they served us. The plain wholesome fare I had scarcely noticed before. It seemed to me now alien. I craved crackneys and fat rascals, sad cakes, oven bottom cakes, rowan jelly, bilberry jam. No other tastes would do. And all must be as cooked at home.

I began to leave my meals. I had no appetite anyway (unless it was for what I craved). At first I was reprimanded, and made to sit with the uneaten meal. But after some days, I found that the secret was to sit next to a hungry girl, who would eat it for me.

Such homesickness. It grew steadily deep inside me – sad, festering version of that which I had felt a year ago. I had had courage then, and anger. Now anger and life seeped out of me, as from a wound.

I remembered little Jane Grimshaw who had died of homesickness at Charles Wesley's school. (Such a spartan school, up from four in the morning until eight at night, and no play – '*She that plays when she is a Child will play when she is a Woman*'.) Had her father not told her, 'As there are none too old for Eternity, so there are none too young for Mortality'? As she lay dying, she had called out, 'He hath loved me, I cried, He hath suff'red and died, To redeem such a Rebel as me . . .' But it had been homesickness killed her. Mercy had said so.

It became difficult to sleep at night (as also it had become difficult to weep). I lay dry-eyed in the dark, staring at the chinks of moonlight through the dormitory curtain. Perhaps just before dawn I would sleep for a while. A confused, light, unhappy sleep. Never dreamless.

Those nightmares . . .

*

I dreamed I was at Polly's house. A grand gathering. Everyone in fine gowns – only I was different, in my brown stuff dress. No one had told me there would be a party. But there was music, and Polly in silk and lace was happy and smiling. I stood with her and Edmund. He was speaking of some illness, but mouthing the words silently so that I could not hear. I looked instead across the room. Two girls and a young man stood together. The man was very good-looking: a head of black curly hair, a lively face. The girls were laughing, hanging on his every word.

I walked over to join them. No one noticed me. Least of all the young man. 'Hallo,' I said, 'and good evening.' I wanted desperately to talk to him, to be with him. But he looked right through me. And went on charming.

Desolation swept over me. I asked someone standing by, 'Who is that? Who is he?'

'But surely you know him? Joshua Woodward. From Apple-yard Mill. The younger son. Has he not grown wonderfully handsome?'

Oh save me, or I shall die.

One morning I could not get up. I lay there with a pain about my heart. Leaden limbs. I felt that I might suffocate.

The school surgeon was sent for. I would not answer his questions, but turned my face away. He left pills for me, and a recommended diet. I was purged. Twice a day, I was made to drink Harrogate sulphur water.

What went on in my head? I was with Aunt Martha in Halifax. I saw the Irish come out of their church – Fergus, was it Fergus? They crowded round me, pressing on me – I was dancing with them. Up up in the air, to the tune of a mouth organ. 'Oh take me home,' I cried – but it was after all the parish church, the bells of St John Baptist, pealing in my head:

'*Daughter of the northern fields . . . daughter of the northern fields . . .*'

'My heart will break,' I said. The pain was in my heart. I knew that if I could not go home, I would die.

They had placed me in a room by myself. But at no time was I alone. All day now someone would sit with me: sometimes one of the great girls, occasionally one of the housekeepers. I could not speak. When I was addressed, I only lay there. No words came.

Food was pressed on me. A spoon held up to my resisting lips.

Oh, how nauseous the smell of beef tea, the slipperiness of calf's foot jelly –

Geraldine came to see me. Sitting on the end of the bed, dressed in sprigged cotton. Or did I dream she came?

Now it seemed to be night always. If there was daylight, I did not see it. There was a lamp always in the room. Sometimes I heard sobbing, deep and convulsive, and knew that it was mine.

And then Jane – Jane Grimshaw – was in the room with me. She came, pale ghost, and sat at the foot of the bed . . .

7

I did not die. But surely I had been about to. My family was
angry with The Beeches that they had not been sent for earlier,
that they had heard nothing until it had become too serious to
ignore.

At home, Mama gathered me in her arms. My face buried in
her neck, smelling her sweet smell, I sobbed noiselessly. 'If we
should have lost you,' she said. And 'If I should lose her,' she
said, as if to herself, 'all I have of him, dear God, all I have.'
She stroked my hair, caressed me, covered me with kisses, then
lifted me herself onto the day couch which had been prepared
for me.

'She'll soon be right,' my father said, coming into the room.
It was with him that I had travelled back, weak, propped up with
cushions. Fainting twice. 'I've sent for Rushworth. I'd told him
to be in readiness – he'll be here within the hour.'

I said, 'And I shan't have to leave? I am to stay – even when
I am well again?'

'Aye. You're to stay, little lass.'

I had not died. But surely I had been about to. I knew now
that I should have to be good. Obedient. Not arguing. Keeping
a civil tongue in my head. Quiet, industrious. Tidy in my appearance. Willing to sew and embroider and to read improving texts.
Above all, I must be a model pupil to the present governess – or
whatever governess might be engaged for me.

Betty, scarcely needed as a nurse now, still had many duties
in the house: sewing, ironing for us. She was there to see Halliwell
and Agnes (and now me?) safely into our beds of a night. Agnes
was just nine and had grown very pretty. She had my parents'
dark colouring (Cousin Millie's blood – not a drop of it flowed
in *her* veins), arched brows, eyes wide apart, a small straight
nose. Her hair grew in the same widow's peak as my mother's.
Already it was possible to see how she would be when grown.

If she was perhaps jealous of the attention I was receiving now
(I was, after all, the prodigal daughter) she did not show it. She
was good and sweet, and had become Betty's darling, just as

Halliwell was her 'little lad', although he had grown so tall. Ten years old now, and sharing a tutor with Phil. I think he did not enjoy his lessons, except for history – and then only when it concerned battles. His happiest hours were spent with his fort, and his ever-growing armies. He tried to persuade Phil to take an interest too, but without success.

With me, he was angry – and scornful of my illness. He waited a while to ask: 'Is it true then, you were all but dead? Betty said . . .'

'Betty knows nothing about it,' I said rudely. I no longer wished to speak of it. I wished others would not. I had become embarrassed by the enormity of it. Frightened. The depths to which I had sunk – the sheer terror of that fall. The ground had opened and swallowed Josh. As surely too, I had been about to be lost.

There was another glad to see me back. One who I knew would have grieved at my death. 'We prayed, Christabel. I asked from the pulpit for prayers . . .' And yet I was shy when he called to see me.

Five days after my return, as I lay in bed – already I was growing stronger by the hour – I listened to the bell calling the worshippers, and thought that next Sunday perhaps I would be in our pew again. Mama, back from church, leaned over to kiss me. 'Mr Hume asked again today we should pray for you. And Kit Ogden,' she said. 'He wanted to know how you were. And might he come and see you?'

'Oh, please,' I said. 'Yes, please.'

I never thought of The Beeches now. And as for Geraldine: my illness had purged me of love for her. I wished her well with her tubby clergyman.

Kit called one evening that next week. He had grown taller still, but a little hunched with it, as if uncertain what to do with such long limbs. He was whiskered now, and quite the man, being eighteen. Long years now since he had sat in the nursery eating our porridge, and long years since Betty had told him, 'You know your place, and mun go back to it.' Long years too since he had searched the conduit for Joshua's small body.

We were awkward still. We said nothing about visits to the farm, or walks together. Yet I supposed the friendship was still there, for he told me:

'When parson were asking for prayers, I were feared. I wanted like to see for missen . . . that you're not too poorly.'

'I am not,' I said. 'I'm not poorly any more. And I don't expect ever to be ill again.' I believed it, even as I said it, so full was I of confidence and good resolutions, certain that it was in me to decide such matters. I had been brought back to life, saved, and now need only be good for ever after. It seemed to me suddenly very easy. I felt that God through Jane Grimshaw was sending me a message. It was thus to be converted. I need not be afraid now: I had been brought back to life that I might have it more abundantly, and might, by my light, shine on others.

'I mean also to be very good,' I told him. 'That is why I have been allowed to live. And I can do it, with God's help.' To speak like that, as if God spoke through me, how easy it was.

Kit was impressed, I saw that. He did not laugh at me, with me, as he might have done once.

'And what of the railway?' I asked him. 'Do you still want to work on the railway?'

'Nay, I don't fret after the railroad now. That's all in t'past. It were a lad's dream that . . .' He said shyly: 'I've other plans now . . .'

'What, Kit?'

'I mind,' he said, smiling now, 'the lessons you gave me . . . I can pen a good hand now . . . I reckon – there'll be clerk's work for me afore long. I mean to get on, you see.'

I was not good for very long. The sweet pleasures of goodness and kindness and submission, they were not for me.

And yet I managed, somehow, to be the model pupil of Miss Milner. She had only a little Latin, and no Greek, but this did not matter since Halliwell studied with Phil, and Agnes would not need it. I was eager (this time) to learn. She was eager to teach. Molineux's *Arithmetic*, Peacock's *Algebra*. She did not like – beloved of The Beeches – Mangnall's *Questions of General Biography*. Instead we sent to Halifax for lives of Nelson, of Mahommed, Washington, Sir Walter Scott. We borrowed books also from the Vicarage. For geography – no more globes. Instead, Captain Cook's *Voyages*, Franklin's *Travels to the Polar Seas*. My head was seldom out of a book.

Mrs Hume was failing. She now did not attend church, or only seldom. When I called to borrow books, or to see my friend, she would be seated, wrapped in a shawl by the window. She would stretch out a hand to me – it felt cold even in the heat of summer, and as feeble as her voice had become. Oh, the sadness of being Mrs Hume. And the sadness for Mr Hume, who never complained – just as she did not.

There she sat, her hands trembling, with a flicker of heavy eyelids. To speak at all seemed an effort. 'Little Christabel,' she said.

A thick manuscript lay on the table beside her. She told me: 'You see, when I have time, and am not too wanting in energy, then this work of Mr Hume's . . . I can fair copy, you see.' She showed me some pages of his black-inked vigorous hand, with its criss-cross of corrections and second thoughts. Some of it was in Latin, but also dotted about were lines in Greek script. Magic, wondrous script. It filled me with such an excitement I did not know whether it was in my head or belly.

After Christmas, Aunt Flora painted my portrait. She had often threatened me with this. I would have liked to refuse but it was too difficult. She positioned herself in the parlour with her easel and her crayons. I sat on a blue velvet stool. I had asked if I might have Trissie on my knee, but was told that she must rest quietly on a cushion behind Aunt Flora.

Aunt Flora liked to talk but required me to be silent as well as still, and since the portrait took many sittings – she was not a quick worker – she encouraged the family to come in while she worked, choosing early evening often when Papa would be home, and Uncle Sutcliffe could be invited over. If it was in the day, Meg came with her. Meg would occupy herself sticking hair pins into Trissie, or covering her with cushions and then sitting on them. When, finally, Trissie snarled, she wailed, crying to her mother, who hadn't been watching, 'Christabel's dog is *savage!*' Once Agnes, who had come in with a doll which she was quietly dressing, spoke up and said, 'Meg was provoking – it's her own fault.'

Behind her mother's back Meg stuck out her tongue at us both, and pulled a rude face.

Aunt Flora told a Mrs Howgate who, coming to call on Mama, had stayed to watch:

'I model my style in chalk on that of George Richmond – you know George Richmond? He is most fashionable. Everyone who is anyone wishes to be drawn by him. He can command large sums for his work. *I* do not do it for money, of course. Mr Armstrong and I are hardly in circumstances which . . .'

She ran on. I could see that she was pleased with herself, and certain of having made a good impression.

While she worked, she would speak of me to others, as if I were not there.

'I have long thought Christabel a good subject. Agnes and Halliwell – they have such natural good looks. Christabel is altogether more interesting . . . The colour of her hair, if I can render that. The height of forehead, the determined chin. I think that is an Armstrong chin – although *you* have not it, Sutcliffe . . . An interesting face, Christabel's, is it not? *Quite* without beauty . . .'

Papa, who bore with her only because Sutcliffe was his friend, tried to avoid the evenings she was there, and usually succeeded. He was often out these days anyway. From something Betty and Mercy hinted, I suspected that he added gaming now to his evening pursuits.

One evening when the portrait was almost finished, Aunt Flora brought Alexander over. He was spending the week with them, on his way up to Scotland.

He at once took notice of me as I sat on the velvet stool. 'Little Miss Muffet,' he said, coming up and stroking my hair. I thought he creaked as he bent towards me, and I remembered that he wore stays, and despised him.

And then my father came in. My mother was already there. I could see that he had been drinking, although supposedly he had come straight from the mill.

Aunt Flora began her attack soon, rattling on:

'My brother has had some more quite splendid notions for multiplying our income. Have you not, dearest? Sutcliffe and I have put ourselves completely in his hands, James. Alexander has a way with money – everything he touches turns to gold. And he is to do the same for us –'

'I heard tell,' my father said, 'when you were on about it, a year since.'

'And I said then,' Aunt Flora remarked, lifting her finger from the box of pastels, wagging it at him, 'listen to this, Alexander – I said if James were only to pass to *you* the gold he hands mine host at the Lord Nelson –'

'And I'll say the same as I said then,' my father interrupted angrily, 'I'd as soon have it liquid –'

Aunt Flora said, not so playfully: 'You sound as if you are just now come from there . . . Is that not so, Caroline?'

'Hold your tongue, you daft woman,' he said sharply.

'Ah!' she said with a little intake of breath.

'James,' began Mama, a hand on his arm.

He shook her off. Then walked up to Aunt Flora, and stood menacingly before her. Alexander, just behind her, had his mouth open, a foolish smile on his face.

'Have you done then?' my father said.

'You have been drinking,' Aunt Flora said primly. 'To excess. It is the only excuse for your manners.'

'Hark hark the lark,' my father said. 'Just listen to you. *Mimmy, mimmy.* Mealy-mouthed mimmy. I don't know which of you stick worse in my maw – you or your fancy-corseted sibling. Both on you, hold your din. And don't be here when I get back.'

'Where do you go?' my mother asked anxiously.

'Where I came from.'

At the doorway he said, 'Aye, and when Sutcliffe comes, tell him – he knows where to find his friend.'

There was no more portrait that day.

Later that winter, Grandma Woodward died. Since her apoplectic stroke she had been a faint shadow of herself. So forceful once upon a time, and lately so enfeebled.

It was I who found her dead. I was leaving that morning to stay with Polly, and went upstairs to say goodbye. I had almost forgotten and would have left without, except that Betty said, 'Looked in on your grandma, have you?'

In the bedroom she had been placed in a chair by the window, looking out and down the ravine (that same view that I had in the room above). Seeing that she slept, I tiptoed to kiss her – although I did not want to. I saw then that she was chill, and quite still. I who was so afraid of death and of ghosts was quite calm now and not at all afraid. I ran up the stairs and into the nursery. 'She's dead,' I cried. 'Grandma is dead. Come quick.'

And so it was that I arrived a day late at Polly's and wore mourning throughout my visit. We were happy just to be together again, and spent long hours talking. For some of the time there was ice enough for skating, and we would go out for expeditions with her governess. Once Mr Liddington took us to an evening party, where there was a bonfire and a sheep roasted.

Mrs Liddington was away. She had to take great care still and was spending the coldest months in Penzance. Next month Polly and her governess would join her, staying until the worst of the weather was over. Edmund was in Edinburgh, beginning his medical studies. He was the youngest of the students in his group. Henry I did not see. He was now at Oxford, in his first year at Pembroke. Already, it appeared, he was active in politics.

Polly was lighthearted. We twirled round on the ice, and then coming to a halt, sat down on chairs at the edge:

'You have your mother,' I said, 'and are a happy person again. We need our mothers . . .'

I told her that my mother was not a happy person. 'It's as if something dark and secret makes her sad.' Even as I said it there flooded into my memory strange remarks she had made. About death, about life. I told Polly of my kink-cough memory. She was surprised, a little incredulous, and shocked.

She said, 'That sounds like Latin. I think that makes you a Romanist? Perhaps you are a Romanist, but do not know it?'

'I cannot believe that,' I said. 'It is not done by muttering a few words . . .' (And yet what was the truth of it all? Had I dreamed it in delirium?)

I said now: 'It is as if there is something dark inside which eats her. And yet I could never ask her. I could sit with her, and we might talk of everything, but I could never . . . I only know she loves me!' I cried.

'Do not all mothers love their children?'

'No,' I said, 'not all mothers. Or perhaps – yes. But not in this way, that she . . .' but I could not finish. I had no words to describe in what way it was that she loved me. Loved me as she did not love the others. It was not right that I should be her favourite when already I was my father's bonny darling.

But for Polly, I should have remembered, people were as in the medieval humours. A choleric, a melancholic, a sanguine . . . Shades of grey worried and puzzled her. So she could make nothing of it when I said:

'My mother has happiness inside her. But something stops it from coming out. I think perhaps it has died, or is asleep and cannot awake . . .'

Soon after my return from the Liddingtons, there was another death. No one known to me this time. Or not directly.

I was sat in a corner reading. *Shirley* by Currer Bell, except that I knew her to be Charlotte Brontë. I was reading it and making little of it – although I recognized the life of the mills, and was interested in reading of the Luddite Riots.

Betty saw me there. I said, 'Listen to this, Betty,' and I read out a passage about two waggon loads of frames and shears that the hero was expecting delivered – and the riot that might result.

'The riots. Do you remember them? Were you there?'

'Get away. Them days. I were only a bairn.' She looked at me darkly. 'What's that you've buried your face in?'

I told her. She said:

'You never heard, she's gone? Mercy spoke of it. Sick since January, they said. Keeping nothing down. Not enough to feed a sparrow, and *should* have eaten for two – but you'll not know what I mean . . . Any road, Mercy had it from John o'Dicks who had it from Sal that Mr Nicholls – that he broke down, did her husband . . . Eight folk when they first come, and now there's only Parson left.'

'And the husband,' I said.

'Aye, but he's a foreigner . . .'

We heard of the funeral through Mercy, some four days later. The same clergyman, their friend Mr Sowden who had married them, now buried her.

Papa had been drinking. Again. It seemed nowadays that he was more often drunk than sober.

I was curled up behind the parlour sofa with a book from Mr Hume's library. Today I had Trissie with me, asleep, so that I expected soon to be noticed.

But it was not to be.

My mother came in first. I heard her cross the floor. And then, just after, his voice. He muttered something.

'Don't you work this afternoon?' she asked. 'If you *can*, that is –'

'Aye, here – I've matters to attend to, in the snug.'

'Smoking and drinking. In that condition you won't get much done –'

'Well I've sorrows to drown, haven't I?'

'If we're to bring all that up again –'

'*I'm* not speaking, I've done nowt.'

'No, but you looked, James. You read –'

'Well, you've a lock and key, haven't you? Instead there's your ruddy words, written in your fancy head, lying about *waiting* to be read –'

'Years of care,' Mama said, her voice thick with tears. 'And then it's left out the once . . .'

'What's all this water then? Repentance, eh? Or vexation you were found out –'

'Of course I'm ashamed. I've said, I've said –'

'Writing all that piss, how you'll not have me touch you. It's been hands off, gone two years now –'

'You keep a count?' she asked miserably.

'Aye, I do . . . Ready enough for me, weren't you, those days on Warley moor? Eh, Lina?'

'That's going back fifteen years, that –'

'Who's keeping count now, eh? And all the while you've this puking mewling pissing *secret* . . . Mind you I don't blame him –'

'Keep him out of it –'

'*You* didn't keep him out of . . . well, did you? Go on then. Lift a hand against me –'

'Haven't you said enough, James? Please –'

'There's not words enough, for what I've to say . . . It's no bloody wonder it's my best friend, is the brandy bottle.'

'It helps no one,' Mama cried, 'that you're seldom out of your cups.'

'Aye. Well, I've to have *some* pleasures. You've taken most else away. And not least my pride, eh? I've done with you. I said that when I read it . . . I've only one more thing to say. Since it's your doing, is all this – I'll not have the innocent suffer. And that's why you'll never see me punish those who didn't ask to be born . . .'

'James, James,' my mother cried, '*try* to forget!'

But he had already gone out of the room.

And of what were they speaking? I had grown used over the years to their bickering. To these accusations I couldn't understand. I think, too, that I did not really wish to know. I just wanted Mama to be happy. And Papa to be once more the man on whose knee I used to sit in the snug. Turning the pages of picture books.

A year passed. Eighteen months. A little before Easter Miss Milner's mother died. And Miss Milner left to go and keep house for her father. A governess was obtained for Agnes. But for me . . . At fourteen, although I was short on some accomplishments, and especially sewing, I maintained I knew enough. I dreaded work on the globe, and *Questions and Answers* again.

And then one evening (he was sober), Papa said to me:

'Well then, little lass, do you still have a notion to learn Latin?'

I was wary.

'It depends –'

'I've maybe not been as kind as I ought. And I'd the notion – well then, Latin. Is it to be Latin lessons?'

'If it's to go to school again –'

'School – what about school? When there's a scholar lives not a stone's throw away . . . I've spoke with Mr Hume. He says if you're willing, he is. I reckon they like to teach, do scholars. Any road, you're to have your way – and if it's Greek you want, you've to have that too . . . Right, eh? Does that suit, little lass?'

Yes, I said, yes, yes, yes. And threw my arms about him. And, for a few happy moments, was his darling again.

8

And so the lessons began. I was fourteen now. Halliwell was to go away to school in the autumn, when Phil, with whom he shared a tutor, went to Rugby. None of the Yorkshire schools were good enough, Aunt Flora said (and Uncle Sutcliffe nodded agreement). She spoke of Phil's attending Oxford or Cambridge. Halliwell was to go to Clitheroe House Academy in East Keswick. That would be quite grand enough, and he would learn there all he would need for becoming, one day, the owner of Appleyard Mill. As soon as he was sixteen he would join his father.

It was not, of course, what he wanted. His heart was not in it. Papa would say, 'Come here, my lad,' showing him a sample of fancy lastings (crape, with gold and silver thread, in designs which I thought quite beautiful). And Halliwell, sullenly impatient, would say, 'Yes, yes,' when my father asked, was it not very fine? Then, 'Can I go now?' and I would know it was back to his army.

He did not care much for reading, unless it was about military matters. He had followed the Crimean War in detail. Now, this spring, he had the Indian Mutiny. Through the months to come, he entertained Agnes and me. He could not be halted.

'Now you see, these Indian troops . . . the Moslems can't eat pigs and the Hindoos won't eat cows, and they heard tell their new rifles had been greased with pork and beef dripping – and that was the spark that has set them off . . .'

Betty, bringing in his laundry, was forced to listen. She professed herself disgusted.

'Nine hundred – almost half of them women and children – the sepoys granted safe conduct, but they killed all the men. Then the women and children who survived – five assassins hacked them all to death . . . When we caught the mutineers, we blew them out of cannons – human cannon balls – while they were alive. Wasn't that a good revenge?'

Thus he regaled us throughout the summer. But I was not with him. I was in paradise.

Of course I could not spend as much time with Mr Hume as I

would with a governess. But I could be certain of three mornings a week. And I had the run of his library – not as before, shyly, but now with his guidance. All that Geraldine had hinted at, suggested for me, all those unhappy schooldays, hidden in the library puzzling out Latin words and, glorious enigma, the Greek, of which I had been able to make nothing but whose beautiful shapes I had traced over and over.

Now I asked, 'And please – might I learn some *Greek* also?' Expecting him to say: 'Ah, wanting to run before you can walk, eh? Isn't the Roman tongue with the simple Roman alphabet enough to be going on with?'

But he did not. My dear friend, standing at the bookcase, heavy black brows raised in amusement, smiling:

'Of course, Christabel, *if you wish*, and don't mind hard work . . .' And then he explained that as a small boy he had known the Greek alphabet before the Roman – and was accustomed to write his name in Greek script before he had learnt his other letters. 'It amused my father to show me off, to exhibit me. A prize monkey . . .

'And then, you see, Mrs Hume – *her* father was a scholar also. It was at Oxford that we first met, when he was my coach. *She* had learned to help him, and latterly, became his eyes. For he was losing his sight, you see, and relied on her totally.'

I loved to hear of other people's lives. To me it was like a story book. It was not at all the world of Appleyard or Horsfield Mill, of Wade or Buckley House, of Wentworth Terrace. And how easily he talked. How happy he was to stop, hand poised on the page, searching for a memory, and then, in his deep voice, giving a shout of delight as he recalled the incident, the person, the time . . . The same shout of delight he gave when I first began to decline in Latin: my first *correct* declension.

At eleven o'clock in would come the tray of tea, we would pause in our labours, and then perhaps I would ask something about his school. *Uppingham*. How much better it sounded than The Beeches! And the work – no tedious mornings with the globe. All seemed excitement. Latin, Greek, algebra, geometry . . .

And then Oxford, and Pembroke College. He showed me engravings of the town, and the university. I heard about the river, where one might sit lazily in a flat-bottomed boat, and the water beside would carry only drifting weeds – no mill effluent or scum, no purple or green dyes. No, Oxford was not at all like Halifax. Then, he had a First in Mods ('whatever are they?') so that must be explained. And when he had won the Latin Essay Prize, there was the pride of Mrs Hume's father, his coach, at whose house he spent so much time. And how he had been congratulated by Mrs Hume . . .

'If we had thought of marriage then . . . A curate's pay . . . We had to wait almost ten years. Mrs Hume, she came of a family – she could expect to make a good marriage, not least because of the wealth on her mother's side. My mother-in-law is confined to her home, an affliction of the legs, otherwise she is in excellent health – would that her daughter were also . . . But *then*, ah, then, Mrs Hume was fit and strong. A most vivacious young lady.' He looked away. 'The sad person you see now . . . She was used once you know, to *tease* me . . .'

I thought of the ailing Mrs Hume – and tried to picture her the laughing tease. I could not.

'How good, how blessed,' he said, sadly yet vigorously, 'if we could give not just our time, our thoughts, to those we love, but also something of ourselves. Our energy perhaps, or life force?'

Mr Hume was a busy man. His day was organized thus: when I arrived, on Tuesday, Wednesday and Friday for my lessons, he would be at work already on parish matters. From half past one, he would be out in all weathers, visiting. (He had a notebook – I was shown it – in which he wrote short descriptions of his parishioners so that he might recognize them all: 'Kit Ogden – extremely long arms and legs', 'Mary Holroyd – thumb missing in mill accident'. He called it *Speculum Gregis* – Mirror of the flock . . .) Or he might perhaps travel to Halifax to visit a parishioner in gaol. And then he had, in the evening, his school. The very one to which Kit went. But it was not too well attended – many of those from the mill were too weary, and in the lighter evenings, the labourers from the farms could work later, so did not come.

Monday and Thursday morning, he devoted to parish accounts and business, with his doors open to visitors. The needy, however, came at any time and it was nothing for a lesson to be broken into with a call. Then perhaps five or fifteen minutes later, he would return, to see how much I had progressed with my exercises, and would glimpse almost before he had sat down, what mistakes I had made.

'Ah, look, you have written *hoc*. And it should be *haec*. Where

is your neuter? I see no neuter – these things *matter*, Christabel!'
And he would smile at me affectionately, approvingly.

With what reluctance I left for home and our one o'clock
dinner. The joy in my heart was the homework he had given me.
And in the afternoons, I might practise on the organ. He had
given me permission, and a key to the vestry. I played with some
facility and no want of confidence. Oh, my happy afternoons,
with Renkes Organ Tutor, and St Mary's to myself.

There came a spell of wet weather. One Wednesday, heavy rain
prevented me from leaving to cross the road for home. I would
not eat with Mr and Mrs Hume, so stayed on in his study.
The fire crackled. Outside the heavens had opened, and water
splashed into the gutters. I skimmed through a copy of the
Leeds Mercury. Lying beneath it were two volumes, *The Life of
Charlotte Brontë*, by E. C. Gaskell.

I knocked on their dining-room door.

'Ah, Christabel –' Mr Hume stopped, fork to mouth. Mrs
Hume was sitting listlessly before a bowl of broth. I held out the
books.

'May I borrow these – as soon as the rain stops? I shall cover
them with my cloak of course, and –'

He craned his head to see. 'They were delivered to me only
yesterday from Leeds. I have not looked in them myself . . . but
yes, of course you may. May she not, Mrs Hume?'

A break in the rain sent me across the road. Thereafter it rained
until nightfall. I read for the remainder of the day. Betty brought
in her sewing:

'Not at your double-dutch today?'

'No,' I said, 'I'm reading about Miss Brontë.'

I read as one possessed. I could not put it down. I read till
late, with a candle. And then the next morning immediately after
breakfast.

I found little, scarcely a paragraph, about Branwell's time at
Luddenden Foot. I had expected somehow to read of Mama and
Papa and Sutcliffe. But then, towards the end of the first volume,
I read:

'The story must be told . . . not merely is it so well known to
many living as to be, in a manner, public property, but it is
possible that, by revealing the misery, the gnawing, life-long
misery, the degrading habits, the early death of her partner in

116

guilt – the acute and long enduring agony of his family – to the wretched woman, who not only survives, but passes about in the gay circles of London society, as a vivacious, well-dressed, flourishing widow, there may be awakened in her some feelings of repentance.

'Branwell, I have mentioned, had obtained a situation as a private tutor. Full of available talent, a brilliant talker, a good writer, apt at drawing, ready of appreciation, and with a not unhandsome person, he took the fancy of a married woman, nearly twenty years older than himself. It is no excuse for him to say that she began the first advances, and "made love" to him. She was so bold and hardened, that she did it in the very presence of her children, fast approaching to maturity; and they would threaten her that, if she did not grant them such and such indulgences, they would tell their bedridden father "how she went on with Mr Brontë". He was so beguiled by this mature and wicked woman, that he went home for his holidays reluctantly, stayed there as short a time as possible, perplexing and distressing them all by his extraordinary conduct: at one time in the highest spirits, at another, in the deepest depression – accusing himself of blackest guilt and treachery, without specifying what they were; and altogether evincing an irritability of disposition bordering on insanity . . .

'. . . When she [Charlotte] reached the Parsonage, Branwell was there, unexpectedly, very ill. He had come home a day or two before, apparently for a holiday; in reality, I imagine, because some discovery had been made which rendered his absence imperatively desirable. The day of Charlotte's return, he had received a letter from Mr —, sternly dismissing him, intimating that his proceedings were discovered, characterizing them as bad beyond expression, and charging him, on pain of exposure, to break off immediately, and for ever, all communication with every member of the family.

'All the disgraceful details came out. Branwell was in no state to conceal his agony of remorse, or, strange to say, his agony of guilty love, from any dread of shame. He gave passionate way to his feelings; he shocked and distressed those loving sisters inexpressibly; the blind father sat stunned, sorely tempted to curse the profligate woman, who had tempted his boy – his only son – into the deep disgrace of deadly crime.

'All the variations of spirits and of temper – the reckless gaiety, the moping gloom of many months, were now explained. There was a reason deeper than any mere indulgence of appetite, to account for his intemperance; he began his career as an habitual drunkard to drown remorse.

'The pitiable part, as far as he was concerned, was the yearning love he still bore to the woman who had got so strong a hold upon him. It is true, that she professed equal love; we shall see how her professions held good. There was a strange lingering of conscience, when meeting her clandestinely by appointment at Harrogate some months after, he refused to consent to the elopement which she proposed; there was some good left in this corrupted, weak young man, even to the very last of his miserable days. The case presents the reverse of the usual features; the man became the victim; the man's life was blighted, and crushed out of him by suffering, and guilt entailed by guilt; the man's family were stung by keenest shame. The woman – to think of her father's pious name – the blood of honourable families mixed in her veins . . . goes flaunting about to this day in respectable society; a showy woman for her age; kept afloat by her reputed wealth. I see her name in county papers, as one of those who patronize the Christmas balls; and I hear of her in London drawing rooms. Now let us read not merely of the suffering of her guilty accomplice, but of the misery she caused to innocent victims, whose premature deaths may, in part, be laid at her door . . .'

'What is this?' Mama asked, coming into the room where I sat. 'What are you reading? Betty says –'

I showed her.

'Ah, no pet,' she said. 'You see, there is trouble about that book. Please give both volumes to me.'

Half an hour later, she brought them back: 'Christabel – how much have you read?'

'I was just on the second volume . . .'

'You must take them straightaway to Mr Hume, and tell him – no, I shall tell him – that this book has been withdrawn. Further copies are not to be published – you must forget what you have read, darling.' She was very white, and her lips trembled. 'Will you?'

'Yes, Mama.'

Of course the next morning when I went for my lesson, I asked Mr Hume.

He looked grave for a moment, then laughed:

'Yes. There is trouble. It seems a lady referred to within, has taken out a writ – a Mrs Robinson of Leeds. But you must forget all this – and not bother your dear little auburn curls with the matter –'

'Do not speak to me like that,' I said boldly. 'My auburn curls, as you call them, are good enough for Latin and Greek –'

'Then begin at once . . .' he said, laughing. 'Let us see. *Supra*. You have given me "above". Yes, literally. But here – "beyond", do you not think?'

That summer I went to stay with Polly. Her family had taken a house at Scarborough for the month of August. It was a happy month. Mrs Liddington was of course with us. I loved her dearly. She was a laughing person (how easy it was, in Polly's company, to think like her . . .), animated, happy. Full of energy, wanting to walk often when we would like to have rested. Sometimes when she and Polly were laughing together, they would seem almost like sisters. Mr Liddington was sterner, graver. Traits that Edmund surely had inherited.

We would have liked Henry's company, but he was travelling in France until the autumn. Edmund came down from Edinburgh for one week. The five of us went on an excursion to Falsgrave. All the way there, he and his father held forth about medical matters, whilst Polly, Mrs Liddington and I pulled faces behind their backs. 'It's so dreary, and quite disgusting,' Mrs Liddington whispered as Edmund related to his father the details of an internal obstruction.

Henry was at least excited, moved by the ideas he held, but Edmund seemed over-awed by a sense of his own worth. He had already written to the *Lancet* about the management of spinal curvature using the inclined plane. 'And they have done me the honour of publishing it . . .' We had to remind ourselves – one would not have known it – that he was not yet nineteen.

'Edmund, dear,' Mrs Liddington said, another time, 'these *organs* you speak of continually – the girls, and your mother too – we have no idea where they are placed, so that your talk is quite wasted . . .'

But Edmund only blinked and swallowed, and then at once offered to draw a simple diagram.

'I think that will not be necessary, dear.'

'Alas, he has become a very tedious person,' Polly said.

Polly was fifteen now. In about eighteen months' time her

parents planned to send her either to Paris or to Brussels to school. Part of her wanted the excitement and adventure.

'I long to see the world,' she said, 'but I fear to be homesick again. Remember how we met . . . if I should have to feel like that again –'

'But that was when your mama was so ill . . .'

'Yes . . . but then – Christabel, can you not ask your mama and papa if *you* could come too?'

Standing there on the sands, poking daringly with her parasol at the small curling waves, and laughing at her little white dog, Jasper, she scarcely seemed to notice that I did not answer her.

The North Sea stretched before me, creamy and peaceful. I busied myself with my bonnet strings, and a shaft of pain ran through me, as if I had already suffered loss. How could I go? What would happen to those dear mornings spent with Virgil and Xenophon? And Mr Hume . . .

'I don't imagine they would allow such a thing, dear Polly. Even Halliwell is to go no further than Wetherby to school,' I said. 'And Papa for one would think it very fancy.'

That evening I took out my books and brought them down as we sat in the parlour of the villa. I did not get far. Mr Liddington said, as his wife sat at the piano, 'Christabel, it is you to play for us next.'

But I was shy and self-conscious of playing before an audience. The organ in St Mary's – that was different, and solitary. I stumbled through a lullaby by Couperin, and then was allowed to get up. But not to go back to my books. I was required to sing a duet with Polly: 'I'm a merry laughing girl.'

Mrs Hume's condition had worsened while I was in Scarborough. I arrived back to find her upstairs and in bed. Mr Hume said little, except that she was too weak now to remain up, and that her eyes were giving trouble also.

'Perhaps it is something akin to the father's affliction – I fear very much that has come to complicate the picture. A fresh burden on her, on us.'

I am not certain whose idea it was that I should read to Mrs Hume. I would hope that it was mine. I know only that it is one of the few deeds of which I remain proud.

She lay in the big room upstairs, facing out towards the ravine, looking down more directly than I ever did, on the churchyard. Mr Hume said that it would be simple to convert one of the small rooms downstairs for her. 'But she would prefer,' he said, 'since she believes it is only for a short while, to be where she is accustomed.'

A short while. But who was it believed that? She or he? That first afternoon, I followed him up into the large back room, its heavy yellow curtains looped back. A fire had been lit, for this early September was chill. The room smelt curious, partly the heat, partly perhaps some medicines which stood already poured out.

She was half sitting up – 'Who is it?' she asked, peering forward.

'I have brought little Christabel, dear. She has asked if she may read to you.'

I read to her. Every afternoon. Only on Sundays did I stay away. Sometimes when I had finished reading, I would take a cup of tea with Mr Hume if he were home, or if not, go into the church to practise the organ. I thought that I made a grand noise.

As I read, the house felt strangely still. Mr Hume was of course out visiting. And the noisy sounds of cleaning, the rattling of coal, were morning sounds. But as I sat by the bed, it felt sometimes as if the world had stopped – so still was it.

And she remarked on it. 'So quiet,' she said. 'So quiet. This house should be full of children. Your parents are very blessed – three strong little ones.' She did not mention Josh and I supposed her to have forgotten.

'Mr Hume would have liked children – a son to share his scholarship with. But God had other plans . . . Are you responsive to God's Will, Christabel? Do you believe and accept that God is All Wise and knows what is best for us?'

'No,' I said. But she had tired herself with talking and did not notice my answer. And in this I was fortunate, for I had answered from my heart, and not my head.

We read, or rather I read, aloud to her the latest issue of the *Cornhill*, the whole of *Little Dorritt*, *Blackwood's Magazine*, and over the next few months each instalment of *Janet's Repentance*, by a new writer, George Eliot.

She lay there, eyes closed. I wondered sometimes if she slept, but if ever I halted, she would say: 'Why do you stop? I am enjoying it so . . .' And then I thought: When she can see so little, and that little not pleasant, why should she open her eyes?

I knew she had great pain now. Two afternoons a week Mr Rushworth called on her. Sometimes as I read to her, I would hear pacing in the hall, or steps down in the study below. I knew that if he was at home, Mr Hume would be walking to and fro, to and fro. Agitated for her.

And so it went on, through the rest of that year.

Mama was not too happy about the reading, saying:

'Is it good, pet, that you are all the time with a sick woman? Poor peopling is right, and part of our duties – so is sitting with the sick – but you are young. A child still . . .'

I protested. *Fifteen* – a child? I knew it was because I was still so very small, and showing no signs of growing, either upwards, or across (even twelve-year-old Agnes had passed me by at least an inch), although just this year the dreaded monthly courses had begun.

'It is not the task of one person,' Mama said. 'There must be women of the parish, persons educated enough to read to her. Her own husband?'

But he was busy, I told her. 'And anyway, she wants me. She needs me. It is me she asks for.'

I was not there when Mrs Hume died. She died during the night. All the rain-lashed afternoon before, the wind scraping the sycamore tree branch against her tightly closed window, we had been reading Stanley's *Life of Arnold*. Her laboured breathing. The long-drawn-out moans. Her hand would stretch out for mine. Thin, transparent hand. Her eyes when she turned them to me were covered with a fine film.

How to explain my devotion? As I sat in the parlour, dutifully sewing, and heard the tolling of the bell, I knew that it was for him I had done it. That he might think well of me.

Melancholy tolling of the bell: I mourned for, with Mr Hume. With Francis. (For yes, I had come to think of him as Francis. Daringly at first, in odd moments, and then always.) In those days after his wife's death, it was not her past suffering haunted me – although God knows I had been witness to that – but the image of his sorrow.

I did not go back at once for the lessons. I was not sure whether he would still wish to teach me. I had seen his grief – so painfully apparent from the pulpit. Meanwhile, a cold east wind, more March than April, moaned about the house. At night in the bedroom which I now had to myself, I lay and listened to its weird cries.

One night I left my bed and crossed to the window. Clouds,

blown across the sky, parted to reveal the moon, casting a strange light on the lane. Every tree bent and creaked and tossed its branches. In the Vicarage – a solitary light flickered in an upstairs window. I knew that this was his room, I thought of him alone, mourning. I was certain that he sat – that he had not lain down to bed.

If I opened my window, if he opened his, I might fly in and comfort him. '*Come to me all ye who are burdened* . . .' he had said on Sunday. But was God comforting him now? (I remembered how once he had comforted me – screaming child, ghost of Grimshaw . . . But I knew about ghosts now. That ghosts were within, not without.)

After a very long time I went back to bed. When I awoke I knew that I loved him.

The lessons began again. I dreaded only that they might ever end. I wanted everything safely mapped out: that that was how it would always be. That my family should not have different plans for me . . .

Aunt Martha for one thought it all very odd, and her brother quite wrong in allowing me to spend my days in this manner. 'She had her chances – at school. But what's the sense of all this? What good will it be when she's wed?'

Wed. Yes, they were already hinting at such matters. One day, with Uncle Sutcliffe and Aunt Flora in the house, 'When the lass is wed . . .' my father had begun.

Uncle Sutcliffe interrupted. 'But she's only fifteen, your lass –'

Papa said, 'By then I'd made sure of Lina, or all but. Any road, the old ones had. It was what they wanted . . . us wed. Never mind if they had it wrong.'

He said it in the bitter way he affected these days, even when sober. More perhaps when sober.

Aunt Flora ignored him:

'I think it quite ridiculous, Sutcliffe. She has a pretty little talent at drawing, does she not? Now if her parents were to foster *that* . . . a little trip perhaps to Paris or Brussels or Rome even? I could easily be persuaded to accompany her. If she is to have a polish or shine, it should not be this ridiculous learning, which will only antagonize any gentlemen who might –'

'How do you know I want to be wed?' I interrupted indignantly.

'Every girl wishes to marry . . .'

'I don't.'

123

'Simply because you are not ready. It wants a year or two. But if when you are ready, you are not suitable – you have traits which make you unattractive to likely suitors –'

Uncle Sutcliffe repeated (he was my friend today), 'The lass is only fifteen. Let her be.'

His intercession earned him a rebuke from Aunt Flora. Meg smirked in the background, then poked a warning finger at me before giving a high pitched giggle. 'Quiet, Margaret! Over excited again,' her mother said sharply.

Love. There was nothing to be done about it. I knew only that I would work harder than ever before at my books. Perhaps I would be the one – why not? – to do fair copies of his commentary? Yes, yes – to sit with him, while the fire crackled in the grate, no other sound but our two pens scratching, our only interruption, the announcement of a parishioner on urgent business. ('Christabel, you will excuse me, my dear? I put a marker now on page 112'), and then a little later in would come a tray of tea, to drink by the fire. And slices of lemon cake. That was how it would be. As once Mrs Hume had been to him, I would be too.

He was still working on his *Aeschylus*. An annotated edition of the *Eumenides*. He had completed, almost, the first two plays of the trilogy: *Agamemnon* and *Choephoroe*. I saw that it might take some time yet, for there was always something else he should be doing. Also, both the commentary and the notes for these plays must be written in Latin. He said this was so that *all* scholars might benefit from new editions.

The *Eumenides*. The Furies: who dwelt in darkness, whose task it was to chase matricides and murderers over land and sea, and even into Hell. Running like hounds, rejoicing in the smell of blood, sucking the blood of men even while they lived – this was strong stuff.

Those warm July mornings. How bright and welcoming he would seem always. I was working then on Virgil. 'Well,' he might say, looking at my yesterday's task, '*Sunt geminae Somni portae* . . . yes, yes, you have "gates of sleep", not "doors" . . . Good, Christabel, very good.'

And then the smile I so much longed for, and loved. He might even seem in fine high spirits. But then, as suddenly, I would see the lines of his face droop, his voice when he spoke would turn down, harden. He would be as if plunged into despair. Pulling himself together, he would get up:

'Enough of books . . . I shall go and visit Isaac Webster. I promised to help him make his will.'

I wanted then to throw my arms about him. As I wrote and studied, I would watch his face: I knew the days when his sorrow and grief were too much with him.

And thus the summer passed. Polly was to leave for Brussels in January where she would attend the Château de Koekleberg. In August, I went with her family to Scarborough. Edmund did not join us. Henry did. And now that I did not, puppy-like, worry at his heels, he was more patient, more willing to spend time with Polly and me. Because I knew that his studies were of the classics, I would like to have spoken of them, but with my little knowledge felt afraid of his scorn. Polly, however, told him of my interests. 'Well then,' he said, 'let her remember the old saw, "There is much more learning than knowledge in the world."'

We were happy all together. But that did not stop me from counting the days until I should be home again. And sitting at the table in Francis's study.

'You're drunk again,' my mother said. 'Stinking with it. And in front of your children –'

'Bairns, what bairns? A great hulking lad who'd as like go for a common soldier . . . *Damn*, damnation, *hell*. If you've not tripped me with that stool.' He fell heavily, then righted himself.

He stood angrily, swaying a little. 'Don't stare at me, don't *bloody stare*.'

'Get away. Get upstairs,' my mother said. 'Full of ale as you are –'

'And brandy, and rum. Dog's nose, eh, bloody dog's nose?'

He would not be moved, standing there aggressively, daring her to touch him. Halliwell, behind her, looked as if squaring up for a fight, but he was not even noticed. Agnes, curled up in a chair, trembled on the edge of tears, and fear.

It was my second day back from Scarborough. Halliwell was preparing to go back to school. My father had not returned to the mill after dinner. Now at seven in the evening, he was the worse for wear. Soon he would leave again – no doubt for the gaming table this time. These days he did not bother whether he shouted at my mother alone, or in company. If we were there, he ignored us.

But today he was not going to ignore me. If he did not speak to me, he would speak of me.

'Where's she been all day then? Your precious little lass? Nose stuck in a book. *Learning*, eh?'

'And why not?' my mother said tiredly. 'It was your idea. You encouraged these lessons.'

'Bloody chip off the old block,' he shouted, 'all that learning – bloody chip off . . .'

'Get away. Go!' she cried out in distress. Agnes rushed up to throw her arms about her, burying her head in my mother's skirt.

'Look how you frighten your children,' she said.

'Aye, I frighten *mine*. Mine are frightened,' he said, turning to go, banging out of the room.

And so it remained to comfort our mother. And to forget as soon as possible.

I did. I would put it out of my mind. I did not want to think of the changed man he had become. Whose darling I had once been, but who sadly now seemed to love me hardly at all. How fortunate that I had Francis, whom I loved . . .

Papa, more and more frequently drunk. Never to be trusted for civilized behaviour. And yet, my grandfather, old Joshua Woodward, had scarcely touched alcohol. Sober, God-fearing, hard-working. But *his* father? There had been many tales of Daniel Woodward, on the ran-tan . . .

'Hark the herald angels sing, Glory to the newborn King . . .'

A new carol. I played it on the church organ that Christmas, and then again on the piano at home. At the beginning of January I helped Francis with the New Year party for the children. The weather that month was extraordinarily mild. Down by Josh's grave, two daisies sprang up, as if ignorant of winter.

My lessons began again. Francis, working with me on a passage of the *Aeneid*, broke down and wept. I was shocked to silence. He said then, recovering himself:

'Please forget that you have seen this. There are some days . . . If you knew of the loneliness –'

I was not able to answer him. I could do nothing but sit, quiet and sad, until he was himself again.

A moment later, reaching out, he placed his hand over mine. It remained there for the rest of the lesson.

At the beginning of February, work began on the new ceme-

126

tery. The old was now too full. There would be a bridge built over on to land the far side of the church.

I was setting to music one of the poems from my mother's blue leather book, *Ode to the Polar Star* ('Lord of the northern fields of heaven . . .'), by Branwell Brontë. It was to be a surprise for her.

Now that I had the key of the vestry, I went in always that way, skirting the graveyard, creeping in, unseen surely. Sometimes before going in with my music, I lingered there. Like the church, it was cold, and it was damp often, but I loved the smell of the vestments, the musty smell of the bibles.

Francis. I could not forget that I had seen him cry. That he had wept before me. I could not forget either that our hands had lain together. I waited till it should happen again. Which it did.

'What is this?' he asked one morning. '*Lugete . . . et quantum est*, etc. . . . "Mourn", Christabel. "Mourn". Not "*listen*".'

'I was thinking of lugs, you see – and so ears. And –'

He laughed loudly, then clasped me to him. 'Stupid, beautiful mistake – oh Christabel, will you never learn?' And then he held me tighter still.

I remained in his arms. Then, as he released me, I saw that he was distressed, and trying to control – what? Tears?

'Ah, dear God,' he said, 'no more lessons for today.' He gathered up our books. 'I must visit Meg Bates . . . Her husband – you'll have heard he's to be transported. A sad business.'

I told Francis:

'My father is drinking too much. We are all worried.' I was ashamed of what was happening in our home, and had never been able to speak of it. I could not imagine he did not know. Nor did I think he would come storming across the lane, to read to a mill owner the Riot Act. A worker, yes. But James Woodward, no.

And indeed, 'I cannot interfere,' he said. 'I know of the sadness. And if I thought a word from me . . . Perhaps there is something he cannot bear? We must all carry crosses, Christabel. Some are better able to bear them than others, who falter by the wayside. Perhaps God alone knows . . . Yes, God alone knows, Christabel.'

*

127

And now, more and more often, he held me to him. Closely. As if he would never let me go. Clasped me to him, on any excuse, on no excuse. Bewildered, yet longing, I said nothing, did nothing. We never spoke of it. I could only feel in him a great strength, a force held back.

Sometimes, the housekeeper would knock on the door – and he would loose me, springing back, rising hastily from his chair to move towards her.

How dear he was to me. So dear. I would have trusted him with my soul.

The icy weather came and went. In March, wicked winds blew, moaning around the house. Night after night, I would wake and hear the wailing rise, and die, rise and die. I slept badly, my dreams unhappy, yet confused. In the morning I could remember only that I had been distressed.

But then spring arrived. And with it a spell of warmth. A little before Easter I had ready for my mother her music, *Ode to the Polar Star*. It was not right, it was not good. I had thought of asking our church organist for help. Today, I decided I would play it through, and see if I could not get it better.

Four in the afternoon, and the sun moving round, casting a long shadow against the church. Walking to the vestry, the key in my pocket. And then inside, lingering a few moments. I counted my sheets of music. I rearranged them together with the poem in their embroidered linen cover. Then the door opened, and Francis came in.

But what was this? Francis, locking the vestry door. Both sides. Francis, groaning, troubled, saying: 'Make haste, make haste.' Holding me to him, burying his head in my breasts, my so small, too small breasts. Kneeling before me then.

'Make haste . . . Ah God, ah Jesus Christ, Christ will forgive . . . How can God . . . Ah, if you knew . . . Christabel, Christabel, little Christabel . . .'

Hands exploring – where was he going now? My clothes. My skirts, my clothes. And the pain.

And what was he saying? '. . . Both of us, closer to God. Ah but if you knew – the life that comes from you, that lies in you, Christabel . . .' His questing fingers. And then more pain. And more. And more. I cannot move. I shall never move again . . .

Then suddenly, he has left me. Is standing, head bent. Turned away. The only sound his sobbing. A great convulsive sound.

128

I could not move. I did not move. We remained there, both of us, for how long?

He was the first to speak. 'How –' he began. 'What is to become of me, of us? I cannot think. I –'

'Nothing,' I said. My voice a dry squeak. I had rearranged my clothes. I took my music and unlocked the door. 'Nothing.'

I went straight up home, and to bed. I had a fever, I said. And my monthly courses. Yes, I was bleeding now, and the fever too was real. For more than a week, I tossed and turned. Mr Rushworth who visited listened to my chest and pronounced it not serious. I asked if I might go to the seaside to recover.

9

An enormous saddle of mutton, waiting to be carved, steamed before Papa's place at the table. He was late home and we had been waiting more than half an hour to begin the meal. As the tray had been carried past me I had felt a wave of nausea at the fatty smell. I began to think of what excuses I could make not to eat it – or perhaps to slip it to the aged Trissie who lay not far from my feet.

It was Saturday dinner time. He usually left the mill in time for dinner at half past one and did not return in the afternoon. But sometimes lately he had not come home for the meal at all. During the week it was more often six o'clock tea that he missed.

He looked round the table, carving knife in hand: 'You'll not have heard the news then?' Then turning to my mother, 'Well, Lina, eh? Sutcliffe's not been this way with his news?'

My mother trembled, as she trembled so often these days.

'Not interested then? You're not interested? You don't have a care these days what becomes of your bonny brother, and my friend, who married a fancy mincing flibberty –' he jabbed at the mutton.

My mother said mildly enough, 'Tell us then. If it concerns Sutcliffe, tell us.'

Halliwell was making bread pellets which he was lining up in formations of four. Fourteen-year-old Agnes, looking straight in front of her, gave a little shiver.

'You asked,' he said, 'I'll tell you.' He laid down the knife. No one had been served. 'It's all up with him. He's done for, is Sutcliffe . . . And it's a sad day to see that happen to a friend. For all that he's been a sackless fool – but that's enough. We'd best eat. And the young ones – it's not fit for their ears . . .'

'Since when have you cared what they heard,' my mother cried, her face working with the suspense, the need to know. 'Many's the time you've treated them to language that –'

'Hold your tongue.'

'Tell me then –'

'I'll tell it – the daft thing he's done. Brass, Lina. Good

130

Armstrong brass, gone for nowt. And you know who's at bottom of it? No one else but that fond brother-in-law of his. Alexander Gilbert they call him, don't they? Alexander *Gibbet* more like.'

'But Sutcliffe – is Sutcliffe all right?'

'Let it be a lesson to all of us that's sat here, young *and* old. What did he do, the sackless idiot, but mortgage all he had . . . That clever Alexander was going to work miracles. Well, he's worked a miracle, for Alexander. He's had the brass for himself – speculating here and there – and he's got it wrong. A lot more wrong than Hudson did.'

'*Where's Sutcliffe?* I must go to him,' my mother said, starting up, her hand to her face.

'I reckon I've little stomach to this meal,' said Papa. 'Sutcliffe's done for. The mill, the marriage settlement – and I don't know what else –'

I dared to speak up from my end of the table.

'And where's Alexander?'

'Ah, that bird's flown. He flew to France or maybe Holland, I don't recall the geography. But I'll fancy the law's arm won't stretch to reach him.'

My mother said, 'Phil and Meg?'

In a satisfied voice, Papa said, 'That'll be the end of his fine school, that's what. And all the fancy notions meant for the little lady. Pretensions. They'll go the way of everything else.'

I thought of my cousin Phil, with his long pale face and weedy body, his sharp nose so like his mother's, his quarrelsome voice. I thought too of Meg, with her heavy looks and her malicious giggle, tee-hee, tee-hee, and the swift jab of a finger to emphasize. I pictured them hearing from Aunt Flora or perhaps from their father the terrible tale of woe. The tale of the wicked uncle. And I felt nothing but pity for them. Affection too. And some envy. They after all were innocent. Wrong had been done to them. They did not carry the burden of guilt.

Ah God, dear God, what have we done, what did I do? I thought, as the carriage drew up, and the bell rang and Uncle Sutcliffe, his cloak almost covering his face, came in alone. And went with Mama and Papa into the parlour.

My father came through with a flask of brandy and saw me standing in the hall.

'Off – away. Up with you to bed. You're not helping, stood there. Nowt said needs no mending. What's done can't be undone – and that's all there is about it.'

131

What's done can't be undone . . .

I stood quite still, trembling. Pain in my heart. My body. *What's done can't be undone* . . .

I was eighteen, the year of Uncle Sutcliffe's disaster. I had been sad for two years now. And ill for many months. Green sickness, they called it. And indeed when I looked in the glass, I saw the sickly greenish cast of my complexion. I was made to force down sulphate of iron pills, to drink Brandish's solution in linseed tea and take powder of savine three times a day. I was threatened too with electrical treatment.

Francis. I had not seen Francis again. When I recovered from my fever, it was to learn that he too was ill. I had been afraid to go to church. In my hurt and anger and pain, I would have refused to go. But I was spared. A locum stood in the pulpit, and at the communion table.

His was a nervous illness. That was what we heard. A nervous crisis or breakdown. Unhinged by his wife's death, some said. It had taken a long time to manifest itself, but perhaps he had not rested as he should? Or taken good enough care.

He stayed indoors. A nurse was engaged for him. At the church, several locums came and went: I do not think I can recall the face or voice of any of them. When he was fit enough to leave his bed, Francis went to Malvern, for hydropathy, under Dr Bilbirnie.

He called to say goodbye, but by this time I was in Halifax with Aunt Martha. I spent three months in Wentworth Terrace – to my parents' astonishment – helping her teach millworkers to read.

The months passed. And Francis did not return. We acquired a new Vicar, a Mr Everett. A ponderous, slow and kindly man whose sermons were full of pauses. It appeared that Francis was now very rich. I learned, I forget how, that his wife's mother had died. Under the terms of the marriage settlement, he now inherited a substantial sum of money. He was to settle on the Continent.

My pain was such that it turned inwards. I did not want to look at it. When I stayed with Aunt Martha, I did not need to. But home again, it was different. I asked if I might change my bedroom. I wanted, I said, to face the hills.

And then, my Latin and Greek:

'You must miss that,' Mama said.

'I was tiring of it,' I said. 'And since Mr Hume is ill . . . perhaps it is best I stop.'

I could not look at my books, corrected in his neat hand, peppered with marks of encouragement. I hid them. But as I put the last book away – Virgil's *Aeneid* – it fell open at the page we had worked on that day.

'*Tacitum vivit sub pectore vulnus,*' I read. 'The silent wound lives in the breast.'

'*In the Court of Bankruptcy for the Leeds District. In the matter of SUTCLIFFE JOSEPH ARMSTRONG, of Luddenden Foot, Halifax, Worsted Manufacturer, a Bankrupt . . .*'

Horsfield Mill was sold soon after Uncle Sutcliffe's disaster. Papa had spoken of buying it, but Mama and I, and everyone, guessed that this was just talk, and that he could never raise the type of money needed. Buckley House was also sold.

My mother was of course very distressed by its loss, and by Sutcliffe's plight. She wept freely. But I could not, as once I would have done, throw my arms about her. I had grown shy – shy of her confused unhappiness, taking her side only when it was apparent Papa was goading, humilating her with his excesses (and there was no improvement there. 'Out of my road!' he had said only yesterday, coming in an hour late for his tea, his voice loud and thick, his manner rough, his walk a caricature almost of his normal confident swagger).

When he first felt able to make plans, Uncle Sutcliffe had thought of starting again in a place such as Birmingham, where he was not known. Aunt Flora turned up her nose at this idea. And it was she – still in possession of some of her own money – who made the decision.

They went to live in Bath. Aunt Flora's money was sufficient for simple accommodation. She intended they should live genteelly, their past shrouded in mystery. She would sell her drawings and paintings. Surprisingly, she bore her brother little ill-will. Pale and plucky, she ever referred to him as 'that scallywag'.

In the summer of that year I went to stay with Polly. She had come back from Brussels at Easter. Henry was not there. He was seldom at home, living most of the time in London, where he spoke of working for the newspapers or standing for Parliament. Edmund was also in London, a physician now, at Guy's Hospital.

Polly and I sat in her room and talked. I told her – for I could

133

never have written it in a letter – of Francis. I wept as I spoke. For I had told no one.

Polly wept too. 'And your mama knows nothing? Oh, darling Christabel . . .'

'I could not say . . . How would I tell her? How could I make her so sad?'

'And you have had all this *alone* – I would have come from school, come from Brussels to be with you. You had only to write. If you could have written . . . It is the most terrible – and you are not ill any more?'

'No, not ill. Only what they call green sickness. I have to take chalybeate waters. They fetch them from Harrogate . . .'

But even as she wept with me, and showed her concern, I could see that contentment lay steady and calm beneath. (Her first words to me: 'I have just become an *especially* happy person, dear Christabel.')

And she told me.

'He is called William. And we are so terribly, fearfully in love . . . Look, here is his likeness in a *carte de visite*. His married sister lives near Liddington, and he was down here visiting and . . . He is only a curate, you see. Papa does not approve at all. That is my only, our only sadness. And they have said already that we may not marry. They *must* change, they will change. Mama is on my side. And so would Henry be if he were here . . . My dearest William is not considered suitable at all. And his background is quite humble. He was a sizar at Cambridge – his sister has married well. But Papa will not hear of my "throwing myself away" as he calls it. And he says that I am too young at nineteen. But I know my own mind, and I know too that if it were Lord Iredale or the suchlike, there would be no forbidding it.

'I had even thought of *eloping* – but that will not solve anything, since William is adamant that all must be with their blessing . . . When I am of age, then I shall do as I will. There are only two years to go. It is just . . . we may not see each other, it is not possible – his curacy is in Gloucestershire. I have no excuse to go there, there is no deceit I can think of. We write of course, although I half-promised I would not. Only his sister is here, as messenger. And, oh Christabel . . .'

Later she said to me, 'It will be all right. I know that it will, for both of us. And you too, Christabel. It is so easy for *me* to be good and to be happy, now that I have my dearest William.'

Oh, fortunate Polly. Who loved, and was loved in return. Who had only to wait, and all would be well.

All was not well with me. It was not love I felt, but hate. I could not understand what it was had been done to me. And often, so often now, a wave of hate would engulf me. Yes, hate – for my dear Mr Hume. For Francis, whom I had loved so.

I would have trusted him with my soul. But it was my body he took.

10

'Right then,' said my father, 'since you'll not listen when you're up there, you can keep your lugs open now. I said two clear months' credit to Joseph Thompson, and threepence in the pound discount – did you have that? You didn't. And what of the six check fancies – gone missing. Missing, eh? And the pattern of imperial crape – they'd been waiting on that past ten days. Have I to sit in my own house, telling a great lad of gone eighteen – *eighteen* – asking him if he can make his letters? What was your schooling for, eh? The simplest task and you can't be trusted . . .'

Halliwell looked away from him sullenly. I noticed one eyelid twitching.

'Nay, look at me. You'll not right the matter by fancying I'm not here. And don't look at your mother either. *She* won't help you – not if *I* can stop her.'

But my mother knew better than to become involved in these, regularly recurring scenes. They happened only when my father was sober. When he had been drinking he could not remember, or gather together coherently, a list of Halliwell's commissions, omissions and confusions. And then Halliwell would always win, leaving my father crashing about, shouting insults and curses. Frightening Agnes and Mama – but not me. I was both sorry for him and angry. But not afraid. My own nightmares were such that sight of his behaviour was no more to me than a spoilt child running amok in the nursery. Foolish, and wicked I would think, but not frightening.

We were sitting in the parlour. Halliwell, holding some brass bearings in his hands, fiddling, let them drop to the floor. One ran under the sofa.

'Go on then. Pick that up. Pick it up.'

Halliwell didn't move.

'Pick it up, I said. *Pick it up* –'

'Let him alone,' my mother said. 'I've said before, you'll do no good trying to humiliate him.'

'Who's humiliated? Aren't *I* bloody humiliated, with a great gawk like that . . . he's nowt but a joke, a ruddy joke at the mill, is that lad. Young Mr Halliwell. When I'm gone, the place'll not last six month . . .'

The words fell uneasily into the warm family room. Papa, Papa. So righteous now, when sober. So seldom sober. If anyone was a threat to Appleyard Mill, it was scarcely that half-hearted employee and reluctant heir, Halliwell.

'*Pick it up*, I said.'

Then Halliwell's answer – shocking in its loudness. Its anger. Its rudeness.

'You're not my bloody sergeant. This isn't the army, more's the pity. I'll not! I don't have to obey orders from you . . .'

'Hush,' said Mama. 'Your own father. Honour and obey, and just let be. For my sake, Halliwell –'

'Shouting at me, like a ruddy sergeant major. I'll not bear it.'

'Like that, is it? Threats, insults . . . If I'd spoken to *my* dad that way, even the once – I'd not be here to tell the tale . . .'

'Well,' Halliwell said, turning to us. 'Why is a drunken man like a Quaker? Mama? Christabel? . . . You don't know? A drunken man is like a Quaker – because *the spirit moves him* . . .'

He spoke with uneasy defiance. An insult that was the only weapon left to him. Papa ignored him. Halliwell said to us:

'You know what I want . . . *He* knows what I want.'

He wanted of course, the army. When had he ever wanted anything else? Sometimes, unspoken, Josh's name would hover. Had Josh lived, and had he been willing, then *he* could have been heir, and Halliwell could have had his way.

These sad scenes were all too frequent nowadays. And since it was his own missing days, uncertain temper and fickle memory that put the prosperity of the mill at risk, it was easier for Papa to vent it all on Halliwell. And if he could catch him here at home . . . With all the family gathered round. A chance then to frighten, to impress on us all that he was, this spring of 1862, still James Woodward, worsted manufacturer, of Luddenden.

Summer, and I was to have stayed with Polly, spending at least half of the time at Scarborough. But as so often nowadays, my plans went wrong. Mama became ill with a quinsy two days before I was due to leave. I stayed behind, willingly, fraught by love and concern. The quinsy was more a nuisance than a danger – except, when did danger not lurk where illness was concerned? I hoped my presence would cheer her.

I would like it to have done. I doubted that it would. Three years since Francis left and although I was still Christabel, what meaning did that have? I could as well have been anyone, so little did I feel at home in my body, so sick did I feel in my soul. Perhaps the sickness was hate, perhaps it was an unhealed wound. Possibly it was both. I could not but desperately wished to speak to my mother of it. Once I came very near, only to have the words choke in my throat. I cried then for the first time in many months. And had then to explain away my tears.

Francis, no one spoke of now. It seemed that the ponderous Mr Everett had been forever living across the road. Aged about forty, he had a wife and a young family. Children's voices piped up in church, calling out 'Papa'. One Sunday the little boy, on his way to the pew, ran up the aisle, calling for his father. The scolding he received as his laughing mother ran after him was full of loving pride. Yes, we had been invited inside the Vicarage. Mr Everett liked to entertain. He liked, he said, anything which took him away from his desk and 'the eternal writing of sermons, and parish business . . .' So far, I had managed never to accept.

Of Francis himself, I dared not think. I supposed him to be still abroad. I heard once a third-hand report of a letter sent from Carlsbad. I hoped that whatever the illness, he would one day recover.

Mama got better slowly. But she could not be said to be well. Nor was it good that she trembled so easily. It seemed to me too, I had noticed it suddenly this last year, that she had aged. She had had her fortieth birthday a week ago, but looked far older. She had grown very grey. Threaded through her black hair the grey might have looked well enough. But the whole had now a dusty appearance which no amount of brushing restored to a shine (and I it was who brushed it often. For soothing, not sheen). Her skin had little life, and she had had trouble this last year with her teeth. The result probably of some mercury which Mr Rushworth had prescribed for recurrent liver trouble. She had lost several teeth through loosening, and her cheeks had now a sunken appearance. And where was the pretty voice I remembered? The voice which had been *Mama*? I heard it now only in memory.

I blamed Papa for all this. Who else? He it was who had reduced her, through his drinking and his rages, to the cowed and exhausted person that was now my mother. About the confusion and half-understood, half-heard quarrels and wrongs between them – I did not want to know.

138

He it was who frightened Agnes, who was trying to break Halliwell's spirit. I could not believe that once I had been his darling. These days I was an accepted irritant. He was short with me more often than not. I was the daughter who would, most probably, stay at home to be with Mama. I never heard nowadays, those words: 'When you're wed.'

And yet at nineteen, I could not, surely, have been placed on the shelf? I think I had placed myself there. I could not imagine being wed.

Earlier this spring there had been some jokes and hints about the Howgate son, up at Warley. A perfectly pleasant and quite harmless, if somewhat stupid, lad of just turned twenty. Matthew Howgate and Christabel Woodward. Why ever? Why should he look at me, who was – and Aunt Flora had pointed this out years ago – no beauty?

Indeed, why should he notice me? If he was to notice anyone, it should be Agnes.

Agnes, at sixteen, was very beautiful. So beautiful that she could ask for a king's son, and get him surely. She looked like Mama must once have looked – the same eyes and hair, the velvety skin – with something of Papa in her vivid red cheeks and shape of face. She had not Mama's cleft chin, for that was mine. She had, though, a dimple, and a small high clear voice. Yes, she was beautiful. And nice with it. I loved her and could have wished to be able to talk to her. I was not at all jealous, nor was she of me. What did I have that she could be jealous of?

I did not have friends. My own fault, I knew. I had not needed them when I had Francis. I did not know how to make them afterwards.

But I had Polly of course. And having Polly, really needed no other. Yet I had never asked her to Wade House. Or rather, in the early days I had asked and for one reason or another it had not been possible. And then later, when my father . . . when the drinking had started – I could not have borne the shame.

So I never did. Nor did we ever discuss it between us. Instead I went to stay once or twice each year at Liddington Hall. We would speak then of Polly's dearest and still secret love, William (less than a year now till she was twenty-one).

Occasionally Henry or Edmund might be there on a short visit. I liked Henry, with his abrupt intense questions. I liked him even though he disturbed me, asking me what I thought about say, compulsory education? Would it be a good thing? (Whoever cared what I *thought* – about anything?) His manner was hasty, the intensity of the questions betokening hurry. For when that question was done, he had another to ask . . . *And* he must be somewhere else: he would need to catch the 9.10 from Leeds if he was to reach Euston in time for . . .

It was difficult to make out what he did in London, unless it was to look for wrongs to right. 'God knows,' he said, 'there are enough of those . . . No, I cannot say exactly what I am doing . . . There are those who would silence me. We are inconvenient, we reformers. Unsettling those who sleep comfortably in their beds, with our tales of those who *have* no beds . . .'

Edmunds looked at no one and nothing else but medicine, and was permanently abstracted. When visiting home, he stared ahead of him at meals, chewing absent-mindedly, stopping only to make some medical observation: entirely irrelevant, totally incomprehensible. Only his father could take up the remark.

I did not worry myself whether he liked me, or resented my presence. As far as he was concerned I was not there at all. I do not think in those years that I knew him, he addressed me directly above half a dozen times. Polly had grown bored with teasing him, or trying to puncture his pride. She announced:

'Once he was a boring person, dearest. Now he has become a *very* boring person.'

And yet she was proud of him, as who would not be? Certainly he was a happier person than Halliwell.

The door of the snug was half-open as I came up to it. I saw the back of Benjamin Mason from the mill, standing just in the doorway. He held a book in his arms.

Papa's voice came from inside:

'What in God's – what the hell do you bring *that* here for? What is it, what are you angering me with now, eh?'

'If you've not your Mill Book, sir – it's the Child Register, sir. Mr Rushworth signed it. And then, the inspector . . . We've not changed sets each month, sir . . . There's children's certificates missing. Age certificates – Mr Spencer thought, if you've them here. Mary Jane Southwell, see here, sir. This page, Mary Jane –'

'I don't want the bloody Child Register here, it's not my bloody business –'

'Begging your pardon, Mr Woodward –'

'What pardon? Pardon, pardon. Why do you come here with it, eh, why *here*?'

'Begging your pardon, on account you've not been at the mill, and Mr –'

'What do you mean, *not at the mill*?'

'This last week, sir. We didn't see you, sir.'

'Frame off, will you? Telling me. Not at the bloody mill, eh? I'll be down there soon enough, and with a stick –'

'It'll need looking at now, will the Register –'

'Why do I employ daft dratted sackless buggers like you, if I've always to be there?'

'You always *was*, Mr James . . . And old Mr Joshua before you. Your dad, sir . . .'

There was the sound of slapping. I turned and ran. Years since I had eavesdropped: this time I had not even realized I was listening. I ran into the parlour. Mama was sitting quietly sewing with Agnes.

'Well,' I said, 'he's shouting at Benjamin. And what's more, I'm not sure he hasn't struck him . . .'

'He's been shut in there all afternoon,' Mama said. 'Doubtless with a bottle for company . . . But if he's not seeing to what ought to be seen to . . . It's not as if poor Halliwell is much help.'

Agnes remarked: 'Halliwell's like a sleepwalker. He told me that himself. He said, "When I walk the mill floor, it's like as if I'm still asleep, but the dream, I never wake up from it. And then," he said, "if that's to be the rest of my life –"'

'Sons are sons,' Mama said. 'Your uncle Sutcliffe – he never wanted the mill either.'

'And now he's out of it,' I said.

But my mother spoke to my father later that evening, reproaching him – something she did not often do, dare to do. 'Benjamin, he's a faithful servant. Forty years or more. I heard you struck him –'

'He told tales, did he?'

'You were seen, James. You were seen.'

I kept out of it, expecting at the same time to find myself in trouble. But the angry fit, the vexation brought on earlier by drink, had worn off. He seemed weak and sleepy, giving great yawns. He could not be bothered with us, and made his way upstairs.

A week later, I went to Halifax with him, alone. We had not been alone together for longer than I could remember. And it happened like this:

He was sober, quite sober. Standing in the hall, seeing out – towards the back entrance of course – a gas fitter over from Sowerby Bridge. Saying, amiably enough:

'Five and ninepence in the weaving rooms, six bob in the spinning. That's my last price. And to be done to satisfaction. Right, then?'

Yes, his mood was good. Or good enough. Although I knew it could change as quickly as the blowy weather outside could turn to rain.

He was dressed for going out. But not to the mill.

I asked him, 'Are you going far?'

'Halifax –'

'Take me to Aunt Martha,' I said.

He didn't look so pleased then. 'I'd have ridden,' he said, 'I'd the grey saddled. Now we've to harness up, take the gig. I don't know –'

But having thought of visiting Aunt Martha, I wanted very much to go. He hesitated a moment:

'Right then. Right. Get your things. We're off.'

Outside it was a blowy September day. In the distance as we drove, the moors were rich in colour, but immediately about us the leaves had begun to fall. We didn't talk much on the way. I didn't trust the half-kindly mood to last long. Then I made the mistake of asking him what he had to do in Halifax.

'Insure the bloody place – that's what. They've sent to say it's up. One on them, or both. Time's up.'

He didn't speak again, except to ask me if I thought Aunt Martha would be at home. 'If she's not, I'll not have you trailing the streets. And I don't want you with me . . .'

'There are other folk,' I said. 'She has friends. There's Mrs Walmsley, three doors up the terrace. She's a cripple.'

'Then not likely to be out gallivanting, eh?'

His physical appearance – as we sat together, I noticed it as if for the first time. How he had changed from the handsome man of my childhood. It was not just my mother who had lost her looks. His was an over-all coarsening. The skin thick and pitted, his fleshy nose red-veined, and the skin under his eyes forming heavy, fleshy bags. His clothes hung badly: a too tight waist, shoulders sagging and loose. I looked at him with sadness. A man with worries, who was more often than not a drunken sot.

'What are you staring at then?'

I feared he felt my gaze. Sadness came over me.

'Just thinking,' I said, 'I was just thinking.'

'You've to pay for that. Everything costs summat these days. I've to find brass for these new gas lights. And –'

We arrived at Wentworth Terrace. It was already midday, after midday. Aunt Martha greeted him.

'Well, brother, what's to do?'

To me, she said, 'Can't you pass a few days, child?'

Papa was eager to be off. I told Aunt Martha, 'He's come in about insurance.'

'Is that Yorkshire Globe then?'

'Aye,' he said, 'and West of England. Maybe. It's spread . . . But I've not come here to stand about –'

'If it's the Globe, up Northgate, we'll go alongside of you. I've a mind to go up to Thorp's, and your lass can . . .'

He was short with us. 'I've other matters to attend to first. I've to meet some folk. As if Christabel's not made me tardy enough as it is . . .'

Alone with Aunt Martha, I told her about Benjamin Mason and the scene in the snug. 'And that's what it's like now,' I said, 'it's come to that.'

She was neither shocked nor surprised. Only resigned. 'When folk go to the bad. She's call to worry, has your mother. A man can drink and work for a while. But this – how long now?'

'Five or six years,' I said.

'It'll end badly,' she said. Resignedly. 'Mark my words, Christabel . . . And now, let's away up to Thorp's.'

My father came for me. He was very drunk and very late. Aunt Martha was disgusted and said, 'I thought you'd forgotten the lass. She's to sleep here.'

I thought there would be a scene and that he would insist on taking me. Indeed he made a movement as if to grab me, but Aunt Martha had taken up the umbrella in the hall (memories of the kirkyard and mischievous children leapfrogging amongst the tombs. Of the bells pealing 'Daughters of the northern fields'). She brandished it. He cursed, not under his breath. She brandished it again. He lurched through the doorway, out back to the gig.

I worried all evening that he would not arrive safely home. Would it not have been better if I had gone with him? Unfolding a huge borrowed nightgown from Aunt Martha, in which I knew I would trip, I came to take a candle for the bedroom.

I worried, how I worried.

'Don't fret,' she said. 'Bad news travels fast. There'll be word if something's up . . . A God-fearing man, our father was. I shouldn't wonder if he's not turning in St Mary's kirkyard now . . .'

Polly wrote, towards the end of November:

'. . . I know you will be discreet and not let anyone see this letter, because it is *very secret*. We have made all our plans, dearest, just two weeks ago. Only seven weeks until I am twenty-one (I have not forgotten *your* birthday on Christmas Eve! and that you will be twenty). Our plan is this: his sister, Georgie, is to invite me over on some excuse . . . I think I am to spend a morning sewing with her, and other ladies. And at once when I arrive a carriage will be waiting . . . And I shall leave at that very moment. I am not an adventurous person, but it *is* all quite an adventure. If it were not so sad . . . William has obtained leave, and I will meet him at York. We shall leave at once for a secret destination . . .

'I shall of course have *no* money – and as you know William has very little. But Papa said quite categorically, several times . . . There is no question. Although Mama is quite the other way. She says only, "I would have been your friend still – if you had done it." Dearest, I *yearn* to confide in her as I do in you. But I dare not. I have on the contrary – I have pretended, you see, to be taken with, yes! Lord Iredale (Maria's cousin, remember? At The Beeches. And the billy dos during the hunting season). He is rather a *silly* person in fact, but very handsome, and very rich, and about twenty-six or seven. Just right they say. (Fortunately he is not at all interested in me!) And just right, I say. And sigh. You would be proud of me, who could not act when we had charades at school. I do not like being a deceitful person . . . I shall never be one again . . .

'I have so wanted to confide in *Henry*. But he is such a *loyal* person and his first loyalty would be to Mama and Papa. So . . . It is all so complicated, dearest. I would wish it all so simple. I love him.

'Please destroy this letter when you have read it.

'P.S. I try not to think how it will be without the family. I do not wish to be a sad person again. But I have been given so much love that I truly believe that forsaking all others, we still *shall* be happy.'

*

Agnes had a suitor. He was Septimus Whitaker, forty-two years old. The new owner of Horsfield Mill and Buckley House. For two months now he had paid suit to my younger sister. Sitting in the Armstrong pew (yes, not only did he own the mill and Buckley House, but he also sat in their pew. It was my mother I think felt most the humiliation), together with his family, he cast glances at her throughout the service. He waited for her, again with his family, outside church. Pressing on her – on all of us – invitations to supper, to a musical evening, to a soirée, it was nothing less than an embarrassment.

Agnes smiled sweetly, and accepted my sympathy and Mama's. At home, she felt free to laugh at him. Perhaps of all of us, it was she found him the most ridiculous.

His family consisted of a large sulky son of fourteen, and two plump little daughters. Aged around ten and twelve, they giggled and nudged each other. There was also his sister, who when he was widowed some five years before, had come to look after his motherless children. In the meantime, letting her own home.

Mrs Green. She was a sea captain's widow, a large, comfortable woman, with a weatherbeaten face. She wanted only to get back to her own home.

I knew this, for she told me so at length one evening when yet again Agnes and I, but not Halliwell, had been persuaded to attend a supper party.

She had sat earlier talking to Mama. Now it was my turn. I saw on the far side of the room, Mr Whitaker bending over Agnes, holding a glass.

'. . . I *long* for the day I return. It is by the sea, my little house. In Whitby. In Grape Lane. I have of course let it only. I would never *sell* our home. But I long for the day . . . As soon as Mr Whitaker has no need of me, back there I'll go . . . My brother,' she said suddenly, 'he's quite enraptured with your sister . . .' She took my hand in hers. 'Can we hope, Miss Woodward? Shall we hear the bells ring, then?'

I said, horrified, 'But she is only sixteen, Agnes is only sixteen –'

'Oh,' she said airily, 'time will cure that. No one is sixteen for more than a year . . .'

She paused a moment, then: 'I must say to you, I've every intention he weds again. I'm past my half century. I want to go home. And if I've to wait while all his bairns grow . . .'

She rearranged her hoops. She was wearing a brown frock with scarlet trimmings:

'Now, would you like to hear how I met and courted the Captain?' And before I had time to nod agreement, or refuse: 'Well you shall, love, you shall . . .'

Her voice went on:

'. . . and I mean, I'd a hard life with the Captain when he was home, and a good life while he was at sea. *Travel* . . . I could make that red hair of yours stand on end with the sights I've seen . . . And seasick! I couldn't keep a thing down. "It's not your ship that'll be a wreck," I told the Captain, "it's your wife . . ."'

Later, Septimus spoke to my father. I understand he asked formally if he might pay court. Papa was angry, but amused at the same time.

'The great gawk,' he said, 'I laughed in his face . . . Fond cheek . . . He's all but a grandad. Happen he is for all we know . . . And the beginning, middle and end of it – it's not love, but brass. I'll not buy him. Just on account of Sutcliffe was a fond bastard, I'll not buy him.'

Immediately after Christmas, I went to stay with Polly. She was quietly happy. A happiness tinged with occasional fear and sadness. ('Mama will be sad.') She told me: 'I am not a secretive person. Just a person with a secret.'

To be able to talk with me was the most wonderful relief, she said. When Henry had come up to them for Christmas, it had been the most tremendous struggle not to confide in him.

I queried this, 'But your own brother, that he would betray you to your parents?'

'Would? I don't know, dearest. It is that he *might*. Once in childhood, you see . . .' And she gave some account of a secret project, something so absurd, was it to gather mushrooms by moonlight? And of how Henry had said, 'I shall have to tell Mama, you know.' And of how she had believed, really believed that he might.

'Then he is a prig, after all that, Polly, a prig.'

'No. No. It was just – he explained – that he was concerned, what might happen to me, and that Mama would worry, and so . . . No, he is not a prig.'

I thought still that he was. And yet obscurely I envied her that. Would Halliwell have cared if I ran off (with whom, pray, with whom?). Would he have cared about Mama's distress?

Polly wished for me just such happiness as hers. 'Soon, soon you too must be in love . . .' (We never spoke of Francis. We never, never by tacit agreement referred again to that dreadful day nearly four years ago now.)

I said, 'I am too ugly to marry. Altogether quite plain. Aunt Flora said so. Years ago. "Christabel is quite without beauty."'

'Oh, such nonsense. And she is a foolish, prissy person, Christabel –'

'I have the evidence when I look in the glass.'

'Dearest, I shall lose patience. They are not . . . You do not have ordinary, everyday looks – "bread and butter" looks as Mama calls them. Yours are different. They are for someone specially your own. Wait and see. Even the glass will tell you you are beautiful, *when you are loved* . . .'

And then as we parted, 'Oh, think of me,' she whispered, 'oh think of me on the eighteenth, fourteen days from now. Think of *us* . . .'

It was a gloomy homecoming. Agnes had gone to Bath, to spend a month with her cousins. (Phil, I knew, admired her. Meg, who had not improved much, would be rather a trial.)

Halliwell was sulky. There had been another row. My father, as I arrived, was calling for hot water and whisky. Mama was not to be seen.

It was Betty who told me: 'She's poorly. Mr Rushworth were here. Two nights she's been poorly. Mr Rushworth says we mun . . .'

I found her, propped up in bed in the green room. Once the room of both my parents. She had this to herself, as she had done for a long while now. Outside the window an icy mist hid the hills, and then the moors up behind the house. A fire roared in the grate. But the room was chill.

Betty had been looking after her.

'What does Mr Rushworth say?'

'That we mun watch her. He bled her, Miss Christabel. And he's to bleed her again. But he'll not blister her while the fever goes down.'

I saw that she breathed with difficulty. I was appalled too by her pallor (but that could have been the bleeding). She began to cough even before she could speak to me, her face contorting. She clutched her hand to her side.

I ran to her.

147

'Mama . . . why didn't you send? I'd have come back, I'd have been back at once.'

When she could get her breath, she said:

'It's not as bad as all that. Rushworth says . . .' and she began to cough again, dry, unproductive, shaking her whole body. I poured her some water from the jug by the bed and she swallowed it greedily, through dried lips. 'I get so thirsty,' she said, between coughs. 'It's maybe the fever . . .'

'But does he say what it is? Does he *say what's wrong*?'

'He says the lungs are inflamed, the pleura really – and that is the reason for the pain. Only that. So *dread* when I breathe. But it is only the swelling of the pleura.'

'And what are we to do? And when will it go? And oh, how dangerous is it? That you didn't *send* for me –'

'But pet, darling . . . listen, don't make me talk just now. I must rest it . . . There goes the cough again. Ah, my God . . . No, Mr Rushworth says it is only time, and rest, and warmth.'

Betty came in then with a kettle, and all the arrangements for steam. She was to have warm water vapour all the time. That would ease the cough and the breathing.

I felt sick, and full of dread, as if I had walked into one of my nightmares. I did not want to leave her side. And indeed for the next two days, I scarcely did so. Only at night could I be persuaded to leave her for a while. And then I asked if I might have a truckle bed made up in the room.

I expected that Mr Rushworth might say we should have a nurse in, so that she was more skilfully taken care of, and never left alone. But the only time I waylaid him and spoke of the illness, he professed himself satisfied with her progress. Mr Rushworth, that slight, now bowed figure from my childhood, who had *always* been there. Who could not be expected to take my questions or my interest seriously.

She never lay down, but was propped up always. Otherwise she would have found it impossible to breathe. She did not seem to me to be making much progress. The first medicine had been calomel and opium, but the evening of my return, Mr Rushworth prescribed tartar emetic.

The dose was very large, even diluted in barley water. She vomited violently, painfully. Again, and again. I asked that she should not have to take another dose. But Mr Rushworth when he called next afternoon insisted. 'If we're to effect a cure – this is the best remedy. An expectorant, after all.'

Betty, distressed by the increasingly unbearable pain in Mama's side, remembered from her childhood: salt baked to a great heat and enclosed in an old sock. She laid this scalding pack on Mama's side.

My father was scarcely to be seen. Occasionally standing in the doorway.

'How is it then? You're doing what Rushworth says, eh? Is she, Christabel? Knows best, the surgeon does. Knows best . . .' He was preoccupied and smelled of drink.

Halliwell grew anxious and could not settle. He rowed again with Papa. 'Is she no better?' he asked me several times an evening. But he did not want to come into the sick room above a few minutes a day.

On the fourth day I made the decision to send for Agnes. I dared to begin to fear the worst. There was no improvement that I could see, and although Mr Rushworth persisted in saying there was no immediate danger, I thought otherwise.

And so did Mama. Putting out a hand, feeling for mine.

'Pet, what time is it?'

'Half four. In the afternoon.'

How it wrung my heart, the difficulty she had now in speaking. Every breath a knife in her side. The words gasped.

'I want,' she said. 'Pet, darling, there is something . . . you should read, must read . . . something . . . for you . . .'

'Don't,' I said. 'Don't speak when it hurts so. *Later.*'

That 'later' might be *too late*, hovered unspoken.

'I tell you . . . where it is, where they . . .'

She spoke then of a small packet, and too, some exercise books in which she had written certain things . . .

'Can you – get them – now, darling – hide them. I don't wish . . . James – it has all been so . . . *Hide them*, pet – please, *please.*'

I fetched everything – the small oilskin packet, and another bundle wrapped in brown paper and sealed with red wax.

'Hide them – hide them – for you, pet . . .'

I left her only to do what she asked, secreting them in my room where no one but a determined thief could find them.

When I returned, she said, 'Thank you, thank you –' then after a moment's pause, with great difficulty, 'I wrote – things you should not read – things there – matters – descriptions. You see, darling . . .'

'Don't worry,' I said. 'It is all right, everything is all right –'

'If something happens – if I – you know that it's no better – I am going to *die* – I cannot, I cannot –'

'You will get better. Mr Rushworth says. Believe him, believe him. It is just to wait for the crisis . . .'

'Die, pet – surely *die* . . . I die – promise to read. Not judge, pet – wrong done to you, very wrong – wrong to him – please forgive, promise forgive . . .'

Her hand lay feebly on the counterpane. And what was the last sickbed at which I had sat? Holding the hand of the dying Mrs Hume. Not an illness of a few days. She had been weeks dying. And I beside her every day. I had not thought, had not dared to think of her for so long now . . .

How glad I was, watching my mother now, that I had not burdened her, had told her nothing, that I had suffered alone. What would she have done with my distress? What would my distress have done to *her*?

I sat up with her all that night. It was very cold. The coldest night I think we had had. It brought back memories of childhood: frozen mole hills, roads like glass. Out at play with Betty, and Josh cracking the iced surface with small determined stamps of his boot. Josh, Josh, Josh. Waiting, waiting, for this death, putting me in mind of *that* one. I thought that soon Mama would see him, and wished that I might too.

During the night the cold had deepened. In spite of the fire, kept burning, and the heavy drapes at the window, the steam vapour, the chill could be felt, biting through my fatigue. Towards dawn I slipped into sleep, head fallen forward. I woke stiff necked and aching. My mother seemed to be dozing. Only the sound of her rasping breath.

Betty came in. I told her what my mother wanted, would need. She told me, 'Master Halliwell's still abed. And the master – he's maybe slept downstairs. There's neither on them left for mill . . .'

The small carriage clock struck seven. I went through and washed quickly, then went downstairs to see the maids. I was running the house now. I did not look to see if Papa was in his snug. Or where.

I was for a few moments in the parlour. The shutters had not yet been opened. I unfastened one pair. It was still dark. Thick frost patterned the glass outside. And then suddenly –

But what was this? What could I see?

A red glow. Perceived mistily, up on the hill. Red glow like a

150

beacon. I could not understand. And then could not believe.

I rubbed frantically, distractedly at the window pane, tried in vain to pull the sash up. I ran to the front door, and flinging it open, looked outside. Then my hand to my mouth, I ran into the kitchen.

'Miss Christabel – what mun we have now, what mun we have now? Is it the missis?'

'Come quickly,' I said, 'come out here. Get your master, get Halliwell, come out here . . . Our mill. It's on fire.'

Mama must not be told. If fetching Papa and Halliwell was my first thought, that was my second, and more important one. She must not be worried. I would sit with her. Whatever was going on in the outside world, I would sit with her. I would be a calm, quiet presence.

And throughout that terrible morning, I would leave her for short intervals – three or four minutes at a time – to learn what was the latest news . . .

I tell you now how it was. It was from Halliwell that I had my account. Some of it he had from others.

Our machines had not been working the day before because of January stocktaking. But this morning the engine had started up at six o'clock as usual. The fire began within the hour, in the carding room immediately above the engine house. Part of this room was fitted up as a devil hole, where wool was devilled before being carded. There must have been a few hundred pounds of wool stored. This room was lighted by a single gas jet from a short pipe fixed to the wall, opposite the end of the machine.

There was a sudden blaze over the gas light. It went directly to the machine, which was revolving very fast. The buckets of water which should have been on the landing, were not. Workers rushed to the yard for water, and returned to find the devil hole full of flames. They raised the alarm. But fierce flames shot now up the staircase. Dense and suffocating smoke blocked the way of those above. The oil on the floors – there was always oil, however regularly it was swept out – fed the flames, shooting them ever higher.

Our fire engine was delayed. The horses were hitched at speed, but so frosty was the weather that the fireplugs stuck fast with ice. Hot water had to be got from a nearby cottage to thaw them. Those who had not escaped by the stairs rushed to the roof.

151

Frantic women and children ran about wildly, calling and shrieking for help.

There was no fire escape. The firemen tied two long ladders, but could not reach the upper storey. Some flung themselves from the roof. One was taken up alive, but mangled. Three others died instantly.

Fire was by now bursting through the roof. Enormous quantities of water were flung at the flames from the high power jets. But the flames seemed impervious.

Halliwell and my father were bringing out documents and files. It was Halliwell telling Papa what to do. My father was stunned, behaving as a man sleepwalking. (He was to be worse afterwards.) Halliwell said with amazement that Papa had obeyed every command. Questioned nothing. Halliwell, marshalling his troops . . .

But the real hero of the day was Kit.

He had by chance been up in the attic, where there was a room in the roof. The man usually in charge there was off sick. The others were one woman and thirteen children. Trapped up there, with the stairs cut off, he assembled them all out on the roof. Then for the next twenty minutes, with the fire drawing nearer, he calmly helped the children down with a knot of twist band, which he had fastened to a carriage frame. Safe landings all – with only friction burns on hands and legs. But when it came to Kit, either the frail rope gave, or (Halliwell was not certain), he lost his nerve, and fell.

'What of him, what of him?' I asked Halliwell. 'What of Kit?' Thinking that I could not bear another death. But he said that Kit had been taken up, and carried to his mother's cottage.

'We'll hear soon enough if he's gone. Mr Rushworth's going up, and there's the surgeon over from Sowerby Bridge . . .'

The alarm had been at seven. By half past seven the roof was falling in. Flames shot out of the windows at greater and greater heights. An hour later, the fire engines moved just in time, as the brickwork of the walls fell in. So great were the flames that the waistcoat of a fireman standing fifty yards away caught fire.

What had caused the fire? Perhaps a gas leak. Or a spark struck from some gritty substance in the wool being prepared . . .

The floors went next . . . By nine, what was left of our mill was wrapped in flames which the engines could not check. Jets played on the smoking ruins until evening.

Six persons were known to be dead, three of them children. Others could die yet from their injuries.

Throughout the rest of that morning, and all afternoon, I remained with Mama. She was conscious only for a few moments, when she spoke to me. I could not make out the words. But although in great discomfort, she appeared peaceful.

In the afternoon she became delirious, her mind wandering. I could make out no words at all. There was a rattling sound now as she fought for breath.

Agnes and Halliwell were with her also. My father, back some time from the fire, walked in and out of the room. I saw that he had been drinking. I did not see how I could stop him. She did not appear to recognize him. When it was apparent, about six o'clock, that she was dead, he wept loudly and clawed at the bedclothes. Then he crashed about the room, calling on God, and then God again.

Betty came to help us calm him. I think he almost certainly drank more that evening.

Night time. Mrs Bennett from the village had laid Mama out. My father lay, as far as I knew, drunk in his bedroom across the way. Agnes, whom I looked in on, lay asleep, exhausted, her face wet with tears. Halliwell, who said he wanted to be alone, had gone to his room.

Alone myself. Dry-eyed, aching, heavy with fatigue. But before I lay down, I took from their hiding place the brown paper parcel, the oilskin packet. I sat on the edge of the bed.

Inside the packet, wrapped in silver tissue, was a lock of auburn hair. And in the brown-paper parcel, three exercise books, in my mother's handwriting.

I shall call them simply, *My Mother's Story*.

PART TWO

My Mother's Story

1

The first time I saw him (you will know soon of whom I speak), it was with my brother, Sutcliffe. Sutcliffe and his friend, James Woodward, brought him to Buckley House, the evening of April 25th, 1841 – two weeks after Easter, and one day after my nineteenth birthday. It was an hour or so after tea and we had just lit the lamps. The evening was damp. It had rained all day. James was first into the room. Sutcliffe and the stranger following behind.

James it was who did the talking. It was always that way. He seemed more at home in our house than its son and heir. He did not appear to have been drinking. Neither did Sutcliffe nor our visitor. They all presented a very sober appearance that evening.

And there we sat: Mama, Grandmother Armstrong (Papa was working late at the mill – nothing new this), dear shy Aunt Eliza, at the piano, and myself.

I had been about to leave my embroidery and join my aunt, because my grandmother had asked that I should sing. Mama had been reading aloud; the book lay open on her lap.

'See what a welcome you ladies give us,' James said, going over and paying his respects to his elders. 'We were Lord Nelson bound . . . when Sutcliffe here had the notion to bring this fellow up to Buckley House for an evening of *refinement* – is that right, eh Sutcliffe? Any road, here he is then, our visitor, Mr Brontë.'

Bows, shaking of hands, introductions:

'Miss Armstrong – Caroline – is Sutcliffe's beautiful sister. But that you can see for yourself . . .'

Explanations:

'Mr Brontë's just been appointed, two weeks since, clerk-in-charge down at the station . . .'

Mama said then that Brontë was an uncommon name and – surely he must be the son of Mr Brontë at Haworth?

When he said Yes, she told him that she was a clergyman's daughter, and knew even now who held most of the livings.

'And we have a servant here, Betty Ramsgill, who comes from your village . . .'

Sutcliffe stood a little behind both the other men, smiling at us all. His face wore its gentle expression. Meanwhile I was looking at our visitor.

He was small in stature – the more so since Sutcliffe was so tall, and James quite a heavy build. Later he was to confide in me that he had not grown since he was fourteen. I judged him now to be of about the same age as James, that is, in his mid-twenties.

But what I noticed first was his hair. It was of a striking colour, some might say red, or auburn; damp where his hat had not covered, it curled. He wore spectacles which hid deep-set eyes, but a few moments into the room, he removed them. When James introduced him to me, he muttered something I could not catch, his voice was so low. After darting a glance at me, he looked away.

So what was this, James was saying to Mama?

'I must warn you, Mr Brontë here, he can talk the hind leg off a donkey – and then sell you the donkey. *And* he's a great Latin and Greek scholar – you'll not understand a word, just as we don't, but there's great learning there. Isn't that true now, eh, Branwell?'

Mama remarked that for a parson's son that was nothing strange. But that she was glad to hear of it all the same. 'Sutcliffe has not been over-fond of his books . . .'

Slight, small, as I said, but not insignificant. Although that evening, at first, somewhat shy. No donkey lost a hind leg. Shy perhaps, in a private house, a strange one, without the tongue-loosening effect of a drink, which to men is so important (although he came, as I soon learned, from a household of mainly women – and was used to shine in company).

But it was not long before he was being gallant. The apparent shyness, it did not last long. Suddenly, he was praising my mother and me extravagantly, flattering us with:

'In the words of Horace, "*O matre pulchra filia pulchrior*", which means, dear lady, "What a beautiful mother, and yet more beautiful daughter!"'

Had I been the kind of girl to be embarrassed . . .

I remember too that my mother in the course of the evening brought out her small gold snuff box – which she did always with a flourish. She offered some to Branwell – she knew that no one else present was a snuff taker – saying:

'Well, Mr Brontë, are you a snuff taker? I fear I'm alone as ever with this elegant habit . . .'

But although he refused, his face lit up. He remarked that his *aunt* was also in the habit of bringing out a little gold box, with just such a flourish and hoping perhaps to shock the company a little. And my mother said archly, 'I didn't shock you then, Mr Brontë? I had hoped I might – there are not many excitements left for an old lady.' (It was not clear whether she meant the snuff taking, or shocking the likes of Branwell. How like Mama . . .)

Grandmother had rung for tea – and something stronger was offered but not accepted. (Were they not after all on their way to where drink flowed?)

Aunt Eliza, who had come over to greet the visitors, was persuaded back to the piano. There I sang (for I was never shy), *Bessy of Dunblain* and *The Wreath*, and then Mr Brontë joined me in *Sweet Home*. By this time, I had learned that his name was Branwell. Patrick Branwell Brontë. (Patrick, or 'Parson's Patrick', in his home village, Branwell to family and friends.) Soon I would call him Branwell as did Sutcliffe and James. And then it was Aunt Eliza with her gently bobbing grey curls leaving the piano, since we had heard that Mr Brontë loved to play. Another duet then, which became a trio when Sutcliffe joined in with his patient bass. *Oh no we never mention her*, we sang, and were encored by James.

And that was the happy picture that greeted my father when – nine o'clock striking in the hall – he strode in, tired and bluff, overweight and careworn, but rubbing his hands and saying:

'Well, you've a merry gathering . . . Nay, I'll not take tea . . . Sutcliffe, who's the visitor? There's a bonny lad and all . . .'

Often this last year, when I have been alone, I have asked myself: how did the happy Caroline Armstrong in the days of which I have just written, become the Caroline Woodward of today? How? And why? My life now – so difficult (although much of that is of my own making). My head, which these days, aches and aches . . .

I have never penned much, although I loved poetry at school. I imagine that those who write verse, and for whom the pen is so important, in their poetry bare their feelings often. *Search* for their feelings . . . I imagine that sometimes they make sense of themselves, to themselves.

Although I have tried (I blush at the memory of it), I cannot write verse. I can only read it. How I love to read it! But because I cannot write it, I thought some days ago that instead I should put on paper an account, a full and truthful one, of all that has happened in my life so far – whilst *standing outside* as much as possible. Since there will be no reader, I must imagine one – who of course knows nothing of us, and must be told all.

To do this will help me perhaps. And so in the end benefit other loved ones. But since my account will have in it *secret matters*, for I mean to write frankly (otherwise what use to do it?), I must keep this exercise book in which I am writing – and any subsequent ones – *most carefully hidden.*

And so to resume . . . Having written of the evening Branwell first came to our house, I shall write now something about us. The Armstrongs.

We were a very united family. A happy family. And that in spite of the sorrows and losses that come the way of everyone. I grew up in sunshine. However dark the world outside, stormy or cold the weather, inside our home the sun shone. It was my mother's doing. It was not my father's, although he would wish it to have been. He would like to have been happy.

My grandfather, Edward Armstrong, was what they called a yeoman clothier, as had been his fathers for generations before. His ancestors had come down from the Borders, moving about the north country generally. At first they were cotton weavers. By the 1780s my grandfather was manufacturing figured material and a sort of bunting called 'Little Joans'. Then around 1805 the family settled at Luddenden Foot where my grandfather, aided by my father Samuel and my Uncle Timothy, established Horsfield Mill. A spinning mill. There was water there to turn the water wheel. Soon they added weaving, manufacturing the heavy watered fabric known as moreen, which was new in the area.

Samuel Armstrong, my father. Hard, ambitious, kindly, unhappy. He was all those things. Uncle Timothy's portrait shows a sharp face: although the younger brother he had been the energetic, pushing one. His early death, unmarried, was a severe blow.

Then, in the year of Waterloo, my parents met at a thanksgiving for victory: my mother, newly arrived in Yorkshire, sang a solo in Haydn's *Nelson Mass*. A year after the bells had pealed for victory, they rang out for Bessie Sutcliffe and Samuel Armstrong.

My mother was an only child: her mother had died in childbirth. I never heard what my clergyman grandfather thought of the match. But whatever the social standing or lack of it in the marriage, it must have been apparent to him that my father would be able to keep her in material comfort.

Indeed. The mill went from strength to strength. The year I was born, they installed power looms, and enlarged the mill. By the time I was seven they had set up one of the new Jacquard looms, and could now weave damasks and figured goods.

It was a time of transition. Handloom weavers and wool-combers were thrown out of work by the coming of the power loom and the combing machines. My grandfather helped those who were fit and able, assisting them to emigrate to Australia, paying others a weekly allowance. But he was a hard man too – as my father was to become – with an eye to profits. By this time also they were employing the Irish, those same ones we have today down by the canal. They had them through Liverpool. The Irish were cheap, and they were hungry.

My brother Halliwell, the firstborn. As I remember Halliwell, he was small and wiry. Eyes wide apart and of different sizes, eagle-nosed, he was a throw back to some earlier Armstrong or Sutcliffe. He was never still. His one desire from an early age was to be down at the mill. Heaven lay in a weaving shed. It became a common sight to see him ride in front of Papa ('Mr Samuel's bairn'). Whenever possible – although at some time he must have done his lessons, for the calculations he could do in his head were a marvel – he would be there beside his father, watching, listening, and above all touching. Cloth between finger and thumb. When he was still a child, my father would turn, and in front of his peers invite Halliwell to 'tell us what you reckon on it, lad . . .'

That was Halliwell – vigorous, impatient, waiting to be grown up, to be a master. My strongest memories are of my father standing, arm about Halliwell ('This is my beloved son, in whom I am well pleased . . .') and Halliwell accepting that arm and that glow of satisfaction and love, but all the while straining to be off, to be about the *real* business of life. Which was work.

Sutcliffe, named as the custom goes, after my mother's family,

161

was born three years later. He was a large, pudgy, clumsy child, with a long mournful face and high pointed ears. Shy and wanting in confidence. Between the two births, there had been a daughter who lived only nine months. After Sutcliffe came two more daughters, one stillborn, another surviving a few weeks. So my arrival, and even more, my survival, were all the more rejoiced in. But I was the last. Some complication after my birth – she never conceived again. Sadly – for I would have loved a sister.

So there we were, a small, but so happy family. Horsfield Mill prospered. It was an exciting time. My father did sufficiently well to build Buckley House (a fine house, but as my mother-in-law tells me so often, nothing beside Joshua Woodward's home, Wade House, already under construction before the century was a decade old . . .)

I was a beautiful child. And a bold one. It was Sutcliffe the shy one. I had all the confidence of Halliwell, but quieter. That I should be beautiful seemed quite natural. My mother spoke of it as a joyous gift. Only Aunt Jessie, long dead now, scolded my mother for praising me. Speaking of the dangers of vanity and the wrong she did in 'puffing me up'. I was surprised and my mother distressed.

And yet it was nothing but a gift. Do black glossy curls, gently cleft chin, dark eyes, fine teeth, bring happiness? Have they brought *me* happiness? I think not. (Then why, oh why do I wish for Christabel something better with her looks. Better than, alas, she has been given . . .)

How happy our days. We had ponies, Sutcliffe and I, hardy galloways (Halliwell too – but he was scarcely ever with us). For all that Sutcliffe was foolish, and weak and clumsy, I did not see him like that (I wish that I did not now). He was my loving companion, my elder, my superior. It was he, as we grew older and might go out riding alone, the one to decide where we should go. Should it be to Hardcastle Crags, Wade Woods – or up on Midgley moor? Once only I remember that Halliwell joined us – and because everything he did, he did to the utmost of his bent, it was a day of ferocious hard riding, of exploration, of challenges. Sutcliffe and I were accustomed to meander, a canter or a gallop was always succeeded, if the weather allowed, by a lolling against a tree trunk, or a lie in the heather, feeling the moorland breeze on our faces, listening, eyes closed, to the soaring trill of a lark. Or, on our ponies again, to watch, heads flung back, the wheeling flight of a curlew.

Loved and cherished by my parents, praised by my mother, petted by my grandfather, grandparents, the proud possessor of two fine brothers, how could my voyage not be calm and prosperous? And would it not always be so?

And other memories of our childhood? What else do I remember? A strange one, this. Was I perhaps four, three? but there was Ada, our grey-haired nurse, fat and forthright and fierce in her love for us, who would allow no one else to criticize or reprimand – scarcely even our parents. We were hers, to be defended to the death. (I think she would have liked the nursery to be under siege so that she might die for us.) She loved us all, but Sutcliffe most of all. 'My bairn, aren't you now?' she would say to him. And he was. More than Halliwell, more than me, however fiercely we were loved.

But all this I realized later, when I was old enough to look back and reflect on how it was. Memories were something else. And one memory is so clear that I know it not to have been false – or a fabrication by someone else, for who would have told me such a thing?

The picture is of Sutcliffe in his crib. Mine is beside him and I am between waking and sleeping. Halliwell has his own truckle bed in the alcove beneath the window, far away from us. The large lamp has been turned down and a small lamp burns at the head of our beds. Sutcliffe is restless, whimpering. Half asleep, I am vaguely aware that he tosses and turns, cannot settle. Then, I do not stir but I open my eyes. Ada is bending over him. She has one hand on his forehead. 'Hush, hush, hush, my little one. Nursie is here, nursie will make it all right.'

Then she is half-sitting on the bed – he has still the bedclothes flung back. I see (my hand is before my face, I see through my fingers), I see that her other hand is beneath his nightshirt. Her hand moves gently, gently, as if stroking, while she murmurs to him. Then her hand moves faster, to and fro, to and fro and then rearing up from beneath the coarse cotton, I see it – a person almost, as if with a life of its own. As if of her own making (and in some way, is it not?). Up, up. And all the while she murmurs her love, her soothing endearments. 'Hush, wisht, hush, my little bairn . . .'

And then I close my eyes, and remember no more. Or do I just fall asleep? Waking a little while later to a still nursery, the lamp burning still, and Sutcliffe, peacefully asleep.

She left us when I was seven, Ada. She had a fit of some sort

– falling to the ground where she lay snoring, causing me, who discovered her, to think her asleep. She recovered, but could no longer manage the work of a nurse and so went to live with a sister in Dewsbury. It was then that Betty came to us, from Haworth. She could have been only eighteen or nineteen then. But already she was able to scare us pleasurably with her tales of elf bolts, and the gytrash, and black dogs who went howling over the moors.

As children, we were not alone, Sutcliffe and I. Amongst those we knew – although too old a playmate for us then, being exactly Halliwell's age – was James Woodward, only son of Joshua Woodward, owner of Appleyard Mill.

Joshua Woodward, scrupulously honest, a zealous Christian, vigorous in business, sober, law-abiding. But the son of a wild father. Daniel Woodward died young, killed by hard living. Appleyard Mill was all Joshua's work.

He did not marry till late. His son James was as strong as Halliwell, as hardheaded, as able, and as much his father's pride and joy – and hope. But how different not only the looks, but also the carefree attitude to life and its problems. (Or so I thought – I was the more deceived, thinking that once.) A tease, with his black curly hair and red cheeks.

He was the younger of only two children. Four brothers and sisters lay in Luddenden churchyard. After James, Kate Woodward buried two more. (I must remember that now when impatient with my mother-in-law. I *have*, but to no avail – her hatred and distrust of me are implacable.) Her first born, Martha, was thirteen years older than me. She seemed always to have been grown up. When I was seven, she married Eli Lumsden, schoolmaster, and went to live in Halifax.

The days passed happily. Sutcliffe and I shared a governess – the more tedious part of our days. I was not a child who read much. That came later. Halliwell never opened a book except to learn his lessons, or unless it concerned work: Baines's *Wool Manufacture* perhaps, or Banks's *Treatise on Mills*. Sutcliffe was the same, and might I think have remained so had he not begun to spend time with James. (Halliwell's friendship with James did not extend to being influenced by him.) For James, like his father, was a member of the Luddenden Reading Society. A society whose members were fined for swearing. Several hundred books of all sorts were housed then as now at the Lord Nelson, in the great panelled room above the bar and snug. He and James might read what they liked – books as sensational as the *Newgate Calendar of Crimes* – without any record of their tastes, for the books were catalogued and borrowings listed by number only.

By the time he was sixteen or so, Sutcliffe had begun to join James and others in the livelier part of the Lord Nelson. Halliwell would be there sometimes, but usually arriving late, leaving early. And always sober.

By then Sutcliffe and I were separated, for at fourteen I went away to school. I saw the family only at Christmas and for six weeks in the summer. My school was in the country outside Huddersfield. For those days, it was an easygoing, kindly seminary and I was very happy. The two sisters who ran it – the house had been left to them by their father – would have liked I think to be mothers of children, and especially daughters. All twenty of us were coddled and fussed over: birthday treats, Easter treats, excursions, primrose expeditions in the gig, fine nourishing meals – and a reluctance to punish us by more than a sorrowful reproach (for most of us quite sufficient).

It was there, at Tolton Hall, that I learned to love poetry. The younger Miss Gardam, Miss Minnie, would read to us as we sewed in the garden in summer, or by the blazing log fire in winter. The poetry of Wordsworth, Coleridge, Mrs Hemans's *Songs of the Affections*, the sonnets of Keats and Shelley – all in a sweet clear voice which never hesitated or stumbled on a word. And afterwards we might, if we wished, borrow any of these works. I acquired the habit then (suggested by Miss Minnie) of copying out, in a tooled leather book bought for the purpose, those lines which most stirred or moved me – the happiest in sentiment or choice of words.

I was happy during those years at school and left almost with reluctance when I was sixteen. It seemed that every girl there was my friend, although I had made no particular one: I did not find there the sister I was missing. Nor sadly, after the first year or two, did I keep up with any of them.

When was it that I first realized James Woodward and I were destined for each other? I use that word 'destined' not in any romantic sense, for it was man-made, this destiny. Those who destined us for each other were Samuel Armstrong and Joshua Woodward.

The purpose was not to unite the two mills (there were after all two male heirs to Horsfield Mills), but rather to celebrate the close ties between the owners. Rivals, yet good friends – would not future blood ties guard against animosity? Healthy rivalry remaining, enmity kept at bay.

Certainly I cannot remember it as a great surprise. Nor as causing me distress. The first joking reference to it came the Christmas I was home again after school. Joshua Woodward, standing with my father before the fire, glasses of punch in their hands, laughing together over some item in the *Halifax Guardian*. Then Joshua saying suddenly:

'Well, Caroline, lass – come home to stop, have you? Young James . . . he'll be glad and all. Only, we've not to send for a Bride cake yet, eh?'

'That's talk she won't understand –' my father began.

But Joshua wouldn't be stopped:

'You'd not fancy that, then, lass – wedding a Woodward?'

Before I could answer, my father clapped Joshua on the back – and took him away to his snug, where he said they might both smoke in peace, away from the ladies.

Mrs Woodward was not there that day – or she would surely have spoken up. She had always disapproved of me. From childhood, at gatherings, there she would be, muttering to her neighbour then looking in my direction with a frown. Sometimes I caught a few words:

'Bold, that little lass . . . Trouble with her more than likely . . . Bessie Armstrong . . . soft with her . . .'

I knew she thought nothing of the way Mama brought us up. She made remarks about Sutcliffe also. Halliwell, she spared. He was the kind of son of whom she approved.

Indeed if it had not been that finally, in most matters, Joshua had the upper hand, she would have scotched the whole idea of marriage, years before. For it appeared that it had been in their minds at least since I was twelve or thirteen. Now that I had returned home a young lady, Joshua felt free to speak out.

He should have waited, my mother said when she heard, displeased with him but not unhappy. She said that she and my father had intended to discuss it with me. But there was to be no hurry, I was not to be rushed. Everyone was happy to wait until I was at least nineteen, and James twenty-five.

'He's too wild, that lad,' Papa told Joshua. That had to be grown out of. But that we were meant for each other, there was no question . . .

I did not mind at all. Nor was I in the slightest rebellious. The idea struck me as both apt and attractive. And when my head filled with romantic thoughts, as sometimes it did whilst reading the poetry of Byron, I was not made unhappy by them. Such fancies were not for every day. They were, and would remain, a private pleasure. And since surely I must one day marry – who better than someone both handsome and kind, who was good company and a friend since childhood? A man sought after as a son-in-law by at least two neighbouring families. James Woodward, a good match. A good catch. And mine – when both he and I should be ready.

He was shy (the only time I ever saw him shy . . .) when we met three days after that Christmas exchange. He came to Buckley House, ostensibly to see Halliwell who had promised to go out with him.

'He'll not be back from the mill,' I said. 'The usual story. But Sutcliffe's about. I saw him go to clean his gun.'

'Well,' he said, looking me up and down, boldly.

I liked that. I preferred it to the embarrassed look he had worn as he first came through the door, asking after Halliwell.

'Well, Lina – it appears we're courting.'

'I've been told so –'

'Have you indeed? And what do you say to it?'

'It might be all right, I might like it.'

'Don't go pop with excitement, will you?'

He looked at me again, that same way, running his eyes up and down me. I blushed. I was not accustomed to blush.

'That's a fetching blush . . . Come here, Lina. No, nearer. Now . . . Nay, a proper kiss . . . That's better. Now for an improper . . . Nay, there's no one about –'

When I sat down again with tingling lips and arms and breasts throbbing, he said with satisfaction:

'Then it's to be Aye? I'm to tell Dad, Aye?'

'It might be and then again – it might not. I'll –'

'Have I to go down on my hands and knees?'

'Anything as daft as that,' I said, 'and I'll –'

But I never told him what I would do – and cannot now remember – for at that moment, Halliwell strode in. Impatient, eager now that *he* was ready, to be off – to begin the evening's entertainment.

The weather was freezing that night. And over the next week it grew colder still. For a while there was snow. Then towards the end of the month it thawed, turning the roads to slush. Another cold spell, and the melted snow froze, rock hard, glassy. On the last day of January, Halliwell rode out as usual to the mill. He left before my father. On the turning, where the road widens, his horse slipped on the ice, and fell, breaking a leg. Halliwell was crushed beneath him.

It was my father who found him. When he came back to the house later that morning, with his overlooker and two other men carrying the body, he was a man in shock. I do not think that afterwards he was ever the same again. Yes, in time, he laughed and joked, but there was a forced quality about his cheery remarks. He spent long hours at the mill. All the enthusiasm and excitement that Halliwell had shown, he now tried to find in himself. And could not.

We were no longer a happy family. Numbed by tragedy, we passed the next six months in limbo.

My mother had lost her first born. She found some consolation in religion, and asked me often to pray with her. Together we read the psalms. 'In thee, O Lord, have I put my trust,' we prayed, 'let me never be put to confusion . . . Be thou my strong hold, whereunto I may alway resort . . .'

Sutcliffe was, if anything, more affected than I. Easy-going, dreamy, he had hoped to amble through his days as a second son, with money in his pocket and not too many responsibilities. A contented second fiddle – to Halliwell. Now everything was altered. He did not know how to deal with this new situation, since he must at the same time mourn. My father was no help, telling him, 'Do this . . . do that,' while being too preoccupied to notice when or if his commands were obeyed. Sutcliffe got no blame, but no praise either. Bewildered, he sat at table, refusing his dinner, growing suddenly thin (he would never be slim again). Sleepwalking. I came upon him one evening – for I could not sleep either – coming out of my father's snug, muttering and shaking his head.

And then he changed. For this we had James to thank. He it was who over the weeks and months persuaded Sutcliffe back to his old ways, mourning or no mourning (boaties down by the canal, the Lord Nelson, the Weaver's Arms – and God knows where else besides), at the same time convincing him of his worth to our father at the mill. Yet he must have been suffering too, for Halliwell had been his particular friend. Now it was Sutcliffe who became his boon companion, and main drinking crony.

Bitter months of winter and then a long cold spring. I saw little of James, and then never alone. Half an hour here and there of an evening when he came round to take Sutcliffe out. Our marriage was never spoken of. It too had gone into limbo. I worked at my embroidery, sewed for the missionaries, visited the sick, and when I could bear it, read poetry. In Wordsworth's *White Doe of Rylstone*, I came upon, with much pain, the lines: 'In deep and awful channel runs, The sympathy of Sire and Sons . . .' My mother and I, grieving together, walked up to visit Halliwell's grave in St Mary's churchyard.

In late June the weather turned very hot. James took to leaving the mill early once or twice a week, inviting me to ride out with him. Gone were the days when Sutcliffe and I had mounted our sturdy galloways. James had now a mettlesome bay and I a small black mare. There was no difficulty about riding alone with him. Although I asked my mother's permission, it seemed scarcely necessary. She saw it as a revival of childhood pursuits (I remember she admonished me: 'No stealing of bird's eggs, Lina dear'). My father, I am not sure. I think to him we were as good as married.

What could they have thought would happen? (Yes, there was stealing of a sort, but not from the nesting birds.) What did they expect? Two young people – and yes, I was beautiful then as well as bold – stretches of empty moorland under a hot blue sky, bees murmuring amongst the pale heather buds that later would blaze into purple. And further down the valley, leafy green woods of ash and hazel with secret hideaways; the broom a rich deep yellow. And by the water's edge too where the ghyll, unpoisoned by the mills, ran clear over the stones, and in the beck below, trout leaping as evening came on.

And so it was that we came together, out of doors, on the heather still warm from the sun, hidden by the high banks of moor about us. Or in the dell, leafy, mossy, only half reached by the sun. What could they have expected else? Myself in black, in mourning still – suddenly, for the moment solaced. How I desired him. *And how he desired me.*

Ah, the pleasure, the abandonment. With him, I cared about nothing but this new discovery. July leading into August, and then September. The heath a stretch of purple now, the bilberries ripe for feasting. Ah, the abandonment – did I not *faint* once with pleasure (coming round to see the concerned face of James). Alone together, away from everyone. The groaning, the moans, my sharp cries. What pleasure, those easy days. What pleasure.

A life had been lost. But what if a new one were made? Lying there, I did not worry. I scarcely knew of such matters. And also, James said that it would not be.

And even if a child were to come from these blissful couplings: 'We're to be wed, aren't we? There'd be nowt to do but make it sooner . . .' He reminded me too: 'There's some can't make bairns. If I was to wed that sort of lass, I'd be in right trouble . . .'

Then he'd say, 'That's chatter enough. Now let's . . .'

And so the afternoon would run on, away, away into the future. Ah, those easy days.

But then came autumn, and little by little the last of the golden days. Wild orchids, growing beneath the bracken that soon would turn to bronze. A chill in the air. Mama saying that sadly the rides with James (never with Sutcliffe – he knew to keep away, and was all his time at the mill seeing how best to wear Halliwell's shoes) must come to an end. And how they had brought 'roses to my cheeks' again.

Short days and long nights of winter. Sutcliffe and James spent time together, but I saw James only at our house or in a family gathering. I wondered if what I had given him, he took now from those girls known as 'easy'. A bit of 'skirt', as he and Sutcliffe would say. 'Skirt' was always there for the asking, for the payment. I knew that. Why should I be missed?

And we were not in love. I had so much affection for him, and even more desire. But for all that I fainted, and panted, and behaved boldly, he was not part of my secret life. He was not in the poems I read. He was not in the dreams I dreamed.

And that was the situation when Branwell Brontë came into our lives, that April evening in 1841.

How often did we see him? In my memory now, perhaps it seems that he came more often than he did. Once or twice a month? His visits were not regular, though the invitation was an open one.

It was not Branwell's first time away. Although his health had not allowed him to go to school (and the trouble? My mother suspected some weakness of the nerves, perhaps even the dread epilepsy) and he had been taught at home by his father – Mr Brontë being a Cambridge man. (I wondered, the son being so brilliant, that such an education should not have been sought for him also? A question I never asked . . .)

I did not at first discover what he had been doing in the years since leaving boyhood. Later I heard that he had been for a time a portrait painter in Bradford, but that custom had not been good enough. Then he was a tutur in an uncongenial family in the Lake District. And between last September and now he had been at Sowerby Bridge as assistant clerk on the Leeds-Manchester Railway. Now, aged twenty-three, he was clerk-in-charge, or stationmaster, here in Luddenden Foot.

'It *looks* like getting on, I agree,' my mother said, 'except . . .' And she voiced her doubts about the suitability of such work for someone so – what? It was not a fit occupation, she said, for a *scholar*.

Sutcliffe expressed an opinion, something he did not often do, arguing with her at dinner time:

'What could be more exciting,' he said, his mouth full, 'than to be in at the beginnings of something? Not mills and engines and the new machinery . . . they're yesterday's excitement. But the railways! What shan't we see with them in ten years' time?'

I did not really agree. I saw that it was indeed possible that by diligent reliable work, by pushing on, a person might end up in charge of perhaps a station such as Leeds. And what then? I did not imagine that those who administered the railways, who directed policy, came up from such beginnings. Nor could I see anything about the person I had met to show him fitted for this life – prospects or no prospects.

But when I remarked that it did not seem a place for scholars, James said:

'Aye, but there's more to Branwell than booklearning. Sutcliffe here will tell you, eh, Sutcliffe? And so will the Thompson lads, and Titterington too . . .'

Branwell had also friends who were nothing to do with us, whom we never met and of whom he never spoke. Only later and through others did I learn of them: it was as if he kept us and them, possibly his family too, all quite apart. Did he perhaps bring out for each of us a different Branwell? It could be so. I must admit the possibility, since what I saw of him, *as much as I was shown*, was not in the end enough. Even in the light of all that happened, it was not enough. I could wish to have known all those other Branwells . . . (And of what use would that have been, since I could not in the end save, or even help, the one that I did know?)

It is difficult now to write without suggesting an exaggerated significance for those visits of his, whose incidence I cannot even be sure of counting. They did not feel important *at the time*. Life was about mourning Halliwell and about healing slowly. About being James's betrothed. About helping my mother, and about sewing, playing the piano, reading to and visiting the sick.

I soon learned that Branwell had literary aspirations, even some achievements. He had written verse, and wrote it still. But I knew that a literary career, except for the few, must be backed by money earned in some more reliable manner.

There was not money at home. His eldest sister, Charlotte, he told us, was presently a governess near Bradford – and most unhappy with it. And his youngest was one at Thorp Green, with a clergyman and his family by the name of Robinson. She was not happy either. His sister Emily remained at home, although she had been for a little while a teacher.

Our station here at Luddenden Foot, what sort of a place was that to work in? It has since improved – at least as to the building of a house for the stationmaster and his porter to work from. But it was and is a gloomy place, dark even in sunlight. Damp, and hidden away. The black rock out of which they had blasted it so recently, I should have found sinister as my daily background, used as I was to the lightness in our own home, raised up on the hill, looking over towards the railway and the canal and river. Neither Sutcliffe nor James would have tolerated it for a day. We were a branch line unlike the busy junction at Sowerby Bridge, our traffic mostly goods. Nor were the intervals between trains really sufficient for Branwell to absent himself. Although later, God knows, he did. Oh, how he absented himself . . .

Certainly up the hill must have looked more attractive. For there of course was the Lord Nelson. And upstairs, the Luddenden Reading Society's room. Why not spend time there? I think he began to do so quite soon, certainly within a little while of meeting James and Sutcliffe. There were *The Newgate Calendar*, *Percy's Anecdotes*, all fifteen volumes, Smollett's novels . . .

And downstairs was the drinking.

Yes, he wrote verse. And no, he would not speak of it. But in a general way he hinted that was where he would in the end make his mark. Then one evening, I spoke of what I loved in poetry, in perhaps a foolish way, with too much enthusiasm and eagerness.

I said something such as: 'I dote on Lord Byron and Shelley and much of Mr Wordsworth, and then Coleridge – *The Ancient*

Mariner, that thrills me so, and *Christabel* – ah, what a haunting tale . . .'

Yes, I prattled on in that manner. But I meant nothing. It was only that I did not wish to be thought ignorant and uncultured. (After all, I have heard it is possible to spend on a young woman's schooling as much as would pay for two or three years at Oxford, and yet for her to emerge scarcely able to pen a coherent line, let alone to love and cherish our poets . . .)

He did not respond as I might have wished. But rather in that way he had of deflecting the conversation and yet keeping up a flow of words. And then the tone changed to something light-hearted. A joke, a tease, I cannot remember. Or was it an anecdote from his new working life – a tale told in broadest West Riding, his forefinger and thumb over his nose the better to render the particular voice? And it would be that voice to the life, so that my mother sitting near gave one of her hearty happy laughs – and then out with the snuff box.

That was how he received my – not timid, but too bold perhaps – comments on poetry. I thought them lost, those remarks. But it was to be quite otherwise.

He was not all of our lives. We were not all of his. As spring turned to early summer, he was off and away on Sunday outings with Halifax friends. To places known to me from my childhood: Cragg Vale, Luddenden Dean, Heptonstall, Hardcastle Crags.

And what was I doing? Visiting, sewing for the missionary basket . . . But then the days grew longer, and sometimes fine, and I began to think of last summer and how it had been. James remarked on it in the presence of my mother.

'Well, Aunt Bessie' (he had for many years called her that), 'here come the sunny days again. If this bold beauty here, if she's a mind to have Minnie saddled up, we could ride up on Warley Moor.' And turning to me,

'How'd that be, eh, Lina? Some healthy exercise in the company of your betrothed . . .'

And I blushed, how not? at his boldness, at the double meaning for me alone. Healthy exercise indeed, I thought, as I flushed and demurred and was thought *shy*. Yes, shy. Mama had to persuade me to go.

I did not blush again, except with delight, those first outings.

'*Miss* me, did you, eh, Lina?'

'I might have done . . .'

'I reckon you did. *Tell* how you did!'

173

'You think well of yourself, James Woodward, if you fancy I've nothing to do all winter long but –'

'That's a fib a yard long. If I didn't see you moping and sighing these dark evenings, thinking what a fine upstanding lover you had.'

'May God forgive you –'

'What for, Lina, eh? If it's for this, there's no need – since we're to be wed. Just hush your fibs and say the truth, that it's the fine upstanding bit you missed? Bonny, isn't he? Tell how you missed it, Lina –'

'I missed it . . .'

'Right . . . And now I'll show you *what* you've been missing . . . Lina . . . Another year and we'll be wed. No looking to the sky then, to see if that dratted rain's coming on. A great soft bed . . . I've said we're to have that green room that's facing back onto the fells. Eh, Lina? I've said we don't want facing toward the kirkyard . . .'

And once more I was held tight in his arms, and he held tight in me. The well remembered thrust for which I had grown to long, for which of late I had *ached*. I did not faint again – I was never to faint again – but how nearly I did. How nearly. Not so foolish as to think that only with James could it happen, but rather, since we were to be wed, that it was with him it would happen. Now and for ever and ever, amen. I was a fortunate girl. (I even thought boldly that he was a fortunate man. How fractious I became on wet days when an appointment to ride out could not be kept, and I was faced instead, for my exercise, with an afternoon's sewing . . .)

But also, I would think: how has it been for you, James, through those long winter months? A question I could not ask – because I guessed the answer. It was dear foolish Sutcliffe who in occasional fits of bragging would speak of 'skirts', and of where a lad might find one. Fond Sutcliffe, my dear brother – half the man of James and nothing beside poor dead Halliwell – I wondered often what would become of this companion of my childhood. Yes, he liked to boast to me sometimes, remarks he would no sooner make than deny, or embarrassedly fail to explain. But Mama had told me a little something about 'loose women', and 'women who granted their favours *for gain*'. 'Easy women and girls.' Any description, every description, it did not matter. It was these 'skirts' surely that had made the winter no hardship for James. And I could not ask. There would never come a time

174

when I could ask. *He* had not spoken of a difficult winter . . .

And so it was for us that last summer of our courtship. And I had no proof that even in summer I was sufficient for him. What mischief, if Sutcliffe's boasts were anything to go by, might James still be up to?

I knew that often he and Sutcliffe spent their evenings (and this might succeed an afternoon passed with me) on the razzle. Sutcliffe, with his large frame, seemed able to consume enormous amounts of liquor. James, though more compactly built, was also a big drinker. The same for the others. Hard heads all – except perhaps their new companion. For now they had Branwell with them. They drank of course at the Lord Nelson, but they were also down in Luddenden Foot at the Weaver's Arms and the Red Lion, where they would drink with the boatees who worked on the barges by the canal.

And the Irish. Those Liverpool Irish employed by Papa, whose living conditions were as primitive surely as anything they might have left behind them in Ireland (although at least they would not be evicted, to shiver under a fuchsia hedge in deep winter). Their homes could barely be called shacks. A roof of rusty tin, leaking at the first hint of rain. Simple dirt floors which they did not attempt to keep clean. No furniture to speak of, and as beds perhaps some bundles of canvas lifted from the nearby barges. When it was dry they lit fires outside. The men drank, how they drank, down at the Weaver's Arms, quenching their thirst from a day at my father's mill.

They were bought cheap, I knew they were bought cheap. Joshua Woodward would not employ them. Whether it was because he saw it as exploitation or because he did not want Irish workers in Appleyard Mill, I do not know. (James today does not employ any. Sutcliffe does still. And how little their lot has improved . . .)

It was there, in the shacks, or more likely the Weaver's Arms, that James's crowd spent so many evenings that summer. It was another world. I saw evidence of it only when Sutcliffe could not be roused next morning. Although I had not to go to the mill, I was always up early: it was for me to go in to him, to take his sponge, and then to trickle cold water down his miserable face. And there I would stay till he tumbled out, often still in shirt and undertrousers. He would stagger down for a pot of ale to quench his dry mouth, to clear his head. I have no doubt James did the same.

They were fascinated I think by the Irish. How different a life from that of Buckley or Wade House – or Haworth Parsonage. They described a visit to me, Sutcliffe saying that at times during the evening, Branwell might as well have been one of the Irish. The brogue, the manner – they had taken to him astonishingly.

James remarked then, 'Well, he *is* Irish, after all. And pisky Cornish. There's not a drop of honest Yorkshire blood in him. It's no wonder the lad can't talk sense.'

'Well,' I said, 'and why should he?'

James ignored me:

'And his temper now . . . we saw some of that a while back. It's your true Irish, is his temper. A burst of gunpowder, and – gone. No grudges borne, no long memories, eh? Not like us. *We* don't forget an injury easily. Nor forget . . .'

The Irish – and their religion. Their Romish religion. How weird, how colourful, how *wrong*. But how attractive, when contrasted with Calvinism: the punishment, the eternal damnation, predestined, irrevocable, inescapable for so many. The impossibility of true intercession. The Calvinism, my father's, that hovered about my childhood. (My mother had no time for all this. And I – I was very much her daughter. How else could I have spent those afternoons in the heather so happily, and known that God would forgive?) Dear, gentle Aunt Eliza who lived in secret dread that she was not, in spite of Christ's death on the cross, one of God's Elect.

One July evening we had, all of us, a religious discussion. It was the evening I sang *When order in this land commenced*, and Branwell proposed the duet *Poor Mary Anne* – encored by all present. His mood was odd but lively; he was in good form as a mimic.

How did we get on to the subject of Popery? Branwell grew over-excited and critical – it seemed to me that he said one thing and meant another. For he confessed that evening that his grandmother had been a Roman Catholic, who had turned away to marry their grandfather. He spoke as if disowning her, and yet could not keep off the subject, quoting his father on the dangers of the present-day revival of Romanism ('"that ghastly Incubus of the human mind . . . which formerly held but a slippery footing in this island . . ."').

James, holding forth, spoke of our Irish workers:

'It's all moralizing and proselytizing, is the Romish religion.

The results are terrible . . . Your Irish, Sutcliffe – they're living proof that Popery *doesn't work* . . .'

Branwell could amuse us. He would caricature not only Walton, his porter (a plodding creature, but sadly put upon I felt – left long hours minding the station whilst its master sat in the snug at the Lord Nelson or upstairs in the Reading Room), but also us too. Once while I sang some mournful song to Aunt Eliza's accompaniment, I saw that he sketched on the edge of the *Leeds Mercury*. James, looking over his shoulder, laughed heartily. When I finished and came over to join them, there I was: exaggerated curls, cleft chin almost cloven and mouth open in high-pitched song . . . Sadly we did not keep the sketch. The talk turned, the newspaper was laid aside. When later I thought to rescue it, it had gone.

They must have been delighted with him also up in Luddenden village. His ready way with a pen, his air of learning, his fast and sure hand, and different styles of handwriting (even that 'circus' trick, as my unimpressed father called it, of writing with two hands at once) led to his being in demand as village letter writer.

October, and we went, six of us, including Mama and Branwell and myself, to Halifax, where the Choral Society were to perform Haydn's *Creation*. The Assembly Rooms they used were next to the Talbot Inn so that I wondered if Branwell would rather be drinking next door? Instead, I had that evening a glimpse of his love of music. And the ferment of excitement it could stir in him. The happiness . . .

The Creation. That sombre opening, depicting chaos – yet full of anticipation. The Chorus singing: '*And God said, "Let there be Light!"*' And then a burst of sound, *fortissimo* – on '*Light!*' Elation, joy . . . From that moment, I saw Branwell taken over: drawn into the music, intoxicated.

After the performance, he seemed possessed still. Excitedly, he spoke of the thought behind the work . . .

In the entrance before we left, he greeted some friends. I was standing a little behind him with Mama. He brought out a notebook (it was one I had seen him with often).

'The Motet Society, 9 Denmark Street, Soho, London,' one of the men dictated. Branwell jotted the address down in pencil.

He was still abstracted, as if taken over by the music. I had the sudden wish for him that he might always be so happy as now. That he might be drunk only with *sound*. (Forget the Talbot Inn next door and his drinking debts. I knew of those debts.)

The dark evenings had begun. I remember on two occasions his reading to us by oil-lamp from *Fraser's Magazine*. A cosy enough domestic scene – if we were not to count Sutcliffe and James with cards in another corner of the room, eager I think to begin the evening's carousing.

Branwell, reading to Mama, Aunt Eliza and me. Did the domesticity appeal? Was it a home, indeed *home*, he missed? He spoke of the Parsonage quite freely, as I remember, and of his sisters with affection and pride. It irked him that they should have to work as they did. I think he would have liked to be able to lavish gifts on them and ensure comforts, even luxuries, so that they need never lift a finger again. From odd remarks he made, it was apparent he thought himself to be a railway clerk only *by accident* and *in passing*. He was one day to be great. One day the world would acclaim him. So why did I have the impression that here was someone for whom *it was already over*? For whom somehow, the best had already been . . .

He did not always speak well of his sisters. On one occasion . . . But perhaps it was a question of his moods – for they were not always agreeable ones. He could surprise by his callousness.

We were all in the parlour. Standing by the fire, Branwell told us how important it was that women should confine themselves to their proper sphere. Indeed they should not and must not even *attempt* higher things.

James was inclined to agree. My mother smiled as if to herself, and then raised a point or two. I sat quiet.

Branwell spoke as brilliantly as ever, capping point after point with wonderful turns of phrase that floated above my head – or ran under the sofa with my ball of wool. But however animated, however inspired, the beginning, middle and end of his whole discourse was that women were not *able*. It was not only 'should not' but also '*could not*'.

Stung, I said, 'How can you, Branwell? Your sisters –' And I thought of what I had heard of them, what he had *told me himself*. 'Why, your sisters know more than that!'

And then he said, looking to James for a laugh (and obtaining it, yes obtaining it), 'Oh, they are so ugly – it is no matter *what* they do!'

That he should speak like that of his own sisters. I remonstrated with him. We exchanged sharp words. I cannot recall what I said, only that I knew I was right to stand up for my sex. Since he was in company he did not perhaps reply as sharply as he would have wished, yet the anger was there. That quick hot flare-up – just as James and Sutcliffe had said.

It happened towards the end of a visit. There was not time left for a smoothing.

The next day an envelope was delivered for me. Inside, in a small upright hand, was a poem.

That poem – how did the words go? I cannot remember one line. It is of no use now that I would wish to have it with others in my book – not only copied, but the original kept safe. *I do not have it.* I must have looked one hundred times, in drawers, cupboards, chests, inside the leaves of books, in the cupboards of others. High and low I have searched. His peace offering is gone.

I had other poems. Copies only, of originals not meant for me. He told me so. Handing me the pages, shyly, but at the same time with a flourish as one bestowing a gift. I was not deceived by the temporary humility. He said to me that time:

'See now. *Ut pictura poesis*, which means, "the making of a poem is like that of a painting."'

'*Caroline, Caroline.*' I saw my name, high up, apostrophized.

'No,' he told me, 'they are not you, Caroline. But then – nor are they any other Caroline . . .' Leaving me to ponder on what could be meant. As I do still. As I do still.

Branwell. At first I glimpsed a brilliant child – a darling, a privileged one, the cock of the roost. Only son amongst girls. It is a man's world, after all, is it not?

Yet what if a man cannot bear the burden? Nature in handing out moral strength does not distinguish between the sexes. So weak, so unstable – his should have been the lot of those women who spend their lives waited upon, their every whim satisfied by some adoring man. Nothing asked of them that they cannot give.

As the months went by, I saw a tormented man beneath the dandified clothes, the fine talk. I knew he was not wild in the same way as his companions: theirs were the wild oats of which my mother spoke, which *must* be scattered if married days are to be undisturbed. In Branwell I sensed only despair. A man driven by demons may not *look* very different from one hell-bent upon pleasure – any pleasure which kills thought, or brings perhaps the solace of an admiring audience. Flattery, so potent a substitute for love, and so easily mistaken for it, when love, especially of self, is in short supply. Drink, yes. And drugs?

I knew a little about drink. Nothing about drugs. I knew what laudanum was, and that for toothache or neuralgia and some other ills it was little less than a miracle. But that it might be abused, might be a crutch which some could not then relinquish, I cannot say I suspected. Yes, I had heard of *The Confessions of an Opium Eater*, but had not read it. I had not thought about the title's meaning . . .

That Branwell took opium, I realized later. But the yellowish tinge of his skin and his puffy face that winter, they were the result of whisky. Did he perhaps try to outdrink Sutcliffe and James?

'Well, Branwell,' I said, one November evening, 'since you are such a fine portrait painter –'

He had been boasting that day, flinging out hints about his great gifts, painting, writing, music, if he cared (always that proviso, *if he cared*). As if the glitter of so many talents dazzled him.

'Well, Branwell,' I said, 'if you are such a fine painter, perhaps you would care to do a likeness of me?'

I thought it would be a good idea. A wedding gift for James perhaps. Did I not make it clear it was a commission, and that we would pay handsomely? At any rate, his answer was Yes, and Yes again, and the impression conveyed that it was what he wanted most to do in the world – except that he had with him no materials, easel or canvas.

I suggested he should fetch them when next he visited home. But he said the difficulty was that in Turn Lea cottages where he lodged there was no space for them. So I told him we would look after them for him here.

But although he went home for one more visit after that conversation, the materials never came. And I was never painted. His promise, made with such a flourish, was not kept.

November. December. Now there was talk of the wedding, planned for May. We would live at Wade House. I had not been asked if that suited me. I thought, surely there was money enough (and I was bringing more in . . .) to build a separate house? But no, that was how it would be. Kate Woodward, *Mrs Joshua Woodward*, had spoken. (I could not believe that, disliking me as she did, she wanted me permanently in her home. And yet it seemed she did . . .)

I knew that substantial sums of money would pass from my family to the Woodwards. Were we buying the Woodward name – or what? Were the Armstrongs not good enough? Hands on the deal were finally shaken, a date fixed and lawyers sent for. After Christmas I was to visit the dressmaker in Halifax. There was so much to be done. Mama said we could not start preparations too early. She longed for this union of the two families.

But Christmas must come first. Winter could only have made gloomier the wooden shack that passed for stationmaster's house. Damp in a way that no fires could dry out or really heat. I am surprised, since I rode out often enough on errands of mercy, that I did not make a visit of cheer.

I had in fact been to the station once, on a dark November day, but found only Walton, the porter. Branwell, he assured me, had just slipped out, but when I suggested waiting, he discouraged me with:

'Then you mun wait all day. Happen all night too . . .'

For one reason or another, we did not see Branwell at all between early December and January. Certainly I never thought he might not have returned to Haworth for Christmas – the more so as I knew he had not been home since July. (And this was a man who hinted he could scarcely bear the separation from those he loved. Yet Mercy Ramsgill holds her sister Betty so dear that never a month goes by but she visits.)

Never imagining he might be there, and alone, we did nothing. Did not even enquire. We enjoyed our usual Christmas. James showed me off with pride. ('Soon to be Mrs James Woodward, eh?') I was very dear to him, and he to me.

Almost certainly Branwell came less often to the house after Christmas. And I noticed his moods more when he did. He told me that Charlotte and Emily were to go to Brussels for a course of studies that would fit them the better for starting up a school of their own. (I found it hard to imagine the daughters of the gentry scurrying to Haworth to be educated, but let that be . . .) He would go home at the end of January to say goodbye.

Mr Brontë was to leave to accompany them. I asked Branwell: 'Would *you* not have wished to accompany them? A gallant

181

and elegant knight companion to ward off foreign devils?'

It was one of those questions he affected not to hear. Beginning at once some long and fanciful tale involving happenings to James, Sutcliffe and him two nights since:

'And the canal quite frozen over, or so we thought . . .'

So I surmised that he wished *very much* to have gone. (Yes, to cross the sea, only gazed at from Scarborough cliffs. To walk the streets of a foreign town, smell the smells, drink the wine, sample a world which, while it might not come up to one of the imagination, at least would be different – oh, how different from the wooden cabin and the five trains up, four trains down, on the branch line station of Luddenden Foot on the Leeds to Manchester line . . .)

It was in the stark cold of February that I was measured for my wedding dress. I had much sewing to do too. The trousseau that had been accumulating slowly over the past few years was seen suddenly not to be enough. Some work was sent out, but that I should do much of it myself was seen as a sovereign remedy for pre-wedding nerves, which were expected of me whether I had them or not.

So perhaps I did not notice. The months passed. I think we spoke to Branwell of the wedding. Certainly he was to receive an invitation. And meanwhile James and Sutcliffe changed their ways not at all. The cold weather kept them drinking in the warm snug of the Lord Nelson. (Was it warm too upstairs in the Reading Room?) James was not expected to change. Wild oats must be sown until the last moment. They both joked about 'sober *chaste* wedded lads . . .'

I was to have a cousin on my father's side as bridesmaid: Cousin Millie Wainwright from Colne. She was herself to marry in June, a mill owner, Willie Oldroyd. I did not want her, having only met her a handful of times, and also with her flaming red hair and comparatively great height of five foot six, she would dwarf me. I was to have also a schoolfriend, Martha Barraclough – for we had arranged that whoever married first would dance attendance at the other's wedding.

These and other arrangements fussed me. Nothing concerned James, of course. My mother, with whom I had always had a delightful and easy relationship, began to be out of patience with me. And at all times, when least expected, there would be my future mother-in-law, with her carping and criticizing and air of overall disapproval. Her half-resigned anger at this, to her, unwanted union.

'I hope, Caroline, your mother has impressed on you your *duties* as a wife – and how you've to behave at Wade House. Wade House, it's not yours, Caroline. And until the day it is, I'll counsel you to walk carefully . . .'

A bitter March followed February. Wedding plans seemed to be turning sour in petty squabbles over detail. I did not have too much time to think, nor did I even see much, of Branwell. By day the trains, with their shrill whistles and clouds of white steam, rattled along the line high above the river and canal. Familiar sight, familiar sound.

Branwell. The world wagged with him, I suspected, not too well. On the one visit that I remember, early that March, I thought him more sickly than at any time since we had known him.

And then, at the end of the month, came disaster.

Papa said, over the dinner table:

'I had it from old Stockwell – the accountants have been in at the station. And none too happy, it appears. The takings and the ticket sales, they're somewhat out of kilter. Young Brontë's for it, I fear . . . It's no king's ransom, maybe a week's wages, but they can't turn a blind eye . . . It'll be the porter, of course. But then it's up to the lad to watch for that sort of thing . . . Too much time spent with you, Sutcliffe, eh? Not sitting where he should be . . .'

He was dismissed at the end of March. Sutcliffe and James and a number of other drinking companions spoke of getting up a memorial, petitioning his reinstatement. How he felt about that, we did not know. For we had not seen him at the house. '

James said he had not yet gone home. 'He's his family to face, and that'll not be easy. Although I reckon there's none there but an aunt – and his dad.'

But if it had been me, would I have wanted to crawl home? Disgrace and failure once, twice, yes, but thrice? (And had there not perhaps been other failures not known to us? What was Mercy's tale of an expedition to London and an art school, and robbed on the coach before ever arriving? Or so the story went . . .)

Yes, James had seen Branwell. He was in a sorry state, he said. Most of the time in his lodgings. Those who knew said that probably he lay abed most of the day.

*

On a warm sunny afternoon, a few days later, I rode out to Turn Lea cottages.

We had heard nothing from Branwell. 'He will certainly call before he leaves,' Mama said.

Sutcliffe said, 'We've left him to get on with it. If he wants his friends, he'll come after them . . .'

This did not seem to me good enough. I did not like the reports and wished to see for myself. Once there, I was not sure what I would say or do. What help could I offer? I could not resecure for him the wretched post, or shield him from the shame of his dismissal.

But friendship. I could offer friendship. And an ear to listen to his troubles (but when in the past had he ever confided in me? Or in any of his Luddenden friends? What grandiose ideas I had of myself . . .).

As I rode Minnie up towards Turn Lea Cottages, the sun came out, suddenly dazzling. From the dock leaves growing by the roadside, a small copper butterfly flitted on to the drystone wall.

I knocked at the outer door. No answer. I was trying the handle, when a man came out from the next-door cottage:

'Mrs Fairley – she's away to Sowerby Bridge. There's only the gentleman –'

'But her lodger. She has a lodger?'

'That one, aye. He'll be there. Nivver saw him come out sin Friday. Mrs Fairley . . . She's had the devil of a time with that one . . .'

But I had tried the handle and found the door unlocked. I thanked the neighbour.

Up the small narrow stairs. The door of the first room was partly open. Neat and empty, with its smooth white counterpane. Mrs Fairley's surely. The next room was shut. I knocked. No answer. I opened the door very slowly.

Yes, he was there. Lying in the bed, head turned away from me. The bedcovers, rumpled, lay in a heap near the foot of the bed. A sheet half-covered his nightshirt. He appeared to be asleep.

I approached the bed. 'Branwell. Here is Caroline Armstrong. I am come to visit you.'

He did not stir. The curtains were drawn against the sunshine outside and the room smelled frowsty. Enough light escaped through for me to see the disorder. Dusty boots discarded in the middle of the floor. A pair of trousers and two shirts piled beneath the window. A necktie, cravat and hat on the cotton rag mat beside the bed. An open cupboard showed similar disorder inside. Under the table which served as a desk lay three empty porter bottles. Several books with the distinctive binding of the Luddenden Reading Society were stacked on the table itself. Beside them some uneaten bread and cheese, the bread curling and hard.

'Branwell.' I tried again. 'Branwell. A friend is here to see you. Do you wake? Can you wake? It is *Caroline*.'

I thought then he stirred. I had walked round the other side of the bed, so that I could see his face, if he were to show it.

'Branwell –'

He lifted his head. The light though poor was quite good enough for me to be recognized. But he gave no indication of knowing who spoke to him. He seemed to me perhaps stupefied. I approached nearer to smell if it was drink the cause. But I had not smelled it in the room and now, as I came close to him, there was no trace of it on his breath. I touched his forehead. It felt clammy.

It was not alcohol coming off him, but despair. It was that I smelled. Despair, hopelessness, in waves. It might drown him.

'I have come to help you,' I said. 'Can you hear me? Do you hear me when I speak? I am here because of your disgrace. To say that it does not matter to us at all. Mama and I – if we can help? If you would wish to visit . . . Or if there is something we can do . . . We think nothing of it, that you should be dismissed. You are as fine and as talented a person, and amusing – oh how you amused us – as amusing as ever, before any of this happened. You have been careless only. It is not the end of the world . . .'

And so I chattered on. A nonsense. Say anything. Show friendship. Try to pierce the drugged, depressive stupor.

'It is not the end of the world, you know . . .'

No, it was not the end of the world, but it might well seem so. Could even become so, if he did not some time soon take at least one step forward.

I sat at the foot of the bed. 'Look at me,' I said. 'Please look at me.'

I took his hand, which lay hanging over the bed edge. He did not respond, but then neither did he resist.

We sat a while. I spoke to him a little more. Outside, beneath the window, in the eaves some birds must have been nesting. I heard the twittering and the rustling. There was no other sound.

Then he began to whimper. To move about restlessly. His hand slipped from mine. He muttered words I could scarcely hear, could not make out.

'Oh, what is it?' I cried. 'Let me help! Speak to me, and *let me help* . . .'

Childhood. Sutcliffe in his crib. Ada, who loved him, and who gentled him. Back in the nursery again, and a calmly sleeping Sutcliffe . . .

I did it only to console. I remember that now. *Only to console.* And ah, but what was this? The same, was it not? The same head rearing . . . I who was so bold and knew, about James, everything. Everything.

So what happened then? How much do I remember? All of course. I remember it all. (He, afterwards, remembered nothing.)

And then I put my arms right about him – overwhelmed by a sudden tenderness (even perhaps, my *own* longing). So bold. So used to be satisfied. So used to make James happy.

What had started out as . . . was to end quite differently. While remembering everything, I shall tell you little more. It was all my work, I, I, I . . . my pity, my tenderness, my desire to console. My desire . . .

It was not so difficult to bring to a conclusion what I had begun. I was without shame. Or I was full of compassion, pity, overflowing with pity, overcome by pity. Does it matter now, which?

I was not gentling him now . . . He was inside me. Mouth on mouth, hands in hair – I wished to be embraced and was not. I embraced. This was not James's loving. No laughter here. The scent of his skin was bitter. I smelled excitement, mine. I cried out . . . I cried out as I had not cried out since summer ended. Taken by surprise. And then his shudder. Shuddering, and then still, quite still.

As he lay back on the bed, the sheet rucked beneath him. Then he turned on his face, with a great sigh. Of peace? Who knows? But he slept. How soon he slept. And now the sleep was peaceful, his breathing that of one at peace.

I opened the curtains almost fully. The sun streamed in, over the crumpled linen, the brass of the bedstead. Caught his hair, damp now and clinging dark red to his scalp.

But before I left . . . and I did not wish to leave, I sat for a while at the table which was his desk, in his chair. I leafed amongst the books. There were some letters, their seal broken. I did not touch or look in these. I would not. There was also his notebook – the one I had seen at the Assembly Rooms last October.

It was wrong to look. Ah, yes. But then . . . I opened it at random.

'Jesu, Jesu, Jesu!' he had written, over and over. Train times, goods deliveries, sketches of people – some I recognized, some not. The address of the London Motet Society that I had seen him jot down. The odd everyday note, 'Curled greens for Mr Woolven.' And everywhere, 'Jesu, Jesu, Jesu!' Some account of squabbling with, not my James, but James Titterington, and of making up later. And of an outing to the Irish. (Ah, how well I knew those outings . . .) A note about *The Creation* that we had both attended. A book title: *Manhood, the Causes of its Premature Decline.* And then again, 'Jesu, Jesu, Holy Jesu!'

And poems. I counted several poems. Not meant for my eyes? Perhaps not. Written surely for a wider public – *if that public would accept them.*

I decided to copy one. I took a sheet of paper and a pen, and saw that the inkwell was not quite empty. When I had finished I folded the paper and placed it in my reticule.

Branwell was quiet still. Breathing very deeply. I thought of one last thing. The cottage was empty still. I went quietly downstairs and returned with a small sharp knife.

'Do not be afraid,' I said, holding lightly one lock of hair, swiftly cutting it. (How like an assassin I must have looked – could I not have passed for an assassin?) I placed that too in my reticule.

I stood there for a moment. Trembling. I had been quite calm as I sat at his desk. But now I shook. It was as if, as I waited there, the future, all his future – the little future he had – rose up before me and said . . .

Outside Minnie waited patiently. I rode back, without meeting anyone.

Of my own future, I did not think at all.

A memorial to the directors of the railway company was presented as planned, by my father, by Joshua Woodward and some other mill owners, and signed also by James and Sutcliffe and their friends. The plea was that Branwell might be reinstated in his post. It was refused.

From the news my father brought back, it appeared that the directors' dissatisfaction had been caused not merely by the missing eleven pounds one and sevenpence. Since it had not been suggested that Branwell had taken it, but rather that his carelessness had allowed it to be taken, the whole question had been raised of his attendance at the station – and his diligence and concentration when he *did* attend. Papa told us:

'I've had this confidentially, but I've no reason to doubt it – the lad's station ledger, it's been nowt more than a sketch book for him. Margins chock-full of fancy drawings – caricatures and the like (an Armstrong or Woodward amongst them, I don't doubt). It's not good enough, not for the Leeds and Manchester – or any company for that matter . . . I've nowt against the lad, he's a good lad, we've enjoyed his company – but he's not suited. That's the long and short of it. We've tried our best . . .'

Meanwhile I was wondering, yet again, what was Branwell to do now? One evening several months ago, Mama had suggested to him the Church. To her, a clergyman's daughter, speaking to a clergyman's son – what could seem more natural?

'The Church,' he had answered, 'the Church? Alas, I have not one mental qualification – save perhaps hypocrisy – which would make me cut a figure in its pulpits . . .'

His reply had not been too well received, although Mama was not one to show herself offended. But I saw then how easily he could become his own enemy.

Certainly he was not suited to the Church, except by early education. His lack of belief was the greatest barrier. (And yet that longing, that attraction always towards the Irish? His own race. Where was the solace he sought in all those cries upon the name of Jesus, unless in Catholicism?)

We discussed together, I remember, what he might do now. Sutcliffe said that surely it must be 'head work', as Branwell always called it. And what head work, if not school mastering, or tutoring – or even another attempt to join the literary world?

Between my visit to Turn Lea cottages and the refusal of the plea, Branwell left Luddenden. He called to say farewell one cold evening. I had not expected to see him at all. He was very subdued. My parents thought him sick and were concerned. He assured us he was going directly home. No mention was made of his disgrace. It seemed better so, although he must have known of the planned memorial. The conversation was stiff and uneasy. I was appalled by his mien, the bad colour, the puffy exhausted face, the trembling hand. Whisky. Laudanum. Too much of both.

And how was he to regard me? I trembled – inside. Outside I was as bold as ever. Attempting good cheer, wishing him well in his next endeavour . . .

I need not have feared. There was no recognition in his glance – in the downcast, quickly averted eyes. *I knew for certain.* (Today, I am still as certain.) There was only general misery and the sour smell of despair.

I had not dared to think what I felt, had not dared to think of the episode at all. It was as if I had been mad for a little. Out of my mind. Almost, out of my body. And yet it had not felt so. At the time I had felt only rightness – and tenderness. And a certain inevitability.

He left our house then. For ever. Although there was polite talk, most of it from Mama, of return visits: of how there would always be a welcome for him at Buckley House. I was surprised he had managed this visit at all, painfully making his way up to us, dragging what shreds of self-respect remained to him.

He was about to crawl home, to take refuge in illness. It was time for a nervous collapse.

For me, it was time to think. But I did not do so. I was too busy.

It is difficult looking back now to see how a wedding still five or six weeks away could have produced such daily fuss and bother. Yet it did. I yearned for all the fuss to be over. I wanted to exchange the wedding ceremony and all its junketings for the actual state of matrimony. James and I were well paired. Let the marriage begin . . .

I was not seeing as much of James as I would have liked. And never alone. Of his mother I saw too much. Since we were to live at Wade House, there were many excuses for summoning me there (with or without Mama, and I took Mama whenever possible), to discuss practical matters. In the furnishing and decorating of our bedroom, known as the green room, I was offered no choice. It was to remain green. She wished only for my approval of the materials she had chosen.

We did not come to blows even when Mama, the peacemaker, was not there. But how unhappy Kate Woodward made me, with her implied criticism, her rumble of disapproval. She was not a comfortable, not an affectionate person. I could not imagine wishing to please her from anything other than fear.

I grew to dread my visits to her: to be told yet again that Wade

House was not mine. And perhaps, for good measure, that neither really was James.

'I hope you'll not nag and torment him, saying "I want this or that, or do this, or do that". I know your kind. Trying to change him, when it's your duty to change yourself. And I hope you have it in mind to change. It's needed.'

But then when she had exasperated me almost beyond bearing, I would remember those dead little ones down in the kirkyard, and I would think: How hard. How hard. I could never have borne it. It is suffering has made her a bitter person.

2

I was not too much concerned when my monthly courses, due in the middle of April, did not appear. Only annoyed. The wedding had been timed so that I should be clear of those expected in May. It would be a nuisance if after all I had mistimed it. But I did not worry since I had heard that it was common for girls about to marry, overwhelmed with preparations, to suffer delays.

About two weeks later, I had the symptoms of a bilious attack and was kept in bed on a light diet. Pills and potions were given to stimulate the liver. But, up and about again, I was left with a lingering nausea: just enough to permeate everything I ate or drank or smelled. Some smells haunted me – I fancied them there even when they had gone. The camphor and vinegar of the sick room . . .

The truth was slow to come. Unbelievably so. When it did, I was appalled. This was something I *must* have thought of, and *yet I had not*.

But even as I was, at last, realizing, Sutcliffe came home with the news that James was ill in bed with a fever. To begin with, it was not too worrying. I went up to see him, Kate Woodward at first trying to bar my way. After a little her angry concern alerted me. His fever had risen dangerously high. Cupping and bleeding had no effect.

For five days and nights, he lay on the edge of death. At first I could do nothing but think of him and pray. But then as the crisis drew nearer, as the dread words were spoken, 'If James is taken from us . . .' I was hit suddenly by the horror of my own situation.

I was almost certainly with child. But frightening as I found that, my situation was not desperate. It was only weeks now before I could be expected to conceive – with James. I had worked it out already. A seven months' child. It would not arouse much remark. And that James should suspect anything – how very unlikely.

But if my dear, dear James were to *die*. Ah then – all the sadness apart, leaving aside the weeping and wailing at our great loss – *what would I do?* I thought and thought in circles. Between grief and worry I scarcely knew who or where I was.

My state surprised no one. The worry went with the grief and had a simple explanation. But *I* knew. Only I knew how it would be for me, were James to die. I knew too that I had only to say it was his child, for some of the disgrace to go. But I would not be able to tell that lie. I, who was prepared to deceive him (who did deceive him), could not deceive the rest of the world . . .

I was frightened too by the manner in which it bound me to him, to Branwell. I could not tell him. Of course I could not. Would not. But ah, the temptation . . .

And, that fearful tenderness. I had thought, had I not, to put all that away? A buried incident, the more so since *he* did not recall it. And it was James I was to marry, James with whom I was to spend the rest of my life. And if he was not part of my secret life – not in the poems I read, the dreams I dreamed, neither was or had been, Branwell. Yet now . . . I did not know *what* I felt.

I sat by James's bedside, in mental torment. I watched two nights with his mother. She would have wished me away (and how much the more so, if she had known my secret), but later, sitting there, she felt I think for a short time some grudging respect, some bond. It was not to last.

James tossed and turned, sweat poured from him. He was delirious and thought that Halliwell had come for him. He did not know either of us.

Then after one dreadful night when it had seemed his fever could go no higher, the illness turned. Morning found him weak, washed out – and alive. From then on it was only for him to recover slowly his strength.

We all rejoiced. Sutcliffe, who had been white with anxiety, grew excitable in his relief.

Saved. James had been saved. I too, had been saved.

Meanwhile, what of Branwell? I did not expect to hear from him, only of him. For this I had begun already to rely on Mercy. She came to visit Betty and I felt able to ask her then. I have done so ever since. It has always seemed natural. 'What news of the parsonage, Mercy?' Sometimes she tells me before I ask. Sometimes she has nothing to tell.

Branwell had been invited to the wedding, but whether he ever received the invitation I do not know. Mercy told me that he had been suffering from a nervous illness, and that it had been quite serious. He had kept indoors. Had not been his usual social self and the village had seen little of him. By her account, he would certainly not have been fit to attend.

Such cold days before the wedding. More February than May. At night the wind howled through the ash trees up behind Buckley House. I lay and worried. I had grown the habit of worrying.

James, convalescing, was weak and irritable. There had been some talk, frankly terrifying, of postponing the wedding. Fortunately it came to nothing.

That month Branwell published three poems. He must have been well enough to submit them, even if not to write them. I, who read all poems, good or bad, in newspapers and magazines, did not miss them. The pseudonym they were written under, Northangerland, I recognized, for he had spoken of it to me once. Poems in the *Leeds Intelligencer*, the *Halifax Guardian* – provincial papers, not national. Yet it *was* publication.

In the *Halifax Guardian*, he wrote of *The Callousness produced by Care*. ('Why hold young eyes the fullest fount of tears?') Writing on *Peaceful Death and Painful Life*, he asked: 'Why dost thou sorrow for the happy dead?'

I admired them and thought them very fine. I also found them sad. Such preoccupation with death and suffering, neither of which I would wish to deny – and yet in the midst of both, we are yet in life. And I had life *in* me . . .

At that time, I did not even consider writing to or calling on him. It was not a thought decided against, but a thought I did not have. And in this I was right. Time has not altered that feeling. I was right.

We were married, James and I. St Mary's Luddenden, and a peal of bells in the sunshine. For the weather had changed. On the morning of the wedding, two pairs of swallows flew and twittered around the roof ridge of Buckley House. A clump of primroses was out in the wooded patch behind.

My dress was very beautiful, of ivory satin. I had no trouble with the fitting, unless it was that I had lost a little weight. I was nauseated only in the mornings now and that for a very short time. Since I never actually vomited, the sickness was easy to conceal. I was certain now I had not made a mistake about my condition.

After the wedding breakfast at home, we travelled to Cumbria. There we stayed ten days in a house on a fell road, looked after by a housekeeper. The house was old: 1687 written on its lintel. Although it rained often, because of this, each morning was a glitter of sun and shower together. The green so fresh. A cuckoo calling down the valley from the fell.

James grew in health and strength each day. When we had been there only two or three days, I became suddenly happy. Away from his friends (and alas, I include Sutcliffe), he was not restless as I might have feared, but for those few days, my loving friend. What matter that he did not come into my dreams? Those ten days my sleep was exhausted, happily so, and dreamless.

Gratitude, too. I felt that in great measure. Dear James, who had saved me from a disgrace, a misery beyond reckoning. Now, as his loving wife, I could *show* that gratitude.

I no longer feared deceit, or childbirth. I no longer feared anything. As if some spell had been woven round me. For those ten days I was bold again – and beautiful: James told me so. Over and over.

He wanted us to make a child – preferably a son. 'But I'm not fussed – not fussed at all.' Such an easygoing, happy James. Even talk like that I did not mind.

Except for a few fishing expeditions James made, we were all the time together, walking or driving in the fells, or by the lakeside. He was pleased and proud, saying:

'Sutcliffe'll find me an altered character. And not before time. Who'd want to stray, when they've a Lina waiting at home?'

But ten days is not very long. And then we were back and living at Wade House: where James was *not* master, and where I was grudgingly accepted by his mother. My unhappiness returned at a stroke, and the nausea, which in Cumbria I had been able to keep at bay – just as I had been able to forget my other fears and worries – overwhelmed me.

James and I had nowhere to sit on our own. I had to ask permission before inviting my family to join us for a meal or an evening at Wade House. And James was restless in the evenings – he was not accustomed to stay in with his parents. Soon he was finding excuses to leave me, sitting there with his mother.

I spent much time, too much time, visiting Mama. Bringing on my head criticism from my mother-in-law.

'Why ever did you wed, Caroline, I'd like to know? I see no good in lasses that wed and then spend all their days back with their own folk . . .'

At Buckley House, I might be lucky and meet Mercy on one of her monthly visits. I did so in June. I learned that Branwell was better, and had made a special friend of his father's curate, Willie Weightman. A lad everyone liked, Mercy said. They went shooting and walking together.

But she did not report any news of a career, or even a post. From other sources, I learned that he had tried again for work on the railways, but without success.

My nausea lingered on. It was the second half of June. James asked:

'Have you maybe news of a bairn – eh, Lina?'

'It could be . . . I rather think –' I spoke of sickness, and other signs. 'Yes, maybe, James.'

His pride, his pleasure, terrified me. It was to frighten me for years after. How could I have thought it would be all right? And yet it *must*. I became determined that in this no one should be hurt but myself – not James, not the child, not Branwell. No one but me.

But if I was to manage, some things must change.

'We must live alone,' I said. 'We must have a home that is ours. However small. I cannot carry the child here. I *cannot* –'

Nothing was too much to ask. He felt the same. He'd be damned if he'd be ruled by his parents – a 25-year-old lad. If he'd known how I felt . . .

Within a few weeks we had the use of a small house near The Broad Flags in Luddenden. Once again it was my father-in-law who acceded, over-riding his wife's protests.

When the child quickened – two months too early for it to be safely mentioned – we were happily settled together. Sutcliffe grumbled goodnaturedly, as did James Titterington and the Thompson brothers, that James was difficult to persuade out.

It was a time of waiting. Only my dreams punctured the peace. They were violent. I dreamed again and again that something happened to Branwell or to the child. Often I could not distinguish one from the other: only the violence, the crushing, the maiming, the cries for help heard as if from a great distance, were the same. Waking in the morning I could taste the fear. I did not know whether it was for Branwell I feared, or his child.

In September, Willie Weightman, the young curate and Branwell's friend, died suddenly of cholera. I heard from Mercy of Branwell's loud unashamed sobbing throughout the funeral service, kneeling in the family pew which he had not been in for years, while his father preached the funeral sermon. Within a month the Brontë aunt, Aunt Branwell, who had looked after them since the death of their mother some twenty years before, was dead also, of an internal obstruction. Branwell, the only child at home, sat up with her during her horribly painful illness . . .

I was appalled at this rush of bad news. I was tempted then – the first of so many times – to make my way over to Haworth, and to offer a listening ear, a shoulder to weep on. Perhaps it would have been possible to find some way of making my arrival not too strange, too ludicrous. But if there was, I could not think of it.

I did not go. I never went – until it was too late.

And what of Sutcliffe, now that I no longer lived at home, and James had grown disinclined to spend evenings on the razzle? Sutcliffe's wild days were numbered. Dear, foolish, easily led Sutcliffe. I have never thought it anything but sad, what happened to my brother.

He went for a visit that December to his godmother in Harrogate. He had had a low fever and it was thought a change of air would benefit. His godmother's daughter, Patty, whom he had known from childhood, was at home and had invited a schoolfriend to stay. Flora Gilbert.

Oh, what a fall. Within days he was at her feet. Besotted. Nothing would do but he must have her. He came home and could speak of nothing else. She was to be invited to visit Luddenden in the New Year. In the meantime, we *must* hear of her cleverness with a paintbrush. Flora's was not any ordinary talent. ('She could be exhibited in any of those big London salons, could Flora.')

I suspect that I had already decided on disliking her well before we met. Certainly no one could measure up to the praise she received from Sutcliffe's lips, that last week before Christmas.

Perhaps also I was preoccupied, only half-listening, sitting there, great with child. *Very* great with child. James, and even Joshua, had begun to tease me.

'It's a lad all right,' Joshua said, 'a regular Goliath. It's a Woodward, that one – they always weigh heavy.'

James said, 'I heard tell – they say I carried nigh on twelve pound into the world.' He looked to his mother for confirmation.

'Daft nonsense,' she said. 'As if I'd mind any such thing. This bairn will weigh what it weighs – and that's all about it.'

I was with James and my parents at Buckley House, Sutcliffe showing us a portfolio of Flora's sketches, when my pains began. I was taken back at once to Wade House where I was to lie in. Nothing was ready. February was to be the month. I lay in the great bed in the green room. I begged James to keep his mother away. To send her to bed, anything. Mrs Foster, the midwife, was with me. Mama came, and told me how my brother Halliwell had been three weeks early, and none the worse for it. She told me old wives' tales: of how babes that came early, came easily. It would not be long, the midwife assured me. I wondered if perhaps I was about to die.

The snares of death compassed me round about: and the pains of hell gat hold upon me. I found trouble and heaviness, and I called upon the name of the Lord . . . For as much as it hath pleased Almighty God of his goodness to give you safe deliverance, and hath preserved you in the great danger of Childbirth . . .

Just before dawn the next day, I was delivered of a six and a half pound girl. It was Christmas Eve. I no sooner saw her – small, screwed-up angry face, bald head, tiny flailing limbs – than I loved her. I knew then, too, that I loved her father.

Such an unlikely love. It could not bear examination. It was not amenable to reason. At the time – no, after the time, after – I had felt towards him, more *mother* than mistress. My memory was of a child I had comforted . . .

But that Christmas Eve I realized for the first time I had new feelings. Tangled emotions I could not, did not dare to examine . . . I felt (and still do feel) a fine gratitude towards James. But this – ah this . . . As I looked at the babe – longing then to show her *at once* to Branwell, I knew. I knew I must keep the secret, but that temptation would always be there. I knew too that from now on, it would no longer be friendly concern I felt for his future. It would be an anxiety. A vivid anxious love. Mistress, mother, anything and everything to the father of our child . . .

What rejoicing though that Christmas in the Woodward, in the

Armstrong home. The first grandchild. I did not know what to say to James, who had wanted a son (and who now had another man's daughter . . .).

'I'm sorry,' I said. 'I'm sorry.'

'Daft – what's all that?' he said, hanging doting over the cradle. If, that Christmas, Sutcliffe was obsessed with Flora Gilbert, it was as nothing to James's worship of that child.

'Woodward eyes,' he said, 'well it's your chin, Lina, and I've studied the hands – they're little small ones yet but they're maybe Dad's . . . I don't rightly know, but I'll wager there never was a bairn so lively. She'll be talking at her christening, won't you little pet? Eh, Christabel?'

As I lay back and suckled her, I wept weakly. If only I could have allowed out the happiness which I felt hidden somewhere deep down, out of reach. Covered over, obscured by guilt. If I could have shared his joy, and pride . . .

He could not have been more understanding of my physical weakness. He surprised me – such a roistering lad – with his sudden imaginative grasp.

'If you laboured, then I reckon you've a right to be wearied – eh?'

Then when he'd asked me what were we to call her, and I had wept only, he said it was for me to choose. 'We'll maybe want Martha or Kate for second. But first is *your* fancy.'

I wept in the darkness for my happy schooldays. Miss Minnie reading to us in the garden.

'Christabel,' I told him. 'After the poem by Coleridge.'

'Right then, lass. Christabel it is.'

I was back home. Having stayed at Wade House for only half the lying-in time. It was a fortnight after Christmas. We had a maid of all work, and a servant for the heavy work, but for the child, for Christabel, I had Betty. I had asked my mother if I might. It was the nearest link I could think of with Haworth.

For as well as Betty, I would have Mercy – and news.

Flora, on her promised visit, was proudly brought to our little house by Sutcliffe. I received her lying on a day bed downstairs. The truth is that then, as today, I did not think much of her. She had a kind of faded prettiness combined with a fussy manner. Her age she could not help – she was almost thirty-one, to Sutcliffe's twenty-three. She was very gracious, and conde-scended to admire Christabel, lying in a cradle beside me. I understood from Mama that she would bring with her only a small dowry, but much gentility.

None of this would matter, perhaps, if it were not for what she has done to Sutcliffe. I saw him in the days after – running behind her like a little lap dog. Wanting only to please, made cowardly through fear of her displeasure. It has not been enough that she has tamed him. She has left him hardly a man at all.

But he *would* marry her . . . Why, though, should she marry him? For her family was socially quite a cut above ours. To Mama and me the answer was quite simple. She saw herself already become an old maid. By marrying Sutcliffe, she would be adored, and well off, and very, very comfortable.

Mercy came over at the end of January, bringing good news. Branwell had employment, at Thorp Green where his sister Anne had been for some time as governess to the Robinson daughters. He would be tutor to the son Edmund.

A new life. Another chance. Or so it seemed to me then. As I nursed Christabel, who grew stronger just as I grew stronger, I felt certain that now all would be well. Schoolmastering – so much more suitable than the railways. I had not to worry. My loving, the best kind, the only kind I could give, would be at a distance. I sent thoughts daily. I watched Betty bathe his daughter and, believing, *loved him and wished him well*.

For the first two and a half years of Christabel's life, I did not worry about her father. I had no cause to.

How wrong. How sad. If I knew peace then – and absence of worry about him – I was never to know it again. But in that brave new year, all that lay in the future. It was a happy time. James loved Christabel. How he loved her! Watching for the first smile, dandling her, wobbly-headed, on his knee, he did not care that he was the laughing stock of his friends – who scarcely saw him now.

His mother too thought him foolish. 'He'd do best to save his fussing for a son. I hope you've that in mind, Caroline.' (Always Caroline – never the affectionate Lina. She has never called me Lina.)

Yes, I had it in mind. In good time. But then in late July whilst I was still feeding Christabel, I conceived again. It was the month Flora and Sutcliffe were married. Soon Flora was expecting too. That next spring, she gave birth to Theophilus. I, too, had a son. A Woodward son and heir. James could not praise me enough.

The babe was to be called Halliwell, after my brother and James's friend.

The months passed happily for all of us. I am not sure of whom I was prouder, Halliwell or Christabel, although I know well whom I loved best. (They say that to a mother each of her children should be equal. But what was I to do, when from the very beginning, long, long before birth, one child had been set apart?) Christabel, so tiny, so active, so enquiring – and yet anxious. It was she and never Halliwell who screamed with night terrors.

Because of these terrors, I wanted to sleep beside her, and when that could not be, since Betty would not hear of it, I arranged that Betty should wake me whenever they happened. Standing there, my arms clasped tight round the small, so small rigid body, I would hopelessly attempt comfort. Trying to make out, through the high-pitched sobs, one coherent word. Nothing. (And that from a child who so very early had formed her words, who had surprised us with her precocious vocabulary. Surprised others, that is – not me.) But there was not one word that I could latch onto. Only terror.

News of Branwell continued to be good. He had been tutor at Thorp Green eighteen months now, and the reports were all of his happiness there, and his employers' satisfaction with him.

I did not see too much of my mother-in-law now. We visited only on Sundays, although I think James often called into Wade House during the week. I had done right by giving birth to Halliwell. And for a while was not so out of favour.

It was late the next winter, when Christabel was two, and Halliwell just one, that everything began to go wrong. A week after Halliwell's birthday, my father fell ill with a fever. No cupping, leeches, pills or draughts were of any avail. The next week Mama and two of the servants went down with it. Ten days later, I had lost both parents.

Throughout that spring I wore deep mourning. I was with child again which should have made me glad, since it was new life, but perhaps because the early months were also those of my bereavement, I felt weak and sick and ailing. We were worried also about James's father, who had dropsical symptoms.

Christabel was a consolation, a joy. As spring turned to summer, she ran about our small house (soon to be too small?), loving me, but calling out for 'Papa, Papa!' Escaping from Betty's grasp to run into his arms. Yes, she was a joy, a consolation, but her love for James and his for her – that was a knife through my heart. On what a fragile base it rested! My deceit. My silence.

Then in early August, Mercy brought bad news. At first I did not want to believe it.

Dismissed. Branwell had been dismissed his post as tutor. Accused of loving too well his employer's wife, Mrs Robinson – or so he himself said. (What am I to make now of that sad story, with all its rumours and counter-rumours? Perhaps one day I shall learn more of it . . . For then it had a sufficient ring of truth. I knew that he was doomed. His was a hopeless love, whatever the rights and wrongs of it.)

The story went that Mrs Robinson would marry him if she could. If her ailing husband were to die . . . But for now they were separated. Branwell was in disgrace, drinking heavily and telling his sorrows to who would listen. Penniless and with few prospects. If he had been in a bad way after leaving Luddenden, how much the worse now. I remembered sadly how I had thought, in the days of the Buckley House visits, that here was someone *for whom it was all over.* And now . . .

What could *I* do for him? Nothing at all. I could be sad that he loved some other woman so passionately, and did not love me at all. So that what I felt then was jealousy. I was racked with it. Torn and twisting with it. And yet if asked did I wish him happiness in life, *happiness in his forbidden love?* I would have cried, Yes, Yes!

How strange, how wrong, how convoluted – almost seven months' pregnant with my husband's child – how *wicked* even to experience such emotions . . .

I did not know which way to turn. And I thought then: if only my grief for him, even my jealousy – if they could be transformed into help . . . If there were something I could *do.* But there was nothing. Or if there were, I could not think of it.

Each month I waited anxiously for more news. Hoping for better, fearing worse. In October, Agnes was born. The next month Mercy told me that Branwell had applied for a railway post. But he could not have been successful for we heard no more of it.

Agnes was a beautiful infant. I fancied Christabel not to be too pleased with her – jealous perhaps? Though without cause, for although James professed himself delighted with the new arrival, he did not hang over the crib. I can scarcely recall him looking into it at all. He did remark that the nursery was growing, and that we must look about us for a larger place. (I myself hoped it would not grow much fuller. I did not aspire to a large family. I *dared* to think, and still think now, that three or four living children are quite sufficient.)

He had been working very hard at the mill all summer and did so throughout the next winter – taking on more and more responsibility from his ailing father. Joshua had swollen now to a gigantic size. His colour was bad, and the cheerful aspect I had taken for granted had left him. Victim of Mr Rushworth's purgatives and diuretics, he seemed not to improve at all. His legs were 'scarified': that is, a T-shaped cut was made below the knee to let drain some of the water – which promptly returned.

He died at Easter. We moved into Wade House the next month. Kate was to live with us, although she would have two or three rooms of her own, to which I hoped she would keep. She was still scathing of me, but just as I had once reminded myself of her sufferings in losing her babes, now I told myself that she had lost a husband. Allowances must be made.

I tried. She gave me no credit for doing so. James, deeply distressed at the loss of his father, was angry and distant with me. Except at night.

. . . Lo, children and the fruit of the womb: are an heritage and gift that cometh of the Lord. Like as the arrows in the hand of the giant: even so are the young children. Happy is the man that hath his quiver full of them . . .

All through the months I carried Joshua, I worried helplessly about Branwell. It was not difficult to be reminded of him. I had only to see little Christabel, auburn-haired, blue-eyed. And his.

I had not wanted to be pregnant. This time it was not my body that rebelled, but my mind. I was strong, and not sick – but from the first moment that I guessed what was to be, I felt something stir, not in my belly but in my head. A whirring, an agitation. Too many sorrows in the family of late. I felt that even now I was inviting another. I did not want a child, so what must my prayer be – that I should lose it? But I could not have borne that either.

Then one bright summer morning, I read in the *Leeds Mercury*, quite by chance since I did not often read the obituary column: *'On Tuesday last at Thorp Green near Boroughbridge, aged forty-six, the Rev. Edmund Robinson. He died as he had lived, in firm and humble trust in his Saviour . . .'*

I did not know what to think. I knew it was what Branwell waited for. I *thought* I wished only for his happiness . . .

I waited then for Mercy to bring me news. She came a week later. I did not need to ask her anything. She was bursting with it:

'Dance! He fair danced down t'kirkyard . . . Annie, that serves at t'Bull, she said it were like he were out of his mind wi' joy . . . But t'next day, she says – a man comes to t'Bull to see him, and it's coachman from this Mrs Robinson's. They were in t'back parlour drinking. Then coachman goes and Annie thinks nowt on't . . . But a while on and she hears this din, like what a calf makes as calls for its mam . . . And she opens t'parlour and there he is. In a fit. Down – in a fearful fit. It were *terrible*, she says. Made her afeard to see . . .'

But whatever was all this? I hung on her words, I asked what was it, Branwell and Mrs Robinson, were they not to be married after all? After a decent mourning period, were they *not to be married*? I knew he had lived only for that. But it appeared the coachman had come to tell him the terms of Mr Robinson's will: if his widow were to marry Branwell, she would forfeit not only her entire inheritance, but also the care of her children.

And then, Mercy said, some days after the coachman's visit, he had heard from the Robinson family doctor an alarming account of the widow's state of health: her mind almost gone.

'As for him,' Mercy said, 'Parson's Patrick, it's drink again, nowt but drink – and other stuff, they do say. *Laudanum* that's to be bought from Bessy Hardacre's . . .'

My own mind was a foment of pity and anger and distressed love. Perhaps if I had not been with child, had not already been in the confused, agitated state of mind that this pregnancy had brought me, I would have known what to believe and what not. His despair however was not in dispute. And succeeding months brought from Haworth only tales of further misery.

I think I was a little mad myself then. How else to account for my behaviour that autumn, when Christabel fell ill with whooping cough? I have always found that carrying a new child heightens rather than lessens anxieties about the others. It was so this time with Christabel.

She was very ill. I sat up with her night after night. Betty disapproved as did James. Kate Woodward told me of my duty to my remaining children. But I could think only: *If I lose her, if I lose Christabel* . . .

It looked as if we might. Mr Rushworth's face was grave. He begged me to rest 'for the sake of the infant'. But he could not promise me that if I left Christabel's side, she would be there on my return.

I would not leave her. Alone with her, beside her crib, I begged her to get well, *begged* her to live. She could not hear me for I spoke only in my mind, yet I willed her, *how* I willed her, to get well.

I went further than that. Perhaps I *was* a little mad . . . For I became convinced that were Branwell to know of this, he would wish for her not good Protestant prayers, nor yet Calvinist or Methodist, but rather, Roman Catholic. Only a Papist God could help. (Had I not always felt that that was his spiritual home?)

What must I do? I was despairing. *Desperate.* I remembered then Martha Lumsden, my sister-in-law, and her grumbling and moaning about the Halifax Papists, now with their own church in Gibbet Lane. I penned a simple message to 'The priest in charge'. A cry from the heart that he should come – and sent it by the early morning carrier.

He was with me by afternoon. I had not expected so prompt a response. He was dressed in black but without a priestly collar. I had been afraid to see him in a black frock. We spoke rapidly – I worrying always that my mother-in-law would choose now to visit the sick room, to come looking for me . . .

He was a good man, a simple man – he told me a little of himself and his work. He explained that since Christabel had been baptized once, even though in the Anglican Church, that would be sufficient. What he could offer me, what would help Christabel most, would be a Blessing for the Sick.

We stood talking in the sick room, our voices low. The small body of my child, lying still now, exhausted by a recent paroxysm . . . I knew that at any moment I would weep, uncontrollably. I knew too that we must be quick.

'It must be now, Father . . . My mother-in-law . . .' I drew the bed curtains round. 'It would mean so much to me. If I am to lose . . . I cannot tell you more –' Had there been time I would have told everything. Everything. So trusting, so desperate was my mood.

'What do you need?' I asked. 'Water, oil?'

And then his voice, the Irish seeping through, thickening the Latin:

'Domine exaudi orationem mean, et clamor meus ad te veniat . . .'

From that day on, she went forward. Three or four days later we had ceased to fear for her. I was weak with relief, only able now to admit my fatigue. I spent a week in bed and from there sent a letter of thanks to the man I saw as Christabel's saviour. I have never been in touch since. I think now that it was a temporary madness brought on by anxiety and my already delicate state. What a risk I took, what a foolish act it was with its possible untold consequences. And yet – Christabel lives, that might have died.

For the Brontë family the next two years were to bring tragedy. But for us, the pattern of death seemed over. Christabel's survival perhaps had altered it. If it had not been for my worry and distress over Branwell, I would have been fast recovering happiness, for that is what Joshua's birth early the next February brought me. He was so much more than I deserved.

Also, he was Christabel's. I think that she never said the name 'Josh', or 'Joshua', without adding to it 'my'. It was so from the first moment she saw him. He was her darling, just as *she* was James's (and that showed no signs of diminishing).

It was not an easy birth, though. Joshua was a large infant, who tore me badly. The difficulties were unexpected after the ease of the first three. I had some fever afterwards and was a long time recovering my physical strength. And there were other complications which I did not fully understand, except that they concerned my uterus. Mr Rushworth explained that it would be unwise, nay positively dangerous, to bear another child. He would speak to James, he told me.

I did not know what to think: grown tired with childbearing – four children in five years – my exhaustion was such that I heard Mr Rushworth's interdict with relief. Also times had changed. I could not believe that once James and I had had a happy secret. That I had lain with him on Warley Moor, and fainted with pleasure. Where was that world? Where was that bold girl?

James said only (I knew he had been for a time worried for my safety – when I was fevered):

'So young Joshua's to be the last, eh, Lina?'

I said weakly, 'But you're pleased with him?'

'Aye. He favours Dad. Clever of you, that was, Lina . . . But Christabel'll have him for her own if you stay poorly any longer.'

'Mr Rushworth –'

'Aye, Rushworth. What he tells me, what he says in surgeon's language is that – it adds up to, we've to, I've to take care.'

'He's made me afraid –'

'You weren't feared those days, before we were wed. We'd to take some care then . . .'

Not really. Not really. No, I had not been afraid. I had known fear only when, James ill and likely to die, I was carrying Branwell's child. Now, was different. It was I who feared death. Later, I was to fear James.

As regards Branwell, I was without hope. From the reports I fancied we would scarcely recognize him now. Wandering the village unshaven, unkempt, his clothes hanging on his wasted frame – an old man. Drink, drugs, debts. The family was having a terrible time with him, Mercy said. She had heard his bed had caught fire while he'd lain in a stupor or fit, not taking note. Parson had him to sleep in his room now, though Mercy doubted he slept at all:

'For he's abed and resting all day. They say as he raves and calls for *her* all night . . .'

I thought too that he must be mourning not only for his love, but grieving also that he could no longer write, no longer create. That the end of it all would be death, I never doubted. Whoever still had hope for him, it was not I . . .

All through the next year – the same. Yes, I knew what the end would be. It was only when, I did not know.

It was a fearful summer. Day after day of rain, and cold. The crops were far behind. The children, kept to their nursery, whined and were fretful. In July, walking to Sutcliffe and Flora's, I was caught in a freak snowstorm. Winter into summer – it was all part of the sadness that year.

It was no surprise to me, the news of Branwell's death. It seems, though, to have surprised some, even amongst his family – that the end should have been so near. But when it came, it seems to have come mercifully. Neither a drunken nor a drugged departure, but rather, a calm and peaceful one almost to the end. The sexton's brother had found him near collapse in the lane going up to the parsonage and had helped him home. The account of his death two days later that Mercy brought was the story of a return to God and religion and family. A loving child again.

But the waste, the waste . . . I could think only of the waste.

205

Sorrow pressed on me. If I felt so its crippling dead weight, what must his family feel? As I watched Christabel run into the garden in the late (too late) autumn sunshine, I felt a mad desire to snatch her up, and take her to Haworth to *show* the mourners:

'Look, he is not dead!'

Then immediately I knew it for the madness it was. I grew hot and cold in memory of how once, I had almost done just this, *while he still lived.* There would never be a time when it was right. No solace, if solace it would be, that I might give his family could outweigh the pain and heartbreak that others would suffer.

I mourned. How I mourned. Since it was not permitted to mourn him publicly, my body mourned instead. My arms and legs, and for a while my face too, were victims of a strange weeping skin complaint, the skin so raw that for a while I was confined to bed. My discomfort was so great, it was not thought strange that I too should weep. Vapour baths, alterative pills, sulphur water fetched from Harrogate – my days were busy with cures.

The weeping ceased, outside. I think that inside it is not done yet. But I have never had a recurrence of that skin complaint. (Mr Rushworth thinks this to be his good management.)

By December, Emily Brontë was dead too. I could discuss her death with no one. James, occasionally sympathetic, thought only that I cared in a general way what happened to the family. He told friends: 'Lina was quite the little mother to Branwell.'

So it took little last Christmas for sorrow to surface, coming up as if from some deep well. Christabel, the birthday girl. The doll she so longed for and which with my newly healed hands I dressed in silks and satins, waiting for her. And then Agnes, only three, wanting to admire, to examine. She is rough, and my little redhead attacks her, viciously. Of course we cannot let it pass. Even James will strike his little darling . . .

She ran from the room. I remember that after a little, I went out after her. Oh, the relief of tears. I was able to weep then over her, Christabel. To take her head in my hands, to smooth back the hair from her high forehead – so high, so like – to weep not alone, but with her. What matter that we wept each for a different loss?

And still the deaths went on. I did not know when I wept at Christmas, that within five months Anne Brontë too would be dead.

One day that winter, confined to my bedroom with a chill, I read through yet again the poems that Branwell had given me. And also those I had stolen: they were all fair-copied now in a blue leather book. I planned to show them to Christabel when she was older.

When I had finished reading – I do not know if it was my illness or what, but I was assailed by a mood of the darkest depression. It seemed to me suddenly that my mourning had scarcely begun. With no one to talk to (and in whom could I possibly confide?), I was doomed to a lonely and secret sorrow.

Once I might have thought it romantic that I should suffer in this manner. I knew now that it was not. I would have wished to have some control over my emotions but I had not. So long as I had Christabel, I would be reminded. No use to say that I realized my true feelings too late. The reality is the same. I did not lose Branwell's love, for I never had it.

Now, I shall never know what might have been. Sutcliffe's hint that Branwell was attractive to other men, perhaps even attracted by them, I know nothing of. And about Mrs Robinson – only as much as I have heard from Mercy. But surely there, at Thorp Green, he was a plaything, an amusement of the moment? I cannot be certain. But of one thing I *am* certain – with me it would not have been like that.

Mother, wife, companion – yes, why should I be modest? In me he could have had all those. *And* the wealth he needed to cushion a writing life. Some are not made for the hurly-burly. Their nervous systems cannot support the excitement, the anxieties. They can barely manage the details of everyday life. When that person is a woman, she will be protected by her husband, or if she does not marry, her family. But if it should be a man, then every weakness that might have been hidden is exposed. And failure is the price.

I see that Branwell was weak and wayward, and boastful and unreliable (and yes, perhaps lazy too). But he had also a loving heart and a yearning for the world of the spirit. Bold as I was (and beautiful, why deny it?), I might have, could have saved him.

This matter of refusing James. Yes, yes, there is Mr Rushworth's interdict – but James is certain he could obey while disobeying. And that all would be well.

So why do I refuse him (if not always, then almost always?).

I think, no, I *know*, that it is fear. That last birth, so different from all the others – what if there were to be another like that? *In which I would die* . . . I am not ready to die, I am quite unprepared to leave motherless my four children. (Oh Christabel, Christabel, who never saw your father.)

And yet . . . Is there not just a little unease? That I am not completely honest. James and I, we have grown apart. We do not seem to be the friends we once were. He begins already to be once more the frequenter of inns – hard drinking, hard headed, hard living. My gratitude, that he should have saved me (and Branwell) from disgrace, although once so strong, is fading fast, killed by his behaviour. I no longer care for or want his body, that once I swooned for. That he should be as he is now – cause or effect? I do not know.

I foresee little for us but that we shall rub along together, tolerably. He with the mill and his drinking companions (but not Sutcliffe . . .). I with my children – and my secret.

'I wish I could trust you, Caroline,' my mother-in-law said.

But why should she? I did not trust her.

And I was right. During the course of that bitter exchange, when she hinted, as indeed she had done several times before, that she 'knew something', I thought: I know something too – that you are a wicked woman. And a spy.

She is insatiably curious, given to opening cupboards and drawers. Out of curiosity, yes, but also in the hope of finding something compromising. She loves the power she can then wield. She has long had access to my escritoire – I have not minded too much since I keep nothing of importance in there. I have put up with her clicking pattens as she creeps about on her meddling forays. But when she spoke to me in that manner ('There is something you have not told me – *or James*'), I felt certain she had been prying.

Already in tears, heart drumming, legs trembling, I hurried up to my room. Looked in my hiding place . . . There, safely – they *could* not have been found – were the poems, the lock of auburn hair, the exercise books. All in a box within a much larger box, to which only I have the well-hidden keys . . . No, she has found nothing. But that I should have had, even for a moment, the terrifying thought that someone . . . Careful as I am, I must yet be *more careful*.

So, of what did she speak? Kate Woodward has always disliked me. I think it is this makes her able to sense there *is* a secret.

Yet I feel certain she will take her guesses no further. The power she has, the misery she can wreak, are for her sufficient. Certainly she knows already that James and I do not sleep together – and why. That is just one more weapon in her armoury.

Now I close my story. I have told my tale. I shall put the exercise books with these writings away once more, *very* safely. Perhaps I shall take them out sometimes and read them. And then again, perhaps I shall not.

I must remember as I write this, in the Christmas of 1849, how much I have to be thankful for. My four children are a joy. Christabel, who might have died, has lived . . .

But Branwell is dead. I must learn to live with that knowledge. It will never become commonplace. Branwell is dead. But his daughter lives.

Now to end, I shall copy a few lines from a poem he wrote that last Christmas in Luddenden:

> . . . *And when I join the silent dead*
> *Their light will all be gone.*
> *Then I must cease to seek the light*
> *Which fires the evening heaven,*
> *Since to direct through death's dark night*
> *Some other must be given . . .*

3

December 1857.

I thought I had finished writing, that I had said all I wished to say. But I did not know and could not have guessed what terrible things were yet to come. So I take up my pen again, to write as truthfully as I can what has happened since.

And what was the worst?

That we lost Joshua.

I who had so feared Christabel's death, who had seen her snatched from the grave's edge, lost my youngest son, Christabel's darling.

Of that time I do not want to say very much. I understood then with my body what I had only known with my mind before. I understood some of what my mother felt when she lost her first born: Halliwell Armstrong, crushed beneath his horse, her *grown* son. Joshua was only a child but ah, God – I thought I would be torn apart.

I said little. My suffering was not worn where it could be seen. And I could not help Christabel, who suffered too. I thought once, wildly, that in spite of the dangers, I should have another child. I know that James, shaken and sobered by the tragedy, thought so too – for a while. But it came to nothing.

How can a new child take the place of the old? No child would have been *that* child. Joshua.

What to say of the visit Christabel and I paid to Haworth? How often during Branwell's lifetime I resisted the temptation to go over there. And how often since his death, I have wanted to. I pictured it, how many times I pictured it! That I should call at the Parsonage *with Christabel*. I would ask for Miss Brontë. She would come into the hall to greet me: a friend of Branwell's from Luddenden days . . .

Then we would go together into the parlour, on the left of the front door. (Yes, I know that house.) We would sit by the fire, and we would talk. And talk. I did not need to imagine, to hear what it was we said. We spoke of Branwell. Easily, lovingly. It could be, it might be that one or other of us would weep . . .

And all the while Christabel would be there. Looking so like. Yet not like. For when persons are not expecting a resemblance such as that – do they see it? She has his forehead, his hair, his small stature – my chin, some of my manner, eyes not unlike my mother's, except as to colour – which is his.

No, she would not be recognized. But might there not be a *feeling*? How often I wove that fantasy – and always at the end, there would be the father. Parson Brontë. How much he had suffered . . . He would know, *without knowing*. His eyes, clear now of cataracts, would show him that after all *his son had not died*.

Oh, but there the fantasy would stop – I did not know, was never to know, what came next. These foolish subtleties, of knowing, yet not knowing . . .

When, in the end, in reality, we drove those twelve miles to Haworth, when I had sat a while in the family pew, when I had thought of his bones beneath the church pavement – what then?

The Parsonage, but no Charlotte. Miss Brontë was in Manchester . . . And then that fearsome, angry figure. So courteous at first, that I thought for a moment: It will be all right . . . But then as I spoke up, when I said 'Luddenden Foot', when I talked of 'friends', it was not all right.

What had Mr Brontë heard of Luddenden? Only about life on the razzle, surely. That way of life and those actions which had led to yet another return home in disgrace (until three years later, the final, terrible one).

'False friends,' he said. 'False friends.' Yet there were homes Branwell visited in Luddenden, hearths he sat by. And ours not the least of them.

Perhaps I should have said something. Fought for myself, and Christabel. But I did not. And the moment passed. I was I think too agitated by then, too emotional. How harrowing the day. Already I felt coming on the crippling neuralgic headache which by the time we had come to the end of the lane, I thought would fell me. And so it was that I had to go into Bessie Hardwicke's in the square, opposite the Black Bull. And buy laudanum, where so often *he* had bought it.

It was a sad homecoming that evening. Failed. Worse than failed. I knew that I would never go again.

And Christabel suspected nothing.

Nine years of putting up with my mother-in-law, nine years of criticism, mischief-making, prying and general unpleasantness: brought to an end by an apoplectic stroke. Afterwards her memory was so bad that I think she did not remember what it was she hated me for. She became a pathetic figure, little more than a crotchety child. By the end – and she lasted some four years – I had it in me to be sorry for her, I felt for her only compassion.

And Christabel – how has *she* been? Such a difficult child, as all the governesses (and there were many) have told me. Only I, it seemed sometimes, could do anything with her. I and Mr Hume, of whom she made a friend several years ago. (And now he teaches her Latin, and she is happy, I think.) James, who loved her so much, could do nothing with her.

Those poor governesses. Except for the irresponsible Miss Dutton, there was not one whose side I was not on. I used to think then of those heroines, Jane Eyre and Agnes Grey, just as now I think of Charlotte Brontë's hardships that I read of in Mrs Gaskell's *Life*.

Ah that *Life*. How well it told the tale of Thorp Green, and

Mrs Robinson. It is a pity to me, since I believe every word of it, that Mrs Robinson's threat to sue led to the watered-down version we have now – and can expect to have for many years to come. (Christabel managed of course to borrow from Mr Hume that first truthful edition. If she had known how pertinent to her was all that she read . . .)

The fame, the praise, the excellence of those three Brontë sisters has given me more pleasure than I can express. It is so *right*, although unexpected – who would have thought it, who was not surprised when they heard? But although unexpected, it was *right*. (And if it is true, as they say, that *he* never knew of it – what of that? Was it not better so?)

Christabel, who ran away and was found sleeping with the Irish down by the canal. And who, because she had become impossible, was sent to school.

And there, at The Beeches, once more *I almost lost her*.

But all that is behind us. I have other worries now, only in part to do with Christabel . . .

There was a poem in *Fraser's Magazine* the spring of Charlotte Brontë's death. *Haworth Churchyard* it was called. No author's name was given. I copied the whole into my leather book. I shall write here only some of the last section. It is about him.

> . . . *Unhappy, eloquent – the child*
> *Of many hopes, of many tears . . .*
> *On thee too did the Muse*
> *Bright in thy cradle smile;*
> *But some dark shadow came*
> *(I know not what) and interposed.*

Of the many happenings, I have left to the last the most recent. And the most terrible.

James knows everything. He has done so for two years now. He learned it from that written story which seven years ago I had thought finished. Which I did not intend to continue. *Which I had locked away.*

I was more than usually careful whenever I took out the exercise books containing my story. How carefully they were kept from peering eyes . . . As carefully as the lock of hair, kept now in an oilskin wrap. And as secret.

What happened? How could I, when so much was at stake, *how could I?*

It had all to do with that poem *Haworth Churchyard*. I saw it first in the morning when the post brought me my copy of *Fraser's*. I had time only to glance at it. In the afternoon I took it upstairs with the intention of copying it out: I was eager to do this before the magazine should become mislaid, or Christabel cut something out from it. I wanted also to read the poem in privacy.

James was home that day. In bed supposedly, in his own room, suffering from a chill (brought on I suspect by too much brandy), but in fact wandering the house in a dressing gown. He had appeared in the dining-room just before dinner time, complaining of the noise.

'It is only Agnes,' I said. 'Miss Milner teaches her. All children when they learn the piano – the sound is never pleasant.'

'It's not that bloody din, isn't Christabel's playing.'

'Christabel is older and has played longer. And besides, you are used to be at the mill when they practise –'

'Tell the kitchen they've to bring my dinner up,' he said. 'And I'll maybe sleep after. If there's peace –'

I hated those days when he stayed at home. If he had been really ill, it would have been all right . . . But this condition, owing so much to alcohol, and full of bad temper, was sorely trying.

When I went upstairs with the magazine, I left Christabel with her head in a book – it would be there all afternoon. James was resting or sleeping. Agnes and Miss Milner intended a walk, if the rain kept off.

I had just copied the poem out when I had the idea of adding just a few of the verses to the account of my life. I took out the exercise books, found where I had stopped, and dipped my pen . . .

There was a frantic knocking at the door. A series of sharp screams. I rushed out.

Agnes stood there. Blood poured into her mouth. She wailed: 'My nose is bleeding to death. It's . . . Mama, *help*!'

I thought at first it was not much. When her face had been sponged and she had been reassured, the nose was seen to be quite all right. A blow from a jammed cupboard door had set off the bleeding. Miss Milner was out of the house for ten or fifteen minutes, and Agnes, who panicked easily, at the sight of all the blood had lost control completely . . .

It was more than that. As she calmed down a little, and spoke more coherently, I realized what she was telling me. The door had made her nose bleed, yes, but also the shaking and pulling of the jammed door had caused a heavy statuette which stood on the top, to fall. It had hit her on the back of the head. There was little to see then, only a fast-growing bump. She was more concerned by her bloody nose which had started to flow again.

But not long after, she grew suddenly very strange. Chalk white, she stammered as she tried to speak. She had difficulty in focusing. Finally she fainted away completely. And would not come round.

By this time, Miss Milner had come to help me. I had not called Christabel from her room for I did not want her frightened. We put Agnes at once to bed and sent for Mr Rushworth.

If I should lose another child . . . I was distraught. For I realized yet again, how easy it was to rise in the morning the happy mother, and go to bed the bereaved.

But I did not go to bed. I could not have done so. I spent the remainder of that day and all the night beside Agnes, never leaving her, watching her each second anxiously, *willing* her to come back to life.

Mr Rushworth could counsel nothing at this stage but patience. If all went well, and she opened her eyes again, the matter would be at an end. If not . . .

Quite early in the afternoon, he had asked me, 'What time do you expect Mr Woodward home? Should he not perhaps be called from the mill?'

James. That I should have forgotten James. Her father. That he too would be concerned . . .

'Ill,' I said, 'not enough to send for you – but he is resting, he sleeps. I did not want at first . . .'

When James came, he too was distraught. But he was not good in the sick room. He could do nothing but pace up and down, peering occasionally at Agnes's face, pinching her cheek, trying to wake her. I had to ask him to leave.

He seemed remorseful that earlier in the day he should have been so irritable. It worried him that I should sit up all night, as I intended.

'What'll you do then?' he asked.

'Pray,' I said. 'And watch.'

'It'll be a long night, Lina . . .'

Not for a mother. Not for a mother. The hours passed. About

two o'clock in the morning, Agnes woke. Very suddenly. Her eyes open wide. She smiled, and asked for her tea. 'Did I sleep through tea? Did I? I was so *sleepy* . . .'

I woke Betty to tell her the good news – she had not slept. I asked her to sit with Agnes while I woke James.

He was not in his room (how long now had we slept apart?). I looked downstairs in the snug. No James. Then coming up again, I saw a light beneath the door of my room. I had not been in there since afternoon . . .

I turned the handle. I walked in. James looked up. The bedspread was in disarray as if it covered something. He stood up and walked towards me.

I do not think I have ever seen him look as he looked that night. Drunk? Ill? *Angry?* Any of those. All of those . . .

'She's all right,' I said, 'Agnes is all right . . .'

'Aye,' he said, 'well, that's good.' Still with that terrible face.

And *I knew.* The room whirled. Everything whirled. I sat on the bed, my heart thudding. I fought for breath. I thought I would suffocate with fear.

It could not be. But then I remembered. My exercise books . . . The box . . . Dropping everything to run to Agnes.

I stood up, holding on to the bed rail. Everything swam. I told myself: The world does not end with this –

He threw the exercise books at me. And then the oilskin packet. The books hit the bed rail and fell to the floor.

Do I want to remember now what he said? What *I* said? For I needed to speak also. I could not sit there and hear the insults he flung, not just at me, but at him – at Branwell.

I said, weeping and trembling, 'Well, you have read some of it, a little of it – you have seen that *I* am the only one to blame . . .'

He called me names then – words I had never heard before but knew to be bad. Words meant for bad women. I thought too he would strike me. I was certain he would strike me.

Then, *he will kill me*, I thought, as he came near, his hand raised.

He said: '*I could kill you, Lina.* What you've done. What I read . . . If I'd known. If I'd known the half, just the half – you'd not be here today . . .'

'What do you do in my room?' I cried. 'Why are you in my room prying?' I said it, asked it between sobs. But I did not feel indignation, only fear.

'Thinking of you. If you must know!' he shouted. 'Seeing as I could do nowt to help with the bairn, and you were to be sat up all night, I thought – daft that I was – I'll fetch her down one of her poetry books to read . . . Then I bloody come in and *what do I find*?'

'Shout, shout, and you'll wake Christabel –'

'Right then. Right. Where is she? *Where's Christabel?*'

'You're not to punish her,' I cried, 'you're not to punish Christabel!'

'Nay, I'll not. I'll punish you. It's you I'll punish –'

'All right. Just let my Christabel alone –'

'*My* Christabel – aye, you do right to call her that. She's not mine . . . I'll let her alone, aye. But that's not to say I'll love her . . . Cuckoo in the nest –'

'If you tell her, if you tell her –'

'Never fear. I'll not tell.' He moved towards the books as they lay on the floor. I thought he was perhaps about to destroy them. And the oilskin packet. I rushed to reach them first.

He caught me a blow across the face.

'And that's for you – cheapskate . . .'

Oh, I cannot wish to remember that night, that early morning, that I thought would never end . . .

And since then? It has not been easy. If I thought that he was drinking before, I knew nothing. Now he is fast becoming the complete sot. So far, I think all is well with the mill. His drinking does not affect his work. But for how long?

Cards, rum and ale, or brandy. Companions who don't care as long as he pays his debts. (With what is he paying them? All our hard-earned money, I fear . . .)

And the mornings . . . In his room, how many times have I found him, sprawled half across the bed, outside the blankets, sodden in sleep, boots on, coat half-buttoned, trousers unbuttoned because of nature only? He who was once the handsomest of men . . .

He has said that he would not punish Christabel for my sins. But he has removed his love. Or most of it. She cannot fail to notice that once she was his darling, and now is not. Yet she has never said a word. And I could not say . . .

I find it hard to think her existence a mistake. Yet when I look at her, I tremble. Such darkness: would she know happiness if she saw it? Such fierce feelings, such passion, such hunger for love. How can she or will she be happy, ever? When I think now of my own childhood: the lightness of it, the brightness of it. Sutcliffe and I on galloways, racing over Warley Moor. And the early, happy days with James: to have been bold and beautiful and to have lost it all – it is sad . . . Christabel, I think, is bold. She will never be beautiful.

Last night I dreamed of him (you will know soon of whom I speak). It was back in his Luddenden days. I dreamed of that overhanging rock, the black cliff face from which our station was hewn. The moisture on the rock glistened. In the blue-black light, the trees above and around were a lurid green.

How huge it had grown. I was standing before it, beneath it, as it cracked. It groaned and rumbled as it was rent – by what? How monstrous the falling apart of that rock, how I screamed and screamed to wake, as it fell, thundering, shuddering on to me . . .

I did wake. I dreamed I woke. All was silent. Trees lay mangled amongst torn boulders and rocks. I lived still. But beside the shattered rock, was his body. Crushed. Crushed body. Untouched face.

> . . . *Then I must cease to seek the light*
> *Which fires the evening heaven*
> *Since to direct through death's dark night*
> *Some other must be given* . . .

Oh, my bonny love.

PART THREE

Out in the World

11

The day after my mother's death, the day after the fire, the household woke early. Except for Papa.

I had scarcely slept at all. I had been reading, and weeping, most of the night. Now I felt strangely lightheaded, numb – but only, I suspected, for a while. It was a merciful numbness, for I had much to do. Certainly no one else was in charge.

Almost at once (I knew that I must), after an hour or so of disturbed fretful sleep, I hid away all I had learned during the night. But '*Who am I, who am I?*' hammered away in my head. Ugly refrain. I ignored it. I hushed it, smothered it. This cold January morning, I was Christabel Woodward. *I am Christabel Woodward*, I said to myself. I hung onto these words. And what they meant.

Papa, I thought. He must always be 'Papa' now. I *may never again call him 'my father'*.

It was a subdued household that morning. We breakfasted early. There was no sign of Papa. Halliwell seemed in shock. Agnes's eyes were puffy with weeping.

Mama was laid out upstairs in the green room. We expected visitors during the day, wishing to pay their respects to her. There were hothouse flowers to be seen to. Catering for visitors. I took up the reins again at once. Agnes there as my right hand. Halliwell was less help. Wandering about in the downstairs passages like a lost soul.

Just before ten o'clock Benjamin Mason and two men I did not know arrived to see Papa. Their faces were grave.

Benjamin commiserated with us over our sad loss. 'Yesterday were a terrible day,' he said, shaking his head. 'And not done yet . . . Not done.'

I had shown them into the parlour, for I did not know the condition of Papa's snug. One of the men coughed now politely.

'My sister has gone to fetch Papa,' I said. I asked Benjamin:

'Have you news of Kit Ogden? As soon as my duties allow, I want to go down to his cottage. He is all right?'

I felt as if my head would fly from my body, so whirling, so confused was it. I thought: I do not know where to turn – Mama, Papa, Kit, the mill . . . And then everything went black.

'Hold on, little lass,' Benjamin was saying, 'whoa there . . .' They had me laid on the sofa. The hardness of the leather pushed me back into consciousness.

Now Agnes was bending over me. 'Papa is coming directly,' she was telling the men. She rang the bell. 'I don't know where the brandy is. You need brandy, Christabel.'

But I was already upright again and angry with myself for the weakness, when there was so much to be done.

I said calmly, 'Did they get word sent to Uncle Sutcliffe? Was that done? And has Aunt Martha come yet?'

'You did that yesterday, dear,' Agnes said. 'Now come, and try to rest.'

Just then the door opened and Papa stumbled in: unshaven, carelessly dressed, shirt bulging and jacket torn. He did not look at me.

'Mr Woodward, sir,' Benjamin Mason began, as Agnes escorted me out of the room.

Aunt Martha arrived. She had been with us only a few minutes when Papa and the three others came out of the parlour. She went straight up to him.

'Well, James, this is a sad day . . . Lina . . . You've lost a good woman there . . .' She who rarely showed affection caught him in an awkward embrace.

Benjamin and the visitors began to move away.

'There's news,' Papa said. 'I've ill news . . .'

'It'll wait I don't doubt,' Aunt Martha said. She turned to us. 'It's no good for sleeping, isn't bereavement. He'd do best to rest . . . James,' she raised her voice, 'James, there's to be no drinking – nothing drunk, do you hear? You've to stay sober while Caroline's lain there. And at the funeral too . . . Now get sat somewhere quiet –'

We went back into the parlour. Aunt Martha praised what I had done, what Agnes had done – but nevertheless took complete charge. I did not mind. Halliwell watched her without speaking.

But however much she might bustle, the news, the ill news, could not be avoided. She allowed then that Papa had something to say.

222

I could have wished he had not. I wondered as he spoke that he was able to make the words. His speech was as broken as he himself.

'All up then, is it?' said Aunt Martha when he had done. 'All up? James, why ever, why *ever* . . .'

Agnes had begun to cry quietly. I sat still, stunned, beyond weeping. Halliwell put an arm round Agnes.

'Not one pennyworth of insurance.' Aunt Martha sounded incredulous. 'Not *one pennyworth* . . . And after Dad, and all the care he took . . . James, I'm . . .'

Two lapsed policies. One of them due that day last autumn when I had travelled into Halifax with him: he had gone anywhere but the offices of the Yorkshire Globe. The second one a month later. The sums of six thousand four hundred, and four thousand eight hundred pounds. And not one penny to come back . . .

Ah, but if that had been all. There was worse to come, learned slowly and haltingly during that endless morning. (I kept thinking: at least Mama has been spared. In all this sadness, here is one sadness the less.) Over the last few years, and increasingly during the last six months, Papa had run up debts. Gaming debts in the main. As we were to discover later, others knew what we did not – no one would have thought of passing on such information, even out of kindness. Others knew the extent of his debts. By how much the mill was mortgaged . . .

Halliwell's inheritance – unappreciated by him, unwanted as machinery, buildings, goods, but still rightfully his – all gone. Wade House would not remain ours for long. The three of us, Halliwell, Agnes and I, would have nothing but our wits to live on. Or charity.

Two proud houses, the Armstrongs and the Woodwards, both fallen in as many years. And Papa, who had scoffed at 'fond sackless Sutcliffe', had fallen the furthest.

I felt physically sick as I looked at him. His mouth shaking, the saliva running, his hands, drooped between his knees and shaking, his bloodshot eyes filled with maudlin tears. I felt sick, and sad. Sad.

'Spilt milk, all this is,' Aunt Martha said. 'Sitting here'll not help . . .' She turned: 'If you look out, there's your vicar coming up the path.'

I have to remember now Mr Everett's kindness, and our shame. He called often – as much as twice daily during the worst time. And it was not only he: Mrs Everett too offered sympathy, support. Those first weeks, had there been no Aunt Martha, I could have given up all pretence of managing and allowed capable and kind hands to take over. But I could scarcely bear to speak to Mr Everett or his family. I could not bear even to set foot in the Vicarage. I was at once afraid, yet at the same time resentful that anyone other than Francis should live there. If it could have happened without loss of life, I would have wished that it had been the Vicarage and not our mill burnt down.

It was a morning of comings and goings. Soon after Mr Everett left, Uncle Sutcliffe arrived. He looked ill, shivering beneath his large cape, his nose and eyes sore and running. He was much distressed and went straight up to where Mama was laid out. I knew he wished he had been well enough to leave for Luddenden yesterday with Agnes. Now, he was too late.

Aunt Martha did not approve of his coming. 'Folk that are sick'd do best to keep off the railways. What with the nasty hot air in and the cold air out, I don't doubt he's made himself a deal more poorly . . .' She told him forthrightly:

'To bed with you now – we don't want two funerals . . .'

But of course he had to be told the other news. I had to watch his face, and Papa's face, when Aunt Martha revealed to him exactly how the Woodward family stood. Mr Everett had been told an hour before. It was now the third time we had heard it this morning.

The hall clock struck the half hour. Soon it would be the dinner gong. Life went on, in that way, as if nothing had happened.

'This afternoon,' I told Agnes, 'I shall visit Kit.' I thought at first she might want to accompany me. But she said only:

'Our hero. Yes, I think it is good you do that, dear Christabel.'

I could not have eaten any dinner. When Uncle Sutcliffe had been sent to bed and while Papa was receiving a lecture from Aunt Martha, Agnes and I went upstairs to Mama.

So beautiful she looked. Difficult now, to believe in her illness. I could have thought she slept.

Mrs Ogden opened the door to me. Agitated as ever, trying to offer sympathy about Mama, whilst talking at the same time of the fire.

'Take a seat then, Miss Woodward – nay, you'll want to see Kit . . . Mr Rushworth says . . . Kit's heard tell your mam's gone. He's that upset . . . I've to tidy him now – will you take a sup while he's ready?'

He was in bed, lying down. He seemed pale – but the light in the room was poor, so that I could not really tell.

'Your mam,' he said. 'I were that sad, Christabel.'

I touched his bandaged hand, which lay outside the coverlet. The bed was not long enough. I saw bandaged feet sticking out at the end.

'Yes,' I said, 'we are in much trouble.' (I could not tell him about the other. About our disgrace. I could not.) 'But you,' I said, 'who are our hero. How are you, Kit?'

His voice was clear enough, though not so strong as usual:

'Middling, Christabel. I'll mend, never fear. It's time needed. Nowt else. Mr Rushworth told mam yesternight –'

'You're not in too much pain? I wasn't certain what to bring with me. I could arrange something from the kitchens when I return . . .'

'There've been many folk come. You're the most – the one I'd wish to see.'

'Kit,' I said, 'if you're expecting Papa to call –'

'Mam did . . . She said to me, "Your master'll be down here to thank you." But that were afore she heard of your mam.'

'He *is* too shocked. He would otherwise, I know. You are our hero, you see . . . And now you must tell me what happened. If you are strong enough . . .'

Sitting at his bedside, I listened to his tale:

'. . . and when I'd got t'bairns onto slates, every bairn wanted to be on t'rope, but I checked them and said I'd let them down as nicely as I could. I showed them how they'd to wrap their aprons round t'rope. It were only loose wool – I don't ken how ever it held . . . When I'd done, t'room were all in a blaze beneath me and I expected *I* should go. I did, indeed.'

'But weren't you very afraid?'

'Aye, I yielded like, after t'bairns was gone. I wondered if t'rope would carry me. I remember resting a moment on t'easing part that takes water off t'roof . . . But then I thought I'd give myself up to God's mercy – and live or die as He pleased . . . I remember I got on to t'rope . . . When I lit on t'ground I thought my back were broke . . . Then I heard someone say, "Take him to his mam" –'

'And here you are . . . Kit, you saved so many lives. Tell me that *you* are all right –'

'My feet and hands, they're burned, and my back's poorly. But I'm not hurt otherways . . .'

225

'Can I come to see you again?'

He smiled. 'It'll be some days yet, Mr Rushworth says, afore I can move. So, if . . . if it's an offer, like.'

I saw that he was embarrassed. But pleased too. Sitting there, I remembered everything – Mama's kindness, and Kit's long stay with us, teaching him to read. Kit trying to save Josh . . . the baby lamb I was not allowed. Our friendship, that had not endured.

'I wish I could ask you up to Wade House, to get well there.'

But I saw I had embarrassed him again:

'There's no call . . . and what I did, any road, it were only what any man . . . I'm not after special thanks –'

The silence was awkward. I felt that I had tried to dispense charity – which indeed I had. I said, at the risk of making things worse:

'I can come and read to you. Your hands – and your back – holding a book just now . . . I expect it is difficult.'

'You'll not have time –'

'I have. I have too much time . . . Oh, Kit,' I burst out, 'we are in such trouble –'

'I don't wonder,' he said readily. 'If I'd lost *my* mam. And then there's t'mill. What with t'mill . . .'

'Yes,' I said. 'Yes, yes.'

And it all came flooding into my mind. All of yesterday. The troubled sleepless night. All that I had read. *My mother's story.* Because I could not tell Kit, and because I knew that I might at any moment break into noisy tears, I left him very soon after.

But first I promised to come and read . . .

While I had been at Kit's, Septimus Whitaker had called. Disliking him as I did, I was glad to have missed him. According to Aunt Martha, he had come to offer his condolences. She had thought that right and proper, whilst being thankful Uncle Sutcliffe was safely out of the way, since he had managed, in all the painful transactions over Horsfield Mill and Buckley House, never to meet Septimus.

We all went early to bed. Tomorrow we were to have a meeting to discuss our future. It would be presided over by Aunt Martha. Uncle Sutcliffe if well enough would attend. Papa who had spent the rest of the day in his snug, was told off to come also.

Alone in my room, I gave way completely to misery. All the

strength I had, artificially, drawn to myself, disappeared in a trice. I lay on the bed, too weak to weep.

Who am I? The ceaseless refrain. Over and over. *Who am I?* It was as if I had been dealt a blow. Had been stunned. But now as I came back to life, I could feel the blow still. That hammering. Thump. Thump.

Who was I? The landscape of my childhood: all the figures in it had changed places. Taken on grotesque shapes. Nothing was still. Nothing, nobody, as before.

Was I Christabel Woodward? Or Christabel Brontë? I knew I was neither . . . Although before the world I would wear the same face, talk in the same voice, *seem* the person I had always been – it would not be so.

And what was I meant to feel towards my *real* father? A person I could only know through what Mama had written, and what I might read or discover myself – later, perhaps years later. And, to read is not to know . . . Was I to mourn him now, some fifteen years after his death – he who never knew his importance to me? He had not loved me, had not known of me at all. He had not loved me as Papa did. I had never been, or was likely to have been, his bonny darling . . .

And what to think of, what to feel towards my lovely Mama, who by her carelessness – an unlocked box – had robbed me of Papa's love?

My God, my God – I scarcely knew where to turn for sorrow, and guilt and anger . . .

Had she truly meant me to read what she had written? I thought so. Her deathbed wish: it must have come from her deep self. But did she know that having read her story, I would love her more not less? Would understand Papa more. And my real father, just a little. *And mourn them all three . . .*

I found strength again, from within myself. Whose it was, from whom I inherited it, I do not know. From Mama? It was hardly my father's, hardly Branwell's. In this respect I could not be said to take after him at all. From the Brontë *family* then? The truth is that I did not crack up. I did not go under. I survived. Damaged – *ah yes*. But not broken.

As I lay and thought of my confused heritage, the refrain changed. Not '*Who am I, who am I?*' but instead, the clanging of St John Baptist's bells. Just as in childhood, ringing the changes:

'Daughter of the northern fields, daughter of the northern fields . . .'

'Of course whoever wishes can live with me,' Aunt Martha said. 'Not that I've the place, mind you . . .'

It was too early really to make decisions. Yet it seemed right and helpful and somehow comforting to sit there with Aunt Martha, planning a future. To feel an interest in that future was more difficult.

There were the three of us and Aunt Martha. And Uncle Sutcliffe, pale and sneezing, but out of bed. There was no sign of Papa. Agnes looked tearful, Halliwell worried and a little sullen. There had been as yet no glimpse of the Halliwell who had saved papers from the fire . . .

'It's soldiering he wants, does Halliwell,' Aunt Martha was saying. 'It's never been other. There's no sense in trying to get him mill work – though I've friends that'd be pleased to help. It'd best be army. Only we can't have him going for a common soldier . . .'

As he watched his dream begin slowly to come true, Halliwell's face changed. Aunt Martha talked on. She would buy him a commission, she said. First they would take advice then she would use her savings to buy him into a good regiment. What was the use of brass if it wouldn't do family a favour?

Did Uncle Sutcliffe feel, I wondered, the humiliation of not being able to help, of having himself no savings at all? It was difficult to tell. Perhaps because of his sickness, he was as subdued as if in Aunt Flora's presence.

But he did make an offer. And it must have been his own, for he had had no time to be in touch with Aunt Flora. He invited Agnes and me to come and live with them. He said it was what Mama would have wanted. He tried, I think, to make it sound as if it was what they, he and Aunt Flora, wanted also. I do not think he succeeded. I could not imagine Aunt Flora wishing to live in the same house as me. And certainly I would not wish to share a home with her – fond as I was of Uncle Sutcliffe.

I refused. Politely. Gratefully. Beside me, Agnes wept.

'Don't you go to your uncle's then, Agnes?' Aunt Martha asked.

Agnes shook her head. She said she did not know what she wanted – unless it was for Mama to come back. And she continued to weep silently.

In the end, it was only Halliwell's future settled upon.

And possibly, Papa's. Aunt Martha thought he should live with her:

'As for James, he'd do as well to come where I can keep my eye on him.'

I did not write to Polly. I told her nothing. Not even of Mama's death. I did not want to upset her, only days before her runaway marriage. And as for the rest, I could not imagine writing that in a letter . . .

We were all at Wade House still. It would be a little while yet before we had to leave, although the terrible machinery of bankruptcy had been already set in motion. Uncle Sutcliffe who could not have borne to see it had already returned to Bath, hoping still to persuade Agnes to join them. My refusal, I think he knew to be definite, irrevocable.

Papa was morose. Drinking still (where did he find the money?), and not inclined to speak to any of us. At the funeral, he had wept noisily, drinking himself into a stupor afterwards.

I kept thinking that day of my mother's exercise books. Since Papa knew of their existence, indeed had read them, must he not wonder where they were?

It was to them, I think, that he alluded, a few days after the funeral. I had been through Mama's effects but had not told him I was doing so. He had not been fit to tell. Agnes and I together had decided what must be done with everything.

But coming upon me in the corridor outside his room, he said, as one speaking through a fog:

'Her things, your mother's things. Bit and pieces . . . They've been seen to? You've burnt what you had to, eh?'

The question was left hanging. I answered briefly, giving nothing away, dreading that he might ask directly for the books. I had good care of them. I would not leave them where they might be found . . .

He shambled away. I would have liked to go after him, but what to say? The days of talking together were long since gone. (And, too, the days of being loved.)

Debts, drink, disgrace – oh, terrible, unholy trio. What was to become of us all?

Kit was making a slow recovery, his burns healing quicker than the damage to his back. For as long as he was confined to bed I went up to the cottage several days a week, to read to him. At first I read newspapers and journals. Then I brought him up *The Tenant of Wildfell Hall* and *Wuthering Heights*. They took up all the time I remained in Luddenden before leaving for Halifax.

I was surprised I could read from those books without distress – disturbed as I was these days by anything which reminded me of my secret.

I resisted the temptation, very great, to tell Kit. Often there were days when I wished to tell, not someone, but anyone. Yet I knew that when it came to it, I would not. Papa and I must share the secret. (He did not know that I knew. Although he might guess. But that we should speak of it one to the other – no, that must never be . . .)

And then one afternoon, with only two more chapters to come of *Wuthering Heights*, we had reached the part of the story where Catherine Heathcliff and Hareton Earnshaw fall in love.

I read out:

'. . . but both their minds tending to the same point – one loving and desiring to esteem, and the other loving and desiring to be esteemed – they contrived in the end to reach it.

'You see, Mr Lockwood, it was easy enough to win Mrs Heathcliff's heart. But now, I'm glad you did not try. The crown of all my wishes will be the union of those two. I shall envy no one on their wedding-day: there won't be a happier woman than myself in England!'

I closed the book and stood up:

'And now, Kit dear, I must go. But before that . . . A drink – can I get you something?'

Mrs Ogden was out and would not be back for another hour.

'Aye. Tea. There'll be tea on t'side . . . But nay, Christabel, I want for nowt –'

I looked at him. He was staring at me intently. His face was flushed.

Then, 'Don't go,' he said. 'Don't go – Christabel, there's summat I want to say –'

'All right. What, Kit dear?'

I saw he was embarrassed. I sat down again. I hoped it would not be gratitude – awkward gratitude for what I had been doing for him.

He spoke. They came, the words, all in a rush. I could not at first believe what I heard.

'. . . and I don't ken how I dare – you've to believe me – I've thought long on it these weeks, and I'd a mind to . . . I couldn't abide how it's to be for you – when you were . . .'

Kit, offering me his hand in marriage. *Kit Ogden*, wanting to marry me . . .

'Oh, Kit,' I said. I could think of nothing better to say. 'Oh, Kit . . .'

'You see, I'd take care of you. And t'sad things – they'd not happen . . .'

And there as I sat, stupefied, he outlined how it would be, what he would do.

'I want to care for you,' he said. 'I ken that it's Kit Ogden and Miss Woodward from t'mill – I ken that. But –'

I had never heard him say so much. I let him talk on, for I could say nothing. I listened to his plans for bettering himself, for working harder at night school . . . all his ideas for making life all right for me again . . .

Silence. I searched for words.

'I've presumed,' he said, 'I ken that. I've presumed. It were just like – we've always been contented together. And so, I reckoned . . . It'd maybe be me that'd take care of you – after t'sad things . . .'

'The sad things,' I said gently, 'I hope so much *they're* over –'

He seemed puzzled, then, taken aback, he stammered: 'But – but . . .'

'But what, Kit?'

'It seems like they've not begun. From what I heard tell –'

'Heard tell. Heard *what*, Kit?'

'Like I heard tell . . .' He was near to tears (and so was I, so was I). 'A chap that were here two nights since – he said as how it were all up with you – t'mill and t'house. That you weren't insured –'

'Yes, that's right,' I said. 'I didn't tell you, Kit. But yes, that's right.'

'. . . and that it's t'workhouse mebbe – that there's debts so bad . . . You'll have nowt – for didn't Mr Armstrong lose all – and that you'd to go out to *work* mebbe, or . . .' He was growing ever more confused and upset. He did not seem to know what to do with himself. Bandaged hands at the end of long arms – he waved them.

'But Kit dear,' I knew I said it badly. 'Kit, it *is* sad, yes, but not so very. Not so very. It is not a world of workhouses and the

231

suchlike. Uncle Sutcliffe has a comfortable home now and has offered it to me. Then Aunt Martha is well enough situated. And too, I can work at something congenial I am certain. It is not as if . . .'

His distress was terrible now.

'I presumed,' he said, over and over. 'I presumed. It were only – I'd this notion. I thought of you . . . that'd nowhere to lay your head. I was heart sore for how you'd be. And now . . . now you'll think, How'd he dare, how ever could Kit Ogden think he were a *husband* for me? I see now, I were daft. If I worked seventy year I'd not be good enough. Never. It were just . . . There's no one I'd rather be all the days of my life with. So when I thought . . . I had it wrong, I ken. But I'd have taken care – I would.'

'I know,' I said, 'I know, Kit.'

How to thank him? I could not. There was no way to thank him. No way to comfort. I leaned forward, put my arms about him – carefully, gently, avoiding his poor back, his hands, I laid my face against his. So gently. It was brother to sister.

'Thank you,' I said. 'You are good, so good. You are a good man, Kit.'

Polly's letter was written six days into her honeymoon. It was ecstatic. There never had been, never would be anyone like William . . . And to have waited so long only made this happiness all the greater. If it had not been for her family . . .

'Oh but, marriage is quite the thing, dearest!'

I was glad I had told her nothing.

Polly and Kit were not the only people with marriage on their minds.

'Christabel dear,' Agnes said, coming into the parlour, sitting down beside me, placing her hand on mine, 'Christabel, I am to marry Septimus Whitaker.'

I jumped, as if her hand had been red hot.

'But you cannot!' I cried. 'Agnes, you *cannot*!'

'I can if I wish,' she said.

'But you cannot wish. How can *anyone* wish to marry Septimus? And you of all persons . . . Have you gone mad?'

'I shall marry him,' she said quietly.

'But why Septimus? When you might have anyone? And oh, Agnes, you were used to laugh at him – and at the very idea . . . It was you laughed loudest of all –'

'I am not laughing now.'

'Nor am I,' I cried, 'nor am I – to see you do something so foolish . . . And the *children*, Septimus has grown children. A son almost as old as yourself. You cannot –'

Her manner was very determined. She said, 'He has asked me already five times. This afternoon I said Yes . . . You see, he will protect me, Christabel.'

'But we can do that. *We* can protect you. Aunt Martha and I, and Halliwell. What are you speaking of? And besides, you are so young. Seventeen, Agnes. And he is what – forty-two at least? Oh, but you *must* not.'

She had begun to weep now. She wept so often these days.

'It is what I have set my mind to do. No one shall stop me . . . *You* think I must live in Halifax with Aunt Martha or in Bath with –'

'In Bath, Agnes, you would meet oh, so many people. You would have such a choice. The men would fight amongst themselves to propose –'

'It is not like that. I know it is not. I have no dowry, a drunken father and – I am *afraid*. I am all the time afraid. And Septimus is so very good to me – he is not like you think he is. Not at all . . .'

'That does not make him the right husband for you –'

'Do not keep on at me so! I thought you were my friend. When you hear,' she was weeping so much now that it was difficult to make out the words, 'when you hear that he is – that I have no dowry, but *he* is to give *us* money. The family. He has so much, and we may have what we like – what we need. Halliwell, you, Papa – we have only to ask . . .'

'You really think we would . . . You are not to do this for us, Agnes. This terrible thing –'

'But it is not – not terrible. It is what I want. What I have determined on.'

'We shall see,' I said. 'We shall see.' And then I threw my arms about her. I said that for a prospective bride she did not seem very happy.

'I want Mama back,' she sobbed. 'If you knew how I wanted Mama back . . .'

The next day was Saturday. I went up to Buckley House in the afternoon. Horsfield Mill was silent and I expected to find Septimus at home.

I waited in the parlour while he was fetched. His sister, Mrs Green, the talkative Mrs Green, I had especially dreaded she might be home. But there was no sign of any of his family.

He came in. Small, already inclined to the portly. Receding hair. Rushing up to greet me. Taking my hand:

'If it's not the wrong Miss Woodward . . . I thought it was your sister come up. But any road, one or t'other, you're both welcome. Agnes'll have told you – what's to be . . .'

He was standing. I had of course not risen when he came in. I said, and I had not smiled at all:

'*She*, Agnes, is the wrong Miss Woodward too. Quite wrong . . . You've no business with her. None at all. And I've come to say –'

But I had scarcely thought what I would say, only that I must say it.

'What's this, eh? What's this?' he began.

'You are *not to marry her* –'

'Hey, there now, lass – what's up? Not wed – what's this to do with you?'

'Papa must stop you –'

'Are you *daft*?'

'He didn't want it before. He won't want it now –'

Septimus, astonished, angry, said:

'He'll not say nay, won't James Woodward. Unless I'm much mistaken. There'll be offers made . . . He's in no position these days to be telling Septimus Whitaker what's what.'

He strutted angrily to the door:

'And now, if you've nowt else to say – or even if you have – I'll bid you good day.'

Anger rose, choking my throat. I said:

'You're not to *buy* Agnes, or me, or *any* of our family.'

'I've had enough,' he said. 'Get out of my house.'

'It makes me sick,' I said, 'to see a disgusting person like you living here in my uncle's house. With your horrid monkey's face and your fat stomach –'

'You're deranged,' he said. 'Get out.'

Perhaps I was a little mad. Certainly when I had started I could not stop. I piled insult upon insult. And all the while I was weeping inside that Agnes should be so wasted.

He grabbed hold of me. I did not struggle. I thought at first he would do me an injury. He pulled me to the door, his hand firm on the sleeve of my black dress.

'I'm glad,' he was saying, 'my lad's nowhere about to hear you. A fine example from an aunt – for that's what you'll be whether you care or not . . .' Then beside the door, before opening it:

'Now get out,' he said, 'and don't let me see you this way again. I want nowt to do with you. Ever.'

I had done no good. Only made mischief. The match went ahead. Papa, when he heard that Agnes wished for it, shrugged his shoulders.

'If that's what she wants – if she wants him.'

Agnes forgave me. She said that I had done it out of love for her – but that Septimus was still very angry with me. She thought it unlikely he would ever forgive me . . .

A date had been fixed for the bankruptcy hearing. Wade House was to be sold. Papa and I went to live with Aunt Martha and Agnes lodged with the Howgates, so that she might be near Septimus. Halliwell, who had enlisted in the Green Howards, was presently at York.

The wedding was to be in July. Because we were in mourning still, it would be a very simple affair. The Whitaker son, Joseph, and the two little daughters had been very kind to her, Agnes said. And their aunt, Mrs Green, was overjoyed at her release.

I told Polly. Of Mama, and the fire and the bankruptcy. But of course not the other . . . Nothing about my new father.

She was distraught for me. Writing me several letters a week until she was certain I was over the worst. And then, a few weeks before Agnes's wedding, I went to stay with her. She was five months' pregnant. Excited. Happy.

'Yesterday I felt the babe move . . . Oh we are such blessed persons, William and I.'

But she continued to worry about me. 'Too much bad has happened, dearest. Are you never to be happy?'

I told her that I had thought of going out to work, since I could not remain idle at Aunt Martha's, and without money. I had thought, I said, of doing governess work.

'You see, I studied so hard with Miss Milner. And my piano is quite good. And I have Latin, if that is needed. And drawing –'

'Oh, but dearest,' she said, 'you cannot do that.'

'Why ever not?'

'You will be quite miserable. Think only of the lives we led *our* governesses.'

It might not be so very bad, I told her.

Then we laughed together – reminiscing about childhood.

'And do you remember,' she was saying, 'our Miss Finch, who drank hollands and could not wake in the mornings?'

Yes, yes. Indeed I did. But I was remembering Kit too. For I had not told her of his proposal. I thought of it often.

Memories of Kit. So many. Myself, snatched from the jaws of death. 'I mean always to be good,' I had told him. And then: 'I do not expect ever to be ill again.'

I could have been Mrs Ogden. Starting again somewhere else. Starting all over again, he had suggested. A new life. And then how he would better and better and better himself again. Even as to speech . . . Kit, who would learn to talk like a gentleman. Who would work all day and all night if needs be, to make a fit life for me – and for our children.

It had been all about marriage . . .

Of course I could not have married Kit. But what sort of terror sent me running from that salvation? It was enough to have read what my mother had to say, it was enough *to think of what had already happened to me*, to know that marriage was not for me. And I was not for marriage.

12

'*You are very small.*'

There it was yet again. Those words I had come to dread.

'For a governess, you are very small,' Mrs Adamson was saying. 'You will perceive my eldest daughter is already approaching her mother in height. And her sister, in another year or so, if she continues at the same rate . . . How will you keep authority, Miss Woodward, when even little Elinor looks down on you?'

I thought then: *She* shan't tell me how I shall manage. I had already decided that they seemed dear little girls. I did not anticipate trouble with them.

'I expect, you see, to be friends with them. To be their friend, ma'am.'

I remembered the respect due to her. (That I, Christabel Woodward, legally daughter of James Woodward of Luddenden, should have come to this – to be saying 'ma'am' . . .)

Mrs Adamson raised her eyebrows. A tinkle of laughter. A cheap bell, it sounded like a cheap bell.

'Their friend!' she exclaimed. 'Why should they wish for your friendship, Miss Woodward? You are to be their governess.' Her lips came tightly together. 'I have not been at all the trouble of advertising, interviewing and engaging, to hear talk of *friendship*. My daughters need discipline, Miss Woodward.'

She was tall and thin and patrician. She had a manner not at all like that of people I had known. It was not the manner of mill owners and their families, or of industrialists. But neither was it the manner of dear Mrs Liddington, whose family was certainly as old as the Adamson's.

I suspected I was about to dislike her – even though I had brought with me a fund of good will. What had it not cost me, proud child, now proud young woman, to make myself subservient, to change from one who gave orders, to one who carried them out?

The trouble was that I had been broken into employment gently. Too gently. This new post with the Adamson family was my second. In my first I had been, if not happy – since it was difficult to be that after the shattering of our Luddenden world – at least not made more unhappy by my employers, or their offspring.

It was surprisingly, Mr Everett, the Luddenden vicar, I had to thank for that first position. I am not sure how in the first place he knew of my decision, unless it was that Kit – I thought it might be Kit who had spoken to him of my plans. Dear Kit . . . But I think most likely it was Agnes (without Septimus. The coldness there would never melt. Septimus would not be concerned with my well-being).

Mr Everett wrote asking to call on me, when next in Halifax. He did not say why. When he came it was to bring me an introduction to a clerical family, a rural dean in Derbyshire who required a governess for a girl and boy of eight and six. Three other children were in the nursery.

As I agreed to follow up the introduction – yes, I would write immediately – I thought what a good man Mr Everett was, and how caring. I had always been awkward, almost rude to him – so full of terror and regrets and memories had I been, living opposite the Vicarage. I had spurned his wife's offers of friendship, ignored his children. Yet after our disaster, no one could have been kinder.

About the Talbots and my year there as a governess, there is little to say – unless it is that both the parents were kindness itself, and the two children I had care of, sweet and loving. I ate with the family, I went on every outing – and they were a family who took to the countryside at the slightest excuse, whenever Mr Talbot's duties allowed. A large family, who seemed always to have visiting members, or old friends staying. And I was always made one of the party. The pleasant deanery hummed. There were more smiles than tears. They knew my background, the whole history. They enquired regularly after Papa, never expressing disapproval, only sorrow that anyone should have come to such a pass. At Christmas time, having nowhere particular to go, I stayed with them. They made a great fuss of me – the more so when they discovered I was to come of age on Christmas Eve.

Yes, I had gifts to remember them by, both that Christmas and later. Also, there, I met young men, plenty of them, almost all young curates. If I had been interested or ready for romance, even a mild flirtation, it would have been approved of. I truly believe that. They were pleasant enough, these curates – and

several of them downright handsome and winning. And certainly
it was not every (any?) governess who was encouraged to meet
and make more of such acquaintances: to come down into the
drawing-room, to meet at the dinner table, as company on picnics
or outings . . . Who knows but I might not have met and loved
a William of my own (and not all of these curates were poor –
two at least were sons of wealthy men), even married one – *if I
had wished for marriage*.

But ah God, how to describe the terror when one of these
young men – the more handsome, the more charming, the worse
it was – when one of them would lean forward in his chair, tea
cup in hand, looking at me not as a fellow guest, but suddenly,
openly, obviously . . .

One tea party in February, just after Agnes's son was born,
Mrs Talbot told the company:

'Miss Woodward became an aunt yesterday for the first time.'

And then Mr Grier, easily the most suave and dandified,
and physically beautiful of the young clergymen, leaning towards
me:

'You did not mention an older sister, Miss Woodward.'

'No, she is younger. It is that – Agnes married young. At
seventeen.'

'So how can it be, that she was *preferred* above you? And do
you like this gentleman, your brother-in-law?'

'Not at all.' I spoke frankly. 'And I was forced to tell him so,
in plain terms. There is a great deal about him to dislike.' My
tone became more spirited: 'We are scarcely on speaking terms,
I am afraid. Although of course I hope and wish to visit my
sister . . .'

'What a little firebrand!' he exclaimed. 'If you had seen your
eyes flashing when you announced, "I have told him so" –'

Well, that was all right. It was pleasant, friendly interest. But
what was this? Leaning forward again now, looking into my eyes,
his own eyes sparkling:

'Tell me, for I think we should change the subject, are you
accustomed to receive Valentines?'

Such a harmless, foolish, lighthearted question, but I – who
had indeed never received a Valentine (from whom would I,
unless Kit?) – could not see it as that. And *it was not that*. He
was by his gaze, his stance, his tone of voice, addressing my heart
– however much in passing. And perhaps my body too. But that
I did not even dare to contemplate.

I shrank away. Feeling myself grow smaller – and more and more afraid. How can I describe the terror: that he might for a second even, touch me, heart *or* body . . .

That conversation was on the tenth of February. On the fourteenth I received no less than five Valentines – exactly the number of young clergymen who had been taking tea that day. The postmarks were thoroughly distributed around Derbyshire. I basked in a glow of friendship. One Valentine would perhaps have frightened – I could have guessed its sender and remembered my moment of fear. But five . . .

Oh happy home with the Talbots. I was queen of the school-room – teaching those children my way, the way I would wish to have been taught. I loved my lessons. They loved the lessons I taught. I took care not to imagine the ending of it all. Perhaps, no longer noticed by curates, I would grow happily grey in their employ.

And then suddenly it was all over. In the autumn we learned that in the New Year, the Dean would have an appointment in Tasmania, in Hobart.

Was there ever any question that I should accompany them? I do not think so. From the outset it was, 'How we shall miss you, how dear little Tom and Minnie . . .' Nor did I even imagine myself joining them. Those few family I still possessed, I would not like to have left them behind. And Polly – as for Polly . . .

I spent that next Christmas with her. The Talbots had sailed at the beginning of December after fond and tearful farewells, and a further showering of gifts. And the curates? It was goodbye to all of them. And no one especially singled out – Mr Grier had understood or sensed my rebuff. I was ashamed of that rebuff and did not want to think about it.

Polly was seven months into her second pregnancy. We were happy to be together. Little Louisa, over a year now, was just beginning to walk. She walked for me. William smiled, looking with love on both of them. No, on all three of us – including me in the smile of pride. I was Louisa's godmother. I was family.

She expected Henry to visit them soon. Edmund had written once, wishing her well, but professing himself too busy ever to call on her. From her mother, she had had letters, and gifts for Louisa, but Mrs Liddington would not defy the ban on visiting Polly, or indeed meet her at all. She had always been one who obeyed her husband in everything. Polly knew, from the letters, that her mother longed to see her first grandchild. And she longed to show Louisa. But that sadness was the only shadow to fall across the sun-filled life of William and Polly and baby Louisa.

Money was still short of course. It could not be anything else, on a curate's pay. Polly said:

'But you know, dearest, William will not always be a curate. He is certain of a living, soon. I think perhaps next year . . . And Papa, if he wished, is not without influence. But he would not think of it. His pride, you see. And our pride. We could never ask for such help.'

'Would you accept it?'

'Oh but *yes*, dearest. I was never a proud person. We are not foolishly proud people . . .'

But one slight shadow to fall over that Christmas was dread – dread of my new position as governess.

At first in the autumn it had seemed that the Talbots would have friends or acquaintances who might need a governess. The weeks passed. I had no luck. The time of their departure drew nearer and nearer – I did not like to press them – but no one at all had been found. Without saying any more to them, I placed an advertisement myself in the *Yorkshire Post*, with the hope at least of ending up back in Yorkshire.

I had one answer. A Mrs Adamson, of Topham Abbey in the West Riding. She needed, immediately after Christmas, a governess to take charge of three little girls. I could offer myself with glowing recommendations from the Talbots. Within days, I was engaged, for a salary of sixty pounds a year.

Now I was here. And she complained that I was too small. What had she expected? I had not enclosed a *carte de visite*. Indeed I did not possess one, or any photograph of myself at all. But it appeared now, as I stood before her in the vast Abbey drawing-room, that I was *too small*. And worse than that, I had spoken of being 'friends' with her children.

She was quizzing me again:

'You have told me little of your *family*, Miss Woodward. Your previous employers speak of "sound background, and Christian principles" – all the usual manner of speaking of the clergy – but I think I have been at fault in not asking more about them. Who is in your family?'

'My mother is dead. I have an aunt in Halifax, and my father –'

She interrupted me:

'I trust you will not wish to be visiting them every second month or so.' She stared at me. 'Yes. And who else?'

'A brother, ma'am, who is an ensign in the Green Howards. And a sister – married to a mill owner –'

'I thought perhaps I detected a slight *provincial* accent. Not what I would wish for the girls . . . However, while they are still young . . . There is no *sickness* in the family, I trust?'

I thought of saying (oh, Papa, forgive me), 'My father is a drunken sot.'

'No, ma'am,' I said.

'Very well then – you may stay.' (But I had thought myself engaged. Her letter had seemed to say so. And I had brought with me all my belongings, and my good will – which I saw I would need.) I bit my lip, the first of many times.

'I have my doubts about you, but you shall stay for the time being.'

How cold she was – I wonder I had not felt it emanating from her writing paper, with its engraving of Topham Abbey. But the Talbots and I had found it only romantic. A house built on the ruins of an abbey! And also it was a part of Yorkshire I knew from schooldays, and from Polly. We consulted the map. Liddington Hall was only some thirty miles away, on the other side of Harrogate. We would be near picturesque Knaresborough.

Certainly Mrs Adamson sounded as warm then, as welcoming, as she ever would, with her talk of a united family, and children in need of a restraining hand. Allurements were held out. I would accompany them on all outings, have adequate free time, and a just amount of freedom. There would be some small household duties, but nothing beyond a healthy young woman's capability. I thought afterwards that she wanted an acceptance so as to be over with the bother of sifting. My credentials after all were so glowing.

I left Halifax on a freezing January morning. Oh, the intense cold of that dawn start. Aunt Martha's robust farewell. Going in to say goodbye to Papa.

He lay very still, snoring heavily. Last night I had heard him stumbling up the stairs. Aunt Martha said:

'He'd brass from somewhere. He has ways. There are always those'll stand him a wet at the Talbot or the Old Cock – for old times' sake . . .'

Looking at him – I did not lean down and kiss him – a feeling came over me, a feeling of anger with my lovely dead mother. Why could she not have *kept* her secret? No pen to paper. No carelessness. A united family. I thought callously: Ah, Mama, was not one person's suffering enough – your own (and my father's, my real father's) – that you must make it three persons?

'Come along, child,' Aunt Martha said. 'The train – it'll not wait –'

Guessing perhaps what was in my mind, she said as we left for the station: 'There's no halting a grown man. If he's a mind to drink himself into the sod, there's none of us can do anything . . .' And then she sighed. 'Where's the sense of it all, child, where's the sense of it?'

The carriage was to meet me at Harrogate station. But before that I had two changes of train. The journey was cold. Although there was no snow, I smelled it in the air. The fields were iced over and there was little to see. Mist covered the landscape as we approached Harrogate.

The Adamson carriage rattled along the icy road. I shivered with cold and fatigue, and hunger. The light was poor, and the sight of Topham Abbey took me by surprise. We went through a very wide, high, iron gateway, along a carriage road far smoother than the road outside, stretches of lawn either side, studded with trees – I saw an oak, a bare-branched chestnut. A grove of poplars.

And the Abbey. A large country house of the late seventeenth century, built on the ruins of a Cistercian abbey. Only a tower at one side remained of the original fourteenth-century building. It was all far, far bigger than I had thought. And far more forbidding.

I remembered the warmth of the September day when I had arrived at the Talbots'. Even more, I remembered the warmth of their welcome.

A footman answered the door. A servant was sent for, to show me to my room, which was right beside the schoolroom. I was not offered any food, neither did anyone enquire if I had eaten.

My room was very small. It led off the schoolroom almost as an afterthought. If I was to sit anywhere and read or sew (I hoped they would not expect me to sew), then it could scarcely be in the privacy of my bedroom. There was barely space for the bed, a small chest of drawers and a washstand. There was no looking glass.

The servant who brought me up was not unfriendly. Very plump, she moved as if her feet hurt. She said:

'You've to call me Annie and I've to call you Miss. And that's all there is to it . . .' She puffed and blew at the head of the stairs before opening the schoolroom door.

As I stood in my room, taking off my cloak, my bonnet, my gloves, rubbing my frozen fingers, she said:

'When you've your things laid out, I've to take you to t'mistress.' But then as she stood waiting, the schoolroom door opened.

'It's the childer,' she said.

There they stood, four girls. Three of them holding hands, whilst the youngest, a baby only, clutched the nurse's hand.

'They have been good today,' the nurse said. 'Here's Miss Susan, and Miss Elinor, and Miss Harriet – say how do you do, little lasses.'

All three bowed and simpered and gave me sweet little smiles, whilst still holding hands.

'And here's Baby.' Baby tried to break away to run towards me, but the nurse – her name was Lily – pulled her back sharply. Baby hid her face then in Lily's apron.

'What do they call her?' I asked.

'Oh, Baby's given name is Georgiana.'

The eldest girl spoke up. 'We call her Georgie. Georgie Porgie –'

'Pudding and pie,' I said.

'Yes, she's remarkably fat. Too plump, Mama says –'

'That's enough, girls,' Lily said. And then to me . . . 'Well, Miss, I believe you're to go downstairs, to the mistress.'

A short greeting first, then Mrs Adamson looked me up and down without speaking. I tried to keep calm. To will my rumbling stomach to be silent. I felt I should sway soon with hunger.

'*You are very small,*' she began . . .

Susan, Elinor, Harriet. Whatever could have led me to think them dear little girls? Those first smiles concealed – what? They smiled I think only out of curiosity, believing that by such quiet behaviour on their part I would be led to reveal myself a little.

At the Talbots' I had been spoilt, receiving in every way so much more than I deserved. Now I told myself that perhaps I deserved this? But who could deserve Susan, Elinor and Harriet?

Oh, Christabel, all that long line of governesses you argued with, tormented . . . Their ghosts rise, righteously, to haunt me and taunt me. Even the fey Miss Dutton was there.

Susan was just the age when I had plagued Miss Dutton. A tall fair-haired child of ten and a half, she resembled a gentle version of Mrs Adamson. I would have thought her an angel if . . . but she disabused me very soon. And yet she wore a smile far more often than her mother. When I picture Susan now it is with a smile on her face. She smiled even when asleep, managing thus to look even more angelic.

She appeared in my bedroom that first afternoon, immediately after I had come back upstairs again. I was not to take charge of the girls until the morning. But in the early evening I was to be with them in the schoolroom, to make their acquaintance for an hour or so.

She came and stood in the doorway. Elinor and Harriet could be glimpsed standing just behind, in the schoolroom.

'Are you a midget?' she asked. Her hands were clasped in front of her, and she was smiling sweetly.

'I beg your pardon – what is that, Susan?' I had opened my big trunk and was lifting out an armful of plain dresses.

'Are you *deaf* also?'

'No, I am not deaf, Susan. But I prefer not to hear when someone is rude to me.'

'It is a very polite question, Miss Woodward. I only wish to know. I am up to the half of your head, yet I am only ten and a half years old. So I think that probably you are a *midget*. Am I not right?'

I was too taken aback, too cold and tired and unhappy, to make an issue of it.

'No, you are not right. And now, perhaps, if you are to stay in here with me, you could make yourself useful, and take this dozen of handkerchiefs to that drawer – over there . . .'

Her smile increased. 'You are the governess, Miss Woodward, and so a sort of *servant*. The servants here work for us, do things for us. We do not do things for them –'

I said sharply, 'If we are to be living together, Susan, if I am to be your governess – and after all your Mama has engaged me – if I am to be your governess then we shall have to find a better way for you to act towards me –'

At that moment, a piercing shriek from behind. And then as I turned round, a thud. Little Harriet lay on the floor while Elinor stood over her.

Elinor was lanky, and tall for her age. She would soon outstrip her sister. She had dull brown hair and a beaky nose. Harriet was more rounded, with large brown eyes and a small tight mouth. She smiled too.

But neither of them was smiling now. Elinor, kneeling beside Harriet, held her arm fast. She was shaking her, while Harriet bawled.

I hurried over:

'Stop that at once. What do you mean by – *Leave your little sister!*'

Useless. They took no notice at all.

I was forced to separate them physically, both of them kicking and struggling – as much against me as each other. When triumphantly I had them apart, one either side of me, I turned to Susan, thinking that in this at least, I might have her with me. She must wish to feel superior to her two foolish little sisters.

But: 'See,' she said, smiling sweetly again, 'what a struggle you have had. They don't intend to obey you –'

'A fight like that must be halted, Susan. It could even end in disaster if no one were to intervene.' I tried once more to enlist her as an ally: 'Are they always so wild?'

'They don't intend to obey you,' she repeated. Both Elinor and Harriet were standing now, sullenly, one either side of me. 'They do what they like. And so shall I –'

I said foolishly, 'I think your mother may have something to say about that. Your mama, even your papa – they would hardly approve –'

'Oh Papa – he wouldn't remember what you told him, he wouldn't listen to a *governess*. And as for Mama – she was very cross with Miss Musgrove who has just left. She said to her, "If you cannot keep discipline, Miss Musgrove, do not come whingeing to me."'

Mrs Adamson, visiting the schoolroom my first evening, asked abruptly:

'Well, do you feel you are giving satisfaction?'

'I hope so, ma'am –'

But it was impossible for me to be demure. I am not demure. My tongue slipped into my cheek. I thought she would surely notice . . .

'I shall see soon enough, by the results you obtain.' She had in her hand a book. She placed it now on the table. 'This is the best work I know for imparting general knowledge. And it is general knowledge the girls will need – rather than any nonsense such as, say, Latin. I noticed you offer *Latin* as one of your subjects. Latin is for young boys, and we have no –' she broke off. 'Look inside this work, please, and you will see what it is I require.'

I opened the book gingerly. I had seen by its title already what sort of work it was. Here again were the dreaded Questions and Answers. I glimpsed:

'Which is the planet nearest the sun, and which the most distant?' And: 'Name the last three Laureates and their chief works.'

'I'm not sure that I approve –' I began.

'I beg your pardon?' Again that tinkly laugh. 'Did I ask for your approval? If a mother is not to decide . . . Are you by any chance one of these persons who thinks she knows better than a parent?'

I was about to say, Yes, when I thought better of it. Sixty pounds a year and regular employ was too important to me. I seethed. She noticed nothing.

'You teach needlework of course? I omitted to ask. You will be training them in stitching and hemming and simple embroidery?'

'Of course.'

Could she not see, feel, hear the boiling up inside me of anger?

'Well, since you are so accomplished a needlewoman, what a waste of your skills, teaching young girls. I shall be happy to give you the opportunity of exercising those skills.'

The next afternoon Lily the nurse came in with a pile, a tottering pile of sewing.

'The mistress says . . .'

Gone my evenings. I had planned to draw – if my cold fingers allowed it. To read. Perhaps, who knows, to write?

To think that I had never been homesick at the Talbots'. Unhappy yes, how not, when I thought of what had happened to our family – but I had not yearned for home. I had no home – and the Talbots had given me one. But Topham Abbey . . . If once the monks had been happy there and at peace with God – no blessed vibrations remained where their abbey had stood.

Long cold lonely evenings, through January, February and into March. Once I had been happy alone in my room at Wade House. But downstairs had been my family. Over the road, had been Mr Hume. Francis – whom I would wish never to think of now. Some of those lonely evenings gave me too much time to remember Francis.

I tried not to think of him, or any of my troubled past, as I sewed. And I was so cold. Ah, the cold as the fire died down, every evening by half past eight – the coal hod empty. The first time I rang and asked for more, Nancy, smallest and youngest of the maids, came reluctantly to answer.

'There's no more while morning,' she said, looking sullen.

'But I have to sew for another two hours –'

'There's none while morning.'

'I could come downstairs and fill the hod myself.'

'Nay, you'll not, Miss!' She repeated: 'There's none while morning . . .'

However I watched that fire and the supply of coal, I could never make it last. Almost every evening saw me cold and cheerless.

A quite different life went on downstairs. I did not want to be part of it, but certainly it was lively. Some evenings when I opened the schoolroom door, I would hear laughing, chatter. A piano and harp, singing. Or suddenly Mr Adamson's braying laugh. *Haw, haw* . . . What a loud laugh he had – his voice too was loud. A large, hawk-nosed, determined-looking man. I had little to do with him. Occasionally, coming across me in the hall, or perhaps out in the garden with my charges, he would speak to me:

'Girls behaving themselves? Come to me if there's any trouble . . . You hear that, eh, girls? Miss – Miss Thungummyjig is to come to me if you misbehave.'

How ever, *when* ever? If I had dreamed of doing such a thing, when and where would I find him? Now, it was the hunting season, when he could choose from the York and Ainsty, the Bramham Moor, the Bedale. Next, it would be the fishing, and then the shooting . . . All overlapping and keeping him busy from morn to night.

In spite of the hearty vacuous laugh, he was a man of uncertain temper. Shouting suddenly at the servants, or kicking his dog badtemperedly (I learned then, as I am sure others had done, to scurry out of the way), making me glad he was so seldom about the home. I do not know how he was with Mrs Adamson. I scarcely saw them together unless it was on Sunday when we went to church as a family. Then she was very dignified, a little cold, the gracious half of the pair. Much bowing and smiling and greeting of acquaintances. She was gracious with him too.

It was the maid, Annie, who in the end redeemed my cold evenings. If Lily the nurse, Nancy the maid, Mrs Burgess the housekeeper, and Green, Mrs Adamson's personal maid – if all of these were indifferent, even hostile to me, I found a friend in Annie. (It was she in the end from whom I begged extra coal.) I certainly needed a friend . . .

Annie was a much plumper, younger version of Betty – certainly there was enough of a look to remind me. She had trouble with her feet – bunions mainly, and also some swelling of the ankles, so that to hurry up and downstairs as she had to must have been torture indeed. It appeared Mrs Adamson had complained to Mrs Burgess of Annie's 'want of good appearance'. So Mrs Burgess had told Annie to eat less food, and to behave in Mrs Adamson's presence as if her feet did not hurt.

Annie was warm-hearted and a gossip. She was concerned that I should not be too neglected up there in the schoolroom. On evenings when there was an entertainment downstairs, she often made her way up to me with some titbit stolen from the dining-room:

'You're such a little small one, Miss,' she would say. 'Here's a bite'll feed you up –'

It was from her that I learned anything that I knew about the family. She it was who told me:

'She's a hard one, that one. T'mistress. But then you've to be sorry for her . . . They need a lad, you see. All the childer – lasses. They need a *lad*. A family like that, that's been all those years . . . Mrs Burgess says there were never a time here, when there wasn't Adamsons. Four childer, and never a lad . . . Mind you, she lost one. Just after I come, it were . . . August, or the like. She were right poorly. The surgeon he were up here and I heard – she'd been expecting you see and her time were come – I heard, the bairn came out dead. *And* it were a lad . . .'

I pitied Mrs Adamson then. I thought that inside her, grown from so little, a seed they said, she had had this babe. And then – nothing. I knew that women screamed, cried out in agony – what was that phrase 'torn from the womb'? A great tearing and rending . . . and all for nothing. Yes, I pitied her then much more than I disliked her.

There was little at Topham Abbey to remind one of the monks whose land it had once been. Some scattered ruins behind the stables. A solitary arch not far from the pond which once had been the monk's fish or 'stew' pond. And of course, the tower.

I had seen a light in the window the afternoon of my arrival. I supposed it to be lived in or at the least used. I was curious to go and look and would have done so if I had been free for even a few minutes during daylight. But from seven in the morning until well after dusk, I was at the beck and call of the family.

The tower.

Elinor told me, 'Cousin Fielding lives there. We *never* go there.'

'Why, Elinor? Why is that? And does she not come to see you?'

Susan broke in: 'Oh, Cousin Fielding, she never leaves her home. She is very bad-tempered. The only time she paid us a visit . . . Such a crosspatch as never was. She is altogether a very odd person. Mama says –'

But I never heard what Mama said, for Harriet, left out of the conversation, had stuck the point of her pen into Elinor's thigh. Susan jumped to the attack, taking Harriet's hair in a handful and tugging, trying to bang her head on the table. Elinor jumped up and down, shouting,

'Stop them, Miss Woodward, it's your fault, Miss Woodward, look what you've done, look what you've done . . .'

Yes, there was some curiosity as to that tower. I had been at the Abbey three or four weeks when one afternoon, the three girls were taken out in the carriage to Harrogate for the day. I was not invited.

Mrs Adamson told me: 'You are so far behind with the sewing. This will give you the opportunity to catch up.'

But I was so poor at sewing. I knew of course how it should be done and, taking far more time than the average person, could accomplish it – but at what great cost and repugnance. Today I propped a book in front of me and tried yet again to do two things at once. I feared that reading would win the uneven contest.

After I had eaten, alone of course, an unappetizing dinner of rusty meat and watery vegetables (the kitchen did not need to bother today, since it was only for me, the governess), I was restless. The icy drizzle of earlier in the day had eased off. Wearing stout boots I thought I would walk a little in the grounds. And – why not? I would look more closely at the tower.

I approached it carefully. I could see no signs of life. But then Cousin Fielding never went out . . .

At the foot of the stairs was a heavy wooden door, with a bell pull beside it. Lying on the stone floor just before the door, sheltered in the inside porch, was a large wooden tray. Tin covers lay over the dishes on it. There was an empty jug covered in buttermuslin. Inside, a few drops of milk. I lifted a tin cover. Some half-eaten carrots, mashed up, and the remains of some creamed chicken: cold and unappetizing but better than I had just eaten. Underneath another cover were the remains of some sago pudding. A pot of tea.

What devil got into me? I began by trying the heavy door. Bolted. Certainly I was the old Christabel as I pulled the heavy rope of the bell. (What, what shall I say when she comes down?)

I waited for footsteps. But instead there was a banging noise and the sound of a window being flung open. A voice called out, quavery,

'Who's that now, who's that?'

I put my head outside. A woman's face topped by a lacy cap hung out of the window. Cousin Fielding saw me then. Her voice was a scream:

'Who's that, I don't know you . . . *Get away, get away!*'

I stood fascinated, for the moment rooted.

'Get away, little redhead! You're *spying*, aren't you?'

Her head ducked in. A moment later, there she was again – but brandishing something. I could not make it out – a small sculpture, a stone? She held it above my staring face:

'Spying, aren't you? I'll *crack* your little red head –'

I ran backwards, out of reach – and then round to the other side of the tower, where I stood panting. Warm in spite of the chill afternoon. Damp dripped off the laurel leaves. From the tower I heard a thin high-pitched wail. Cousin Fielding's frustration that she had not crushed my skull? Then the slamming of the window. And silence.

I went at once indoors, and up to the nursery. What matter that Lily disliked me and would if possible have forbidden my visits?

'Have you done the sewing?' was all she said now. 'Have you got on with the stitching?'

'All work and no play. We don't want that,' I said, dandling Georgie on my knee.

Lily made a gesture of exasperation, sighing and clicking her teeth. She busied herself with tidying up.

'Make Gee Gee a picture,' the child said, jumping up and down, 'make a pretty picture –'

I had nothing with me, but to Lily's tut-tutting I took up some of the child's own wax crayons and drew her a large and gaily coloured boat, on the sea. The sun shining, and then the rain coming. 'And up and down goes the boat in the storm. And look here is an *island* – and they are all to be saved . . .'

How long since I had told Josh stories? When Georgie's fat arms encircled my neck, when she covered my face with kisses – it was Josh again, it was the years rolled back, when I was Josh's beloved Cisty. I longed with a desolate passion now to have Josh back. (That I might ever one day have a Josh of my own, was not part of my imaginings, that was not my hope.)

Or perhaps, I wonder now, was I remembering the seven months' child who had been Papa's darling?

At the end of that month, Polly's William wrote to me:

'A son for us, dearest Christabel, and a brother for Louisa. Benjamin Charles was born yesterday morning – Polly would write but she *must* rest. I wanted you to be amongst the first to hear. Forgive me that I write no more. Polly wishes you to know that he has a fine head of brown hair and a determined mouth, and looks already as if he wishes to *talk to us*. She says he greatly resembles her brother Henry, and I say he favours an uncle of mine who was a naval man. But that is another story. And now I must put down my pen and take evensong. Visit us soon . . .'

'Who are all those strange persons in framed pictures?' asked Susan, appearing suddenly beside me in the bedroom one afternoon. 'Who is that for instance?' and she stabbed a finger, smiling the while, at the now faded daguerreotype which was all I had of my mother.

'My Mama – who is dead, Susan.'

I thought for a moment that she would say something foolish – something derogatory, or mocking. Had she done so, I would have killed her. I would have laid about her angelic little face and head, scratching and pummelling . . .

But she passed on, pointing to the *carte de visite* of Polly: 'Who is *this* lady?' And then Agnes, in wedding dress: 'Is this your sister? She is much prettier than you, you are not pretty *at all*.'

Then she spied my small ivory thimble-box with its minute flower engraving – one of the many gifts from the Talbots. Picking it up before I could protest she removed the thimble. Although slim, she had large hands. The thimble would not fit. She said irritably, putting it away, 'I forgot – it must be a midget's thimble.'

'Perhaps you could leave my possessions alone, Susan? You would not like it if I came to the night nursery and looked amongst your treasures – passing personal remarks.'

But she was distracted again: 'And this fan, what do you want with a fan? Do you expect to be invited downstairs when visitors come?'

Elinor had joined her. Harriet fortunately was nowhere to be seen. 'Have you no curling papers? Has Miss Woodward no curling papers, Susan? Where are they, Miss Woodward?'

Susan, I saw, was playing with the fan, opening and shutting it. Then acting the grand lady, waving it affectedly.

'I have my own curls, Elinor. I do not use curling papers.'

'Mama does. Mama does.' She repeated this several times, since she apparently could not find anything wrong with my hair curling naturally.

As I came over to remove the fan from Elinor (she put it down pettishly as she saw me approach), I could be glad only that my mother's legacy to me, her story, my father's lock of curling hair, were safely hidden where these prying eyes could not find them.

Why did I not simply leave, and try for another post using my first testimonials? Why not crawl back to Aunt Martha? I have asked myself that often since, and yet the answer is probably simple enough. It was pride. I could not have borne to admit that I had been beaten by ten-, eight- and six-year-old girls. I told myself that if by Christmas I was not in charge, if my life here was no better, then I would leave.

Evening, and Annie sat the other side of the fire, for which she'd brought up more coal. She loosened the laces of her boots. 'Swelled,' she said. 'Me ankles. Swelled right up.'

She had brought me a slice of plum cake from downstairs. We sat together, companionably. She told me about herself: that she came from Starbeck, near Knaresborough, and was the eleventh of thirteen children. Three of her brothers had been soldiers – her father had been an army man. Two brothers, gone to the bad: one in and out of jail, another transported to Australia.

Three of her sisters had been in service like herself. One had married a footman and gone to Boroughbridge.

For herself, she'd never wanted to marry:

'I've seen how it is, and I reckon nowt to it. If I could of had childer – childer, that's a different tale. I reckon we'd all like childer . . .'

She asked me about my life before I had come to Topham Abbey. And drew her breath in sharply with wonder, when I spoke (why hide it?) of Appleyard Mill and Wade House.

'I seed when first you come – she's never a parson's lass, I said. A fine lady, a grand lady – they ought . . . The missis, she kens?'

'But Annie,' I said. '*Mill* – that is not very grand. A clergyman is far more respectable . . . But the truth is, I talk very little about my past. I tell you only because you are my friend. But I don't expect it to be spoken of in the kitchen.'

I wondered sometimes what they said about me there. I knew Annie's friendship with me was tolerated. That they disliked me was also clear. Not I think for anything I had done. But rather for what I was. I heard stories of the 'put on airs' and 'tittle-tattling' of earlier governesses.

But worst of all, I was a nuisance with my requests for coal, with my suppers to be brought up to the schoolroom. And the respect due to me (that I did not want). In no way the equal of their master and mistress, yet to be addressed as 'Miss'. Not to be consorted with (which was why I worried about Annie). Merely an irritant. And how could I be respected, since I could not keep order? They could not help but hear Susan or Elinor (and Harriet too now – she was developing a line of her own) mocking my authority, saying and doing whatever they liked – often by design exactly when Lily or Nancy was in the room.

I was indeed a nuisance. A nuisance who was also a nothing.

I said to Annie now:

'You're certain you won't be in trouble for sitting here with me?'

She laughed, warmly, a conspirator:

'They'll not tell on me. They think me daft I'd even pass time of day with you, but they'd not tell. And Mrs Burgess – she's in her room, she likes a sup or two nights – afternoons too sometimes. She sleeps heavy.'

I knew about Mrs Burgess and her drinking – although I

suspected the Adamsons did not. I was grateful for it, since it kept out of the way yet one more person who might find fault with me . . .

'A queer one, that Mrs Burgess,' Annie said. 'But never as queer as that Miss Fielding.'

I asked:

'Why ever does she hide away up there? They let her. There must be a reason.'

'Aye. She'd her heart broke. Or that's what they say. But I reckon it were a while since. There'll've been no lads paying court this thirty year . . . But that's what I heard tell. Her heart were broke. So she's to be alone . . . She hates them all. All folk.'

'That's plain to see. The one time I tried to visit –'

'And she's poorly too. You ken, Doctor calls – he allus comes by Mondays . . . They say she's poorly top *and* bottom – if you take me. Like, you've never to speak on it, but washing that comes out of there – some of it, rags like – rags not clothes –' she lowered her voice, 'they're *soiled*, they've to be burnt allus. It seems she can't – you'll know what I mean –'

I was nauseated and fascinated. This incontinent recluse, ready to crush my skull, tucked away – and seeming not to occasion Mrs Adamson much worry at all. I wondered if she ever visited her cousin, other than with the doctor? for I had seen her accompany him up once. And the cleaning of the place, since she allowed no servant upstairs? I could not imagine what it must be like up there.

But when I mentioned this to Annie:

'Aye, but there's Mrs Varley, Lizzie Varley from t'village – she comes in. I never spoke with her, keeps hersen to hersen – she takes t'washing, and cleans through Mondays, afore Doctor comes. Queer soul, she is and all. Well suited. Comes in here for a pot of tea and a smoke and says nowt, unless it's to wish us time of day . . . She cleans, aye – but I reckon it'll be fit for a pig again up there, come the sabbath . . .'

She winced, easing her boot off.

'Now that bite I fetched you – nay, it'll not be missed, don't fret – but get it ate. Go on, eat it . . .'

At the end of February Mrs Adamson took to her bed. There was much scurrying round. I wondered if it was serious, and if so, how serious. I was charged to go to Harrogate with the girls in the carriage. They were to meet some cousins. It was a tedious journey, cooped up alone with them. Elinor kept up a chant for much of the way, talking about the waters at Harrogate, telling Harriet (who believed her) that there were waters there which made people grow.

'Shall you want to drink some, Harriet? Miss Woodward, she'd *dearly* love to, since she really needs to grow – but she is too poor to buy it. The water is *very* dear. Is that not true, Susan? She will have to stay small, shan't she?'

I was exhausted that evening. And looking at the never diminishing mound of sewing, rebellious too.

Annie joined me on her way up to bed. She had brought me up some sponge biscuits. Poking the fire for me, then falling back into the schoolroom rocking chair:

'Ye ken what's up wi' t'Missis – why she's poorly?'

I shook my head. 'No, I just like the peace and quiet. Knowing she will not walk suddenly into the schoolroom –'

But Annie was bursting with her news. Kitchen gossip.

'Expecting. That's what. Expecting again. Lily's pleased enough, I can tell you. For when Miss Georgie's gone from t'nursery, if there's not a new bairn . . . Mrs Burgess told Cook, she heard Doctor say – t'Master were there – Doctor said, "Keep her quiet . . . It'd not do to lose it. *This* time," he says, "you'll have a fine healthy lad."'

I said, 'But, Annie, no one knows beforehand if it's to be boy or girl –'

But I realized even as I said it that of course the doctor knew nothing, but only wished to be reassuring. 'This time, a fine healthy lad.' I felt a pang of compassion, remembering her earlier loss. How it haunted me – that coming dead from the womb. Now, must she not be fearing the same?

A cold morning in late March. Nancy, standing in the doorway of the schoolroom, said:

'There's two gentlemen – nay, army folk, soldiers like, asking for you, Miss.'

The girls looked up at once from their books.

Harriet said, 'Some men have come to take you away. Goody, goody.'

Susan interrupted coldly – I caught her smile, directly at me: 'That's peelers, silly. Nancy said *soldiers*.'

'What have I to do wi' em, Miss? T'mistress is out.'

'Show them into the drawing-room,' I said, 'I shall come down directly.'

I did not answer any of the girls' questions, but set them some work which I did not expect they would do. I feared at first they would follow me down – since their mother was not there to stop them.

In the drawing-room, Halliwell stood examining a painting above the fireplace. Hounds meeting at Topham Abbey. He was in the uniform of the Green Howards. Another soldier stood beside him. Two blue cloth spiked helmets lay on the table nearby.

The door was open and I had come in silently. They both turned.

'Christabel –'

I rushed over then and threw myself into Halliwell's arms. He was for a moment surprised – stiffness of shoulder and chest. But then he kissed me heartily, holding me close. I think I had never really kissed him before. Those years of childhood – not enmity, but indifference. (Domineering Christabel who was Papa's darling. Army-loving Halliwell, destined for the mill and never allowed to forget it.)

A voice beside said: 'And what about me?'

'Here is my friend, Watkins. Ensign George Watkins . . . George, my sister, Christabel.'

George was not so tall as Halliwell. Tow-coloured hair to Halliwell's dark. He clasped my hand, both my hands, firmly in his. At the same time he stared hard at me, with probing blue eyes. I was made uncomfortable.

'What a grand home you are living in now!' Halliwell said.

I said, 'It is *not* my home. Just my place of employment. You know I am governess here . . .'

'Oh, we don't care for that,' Halliwell said. His friend made no comment. 'I learned of your address from Aunt Martha and was determined to see you – we're only a week in York.'

'And then – where then, Halliwell?'

'India,' said his friend George. 'We sail on the twenty-fifth.'

As Halliwell spoke, George watched me closely. I became self-conscious. Not quieter but louder. My voice more excited. And of course I *was* excited, and warmed by this visit with its breath of a past life. This proof that the family Woodward still, after a fashion, existed.

We were all sitting now. I would have liked to ring the bell and order tea, or even Madeira and cake – but I could imagine how the kitchen would receive my request. (Might not Nancy even now be telling Mrs Burgess: 'Miss Woodward is sitting with two soldiers in the *drawing-room*?')

Fortunately the room was warm – the fire was lit always at nine in the morning. Halliwell did not want to talk about my present life, or about Topham Abbey at all. The soldier's life was the only topic to engross him. If ever any one had been made for an institution, or an institution for that person, then it was the British army and Halliwell.

'Hang on,' George interrupted, as Halliwell gave some long account of army exercises, 'hang on. Now that really was misery at the time. The conditions at camp . . . Don't you remember? And anyway, your sister – Miss Woodward won't want to hear . . .'

Halliwell looked, for a second only, abashed. 'I don't recall I was miserable,' he said.

'Then you ought to have been,' George said, laughing.

'Well, maybe . . . But like I was saying, there we were, and it was those few days of really thick mist. We'd the time of our lives . . .'

All the while George's gaze never left my face. I did not like it. It was once more the charming curate, Andrew Grier – and God knew who else yet to come.

I wondered desperately what made me worthy of notice ('Christabel is quite without beauty'), when everything about me cried out, Oh leave me in peace . . . If you have anything more than friendship to offer, *I am afraid* . . .

Halliwell said, as we exchanged family news, that Yes, he had spent a week's furlough with Agnes, and that 'terrible, dreadful, little man'.

'And I can tell you, he's not forgiven you, Christabel.'

They had ridden the eight miles from camp and would soon have to leave. We decided to walk, cold as it was, for a little while in the grounds. Then I would have to get back to my duties.

I told them about Cousin Fielding. They asked if I had been up in the tower yet.

'No. Nobody goes. My employer is adamant that no one –'

George interposed, with a smile:

'Mrs Adamson is adamant – but is adamant Mrs Adamson?'

All was quiet as we walked by and round the tower. I made

them both laugh with my tale of 'an old witch who calls *me* a witch, and who threatens me with . . .' I did not say she had meant to crush my skull. I did not want to spoil the laughter. Halliwell was for ringing the bell 'just for a lark', but I protested, horrified. George said it would be cruel. He added more lightly that if she was up there on account of a broken heart, then what an extra cruelty it would be to see a handsome fellow like Halliwell . . .

Time for them to leave. India beckoned. I could see that Halliwell, his mind leaping ahead, had already set sail. (Nearly ten years since the Mutiny, whose course he had followed so assiduously.) I kissed him again. Clung to him a little. Halliwell, my half brother.

George clasped my hand, looked into my eyes, and asked if he might write to me from India. 'I have no sister,' he said.

'You may write. I cannot promise to reply.' My voice had a tremble to it. I meant it to be severe. For I was frightened.

When I returned, my thimble from the ivory case was gone. Susan said, 'If you look you will see that Elinor is wearing it. It fits her well.'

Elinor said, 'It is mine now. Susan gave it to me.'

'Go on then,' Susan said, 'ask for it back. Ask for it, and see what happens . . .'

But even while I was listening, and deploring the little silver thimble rammed on Elinor's finger, I had seen my fan. It lay beneath the schoolroom table, its ribs broken and bent, the net cut and hanging bedraggled.

'My fan! Susan, Elinor – my fan!'

Susan smiled then. Her sweetest smile. 'The cat got it. A cat came from downstairs and went in your room and took it. And destroyed it here.'

'How dare you – *wicked* girl!'

'Oh, oh, oh – you don't believe about the cat, do you? What are you going to do about it? Shall you tell Mama? Papa?'

'Indeed I shall tell your mama! Destroying other persons' belongings . . .'

'And shall you like it when *we* tell her that you have been talking to soldiers and sitting with them in the drawing-room, when you should be giving us lessons. And . . .'

I rapped her knuckles hard with a wooden ruler. And then I rapped Susan's, and Harriet's too for good measure. I laid about

259

me with the ruler. Hands. Heads. I was like a fiend. Then I gathered up the broken fan and removed it to my room.

'Keep the thimble,' I said. 'I would not want to wear it after it had been on your hand.'

They were all of them wailing. A great caterwauling set up. Each encouraged the other to greater heights of moaning and shrieking as they nursed their hands and cheeks.

After some while, attracted perhaps by the noise, Lily appeared with little Georgie. All three girls ran into Lily's arms.

'I have punished them for stealing and destruction,' I said. 'And they are great girls to be crying about that.'

'I never seed them so upset, what will mistress say?'

'She may say what she pleases.' I took Georgie up. She put her arms about my neck, and whispered a secret. She did not appear to care about her sisters' crying. Then she tugged at my curls and made me kiss her face.

'Baby should be rightly afeard of you – laying about like that,' Lily grumbled. But she did little to comfort the girls.

I was to be paid each quarter. Easter came and went and I saw no money. I did not see how I could ask for it. I had no guidance as to how these matters should be conducted. I could not imagine saying to Mrs Adamson, 'I think you have forgotten to pay me.'

I was not in absolute want. I had food and a roof over my head and a few shillings saved. But if I wished for instance to buy a present for Polly . . .

In the end I asked Annie's advice. She screeched with laughter:

'Ye'll get nowt from her. Best ask t'Master.'

When at last I came upon Mr Adamson – and he was not easy to find, I began:

'In the matter of my salary . . .'

He gave his loud braying laugh:

'But that's none of my business! I don't pay governesses. You must speak directly to Mrs Adamson.'

I heard him mutter to himself, 'What damned thing will they bother me with next . . .'

Later that evening, Nancy brought a tray up to the schoolroom. On it was an envelope, and inside, fifteen pounds. Nothing was ever said.

In June I was given leave for two weeks, to go and stay with Polly. I thought seriously then of leaving the Adamsons'. Apart

260

from Annie's friendship, I had little reason for staying, unless it was my pride. I would not allow the girls, or their mother, to win. I would leave when *I* chose . . .

Probably that would be at Christmas. And then I would begin again. In certain moods I thought even of leaving England. Not as far as Tasmania, but perhaps Italy or France. Wild restless ambitious thoughts. No sooner did I have them, than I would feel a return of the familiar concern. How could I leave Papa? Agnes, who might need me. Aunt Martha.

All those who might need me. It was still I the head of that family. Not Halliwell.

To be with Polly for two weeks, Polly and William and their children, was like walking out of darkness into sunlight. And indeed the sun shone throughout the whole of my stay. We went out each afternoon in the dogcart with the nurse, little Louisa, and baby Benjamin. We would stop and Polly would sit under a tree, suckling Benjamin. I sat beside her. Sun dappling the leaves, no sound but bird song, the cooing of woodpigeon, far cry of a cuckoo – and the babe's contented sucking. A little way away, Louisa and the young orphan girl who was her nurse gathered daisies for a chain.

It is easy to turn memory into an idyll, but surely that was one? If I could not quite yet be happy, how wonderful to see the happiness of those I loved . . .

On those outings we spoke little. It was enough just to be. Polly had said earlier:

'I am all the time now, dearest, such a happy person. And it seems to me so important I should *realize* it. Mama and Papa will welcome us one day, I am certain. So many persons, dearest, do not know they are happy, until they are not . . .'

William had been promised a living in Essex, and had already been to see it. The parish was large and straggly and the rector he was to succeed had burdened him with a list of problems he was likely to encounter, but neither he nor Polly were of the kind to be discouraged. They expected to go after Christmas.

'And when you leave Topham Abbey – for they seem to me such mean-spirited and malicious persons, dearest, that really you must not stay – when you are finished with them, then we shall expect you with us.'

Dear Polly. Although I discouraged her endeavours to find *me* a William, she still could not keep from lecturing me:

'You are to forget, you *must* forget what was done to you by

261

an unhappy person. And look – yes, you will find, I know you will . . . There *is* someone for you, Christabel dearest.'

But even supposing I wanted him, how was I to find him? And when, or rather if, I found him – what then? The fear, the distaste I felt, was for ever, surely?

'Promise me you will try, dearest – your heart always open and free, so that you do not miss him when he comes into your life. Oh it is so important . . . *promise* me?'

'I promise, Polly. I promise.'

I told her of Halliwell's visit, and of George's request that I write to him. I wished I had said nothing, for she became at once so eager and excited.

'A friend of your own brother, a family person almost – that is so perfect. And that he should say such a thing after less than one hour . . . Oh Christabel . . . Let us think now what may happen in the case of George. How long is he in India for? When can you expect . . .' She could not be stopped.

How hateful it was to be back. How I regretted my decision. Nothing had changed. It only seemed worse, because I had been happy and now was not. The girls greeted me with the news that they wished I had stayed away.

'You shall have a new governess sooner than you think,' I said angrily, painfully.

Mrs Adamson's condition had begun to show markedly. I pitied her still and wished to be sympathetic. If what had happened before . . . If the child were not a son . . .

The sympathy I felt did not survive two minutes in her presence. The second day back, she accused me of 'maintaining poor discipline'.

'I have had a chance in your absence to see how these children have been handled. I intend very soon to hear their lessons. We shall see then if you are doing it right . . .'

But what was right? I thought how happy I would be if I could have had Georgie as pupil. (For that I would have to stay another eighteen months.) I would use apples and oranges for counters, and make colouring-in books, and models for the alphabet. She would *love* both her studies and her teacher.

I saw little of Georgie these days. Lily was, perhaps not surprisingly, jealous of the ready and unexpected affection (even I had not expected it) baby Georgie showed me.

The fine weather came to Topham Abbey. I asked leave to

take lessons outside on the lawn, or in the shade beneath the large chestnut tree. Mrs Adamson refused.

'They would be running wild, all about the garden. And constantly distracted . . .'

I walked out myself sometimes in the evenings. It was light now till quite late. Once I saw the high window in the Tower open a little and a head in a white lace cap peer out. I kept out of the way.

Mrs Adamson kept her word that she would hear their lessons. Coming into the schoolroom soon after nine one morning:

'Very well,' she said. 'Pass me the book, please.'

She was very pale, and wore a cashmere shawl wrapped tight in spite of the warm July weather.

That wretched list of questions. And answers. She read out at random. Question Four. For Susan:

'"Mention the chief generals of Napoleon I."'

'Byron, Shakespeare, Pope and Wordsworth.'

'Susan!' said her mother sharply. 'What *are* you being taught?'

It was I who winced. Remembering now Question One: 'Name the authors of the following works: *Don Juan, The Tempest, The Rape of the Lock* and *The Excursion* . . .'

How rarely any of the girls learned the lessons set – when they did, it was always by rote, beginning with Answer One. The questions they did not bother with at all.

'You have no idea how to teach. If *this* is what is going on . . .'

I was standing. She was sitting. I wilted, there in the warm schoolroom. Susan, who had got her answer so very wrong, was smiling. She smiled sweetly. And so did Elinor. Harriet scowled.

Once again there was no sign of my salary, due at the beginning of July. I wondered what I should have to do to obtain it this time.

It was August now. The family had left for Filey. I had imagined I was going with them. I had not visited Filey since the days of tormenting Miss Dutton and I looked forward to sea air, and perhaps some time free when I might wander on the sands. But I learned even before the packing-up began that I was not to accompany them. Nor on the other hand was I to be free to visit my family or Polly again. I had already had the vacation allotted to me, Mrs Adamson said . . .

They had been gone already a week now. The weather had

grown steadily warmer. I walked out every afternoon, often for three or more hours. I worked on my drawings. I wrote letters, to Polly, to George, to Aunt Martha. I read verse and biography in beautifully bound editions from the library at the Abbey (I had not asked permission, so certain was I that it would be refused). And occasionally I worked at the mound of sewing left behind for me. It included a few items from the layette for the new infant. In this I took a little pleasure and some pride.

I thought several times of making my way to Luddenden and Halifax (I had sufficient money), where I might surprise them all. Even dear Kit . . . although I would not expect to see him. As for Septimus – he *must* be avoided. And to see Papa could only cause him distress. I would only make everything worse . . . And, and . . . There were a thousand reasons why I should stay quietly here. Not the least was that I did not know which day they would return. When I had dared to ask, Mrs Adamson said,

'When it suits us, Miss Woodward. When the girls and I have had enough *sea* air . . .' She said nothing of Mr Adamson. He was away shooting and would join them only for a day or two.

Annie, coming up to see me in the empty schoolroom, told me:

'She went, did Miss Fielding . . . Gone away. And wi' nowt said. She weren't never one for words . . . Sudden enow, any road, and I'd not like to think how t'rooms is up there – and Mrs Varley not in while Monday . . . You can reckon it'll be like a pig's . . . Doctor were in. He were in yesterday –'

But I had seen Miss Fielding go. Had seen her leave that morning. Hot August day, and wearing a fur pelisse, and carrying a small leather bag only. She had called for the carriage – I saw it come round to the front, and then saw her climbing in, helped by George, the coachman.

She had asked to go to the railway station, that was all Annie knew. She had had it from George. I worried that perhaps I should get a message to the Adamsons – feeling that in some way I might be held responsible for anything that might happen to her. Dr Calvert – perhaps it would be wise to send news to him?

But I did nothing. It seemed no business of mine. If she was well enough to come down, and well enough to order the carriage . . .

She left on the Tuesday. By Friday afternoon I was no longer worried for her. The coachman had after all reported seeing her safely on a train. She had *seemed* normal.

264

Now, instead, my curiosity got the better of me. Perhaps she had left the wooden door unlocked? And since her apartments would be empty, I might go up and spy. Might do exactly what she had accused me of.

I did not expect to find anything very interesting. Why should there be any clues to her past? And yet, I romanced, reminded irresistibly of Mr Dickens' novel of a few years before, *Great Expectations*. Would she be another Miss Havisham? Cobweb-covered wedding cake, wedding dress . . . What might I not find?

The sun came late to that side of the house. It was just moving round as I reached the tower. I thought myself in luck, for the heavy door yielded at once. Inside, out of the sun, was darkness. Gloom. I left the door ajar as I made my way slowly up the winding stairs. It was further than I thought. And in a foolish way, I expected at any moment the door above to open and a voice to call out: 'Get away! You're *spying* . . .'

There was only silence. But then I thought, as I approached the top: She will have locked the door. Of course she will have locked it. And that will be that.

It was open. I pushed it wide and walked through a small anteroom. It was sparsely furnished. Only an oakchest and a chair. There were two other doors leading off. One had a red ribbon hanging from its handle.

I turned the knob of this door. It was unlocked. I walked in. And then I saw . . .

Ah, dear God, if I live to be a hundred . . .

13

I lay in bed at Aunt Martha's. I saw that the daylight was going, and wondered if I had been asleep. The counterpane, turned back, gleamed white. There were footsteps on the stairs. Heavy. Papa going in or out. Otherwise the house was quiet.

It was all right now for me to be left alone. Aunt Martha had had a nurse in for a week. For I had had some sort of nervous collapse. I could remember very little – only that it had seemed always night time, always darkness. I had gone in and out of some troubled, nightmare sleep.

Now I must keep calm. Lie very still – and try not to think. But already there was a flutter of memory . . . Of my scream. Of what I saw. Screaming and screaming. Standing in the bedroom of the tower.

Now I turned my head from side to side, so that never still, it would not hold its pictures. So that I would not see again what I saw.

What I saw . . .

He had gnawed his fists. Yes, poor babe, lying there on the bed – through hunger he had tried to eat his fists. A child of – what? Perhaps a year. Wearing only a skimpy vest. Below the waist, bare. Small shrunken legs twisted at an angle. The head, monstrous, swollen. The veins showing. Mouth open, and one fist crammed in. The eyes staring.

A man child, and very, very dead.

I had not known what to do. I began to scream, and scream. Running now down the tower stairs – how did my trembling legs hold me up? Rushing to the kitchens looking for Annie, for Nancy, for anyone, anyone who could help.

A strange sight I must have been in the kitchen doorway, screaming, hardly able to get my words out. Babbling about a dead babe . . . About a smell . . .

One of the gardeners was in the kitchen drinking tea. Cook sent him and the footman up to the tower at once.

'Ye mun see, what have we. What's to do . . .'

And the doctor . . . Word went out to the stables, and the

groom was sent riding the three miles. Mrs Burgess, the house-keeper, where was she? Cook was for sending for Mrs Burgess. She would know better what to do. But it was mid-afternoon. She would be asleep, after a generous amount of Hollands.

Annie had her arm about me, calming me, saying, 'Wisht, wisht, *hush* . . .' By the time the footman and gardener returned, white-faced, she had calmed me enough, so that I could both speak and listen . . .

I was being fed with sips of cognac and hot water. The trembling began to ease a little. But I was still in shock.

Annie said she too was all of a shake.

'I mun go up there – but I cannot,' she said.

'No – there is no need,' I insisted. 'It is dreadful, dreadful. Others will sort it out. Dr Calvert . . . It will be all right.'

Perhaps I had now become *too* calm . . . What did I mean by 'all right'? Nothing was going to make it all right. Nothing was going to bring back to life a deformed child, starved to death and, in the sultry August heat, decomposing fast.

They were not my enemies in the kitchen that day. No longer my enemies. (Might Lily have been? But she had gone with the children to Filey.) Not even Nancy, who had refused me coal. No one. We were united in horror and shock . . .

And yet it was a long while before any one voiced the obvious question. It was as if the sight and smell, reported, and by some of us experienced, had so numbed our brains and senses, our thoughts that . . . Yet in not sending for the police – and this had been agreed on from the beginning – we had shown already what we believed.

A child. What child could it be, but an Adamson?

As we waited for the doctor's arrival, and while Mrs Burgess slept on (a knock on her door had brought no answer), I said:

'It was . . . *he* was . . . the child –' But I could say no more.

Annie said then: 'It'll be that bairn t'missis lost. Has to be, I reckon.'

'That's right, aye,' Cook said. 'The bairn . . .'

'Yes,' I said. A wave of horror swept over me again.

Cook (how many meals must she have, grudgingly, sent up to the schoolroom?) placed a newly baked teacake before me. My mouth shook and would not bite as I tried out of politeness, out of gratitude to eat it.

'It weren't . . . Last year, when it were borned – it never come out dead after all,' Annie said.

Cook said, 'If the bairn came out alive – what were it up there for?' Her voice was almost a whisper. She asked me, peering near my face:

'Were it – were he *grown* at all?'

'He was a monster,' I said.

It seemed an age waiting for Dr Calvert. Three miles there and three miles back – if, of course, he were to be found at home. Meanwhile naturally no one seemed able to settle to anything. Cook wondered if the Vicar should be sent for also.

And all the while I kept up my unnatural calm. Cook kept asking me, why had I gone up there? Why go up the tower?

Curiosity, I told her. Just curiosity. Miss Fielding gone. The door at the bottom unlocked. Yet I asked myself too now, why ever had I gone? If only, if only . . .

'Well,' Annie said, 'if there'd been no one go up while Monday, when that Mrs Varley come in. If Miss Woodward, if she'd not found . . .'

'It doesn't bear thinking of,' Cook said. 'In this heat. It doesn't bear thinking of . . .'

They murmured on:

'That Miss Fielding – whatever business had she? Allus queer, weren't she . . . Who'd ever think her fit to take care, charge of a bairn? Even a bairn that . . .'

Fred, the young gardener, was saying, 'Never right – with a head that size. Hardly human it were . . .'

And Nancy, 'Good riddance, we thought, when Miss F. went. If we'd known . . . If anyone had thought to go up, like . . .'

Voices. Voices. Louder. Now softer. They grew nearer, then receded.

I slipped from my chair in a dead faint. I remember the suffocating, whirling blackness. Then coming round again. I heard a low moaning sound. I made it myself. And then again blackness.

I had been put to bed in one of the guest rooms. Dr Calvert was standing beside me. White-faced, he held a glass with some dark liquid.

'Take this, Miss Woodward.'

I said to him (I heard my accusatory voice):

'You must have known all about this . . .'

And then I slipped back into darkness.

My nervous collapse, for that was what it was, took the form of a fever. That is why I remember so little, except that I screamed, and was hot and cold by turns. I could not distinguish my nightmares. I called for Mama.

Once, I swore, she stood by the bed. I was certain that I saw her. In corners of the room I chased the ghost of my father. Branwell, my father. I tried to climb from the bed, certain that if only I searched, I would find him. He was there, he was there.

'My father!' I cried, as I felt arms pinning me back to the bed. 'My *father* looks for me . . .'

Once, I heard someone (myself?) call out:
'*Jesu, Jesu, Jesu!*'

I could have wished they had sent for Aunt Martha. But they did not. As soon as I came out of my delirium, I wanted to go home. There was no question of my going alone.

Nor probably was I fit enough. But I insisted that I must go. I am not sure who arranged everything. Dr Calvert, I think. Mrs Burgess came and spoke to me.

Annie was the only person I seemed to trust. Swollen feet, aching legs, awkward weight and all, she was detailed to take me home, to Halifax. I had not seen the Adamson family. Only Mr Adamson I think had come back. I did not want anything to do with him. Nor did he come to see me.

I walked only with difficulty. The Adamson carriage took us to Harrogate, then a train to Leeds and another to Halifax. I remember little of it because I hid my face throughout. ('Shame-faced', Mama had said, when on the visit to Haworth I had shyly hidden my face with my reticule. This was not shyness. But something much worse.)

Annie delivered me to Aunt Martha, and returned to the Abbey.

Dear Annie, what became of you? I never heard of her again. It is not to my credit that I did nothing about it.

In the *Yorkshire Post*, at the beginning of November, I read: 'On Tuesday last, the lady of Mr Percy Adamson, of Topham Abbey, delivered of a son.'

And so . . .

I had been living four weeks now at Aunt Martha's. I had grown stronger and no longer had to stay in bed, although Aunt Martha would send me up there whenever she thought she saw signs of my: 'running to and fro, when you're barely fit to walk.'

She shook her head over the whole business. She was certain that I had fallen ill through 'miasmas', as she called them, up in the tower. My sickness could not have been precipitated by what I saw there ('I don't doubt it was a nasty sight – but scarce enough to bring on a fever'). Rather was it caused by the noxious gases in the room where I had found the body.

'A sad tale, child. It was a pity altogether you saw fit to meddle . . .'

Noxious gases. I knew better – but said nothing. I would not disturb her notions. She was too dear to me and had been for too long my support. And now that I had so little family, she was all the more precious.

Also, she looked after Papa. Or had done until last week. Although he had been there while I was ill, I had seen little of him (if he came into the room, I had not noticed).

When he was in the house, he spent most of his time downstairs, in the small room at the back which had once been Uncle Eli's snug. There he smoked, looked through papers and dozed. Aunt Martha made sure he did not drink in there. 'Raiding' the room frequently as well as going through it with a fine comb when he was absent.

'Not in this house, James. While you're out, it's as you like. But not a drop here.'

She was speaking to a broken man. He had little rebellion in him now and, in Wentworth Terrace, no spirit – either real or figurative.

Much of his time was spent sleeping. Outside he drank I suspected, if not as much as before, heavily enough. What he used for money I did not know. I imagined old friends and acquaintances helped as often as not.

A few days before, he had announced he would be moving out. He made me the excuse, partly. He said hurtfully, speaking of me but not to me:

'It vexes me. I'll not have that lass, that sickly lass, staring at me. In and out of the house – passing judgement. She's not poorly now, Martha. And what's more, I don't need Miss High and Mighty's pity –'

Aunt Martha said indignantly, 'Is that the way to speak of your daughter? Your own lass –'

'Aye, my *own* lass,' he said, with ugly emphasis. 'My own lass. I'll say what I like . . . what I care to say . . .'

270

An ugly emphasis indeed. But one that went unnoticed by Aunt Martha – who thought she was looking now at her niece. Ah yes, he knew what he knew. And how bitter he was still.

We never spoke directly. I was not sure that I wanted anything out in the open. I could not have borne it – for him or for me. Since I could never be his darling again – worse, since he would never now love me at all, I wanted nothing of it. I thought once more, as I had thought those days after the fire: I am a woman with two fathers – *and no father*.

'Well then,' Aunt Martha said, 'you're moving out, are you?'

'I've work. That's why. And wipe that look from your face, Martha lass. It's *my* concern is this work, and none of yours.'

He told us: 'It's to do with the canal – and that's all I'll say. It's none of your concern. I'll be gone soon enough.'

'Please yourself,' Aunt Martha said. 'I've done what I can. I'm not one to expect gratitude.'

He surprised us by this show of spirit. A few days later, when one of us made some mention about his work, he said it was nothing to do with the Calder and Hebble, the canal. He had never said any such daft thing. It was to do with Crossley's wool mosaics, that were selling so well. Reproductions of popular art in wool. Warm cosy comforting pictures to hang on the wall. His expertise was wanted – he'd been up to Crossley's. Some technical matters and so on. He reckoned we neither of us listened when he spoke . . .

Autumn. Obscured, yet sensed beneath the smell of the mills and the dirt, the refuse and the nuisances Aunt Martha so deplored, was the smell of autumn. I was helping once again with classes at the Mechanics' Institute. I had not thought and could not think properly of my future. I saw the days running, dragging on endlessly. Aunt Martha said nothing. Papa had left the house. I did not believe in his 'work', and wondered where he was and what he was doing.

Aunt Martha suggested the Halifax School of Art, that I might wish to go there in the New Year. Yes, the money could be found. We visited it together. But the work – mainly technical, and for textiles, was not perhaps for me. At any rate, nothing came of it.

I shall marry Kit, I thought wildly. Remembering, regretting, the loving companionship I had spurned. Wanting to be back with

271

him. Friend of my childhood. Hero of the mill fire, who had loved me when I did not deserve it.

But then I remembered how it was (and would always be?), that I could marry no one. Could not, should not, did not wish to marry.

And yet? If ever it was to be different, if ever it could be possible . . . I am ashamed to say I thought then: Might we not be like brother and sister? Could such a thing be? If he loved me enough – we could be together, two against the world and all its storms and troubles. We would be happy for I would be such a good wife, so loving in every other way – only so that it *would not be as it had been with Francis*. And as I sat in my small upstairs bedroom at Aunt Martha's planning all this, I felt that cold clutch of fear, then the hot wave of shame. So familiar, too familiar to me now . . .

I would go to see him, and tell him, 'Kit, if you still wish – what you offered me that time, after the fire. I am willing . . .' And then, I would tell him of how yes, it could be. But only if we could be as brother and sister. And how he must say if this sort of half-marriage, if it were not possible . . .

How could I ever have allowed so wicked, so selfish, so thoughtless, a notion? But I *did*. And in the days that followed, I knew a strange sort of peace. *I shall marry Kit.* As if I had come into calm harbour after a storm. I began to think how I could make him happy. How I could make him proud to have me for a wife. And then of practical matters: where we would live, what work he might do . . .

It was as if all common sense deserted me. As if my recent experiences had induced a folly not of grandeur but of its reverse. I really believed then that our two so different backgrounds could somehow be reconciled. The millworker and the mill owner's daughter.

And all the while I thought of these matters I was able to chase out of my mind Topham Abbey and the child – the fire, Papa, Mama's death. Ah God, so much, so much . . .

Even while I was making my plans, a note came by carrier from Agnes. She had arranged to tell me if ever Septimus were away so that I might come to stay. He was to spend four days in Liverpool on business. Their second son had been born only six weeks ago and I had never seen him. She would be so happy if I would come and keep her company.

As ever, it was strange yet familiar to be in Buckley House.

And sad. I missed Uncle Sutcliffe. But on my first visit it had been Aunt Flora I had expected round every corner, waiting to see her sharp face or hear her genteel tones. Now it was Septimus who had imposed his personality on the house. His fussy angry presence seemed everywhere.

Both the Whitaker girls would be away at school now until Christmas. But the son, Joseph, was there when I arrived – come from the mill for his dinner. He was a large boy of seventeen, still with the same sulky face and manner. He took little notice of me although when answering my questions was not too unfriendly. I wondered if he would report back to his father. Agnes said:

'Septimus will know. I shall tell him. There is no need for secrecy. I expect him to say only that it is all right *so long as he is not there*. You see what it is all about. He never forgives. I take care never to offend.'

She looked well enough, in some ways more beautiful than before. It seemed childbearing suited her. The new baby, Matthew, was large and hungry. I sat with her while she fed him, and thought of Polly who expected her third child in the spring. This world of babies and children – so dangerous and dark and yet so warm and loving. Satisfactions and joys which neither Polly nor Agnes did more than hint at, yet were so obviously there . . .

And I was about to consider a life without all this. And for Kit too. I felt my resolution waver and then I thought, it must be. It is after all, most of it, *what he wants*. And for the other – are there no homeless children we might take in? Surely there are motherless children in need of loving arms?

And so I consoled myself, and Kit in advance, and justified my actions.

'You see,' Agnes said, 'it is not so bad. I have baby Edwin – my little Ned – and now Matthew too. And even though the girls will come back from school to live, I should expect them to marry soon. They are quite a catch, you see. There is so much money.'

'And Joseph,' I said. 'Joseph is always there.'

'Joseph – one day he too will marry and go. But in the meantime he is not so great a nuisance. It is not as if Septimus and I are always wishing for intimate conversations. And Joseph and his father, they are good friends, of a like mind. And that is good. You remember Halliwell and Papa?'

We spoke then of Halliwell in India, and of how well in the

end everything had turned out, that *might* have been so ill.

I mentioned then that I had received letters – two so far – from a friend of Halliwell's who had visited me at Topham Abbey. George. I saw her thoughts leap at once to a wedding, however far ahead. For her thoughts were fixed permanently, irrevocably now on marriage and children. But I dismissed this one quickly, firmly (she did not know what I planned this very evening).

George's letters had been accounts only, first of the voyage, then of the early weeks in Agra. Factual only, and none the worse for that. They were vehicles too, I suspected, for some homesickness. And as he confessed in the second one, 'I have always wished for a sister, as some wish for a brother to talk with. I have now more than forty brothers (of which yours is the best, most congenial!) . . .'

No, here I did not need to be afraid.

She gave me news of the Armstrong cousins. I had not kept in touch at all. Meg had become quite the blonde beauty. Agnes showed me a *carte de visite*: the giggling little girl was nowhere to be seen. Indeed she must have done something other than giggle, for she was to marry soon the heir to a Scottish estate. He had spent the summer in Bath for his health. Her lack of dowry had been no impediment, and they were to wed in the New Year. As for Phil, he was doing well, studying law. His godfather, who had had little to do with them in their days of prosperity, now offered substantial help to Phil until he was set up for life.

'But you,' she asked. 'What shall *you* do now?' She had been appalled by the Topham Abbey story – as much as she had heard. (I kept back from her details that might distress: at the time she had been expecting Matthew, and was now feeding him.) 'You have grown stronger from your illness?'

I knew what she thought. That here was I, older than her, with no marriage prospects, no dowry, no influential connections, and only Aunt Martha – who did not need me – to live with.

I could not tell her about Kit. Time enough when I had seen him.

'There is always work for a single woman,' I said. 'It is just to find it. You will see that at the moment I am not hurried.'

'You are brave, Christabel, brave. I could not have thought . . . the very idea of employ in another's home –'

She broke off. Edwin had come in with his nurse. She became

distracted, moving little Matthew now to the other breast, but smothering him with kisses first.

Edwin stood a moment, sturdily, watching us. I turned my head away. I could not bear to see him. For I was looking at Josh.

Once Agnes had asked, 'Does he look like anyone?'

I denied knowledge. I lied. 'No,' I told her. 'But certainly not Septimus, or his family.'

Agnes said then, 'I cannot pretend truthfully I remember our little Joshua. Only the drawing which hung at Wade House. But is not little Ned wonderfully like?'

'I think that I shall visit the Ogdens,' I told Agnes that evening.

'I have no news of him,' she said. 'But he was always your friend. He is a good man, and many mothers must have cause to thank him . . . You must see that he is fully recovered . . .'

If it was strange to see Buckley House, it was stranger still to be in Luddenden village. Those straggling grey roofs, the steep narrow streets with their sharp corners – all hemmed in by the fells.

I did not go near Wade House – or that which lay opposite it. It was, thank God, not necessary.

The long upstairs windows of the Ogden cottage were in darkness but downstairs a light shone. I saw Mrs Ogden before she came to the door. As always she was flushed, and fussed. She hurried me in:

'Tak a seat, Miss Christabel – here by t'fire. It were clean today that cover, you can rest your mind. A sup? You'll take a sup . . . Kit'll not be long.'

I had removed my gloves and my outer clothes, I was seated by the fire, she was fetching me some tea ('t'cold, eh, t'cold – you must be starved wi' it'), and she had not once stopped talking. But she had told me nothing. I knew no more of anything than when I had come in.

'Miss Agnes – what a bonny lad, her bairn – I seed him the once . . .'

She asked questions but would not stay for an answer. 'And Mr Woodward, your dad, is Mr Woodward poorly? Is –'

The outer door opened, and Kit stepped in.

I had forgotten (why did I forget every time?) that he was so tall. So very tall that he had to stoop as he came through the doorway.

He was surprised to see me. Surprised and pleased. He had coloured. I got up from my place by the fire and came towards him. I took his hands in mine, and kissed him on the cheek. I had to stand on tiptoe.

He seemed to like the kiss. I thought of how that was only the beginning. Of how very soon (difficult perhaps with Mrs Ogden hovering – but we would manage somehow), I would tell him: 'Kit, I have thought again and Kit, dearest, if you wish it still, and *if* . . .' But how was I to make my impossible demand? I was not even then too worried. So arrogant was I, so confident that he would agree. I deserved all that happened to me.

Mrs Ogden was chattering still. Saying how glad Kit was to see me again. And over and over, how kind it was of me to come out of my way . . .

'Have done,' Kit said to her, but not unkindly. 'Have done and let your son speak . . . Best of all now, let *Christabel* speak.'

He asked me questions then, and *did* stay for an answer. He wanted to know all about the positions I had held – for he had heard that I was a governess now. I spoke freely of the Talbots, less so of the Adamsons. I summed up my time there only as 'unpleasant experiences, such as you would not believe'.

'I heard tell that you've been poorly lately?'

'Yes. Yes. But see how well I look now. And you –'

'Do you mind, Christabel, when you said to me, "I shall never be ill again" . . . Do you mind that? It were when you came back, when they fetched you back from that school . . .'

I saw he was teasing me. I liked so to be teased.

'. . . so what were you doing then, getting poorly again?'

The heat of the fire had brought a flush to my face. A ginger cat lay curled on the cotton rag rug at my feet. I leaned forward, stroking its fur. Kit was saying:

'And what of your soldier brother? We'd hoped he'd come marching through Luddenden so that we'd sight of him – he'll carry a sword, will Halliwell?'

The door opened gently. A shawled head came round it.

'Eh, Ellen,' Mrs Ogden said, 'if it's not Ellen. We didn't expect you, love.'

The girl was tall, dressed in a plain dark dress. As she greeted Kit and his mother, as they welcomed her in, she threw back her shawl. Her head was a thick mass of light-brown curls. She had very white teeth when she smiled. I thought her quite beautiful.

Kit was saying, shyly, 'Here's Ellen Harwood – Ellen, this is Miss Woodward, that used to . . .'

'I ken,' Ellen said, smiling at me, but gently. 'T'mill. My uncle he worked for your dad. I'm sad . . . it were sad.'

Mrs Ogden fussed her to sit the other side of the fire. Kit had risen. He took her shawl for her now.

'I were free,' Ellen said comfortably, 'there's me antie come to mind the bairns, so I thought – why not go up to Kit's?'

'Why not then?' Kit said. 'That were good. That's good.' He told me, in explanation: 'Ellen were Ellen Blake – she were that family. It's marriage made her Harwood . . .' He turned to Ellen. 'And the bairns then?'

'Gradely. Luke's chest, I've to watch it, but there's nowt to fret about.'

'Eh, bairns,' Mrs Ogden said. 'It's fret, fret, fret all t'day. I'd only t'one but . . .' She took the kettle off its hook above the fire: 'Kit lad, did you not tell Miss Woodward your news? You're never shy?'

Kit smiled. He had coloured again. He stood opposite me and just behind Ellen. His hands were on her shoulders as he said,

'Well, aye, we think it good news, eh, Ellen? You see, Ellen and I . . . Ellen were widowed five year since, and then like, I'd known t'Blakes – and come this summer –'

'Oh, give ower,' Ellen said laughing, 'give ower, and get on wi' it . . . Have I to tell it for you?'

Kit said proudly, 'We're to be wed, that's the head and front of it.' His hands were resting now on the brown curls, so like his own. 'We're to wed, Ellen and I.'

When, during the chill, disconsolate month that followed did I conceive the idea of visiting Haworth? Twelve years at least since I had been there. A year for every mile between our Luddenden home and Haworth Parsonage – a house which had for me now quite a different meaning. To visit Haworth should have been my first thought (and may have been for a fleeting hour or two) after I had read my mother's story. But as time passed and my feelings swayed now this way, now that, the whole idea had seemed too painful. And pointless.

But now . . . I wished suddenly, passionately, to go. The idea must be followed fast by its execution.

Earlier, I had been reading, and re-reading, then reading yet again, all the novels (even Charlotte's tantalizing fragment,

277

Emma – I had the copy of the *Cornhill* in which it had been published a few years before). I re-read Mrs Gaskell's *Life* in the bowdlerized version which was all I could obtain now. Making part sense at last of much that had puzzled me. Read, together with my mother's story, the whole made for me a new world. A world to which I did not belong, but to which surely I could not be denied entry?

It had been a dark and desolate November. I tried to do the best that I could with my life: to be of some use to others, since I was none to myself. I helped Aunt Martha at the Mechanics' Institute and got some consolation, some satisfaction from my teaching of those skills I had taken for granted – so precious now to others. Teaching these grown men, I was patient in ways I could not have believed of myself. Once, many many years ago, I had helped Kit with his letters.

Kit, Kit, Kit. I had lost Kit. All my good works, and my false courage, yet I could not shake off my terrible sense of loss. It had not been love, it had not been the outrage that was Francis, but surely it had been something else, something that I could not afford to lose, but now must live without.

I knew how it would be, the future. *His* future. Kit, the family man. Two little stepsons already, stepsons. Then soon, some of his own – a little girl to dandle on his knee, her father's darling . . . Ellen was a good woman, she was his own kind, she would make him happy.

Oh, how I disliked myself even in my unhappiness. Just as a little while ago, I had thought, *I shall marry Kit*, so now, sitting alone in the small back bedroom at Wentworth Terrace, I thought, I shall visit Haworth.

An excuse for going there was not hard to find. Parting from Betty, had I not promised, as one does, as one does ('I shan't forget you, Betty!') that I would come to see her? Would not lose touch with one so much part of my childhood (and my mother's too).

So I sent a note that I would be coming to visit both her and Mercy, in their little home in Haworth.

And what did I plan? Some sort of pilgrimage to find out more about my father, my aunts, my grandfather? (How hard to think of him as Grandfather. Obstinately he stayed 'Mr Brontë'.) Or to discover something about myself? I had little hope of doing either. Yet I knew I must go.

The bells pealed that Sunday. The sound muffled, halting

almost in the incessant rain. It had rained it seemed all the week. They rang their familiar tune – '*Daughter of the northern fields, daughter of the northern fields*' . . . Clanging in my head, hopelessly.

November. How different from my last visit. Then it had been a beautiful June day, almost unnaturally warm. Sun had softened the millstone grit, just as it softened it in Luddenden. A strong sun had beat down from a vivid blue, cloudless sky. A bird had sung in the bush before the Parsonage as we stood waiting for old Mr Brontë to speak to us. To snub us.

Now he was dead. Four years dead. And Mr Nicholls, my Aunt Charlotte's widower, gone back to Ireland. Betty told me all that.

How good it was to be with her again. She was indignant that I had not been before. 'A promise is a promise . . . and as for Agnes, Miss Agnes . . . I'll not call on the Lord in vain, but that man, Sir Hoity Toity Whitaker . . .'

'She's happy,' I said, 'she has two lovely boys . . .'

'Bonny lads, are they? And what of you, Christabel? When are you to wed?'

Always the same questions. I was almost twenty-three now. Agnes was both wife and mother. So . . . Something was not right. Betty worried for me.

I forgot that often she had been harsh, rough in manner, that she had frightened me out of my childish wits and been the cause of many a sleepless night. I remembered only that she had loved us all, fiercely. And not least, my mother.

We did not speak of Papa. Or only when recalling happy times. Of Papa in the present she did not wish to hear. She had asked me quickly when I first arrived, then, like Mrs Ogden earlier, not stayed for an answer.

Mercy watched me from a chair by the fireside. For Mercy, who had made the journey to Luddenden, rain or shine, all through our childhood, was now crippled by rheumatism. She was looked after by Betty. I imagined them gossiping together all day, just as I had overheard them once upon a time in the nursery.

The weather, icy, promising sleet during the journey, worsened as we sat talking. They had asked me when I first arrived if I would not stay the night. Now they asked again. I accepted. It was already midday and I could not hope in the few hours left to do even half of what I had planned.

It was not hard to turn the conversation to Branwell. It was necessary only to return to their favourite topic – my mother. In the end it came from them. From Betty.

'She'd a tender spot always, had your mother. A tender spot for that wild lad. She'd only to see Mercy and she'd ask for news of him. I think oftentimes if he'd spent more time at Buckley House, among us, and less at the Lord Nelson –'

A village full of people. So many of whom must have known him if not well, well enough. In the last few days I had pictured myself, believed in myself, knocking on doors, asking: 'What are your memories of Parson Brontë's son?' Now I wanted wildly to rush from the small warm cottage, to charge out into the street, knocking at every door, declaiming passionately:

'Here I am, daughter of the northern fields, of Branwell Brontë, of Parson's Patrick – tell me something of him! *Tell me anything of him* . . .'

I did not. And knew I would not.

All afternoon a steady, icy rain fell. It was not possible to walk out. Perhaps it would have to be enough, *tonight* rather, that I should sleep in this village, which had seen my father's greatest hopes, and misery. Where, if anywhere at all, his ghost would walk.

And then at teatime, a knock at the door, and the wet, freezing-cold figure of Betty and Mercy's niece, Mary Ann. She came often ('All of four times in the week,' Mercy said proudly) to see that her aunts were all right. Fresh-faced with Betty's mouth and Mercy's eyes, she was married with four small children. But since her mother-in-law lived with them, it was always easy to go out.

Mary Ann talked. And talked. Nonstop chatter interspersed with concern about Aunt Mercy's health. For me, she was exactly what I wanted, since she had been taught in Sunday school by my aunts. And even on occasion, by my father.

I hung on her every word. Trying too hard to remember all, and likely to lose most. I wanted so much to know, as well as to feel, 'This is my family . . .' I needed to – surely. For I had for certain lost my other one.

Mary Ann talking:

'Me and Martha and Jessie, at school . . . Mostly it were Charlotty teached us. Sometime it were Annie, and afore Christmas one year we'd the son. Parson's Patrick. If Charlotty, if she were fierce some time, that's nowt as to how . . . A little small lad – my head were all but up to his even then, little one that I were . . . And vexed for a nowt. Snap, snap, he went. Clack, clap. "*Now*," he'd say, "*now* . . . Get it right now!"

'Mam said, if he'd been as fierce wi' hissen, as wi' us, then mebbe he'd not've ended badly as he did . . . But then it's a sad tale and who kens the right and wrong of it?

'. . . She didn't see well, didn't Charlotty, and I'd this knitting – how I'd fash missen wi' that knitting! She'd want to inspect it like – so she'd have it held up right close, afore her eyen . . . like this . . . And then, "Yes, Mary Ann," she'd say, "that's all right, Mary Ann." Jessie, she couldn't manage her needle. Charlotty'd help . . . Then one time she give our big sister, Sarah, she give Sarah a bonnet of hers. And Mam says, I mind her saying it, "Whatever use is this, Sarah? Who's to wear the likes of that *here*?" I mean . . . It were pop. There were nowt we could do wi' it. So Mam burned it . . . But now that Charlotty's famous for book writing, I reckon we'd have done right to keep it . . .

'Jim – that were our eldest – he seed once t'landlord of t'Bull and Parson's Patrick, they was stood afore the shop window and inside were this toy, that were a man sat on a *donkey*. Landlord says, "Why, that fellow there, he has a look of you, Mr Branwell . . ." And then what does Patrick do but jump on the landlord's back! Jim had to laugh . . . Aye, there was pranks and laughter in them happy days . . .'

On and on and on. I could have kept her there all night.

I knew that I must treasure every scrap of memory, however small or trivial – or unattractive. A portrait was emerging.

And what had I found? What portrait emerged?

A small man. Small, small – as I was small. And minding it, yet causing people to forget, distracted by the flow of talk. Amusing, witty. Full of flights of fancy (*not* over his listeners' heads, or at the most, flatteringly so). *Wanting* to amuse and to be amused, and more than earning any round of drinks that might be offered. Kind-hearted (sitting by the bedside of a sick and dying Sunday school pupil), even warm-hearted. Coldly selfish and calculating in his own interests. Unreliable, scarcely to be trusted. A liar and a braggart, and in need of a firm hand. Emotionally excitable with nerves drawn tight, ready to snap. Moods – now in heaven, now in hell. Rarely if ever rooted to the earth. Irish and Cornish – not Yorkshire at all – and with the worst of those two heritages. It was my aunts, his sisters, who had the best. And used them.

That night, I slept in a small box bed downstairs. Mercy slept upstairs in the big bed with Betty: the climb up the narrow steps was a slow business and painful. As I undressed, stepping into a borrowed nightgown, its ample folds falling about me, I thought that tomorrow I would spend time out of doors, whatever the weather, unless it was time to go. Warmed now by the dying fire, I fell asleep almost at once.

I dreamed, and knew that I was dreaming. The box bed rocked as if it were a boat. I was on stormy seas. But even as I tried to save myself, I was swept, now up, now down. But still my frail boat kept upright. The waters about me were grey. And the sky above growing dark. Who were these drowning? Faces. Heads bobbing above the waters. Then hands raised, in pleas for help. A wailing sound, the wuthering of the wind – or their voices?

'I am dreaming,' I said out loud. 'This is a dream.' A face here and there, that I knew. Mama's, yes, Mama's. 'I am coming!' I cried, I am coming. But first I must save myself, and then there was Josh, now near, now far. Josh, recognized first with joy, then despair . . . How could I save Josh?

And last of all, my father. How did I know it was him? How could I *not* know?

Then the bells began to ring. They rang in the distance, over the water, which muffled their sound. *Daughter of . . . daughter of . . .* As I fought for life – my own and others', before we should all go down, I grew ever more frantic. In my terror wishing to jump out into the waves. *I cannot save others, who cannot save myself* . . . and I clung to the sides of the box bed as it rocked with the waves.

Just before going under, I woke myself – with a scream. The quarter-hour chimes were sounding from the church clock. I lay awake trembling in the darkness. Upstairs Mercy or Betty coughed. Then after a little, I heard the clock chime the hour. Four o'clock.

The wind whipped round the corners as I set out mid-morning. 'I shall go for a walk,' I had said, impatient to be off, impatient of Betty's fussing about my clothing. 'I'm not in the nursery,' I told her affectionately.

'Have done. You're still a bairn . . .' She fell then to reminding Mercy of how I had been as a child:

'Back answering – there never was such a one for back answering. The master, the mistress, that governess – Miss Dutton did they call her?'

It was a wild blowy day, cold and surely likely to grow colder, but as yet, no signs of rain or sleet. I walked the little way up Kirkgate till I came to the Black Bull.

Yes, the Black Bull – scene of my father's triumphs and disasters, successes and failures. Stimulant and solace. Inside those walls, how many ideas were plucked from the air and toyed with, juggled with – and never realized. Gone, gone, gone. My poor father sent for to entertain the jaded traveller. Guaranteed to dazzle. Then tumbling, alcohol fired. Swinging up up up and down down down.

Scene of empty public triumph – the only triumph, since all else was failure. Scene too of the last terrible years. When the day only began at the onset of darkness, when hell, or something like it, yawned beneath his feet.

I stood for a moment outside. I would not go in, even though I knew that his chair, the chair in which he sat always, remained in its place. Inside it would certainly be warm, the sounds that came out were hearty. But standing there, lashed by the wind, I felt coming through the door, seeping out from the walls, not only the despair, but all the angry waste. And how angry he must have been . . . What *anger* there must have been deep inside.

And through the tall iron gate, into the church. A few moments only. I needed no more. I sat in the family pew, where childhood outgrown, he had knelt so seldom. I remembered his noisy heartbroken sobbing for the death of Willie Weightman. I remembered too that on our visit, Mama had sat there. And I had not known why. I thought it somehow right that as their child, I should kneel here now. I said too, also to myself: my father's bones lie beneath the church pavement . . .

How much did I remember of the Parsonage, and how might I look without going in? I could not think of any excuse to speak to the new incumbent. In any case, I did not wish to assume the role of common visitor, curious to see where the Bells had lived. In this way, I was proud.

I saw some changes: the small windows that Mama and I had stood before, waiting for the door to open to us, had been replaced by great sheets of plate glass, altering the whole aspect.

I would walk, go where my aunt took her last walk. I went through the graveyard, not as I remembered it, but planted now with young trees. Bleak still, though not so bleak as once.

The moors stretched out, beyond the Parsonage. Stretched for twelve miles. Behind I could see over the valley as far as the hills above Ilkley Moor.

I met no one as I went. Only the sheep of my childhood, staring black-faced. Once a grouse started up. On the edge of the heath grew a ring of thorns, several of them bent in their fight against the wind, bent like aged persons. Then the distant dark shape of a farmhouse or two, a white-washed cottage. I climbed upward, a stone wall on my right.

The view widened to a great sweep of moorland. The waterfall valley lay before me. Then the path dipped down again. On my left were wet, faded heather, dark patches of bilberry, and on my right green-gold bracken. The track narrowed. Now I could see the beck, twisting and turning in the hollow below, beneath the tree boughs which grew out of the bank.

I climbed down through the tall crackling bracken, sodden with rain. Watching for slippery stones. Then I reached Sladen Beck. How the water roared . . . The beck was in full flow after the week or more of rain. Now the wind sent the spray up like diamonds. It was a wild and beautiful sight.

There was a boulder of millstone grit, the shape of a natural chair. But I could not have reached it without entering the water. I looked up now to the main waterfall. Before it stood three silver-birch trees. The water cascaded, a white mighty torrent, down into Sladen Beck below.

I felt alone, as alone as I had ever felt. Not afraid. There seemed no ghosts here.

An ice-tinged rain fell. I grew wet. But still I stood there. No, no ghosts. My father was not here. Branwell was not here. I thought instead of Emily. Here I stood, in wild, harsh winter. I thought of her bleak strength. I thought then that if I were to have, were to be offered something from all of them – my three aunts – then I would ask for, desire some of that strength, so wanting in my father.

How long did I stand there? Too long. Growing cold and scarcely noticing it. Ice-tipped fingers and nose. The sky had darkened, it rained in earnest. I felt then a strength – it could be nothing else – come into me, as if brought by the rain, blown by the wind.

I left that beck, that moorland. Rarefied, uplifted, infused with this new spirit. This strength.

But somewhere beckoning in the distance, was – what? A

sacrifice? I only knew something was to be asked of me. It was *for* something that I had received this gift.

Walking back, lightfooted now, over the slippery boulders, through the wet, bent bracken. Carelessly, confidently, I dedicated myself to whatever would be asked of me.

Betty told me off when I stumbled in only half an hour before I should leave, no dinner eaten, and drenched through to the skin. She shook her head over me. A grown woman and yet not improved at all:

'Worrit, I were. I thought mebbe the gytrash had you.'

Baby Benjamin took two steps, stumbled and fell into my arms. I snatched him up.

'Oh but fancy – *is* he not advanced!' exclaimed Polly.

Benjamin played with my fingers. Two-year-old Louisa, my goddaughter, stood by, her head on her mother's shoulder.

As usual, almost a habit now, I was spending Christmas with Polly. She was in the sixth month of a new pregnancy. This too seemed almost a habit. She looked well on it.

We had had news of Edmund ('I told him he has become quite an alphabetical person – he has so many letters you see after his name') and of Henry, who was safely friends with her now but so busy, too busy, so that he had only once seen the children. I had given an account of Halliwell, and Agnes.

'And your Papa,' she was asking now. 'There is nothing good of him?'

'I don't know where he is. Only that he is not at Aunt Martha's. He is almost certainly drinking – somewhere.'

'And you, dearest, we must speak of you. What shall *you* do now?'

She knew the story of Topham Abbey. By common consent we did not refer to it. But she was insistent I should not become a governess again.

'Why not? Since I must earn my living? The Talbots – that was a happy time –'

'Oh, the Talbots,' she said, 'beginner's luck, they call that. You should not expect to be a fortunate person in this regard. Governesses – how unhappy we made our own . . .'

'If not a governess, then what? *You* are all right, with your Louisa and Benjamin –'

'Something quite different. You must do something different. We shall look in the *Morning Post* . . . Promise me, dearest, that

amongst the advertisements, the first reasonable one you see –
that you will do something about it?'

'I promise.' How could I ever refuse Polly anything?

Later that day, we looked. Polly running her finger down the
front page:

'There you are,' she cried. 'But exactly it!'

I looked where her finger pointed.

Companion housekeeper wanted for Invalid Gentleman. Seaside house. Some sewing and other duties. Nurse resides. Write
with references, Mrs Butler, 15 St Nicholas Cliff, Scarborough,
Yorkshire.

'The sea,' she said. 'And Yorkshire. *And* Scarborough. What
more can you ask?'

PART FOUR

Scarborough

14

The hackney took me at a brisk trot along St Nicholas Cliff. Too fast I thought for the icy cobblestones. A January sea mist hid all sight of the water in the bay below us. It was scarcely midday, but it felt as if the day were dying fast already. Some little green could be seen behind the iron railings of the gardens.

I had kept my promise to Polly and immediately after Christmas had applied for the post as Companion to an Invalid Gentleman. For testimonials and references I had not had to worry – the Adamsons were not needed, for I had the Talbots. I had also Polly's William. With his own parish now, he sounded sufficiently impressive.

The answer took a long time. But when towards the end of January, Mrs Butler wrote, it was to ask me to travel as soon as possible to Scarborough, 'that I may assess your suitability *in person*'.

Aunt Martha thought it all a nonsense. 'Even more daft than this governess notion.' She pleaded: 'Settle with me, child, and sooner or later, we'll find a lad to suit . . . You'd do better getting yourself asked down south to Bath. Your uncle and antie – they'll know fine folk . . .' Useless to tell her for the twentieth time that Aunt Flora and I could not spend so much as an afternoon together without friction.

It was a trying journey. Inland there had been much snow. I thought at one time that the railway lines might be blocked. At York, I spent the night at the George, so as to catch the 9.45 the next morning. And then, the welcome sight of the pleasant Grecian-style railway station. The first glimpse, through mist, of the sea. Oh, happy past days in Prince of Wales Terrace. Polly and I, and dear Mrs Liddington. Boring Edmund. Little white Jasper running at our heels.

Mrs Butler was a comfortable body. Dressed in black silk, a small kitten sitting on her generous lap. She knitted some shapeless garment in grey as she spoke:

'You are very young.' (I had thought it was to be yet again, 'You are very small . . .')

'Twenty-three –'

'I had thought less. But then that is my carelessness in not asking for such details. And I think in your letter, you did not inform me?'

A servant brought in a tray of tea. Mrs Butler said:

'Should you like something stronger? Negus, hot brandy – to drive out the cold?'

'My age,' I said. 'I had not meant to deceive.'

'Ah, there is no question of that. I think only of suitability. And from your letter, and now that I see you in person . . . The family disgrace you mentioned . . . It must have been very hard . . .'

She was comfortable, comforting, such a person as one confides in (what Polly called a 'confidant person'). I found myself telling her already, when we had hardly spoken of the post or what my duties would be, the tale of Topham Abbey. The tale of the babe, of what I had seen, of the sadness and horror of it all. I who had wished never to speak or think of it again.

She murmured dismay, sympathy. 'Such sights and experiences, they mark us . . . I can see you would wish to try a position other than governess. It is not a question of reason, but of emotion.'

Yes, how well she understood . . .

'My husband and I – there are no children, but I know of their loss . . .'

If I were to live with such a person – and if her husband, although ill, were of a like disposition – how well all would go. I would be the daughter they never had. I would . . .

Relief, hope ran through me, ran away with me.

'. . . and your duties, if you are agreeable and wish to come . . .

'Your interest in reading, your studies, they recommended you. You will find your employer a very cultured man. In the way of reading to him – which would be the greater part of your duties – there would be no frivolous matter, material. And you should be able to converse. Not on political matters, for these do not interest him at all. But literature, the classics . . .'

I thought then that I should ask, 'What is the nature of the illness? An invalid – I take it that he cannot walk?'

'No – that has not been possible for the past year. He has tried treatments both in Germany and France, and all without success. It is an affliction of the muscles – I daresay the medical men have a name for it but it is not known to us, and would not help in a cure, which he seeks in vain. Just now he is in Cheltenham, to see if some spa treatment there may alleviate . . . You see how hopeless persons move from cure to cure.

'He has a nurse with him, always. But, you understand, she is no companion. She is a Scotchwoman of middling age. Most able – but I think our invalid tires quickly of her conversation. There was an experiment in reading to him. But I fear, her voice . . . So you will see why it was so important to meet you in person. And to hear, which I do, my dear, that your voice is clear and sweet . . .'

By now we had been called into the dining-room. The table was laid only for the two of us. I made a good meal. I had been cold, but now was warm and at ease, and very hungry. Mrs Butler told me that she liked to see a healthy appetite.

'Some more apple pie? The cream here is excellent. You will see that everything is of the very best.'

I looked down at my full plate. 'I can see that you mean to fatten me. Has your – has Mr Butler a good appetite?'

'Oh excellent. Very healthy. It is all the fresh air. And the many miles he must walk . . .'

'Walk?' I queried. 'But he is an invalid. You –'

'Mr Butler?' She laughed, but kindly, affectionately. 'My husband an invalid?' She hesitated, the spoon to her mouth: 'It cannot be – surely, you did not think it is *Mr Butler* to whom you are to be a companion? Oh, my dear . . .'

'I had not thought – I understood, assumed. I am so sorry . . .'

'Oh but it is I who have been foolish!' she cried. 'How could I have not made myself clear? Mr Butler and I – Mr Butler is a civil engineer. We live at Falsgrave, but he and I caretake these premises when required. And it was I who said I would engage . . .'

Although she had taken the blame, I felt foolish still. I asked, 'Who then would be my employer?'

'His name, my dear, is Hume. A Mr Hume –'

'From where, Mr Hume is *from where*?'

'My dear, you must not look so embarrassed by your mistake . . . Mr Hume is a clergyman. Before his illness he was in the West Riding somewhere, I believe . . .'

While the blood thudded in my head, and my fingers and legs

grew strangely numb, I thought: It cannot be. It *cannot be. And yet it was.* (There was not the slightest doubt that this Mr Hume was my Mr Hume. Francis.) Oh, *what* to do?

I was trapped. I could scarcely speak. My voice when it came out was low and hoarse.

I asked some questions – but only to gain time. (When might we expect Mr Hume back, was this northern climate the best for his complaint?) I hoped that how I felt did not show, or if it did that it would be taken for awkwardness still at my mistake.

Yet all I need do – so simple, was it not? – all I need do was thank Mrs Butler, explain that suddenly I have changed my mind, that I am so very sorry for the trouble I have put her to, refuse all expenses – and go. Simple if a little unpleasant.

I could not do it. I could do nothing. My hand, reaching for a glass of water, was stiff and numb still.

'Miss Woodward – are you well? Are you all right?'

'It is just –' I said. 'Perhaps it is the travel.'

'It is nothing with your health?' I heard the anxious note in her voice.

'No. No. Only after travel. A little rest and I am soon recovered.'

She suggested that I might like to lie down in the room that would be mine.

'What time should you leave? If there is time before your train –'

I sat by the window. The view was mainly of an enormous, half-completed hotel, in the Italian style. Mrs Butler had already spoken to me of it. It was to be one of the biggest in Europe, with over three hundred bedrooms, and a dazzling view of the bay. The original company had run out of money and work had ceased on it. Now, after sale, a new company had been formed. The hotel was to be known as the Grand, and would cost sixty thousand pounds to complete.

I had a shawl about me as I sat there. I did not lie down. I felt sick, sea-sick almost – tossed on waves of revulsion and terror. Oh, for someone to turn to. Oh, for someone who would help me. And yet I did not have to make a decision immediately: I might say Yes, and then on my return, write to say that I had changed my mind. The possibilities were so many.

Go, go, go. Why, when it was so easy to go, did I not do so? The person who that afternoon made the decision to stay, is not the person who writes now.

I think that I was still full of some of the strange elation I had felt during and after my visit to Haworth. Almost three months now and there was a glow still – the glow of sacrifice, of what you will. I had not stood by the waterfall, drenched in November rain, dedicating myself, receiving strength, for nothing. Why this chance encounter? *Why* should it have been Francis's advertisement I answered – if it was not especially *meant*? Surely this, and this alone, was the something, the sacrifice, that was to be asked of me?

When the first shock was over, it would all seem different. It would not be so bad. This distress was only the upheaval, awakening of memories, of old fears. Shock too of the unexpected. It would not last.

But what of Francis himself? Perhaps when he learned who Mrs Butler had engaged, *he* would not wish to employ *me* . . . If he did not, then that was my answer. I would have done what I should, the best I could.

I will do it! I cried, getting up from my chair, and going to the door. I will be brave!

'You are rested, my dear? Certainly your colour is better . . .'

'You will arrange then with Mr Hume?' I said. 'I can come in about a fortnight. I believe you said he returns about then?'

'If the snow allows it. Although we must not be pessimistic. Winter is a hard time for us all, but I think invalids feel it the worst –'

'I knew a clergyman once, by the name of Hume. I have been wondering if possibly . . . How interesting it would be,' I said, 'if he should prove to be the same.'

When I arrived back at Aunt Martha's, Papa was there. He had appeared late the evening before, giving no account of where he had been living, or with whom. From the look of him, he had not been amongst his own kind. By the time I saw him, Aunt Martha had cleaned him up.

'Seventy times seven,' she said to me briskly, tossing on the fire some ragged material, evil-smelling and greasy. It was too wet and cold outside to light a fire. The foul stench of their burning filled the room. 'A dolly peg on your nose if it fashes you, Christabel child . . .'

But I was not fashed. Only sad. He lay upstairs in bed, sleeping it off, whatever it was: drink, degradation, or both. And semi-starvation. When he stumbled downstairs late the next evening, the new clothes Aunt Martha had sent out for hung from him in miserable folds.

He stared at me oddly through bloodshot eyes. But he did not speak. It was almost as if he did not know me. I turned my face away, for the tears had started up. I busied myself with a piece of Aunt Martha's sewing which lay by the oil lamp. She was out of the room for a moment.

I heard him sit down heavily in the rocking chair to the left of the fire – it had been Uncle Eli's once. He began to cough. For a while there was no other sound but his cough, cough, cough.

'Did you get a chill? You're poorly,' I said. 'Coughing like that –' I spoke slowly and with care. I did not trust my voice. The tears ran now into my mouth.

'Christabel, is it?' he said after a moment, stopping his coughing. His voice was hoarse, and feeble. 'You've not a telling off in mind, have you? You that knows nowt about owt. I'll tell you – listening are you, lass?'

'I'm listening –'

'I'll tell you. Again. Nowt said, needs no mending. Mind that, miss, afore you let your tongue run . . .'

I did not answer. Though silence might provoke, it would not provoke as much as an answer.

He had dozed off now. Sitting there, I wept for the waste. The terrible waste. Thinking of the man he had once been – notes caught in his voice, the fleeting expression on his face belonging to happier times, stronger times.

I had a double waste to mourn. Papa's end did not seem likely to be any improvement on my real father's. I felt that evening, not only sorrow but also guilt. I did not seem to have brought either of them good fortune . . .

Aunt Martha still disapproved of my new post. It was not that she wished me to stay and help with Papa. On the contrary, she said that my presence was bad for him, making him edgy, bringing out the worst. For her part, she must ensure he did not wander off again. There had of course been no work, who had believed such a fairy story? Now there must not even be pretence of it.

'He's all I have,' she said, 'if I'm not to count you, child. And I'd best be caring for him. There's no one else will . . .'

She thought that I would be putting myself yet again somewhere where it was difficult to meet 'lads that'll likely court you'.

I reminded her I would be in Scarborough during the Season. So, who knew?

I had not told her exactly who it was I would be companion to. In any case, the name 'Hume' meant little to her. But Agnes I told, visiting her one day that next week, while I knew Septimus to be over in Halifax. I said, as easily as I knew how, what a strange chance it was, that it should be he, Mr Hume.

'What a *happy* chance,' Agnes said, correcting me.

I wrote to Polly. Now only a month away from her third child. But I could not bring myself to tell her anything. I thought: If all goes well – or does not go too ill – I shall tell her when we meet.

It was spring sunshine the day of my arrival at the Cliff. Little of February about the weather. A gold light bathed the great terrace houses, and the pavilions of the Grand Hotel opposite. The salty air was fresh. Fatigued by the journey, nauseous with apprehension, I took great gulps of it. I told myself how happy I should be to leave smoky Halifax behind. And was not comforted at all.

Mrs Butler welcomed me. She was packed and ready to go, but wished first to introduce me to everyone.

There they stood to welcome me. The staff. Mrs Craker, a small somewhat timid-looking woman, newly the housekeeper. Mrs Green, the cook, red-faced and white-haired. Mary and Eliza, the maids, and the twelve-year-old servant of all work, Fanny. And Miss Hope.

'Miss Hope is nurse to Mr Hume – she has been with him almost four years. I don't know what we, what *Mr Hume* would do, without Miss Hope . . .'

I shook hands along the line, little Fanny curtseyed, Mary and Eliza bobbed. Evidently my status was to be much higher than that of a governess.

Miss Hope's hand was cold, as if she had just come from outdoors. Her smile was the same. I remembered Elinor Adamson's smile which had so deceived me. This one I thought was not intended to deceive. It was the frosty grimace of one not given willingly to smiling.

She was tall: tall enough to make me feel my want of height. Thin also, with a long, hard face. High tight cheekbones and curious eyes – a watery blue, set close together and slanting downwards.

She it was who would take me in to meet Francis:

'The Reverend is just about to have his dinner,' she said, in her Scots accent. 'You must be with him only a few moments.' Her voice grated. It had a raucous note. I could not think it good for an invalid.

'Come, please. This way, Miss Woodward.'

His room must have been the best in the house. High-ceilinged, white and airy. I wanted to look round it, at the furnishings, the view from the window – anything. Anything but its occupant, sitting covered by a rug to the left of the large mahogany table.

'Here is The Reverend,' Miss Hope said. She raised her voice: 'Here is Miss Woodward, Reverend.'

She pushed me forward a little, impatiently, with the edge of her hand. I could see already that I annoyed her.

'Ah, Christabel,' he said.

'What does he try to say now?' exclaimed Miss Hope.

'My name,' I said. 'I am called Christabel. Mr Hume and I – Mr Hume was once vicar of our church. He knew me, you see, as a child.'

I heard my own voice. Listened as if to a stranger.

'Och – and you never said a word, Reverend! Is that not a wee bit mischievous?' She leaned forward and rearranged the soft angora rug so that it covered his hands also. 'Say good day now then to Miss Woodward – but be a little quick about it. There's your dinner ready, and Cook's made you hare collops – all nicely minced up, and with port wine gravy . . .'

'Ah, Christabel.' He brought a hand from under the rug. It shook a little as he tried to hold it out.

The voice was his. It was Francis's voice. But slurred and thick. He spoke only with difficulty. And the rest? I could not believe that disease could make such ravages. He seemed to have shrunk: that was perhaps the worst – that he should be so wasted. I could not see the legs beneath the rug, but his wool jacket hung loose. Strands of thin grey hair lay across his scalp. A drawn, ashen face, the eyelids markedly drooping.

'Not one of my good days . . .'

I knew that I would have to take his hand. It was dry and weak, and not frightening at all. My only emotion – which took me aback completely, sweeping over me in a flood – was pity. To have come to this pass . . .

He was speaking to me again.

'Not good day. Later –'

'What's that now? What's that?' Miss Hope had begun to

bustle me out. 'Miss Woodward must go, and you must have your dinner. If I tell you now Cook's made orange custards to follow your collops . . .'

It was late afternoon before I saw anything of Francis, without Miss Hope. She seemed angry with me that I had known him before, however superficially. Or rather, she was angry that he had not told her. She hinted as much:

'Och and it's very strange The Reverend – that he knows you the while . . . I think now that he must have been an excellent vicar – he does not care for me to tell him that. "Please, Miss Hope, please," he says. Always courteous. I have never found him any other – whatever the pain or discomfort . . .' She looked at me sideways, with her slanted eyes. 'Of course The Reverend is just the sort would remember *everyone* in his parish – right down to the Christian names of wee girls. I think now you were not very old?'

'I was a child,' I said, wanting at once to be done with the subject. 'A child only.'

After dinner, I drank tea with Mrs Butler, while Francis slept. She was concerned that I should not feel I was taking on too much. 'Now you have met our invalid . . .' She remarked on Miss Hope. 'Such an excellent nurse. So devoted. She scarcely leaves his side.'

I suggested that perhaps she would not care for my presence most of the day, but Mrs Butler dismissed the notion.

'She will be glad to be free a little . . . I know too, that she *feels* her want of education in his regard, and that is not good.'

I sat with Francis. Alone. And now I was afraid. I would have been less afraid if I could have felt any of the expected emotions. I could not believe that pity was all I was to feel. A pity that carried forgiveness. I suspected that other emotions lurked.

My chair was by the window, not far from his. When the covering slipped from his wasted legs, I was quickly up to replace it. We talked quietly.

His voice, so weak, so monotonous. Where was the voice that had rung in the pulpit – the great laugh, suddenly bursting out. Once his voice had thrilled me. Surely it was *that* voice I feared, dreaded to hear again. This one, with its pitiable sound – it stirred scarcely a memory.

He spoke with difficulty, slowly – I did not wish him to grow tired – of what duties he required of me, and in what way I could best be a companion. We spoke too of his illness. (Lurking unmentioned was that first nervous collapse – and its causes.)

'You will – see . . . Little I can do for myself. Want of strength – in all the muscles. Only the *mind*, Christabel – mind is active.'

He told of how he had tried the most advanced treatment obtainable. But that little seemed known about such wasting diseases.

'Electricity – God's gift. No good for me. Electrical current – stir the muscles. Galvanism . . . Prayers not answered. Have tried every spa in Europe – money, no want of money. Not – not bought health, Christabel . . .'

But he had tired himself with so much speaking . . . I suggested that I should read to him a while before tea.

'I think Miss Hope brings your medicine then?'

'Miss Hope, so kind – but voice . . . Voice, no. Good hear your voice again – Christabel.'

Ah, these glancing allusions to the past . . . So careful, so prepared . . . (We had both to defend ourselves against the other. It would not be easy.)

As yet, we had not spoken of Wade House or the disaster. Mama's death. Agnes's marriage. Nothing. Did he not wonder why I should have applied for such a position? Self-absorption of the invalid perhaps? But ignorance of all this did not seem to worry him. And it was to be several days before we discussed recent events . . . It seemed that his mind, eager for the meat of reading, was not yet up to discussing (or remembering?) the fortunes of the Woodwards.

'Reading – not easy. See double. Grand Latin name – *Diplopia*.' He attempted a smile. Then, 'That book there, second from left, on table – pile on table. Pliny . . . *Letters* . . .'

But just then we were interrupted. A knock on the door: Miss Hope bringing in Dr Timpson.

The doctor's manner was cheerful. He strutted into the room, small and self-assured. It was as if a window had been thrown open. Miss Hope said:

'The Reverend's a wee short of *rest* today, doctor. He has a visitor. The lady companion I spoke of . . .'

'Good, good. Very good. Exactly what is needed.' He came up to Francis and took hold of his hands, raising them up, then letting them fall. 'No examination today. No need to clear the room. We are doing well. I'll just have a word with Miss Hope here. Then it's back again Wednesday.'

Miss Hope plucked at the doctor's sleeve:

'Doctor, will you tell him now, he's not to excite himself with learned matters? If he goes beyond his strength –'

'Can speak for myself,' Francis interrupted. His voice was faint against her harsh one. 'Not tired, Timpson – not tired at all.'

When they had both left I read to him from Pliny. About a brave woman.

Only in the evening, alone in my room, did the day's events overwhelm me. I thought at first the journey had caused a chill on the liver, so sick did I feel. But after I had undressed and lain down a while, I realized that it came from my mind, the sickness.

It was better not to lie and think. I rose and began the unpacking and arranging of my things that I had not had time for during the day. Soon I had everything arranged – my books, photographs, portraits. My few clothes hung in the wardrobe. While I was doing all this I had been able to smother thought. Now I felt only exhaustion and a strange peace. I sat for a while at the table, the lamp beside me, reading Tennyson.

I could not but like the room with its simple rosewood furniture, sofa covered in light chintz, the lightly flowered carpet, and pale green walls. A small carriage clock ticked above the fireplace: such a warm room after my icy box of a bedroom at the Abbey. The fire roared still. A scuttle piled high with sea coal stood alongside.

And behind the high shutters was the sea.

Perhaps I was making a sacrifice, but I could see that it was to be a comfortable one.

I woke full of hope. Throwing wide the shutters, looking out at the magnificent, half-built hotel, and at the sea, hidden now by an early fret. Opening the window a little – smelling the mist, hearing the gulls just beyond the terrace. Yes, I was full of hope.

Hope. Janet Hope. And then as I shivered in my light wool wrap, there at the window, I thought: How ever are we to get along together – Miss Hope and I?

She had been four years with Francis. And would, I am sure, have liked nothing better than to read to him, write his letters, and talk with him – all in addition to her other duties. Devotion. There was no lack of that. So what must she think of this 'lady companion' who when engaged was found to be part of his past?

How much a part she could never know. Yesterday had been enough to show me how angry she was at my arrival, how simply (and understandably) jealous. I saw that it would take all I had of tact, and thoughtfulness, if we were not to come to blows – if both our lives were not to be made miserable. And Francis's with it.

It was her footsteps I heard now outside the door.

'Good morning now, Miss Woodward. If you'd thought of going into The Reverend – best not till he's had his breakfast. I stay with him to feed him. You'll have noticed now, there's a wee difficulty with eating . . .'

She had come right into the room. I saw her looking around as she spoke, craning her neck a little to see my treasures laid out on the dresser.

I was to breakfast by myself. But dinner at two o'clock I was to take with Miss Hope. When Mrs Butler had spoken of this arrangement it had seemed to me reasonable, in a small house-hold where it would be all too easy to be lonely. Now I wondered . . . If we were to sit in that large dining-room together, Miss Hope resenting me and the only topic of conversation in common – Francis. How ever would it be?

When after breakfast I went into him, she was there.

'Ah, Christabel.' The same greeting again. Pathetically glad.

'Miss Woodward is early, Reverend. The clock may *say* half after nine, but we are all the same not quite ready, are we?' She watched me through her slant eyes, as she spoke. 'The Reverend really enjoyed his breakfast. Did you not, Reverend? Mrs Green cooked him some scrambled eggs and bloater to his breakfast – the bloater is there for flavour. Cook is very particular to get all the bones out. But he likes his bloater, do you not, Reverend?'

'It is no trouble,' I said, when I could get a word in. 'I can take a little walk and return later.'

'Och, but there is no need for that – there is our medicine to take yet, Miss Woodward, and then we are ready.'

I watched while she held for him a small measure of dark liquid. In spite of his swallowing difficulties it went down quite easily. He grimaced involuntarily.

'Nesty,' she said, 'isn't it, Reverend? But it helps the tremor. The Reverend is very good about his medicines. Dr Timpson's bitterest potion, and he downs it like a lamb. I've never had a patient like him – have I, Reverend?'

When she had gone, Francis said:

'Managing woman . . . Good woman . . . Grateful, Christabel. Can't manage without . . .'

He asked me to bring over his portable writing desk. Inside the mahogany box was a great pile of letters, mostly still in their wafers. I was to answer them at his dictation, a task beyond Miss Hope.

It was slow work, for although his mind was clear enough, his speech was not. Later, when I became more used, if it was something within my competence, I would suggest what it was he might wish to say. I would be curiously touched then, seeing the humble way in which he accepted. He who had once been so strong, so proud . . .

For today I made no suggestions. But carefully in my best hand wrote to The Reverend Jasper Minott of Pembroke College, Oxford. 'You asked after my *Oresteia* . . .'

Miss Hope was there with his mid-morning drink. Afterwards I read him two articles from *The Times*. I saw then that he slept. How vulnerable, how wasted he looked . . .

He was still asleep when Miss Hope came in, this time with a decanter of Madeira and three glasses.

'Och, you have quite tired him out,' she said. 'He is never asleep just now? At one o'clock. Wake up, Reverend . . .'

Yes, we must live together, Miss Hope and I. I vowed then and there that I would turn the other cheek, ignore her barbs – which sprang after all from excessive concern for Francis. It was likely too that she had realized her attempts at providing culture as well as care had proved unsuccessful. Indeed I wondered that first week if she possessed any life outside of caring for Francis.

Later that day she invited me to the medicine room. 'Come,' she said, 'come, Miss Woodward. It is best you should know what The Reverend is taking . . . Dr Timpson likes to keep the medicines to a reasonable number. There is no need to be wasteful as many doctors are, trying any remedy of which they have heard the *slightest* good. Perhaps used with success for some wee soul in Mongolia or Peru . . .'

But, I asked, was Dr Timpson not attempting to cure him?

'Cure?' said Miss Hope. 'Surely you see that his disease . . . He has tried everything. It is only to wait for death – which will be a release, the dear Lord knows . . .'

We had arrived in the medicine room now. It was really a small scullery in which she prepared everything for him – medicine, drinks and so on. Some hothouse flowers stood in a container in the sink. Towels and dressings, a chamber pot. Altogether it was not as neat as I would have supposed.

'No,' she was saying, 'there is no question of cure. It is to make him as comfortable as possible . . . you have seen that I do my best. And och, in the way of medicine, they are all palliative . . .'

She opened the cupboard. It was dark inside. There were three shelves: the centre one full of ointment jars, pillboxes, china bowls. The top and bottom shelves contained the familiar small blue fluted glass medicine bottles, together with a few large ones of dark glass.

She took one of these from the bottom shelf. 'And here is the liniment – The Reverend, he is such a one for toothache and neuralgia. As if he hadn't enough . . .

'But this is what The Reverend finds the most helpful – this is what Doctor has prescribed, a draught for the nerves.' She took down another dark glass bottle, from the top shelf. 'It is so bitter, not much is taken. A small measure. But the good it does. It stills the trembling – for a wee while anyway . . .'

There was no label on the bottle. 'What is in it?' I asked.

She pointed to the blue bottles. 'See there. I make it up from those. Valerian – that is what is so bitter – and aloes also, and camphor and then Peruvian bark. You see it is all very simple. If there should be any need for you – I don't think it would happen, but if – then a dose is two teaspoons of the mixture with a wineglassful of water. He takes it like a lamb. Indeed, The Reverend, och now, he is like a lamb, is he not?'

My sacrifice was not after all so terrible. I was not one now for looking too far ahead. I thought too that perhaps, slowly, I was being healed. Perhaps since the shock of meeting and being with Francis was so much less than I had feared, I was already nearer to a cure than I realized? It seemed to me that if I thought *all the time* I was with him, of him only – never myself, never my wants or pains or memories – by that utmost concentration, all would be well.

A contented enough life, for now. Through Mrs Butler I had been invited to a teaparty where I had met several young married women. A Mrs Griffith, nearly as small as myself, with three lively children, and Mrs Mitton, a solicitor's wife, pale-faced with sad eyes who said she found my talk – for I was inclined to chatter on these occasions – 'very enlivening'. She and Mrs Griffith wished me to accompany them on expeditions to the sands as soon as the fine weather came. And anyway, they said, it would soon be the Season – when Scarborough would quite come to life. 'Many visitors, and so much happening . . .'

Meanwhile there were visits to both their houses, which I enjoyed. Between them they had seven small children for me to love.

Agnes wrote: 'What do you say to another nephew or niece? It is possible, in the autumn. Septimus has been very kind to me. He does everything to keep me happy, and I have only to voice a want for it to be fulfilled. Joseph is giving us a lot of trouble just now. Septimus will thrash him soon. It is the only way. I am feeling well and of course always kept busy . . . To be the mistress of such a large house is not nothing, you know . . .'

And there, I thought, was one aspect of it all. Whatever she felt deep down about this match, she loved to be Mrs Whitaker of Buckley House. And was it not good also to be Mrs Whitaker, mill owner's wife?

Polly wrote. Answering my letters almost by return. So busy, but always time to write.

And then there was George. Once a month there came an epistle from India, from Peshawar where he and Halliwell were stationed. He wrote as if to his family – except it appeared that he did not have one. I had had already seven or eight letters. At the end of each Halliwell would scrawl, in his ugly unformed hand, a few lines, full of affection – telling me how happy he was and of what an adventure India was.

Unlike Topham Abbey (put so far out of my mind, it was remembered only in nightmares), I got along well with the staff. I was in the kitchens daily to praise and encourage Mrs Green in her efforts to tempt Francis's palate.

And Janet Hope? I trod carefully, and it seemed to me that, after the first few difficult days, she had decided to do the same. Whether her more pleasant manner bore any relation to what she was actually thinking, I did not know. But at least it enabled us to live together without too many sharp words.

Sitting opposite each other at table, what polite conversation we made . . . I was led gradually, as discreet question was piled upon discreet question, to tell her a little of myself. The mill, Mama, schooldays, Aunt Martha, the fall of the house of Woodward. Halliwell in India. I was able to tell it all with little or no emotion. I recounted how hard times had led to my being a governess. I said nothing of Topham Abbey.

'I have had two positions only – and both of them in beautiful countryside.'

'What good fortune – and were they good, the wee lasses that you had the teaching of?'

'They had high spirits,' I told her.

'What a blessing they are, high spirits – to those who lack them, they seem especially blessed . . .'

She paused, a noisette of lamb, gently pink, held on her fork: 'And a brother then, in India? Do you not all lead *interesting* lives?' The lamb went in. After a moment's chewing, she said:

'I have a brother has been three years in India – he is army too. But a sergeant, you know . . . For us, you see, there was no one to buy a commission. *We* all had to make our own way in the world. Och, and is it not a cruel one, Miss Woodward?'

Her voice, so harsh and shrill, seemed somehow to convey this cruelty.

But she had a longer tale to tell.

'Will I tell you now, we were Jamie and I without a mother – and I was only three and he one. Our father was a sea captain – we were as good as orphans for we never saw him. And we were glad of that. He was a cruel man, Miss Woodward, a cruel man. I've thought sometimes that perhaps our mother wanted out, and it was for that she took the galloping sickness . . . For he was hard with his fists and hard with his tongue – he thought nothing of lifting his hand to a wee girl that had done nothing wrong. And as for Jamie, poor wee lad – I tell you now, Miss Woodward, it was enough for that lad to sneeze when his father wanted quiet – the stick or the fist, it was.

'And then he was back from China, and he had the accident on the ship, something with his leg and back and it was no more going to sea. We were the while staying with our auntie in Bathgate, in Lothian – and he came then to live.' Her voice struck an even harsher note. 'Beat, how he beat us . . . for this, for that – och, it was terrible . . . There were some fibs told in those days, Miss Woodward – we soon found a fib at the right moment and we might escape the stick. Och, I'm a truthful person, but the fibs I told then . . .'

She had become very animated and flushed telling this saga of her family. Poor dead mother, cruel father, persecuted children . . .

'But God smote him a mighty blow, Miss Woodward. One afternoon it was. He'd just that moment taken a big stick to

Jamie – there he was with his stick, and Jamie crying out – the poor wee lad, he can't have passed nine years – och, it was a sound to break your heart – and then down Father falls, all of a sudden – *dead* . . .'

She paused for effect.

'No, I tell you we never missed that man, never for one day. The Lord on our side. God is not mocked . . .'

'And Jamie –'

'No question of Jamie going to sea. He went for a soldier . . . But there I go rambling on – and the poor Reverend . . . did he tell you of his tooth this morning? I don't expect he'd speak to you of such intimate matters. He has a very painful tooth. I think some embrocation on a wee cloth.'

I read to Francis from Lucretius *De Rerum Natura*. His red-leather-bound copy, battered with torn fly leaf, from his college days. Outside it was surely the first morning of true spring. The air outside the sick room would I knew be salty fresh, but with the smell too of spring. In the oval gardens opposite, purple, yellow and white crocuses made a carpet. On the scaffolding of the Grand Hotel, all was bustle. Work had begun again in earnest.

I glanced over at Francis. He sat not far from me, wrapped as usual in his soft blanket. His hands, lying on his lap, shook. One eye drooped this morning very badly.

He caught my glance. 'Christabel,' he said, with difficulty. 'Christabel –'

'Yes?' I held the page, half-turned.

'Christabel . . . Want to say – sorry . . . *Sorry* –' He struggled to emphasize the word: '*Sorry* . . . Luddenden . . .'

I could say nothing. Yet must say something. I said,

'All that, what you speak of, it is so long ago . . . It is nothing. Quite over. Forgotten –'

But even as I spoke, even as I lied to him, I saw that he would not let it go.

'Forgive me, Christabel. Forgive. *Say*, forgive . . .'

I would have wished not to look at him, not to see his face. But I could not turn away. In common humanity I could not.

'If you wish to hear it, yes, yes. I do, I do . . . But it is the past, you know. It is all past. I was a child –'

'So wicked, a child . . . a child . . . Called on God, Christabel

. . . Called on God. God forgives. Want *you* forgive, Christabel. *Forgive*.'

'Oh, but I do, I do!' I cried.

He was silent. As he sat there, his face worked, as if he tried to speak again and could not. From beneath the drooping eyelids, tears began to fall. They coursed weakly down his twisted face. If I could have touched him then, could have embraced him, I would. But I too was troubled.

'Please, calm yourself. I am here to read, to be with you. I am here to be your companion.'

He groaned, he wept. He groaned.

'Please, you must be calm. You must not distress yourself so . . . You wanted me to read . . . See, Miss Hope will be in soon with the Madeira – and we shall be nowhere.'

I took up the Lucretius, and read, falteringly, against my own racing agitated heart.

Easter that year was on the first of April. April Fools' Day. In Scotland', Miss Hope told us, an April Fool was a 'gowk'. She sounded almost skittish as she said to Francis, 'I hope you haven't in mind to make a *gowk* of me next Sunday, Reverend!'

Her mood was altogether lighthearted. She had had good news. She showed me an envelope from India. She said proudly:

'And you're not the only one to get letters from *India*, Miss Woodward . . .' She waved the envelope at me. 'Sergeant Hope – you've heard me speak of my brother Jamie that went out there? Here he writes to say, "We're to sail for home the first of August"! He shall, he must come here to spend his leave. The Reverend will allow me time off.'

She said to Francis, excitedly, although it was still five months before the event:

'You'll not grudge me a few wee hours free here and there, Reverend?' She said righteously, 'Och, there's nothing would take me from your side. But Jamie, my brother – all I have in the world . . . You won't know really how that is, Miss Woodward – you that have a brother *and* a sister and a father. Och, and a nephew too.'

There seemed nothing much to say to all that. Although I might have added 'and a friend too . . .' Polly. The Tuesday before Easter, William wrote proudly of the birth of another son, Charles Edmund. Polly was well and happy . . . And what was

I doing about visiting them? 'Come soon, we all say! A special kiss from your little goddaughter . . .'

'Christ our passover is sacrificed for us: therefore let us keep the feast; Not with the old leaven, nor with the leaven of malice and wickedness: but with the unleavened bread of sincerity and truth . . .'

Easter came and went. No one in the house was made a gowk. The atmosphere, as far as possible, was one of peace. I congratulated myself, at times, on being able to live so successfully with Miss Hope. Once or twice, Mrs Butler, when I had been visiting her, had reproached herself for not warning me that 'there might be trouble there . . . She has had the caring of him all to herself for several years now. Such devotion. She is bound to resent a newcomer . . .'

'Now, all she thinks about,' I said, 'is the arrival, the return to England of her brother . . . She will be glad of my presence, when she wishes to stay out late, or be with him.'

I began to take an interest again in drawing. So long since I had done any. Mrs Griffin had quite a talent, and was to have a drawing master in from now until the autumn. She invited me to join her. She would not hear that I should pay anything. The times were not convenient – I could manage only occasionally. Francis had become so dependent on me for everything to do with his needs of the mind that I did not like to disappoint by my absence.

After an early promise of spring, and even summer, the weather turned cold, with a cutting north-east wind. From my bedroom window, one storey above the room in which I sat reading to Francis, the sea far below me rode high, with great white horses. The sky behind, a metallic grey.

Although the rooms were kept warm with roaring coal fires, the wind cut through everywhere – howling in when a door opened, whistling through cracks in the window fittings. Francis was troubled with neuralgia. Miss Hope mentioned it to Dr Timpson, and I went myself to the dispensing chemist to collect the pills which he prescribed. She herself swore by the embrocation, which was used also for his frequent toothaches.

I would be sent to fetch it from its place on the bottom shelf of the medicine cupboard. Then from the dark glass bottle she would pour some liniment into a dish and dip into it a cloth which she would lay on his face.

'It always does the trick, is that not so, Reverend? Wait a while, Miss Woodward – he cannot answer us with the cloth laid on . . . Does that sting now, Reverend? Och, it does . . . it's the stinging does the good. When we have it off, he'll find the pain quite soothed.'

It was a tincture of aconite with morphine, she told me, and there was nothing like it. Poor Francis put up with all her ministrations, agreeing often that 'Yes, better, much better, dear . . .' when I did not doubt he still suffered severely. I would have thought laudanum a better remedy.

I did not read to him only the *Morning Post*, the *Leeds Intelligencer*, the *Spectator*, Lucretius, Seneca, Statius, Tacitus, biographies of poets – but also the Bible. I read aloud from the Book of Common Prayer. I read the Psalms. Sometimes, like that time not long ago, when he had apologized to me, he would weep. As if he remembered when he had been a clergyman.

On Sundays I attended St Mary's Church on Castle cliff. It was in the graveyard of that church, within sight of the sea, that my aunt Anne was buried. I had been to visit the grave. How many times could I not have visited it with Polly? *If I had known* . . . And I would think occasionally – at once battening down the notion – if only I could tell someone. The principals were all dead, but surely there were cousins in Cornwall, in Ireland? It would not be too difficult to find out. But the thought for some reason did not draw me. What should I say, if not the truth? And what good would that do anyone? (I write this now, who have never looked for, who would be afraid to find, the rest of the family. As I write today, I have confided my secret in *only one person*.)

I came in from outside. Today a warm west wind was blowing. I had been down onto the sands. The tide, freshly out, left little streams and pools where the sand dimpled. I had walked quite far in the light sunshine. It was early yet in the holiday season, but a few donkey carriages rode over the sands. The bathing machines, all with their distinctive markings, had been wheeled down.

This morning Francis wished for some letters to be written. I took out the portable writing desk and wiped my pen. Outside the sun shone still. I read aloud the letter I was to answer, so that he would be reminded of the contents. It was from an Oxford

Fellow, and spoke of the writer's distress at learning of Francis's illness. Of planned travels in the Mediterranean this summer. And of a new translation of Plato's *Phaedrus*.

I began to write in a fast, sure hand.

Dear Michael,
Once again this letter is written for me by a good friend. I am unable to hold a pen, and can express myself only with difficulty. It is a double cross I bear . . .

Usually I would suggest some wording; then he would nod approval. Sometimes he would manage to deliver his meaning, or almost all of it, in one of his broken sentences. For us both, it was tiring work.

. . . If you can arrange for a copy of the Plato as soon as it is out . . . I shall be interested, since Frobisher showed no gifts in our day . . .

I paused to dip my pen.

'Christabel,' Francis said. 'Leave letter . . .'

'But we are almost done, and I think I have exactly – Shall I read aloud what I have?'

'No. Leave letter . . . Want to talk. Talk to you, Christabel . . .'

Ah, pray God, he would not say again that he was sorry. I did not wish to be so moved again.

'Rich . . . worldly goods . . . Am very rich now . . .'

'Yes,' I said awkwardly. 'But that is good. You are able therefore to be ill in some comfort. You have said so yourself. How would it be if like some of your parishioners – for some it is the workhouse. You have remarked that. And that you must thank God. I know that you do – thank Him.'

'I want, Christabel, I want . . . want to give . . . When I go . . . all yours . . . Money all yours –'

'No!' I cried. 'No, that is not at all right –'

His words alarmed me. I did not want his money. Of course I had nothing, and was dependent on my earnings, but I did not want his money . . .

'My wishes . . . Own money, must do what wish . . .'

Surely he could not mean to leave me everything?

'But you have relations –' I remembered it had been said the money came through his wife, that it had been part of the marriage settlement and had fallen to him on his mother-in-law's death. 'Mrs Hume – her family . . . Are there not nephews and nieces on that side?'

'No . . . No . . . For you . . . Miss Hope – small legacy, three years ago – arranged. Rest to you, all for you. Now – want write letter lawyer. Write for me, Mr Russell, ask come visit . . . Soon.'

'Please,' I began, '*please*, I implore you –' But then I saw his distress. His hands on the coverlet had begun their trembling. He breathed as if in distress.

'It is all right,' I said, 'all right. Of course, your wishes. It is just . . . you are too good to me, you see. I could not allow but of course . . . If it will make you happy. We will write the letter now together, as soon as I have the ending done to this one.'

'Good, Christabel. Made me happy, very happy . . .'

His breathing was better, but his hands shook still. All of him shook.

'Medicine,' he said, 'Miss Hope. Medicine.'

But she was out in the town and would not be back for another half hour, when it would be time for the decanter of Madeira. I would give him his medicine, I told him. I had done it twice before. It was not difficult.

I hurried out to the little scullery, and there from the top shelf took the bottle of his draught. I measured it carefully and added a wineglassful of water. He took it readily, wincing a little as usual at the bitterness of it. I held the glass and hoped that in his trembling he would not spill too much.

'And now,' I said, 'we really must finish this letter. I remember that when we read first of the translation he mentions, you had comments other than those we make today. Can you remember them now? I think that you were dry and witty.'

And so I jollied him along. That letter was finished, and the one to his lawyer also, by the time Miss Hope, with the decanter and three glasses, had arrived in the room.

A week later Mr Russell, Francis's lawyer, arrived to see him. It was a morning visit. I would normally have been with Francis. Instead I went for a walk, visiting the small circular museum. It was another blustery day and the wind tugged my hat ribbons as I crossed the Cliff Bridge.

As I came back into the hall, Mrs Craker, the housekeeper,

and Mrs Green, the cook, were just coming out of Francis's room. Mrs Craker said:

'He still has the gentleman with him. They talk privately I think . . .'

Miss Hope was nowhere to be seen.

But later, at dinner time, sitting across from me at the table, picking at a dish of turbot, she said:

'Well, The Reverend hadn't much appetite just now. And Cook has been at the trouble of such a delicious chicken turbot, and his favourite shrimp and egg sauce . . . And then the rhubarb pie, Cook's finest, made with beer, that used to be another favourite . . . No, he is not at all himself today. But that is not to be wondered at, *is it, Miss Woodward*?' Her voice rose, as often when excited.

I said, 'I haven't seen him since ten o'clock. He seemed himself then. Perhaps his visitor tired him –'

'*You* would know of course, Miss Woodward, how he is when he *is himself* – you would know what that was, having known him so very many years. As a wee child, did you not say?'

'Yes, I was quite small . . .'

I thought: The only way to behave when she is in one of these strange moods is to be agreeable, placatory even.

'Since you are so sound on telling now whether the dear Reverend is himself or no, perhaps you would care to venture an opinion about his illness . . . Do you think he makes progress?'

'How can he?' I said. 'Surely you told me, and I have heard Dr Timpson say, there is no question of improvement. His condition can only worsen now.'

She moved to the sideboard. 'Will I serve you then with rhubarb pie, Miss Woodward? Eliza has laid it to wait. And so there, a large helping, for I see there is nothing wrong with *you*. *Your* health is all right, Miss Woodward. You have plenty to live for – och, and I daresay every intention of staying alive to enjoy it. Whereas the poor Reverend – it is not so for him, *he* has nothing to stay alive for. Do you not think it will be a mercy when he goes?'

I said carefully,

'Since his life is not at all pleasant – he suffers so – one would not wish it prolonged –'

She cut in with a harsh expletive, lifting her fork as if it were a weapon. Brandishing it before my face:

'Certainly *you* would not wish it, Miss Woodward – *you* are only too eager that it should soon be over. Is that not so?'

She frightened and shocked me with the violence of her tone. Her voice had grown now high-pitched and raucous.

'I don't know what you are saying . . .'

'Och, but you do! *You* know fine why you wish the Reverend already in his grave. And gone to his Maker. How well you'd suit that –'

'Stop this! Stop it!' I could think of nothing but to get up from the table. I did so at once. But she darted up, and catching me by the arm, pulled me towards her.

'Let me alone,' I cried, 'are you mad, Miss Hope?'

'Let you alone, indeed . . . I know fine what you're up to! Isn't it enough now that you've wormed your way in, a lass that wasn't here six months ago . . . *I've* cared for The Reverend *four* years – do you hear that now? *Four* years. And after all that – I know what I heard today. I heard –'

'Were you eavesdropping?' I tried to slip from her grasp.

'As if I ever would. How *dare* you – as if . . . Anything so despicable . . . Was I not at the door about to go in – when I heard, what I heard? *You* know of course. *You* know that after all my care of The Reverend, it's to you, *you* that everything's to go . . .' She shrieked at me: 'Scheming little . . . och, there's no word bad enough –'

I tried then to leave the room, but she had me pinned. I must listen. I must hear all her jealous hate poured out.

'And you that have a family of your own . . . insinuating yourself, that's what – none of the hard work or the real caring, och no. It's just, "What shall we read today?" and turning the pages of a fancy book, or it's to write a wee letter. Whilst I, I, I've to slave, I that never had a chance in life . . . If he's to show gratitude to any person, then is it not to me? *Me?* You're a wicked lass. I knew fine the moment you walked in. So pleased were you not? *Were you not thinking even then*, I'll have it, *I'll* have The Reverend's money –'

'Stop – you're mad, you're overexcited . . .'

'Mad? Mad, that can see wickedness that's right beneath my nose? A fine smell comes from it . . .'

I struggled free. Had I been the person I was even a year before, I would have attacked *her* – hitting out, hurting in the struggle to be free. Telling her what I thought of her. Accusing her of the ugly jealousy she so clearly felt.

But since for many reasons I was not that person, I said, firmly yet mildly:

'I leave soon for a holiday – at the end of the week. You know that. I shall not be around for a while to disturb you –'

'Och, yes, go!' she shouted. 'Go and don't come back!'

Tears of rage stood in her eyes.

I left the room shaken. She did not follow me. I shut myself then in my bedroom until it was time to be back with Francis. I did not go out, even though the afternoon was sunny. I felt sick and shaken. And unclean.

It was good to get away. And best of all that it should be to Polly. My conscience murmured sometimes that perhaps it should be Halifax and not Essex – but the accounts I had of Papa from Aunt Martha did not suggest there was much good in my coming. In her last letter, she had said, 'Breathe in all the good sea air you can, child, and don't come running here out of duty. There's little you, or others, can do for him these days . . .'

Just as on my last summer visit, the weather was almost perfect. We were able once more, in spite of all the other claims on Polly's time, to go out into the country. They were not far from Epping Forest. Last year she had been feeding Benjamin. Now we took with us the infant Charles. She told me that last year, she had already without knowing it been expecting Charles.

'I went, you see, dearest, straight from one to the other. And had of course to cease feeding him when we realized. It would not do . . . one cannot – but of course we were delighted all the same. They are all so close and will be such companions.'

'And are you never afraid?' I asked.

'Of what, dearest?'

But I could scarcely voice it. Perhaps it was the happenings at Topham Abbey, perhaps my own apprehensive nature, but lately I had grown to fear for her. Worrying obsessively about what might go wrong in childbirth. Remembering how easy it was for death to follow, almost without warning, what might seem a natural process.

'If you mean – giving birth . . . But that is soon over. Half a day perhaps – and look then, what joy!' She turned her radiant face to mine. 'Look then, what joy!'

She did not mention money. Although William had now his own parish, I knew they had still to live very carefully. The more so since they were both extremely generous, far above the calls of duty, and were forever helping needy parishioners from their own pockets.

As we talked together, she was still amazed that it should be Francis – that same Francis – to whom I was companion. But she understood, yes, she understood how his illness had altered everything:

'All the same, dearest, I could not have done it. What you are doing – I could never be such a *forgiving* person.'

Not so. Not so. Oh, Polly, I thought, how little you really know me.

Yet all that she spoke of seemed so far away. Francis, Scarborough – Janet Hope.

'Cook has done The Reverend such a delicious crab dish,' said Miss Hope, 'the meat all nicely chopped with parsley and mushrooms. He has really eaten well of it, have you not, Reverend?' She was all smiles.

She turned to me: 'Miss Woodward, tell us now, does The Reverend not look rested? I said to him, with the coming of the fine weather, "Reverend, you . . ."'

And she prattled on, her hands clasped in front of her, her head to one side. Since my return two days ago, she had been as affable to me as she had ever been. It was as if the quarrel had never happened. She made no allusion to it. We were back in our state of truce, making the best of our enforced companionship.

Much of her talk as we ate together was about the return of Jamie, her brother. He would come immediately his leave began to Scarborough. Then after a few days, they would go away together for a short holiday in Scotland.

'The Reverend says . . . Mrs Butler is to find another nurse, just while Jamie and I have a wee holiday. Four years now, Miss Woodward, and scarcely a day away from The Reverend. I know his need of me, you see. We can't all take holidays, like you, Miss Woodward, that was here less than four *months* and had to be away . . .'

I had come back to a changed and much livelier Scarborough, for the Season had begun. All the bathing machines were out now, with their gaily striped roofs, donkeys pulled carriages across the sands, and in the Spa Saloon with its towers and spires, the orchestra played Donizetti and Strauss. I remembered how the Liddingtons had taken Polly and me to listen to just that same orchestra, to those very waltzes and polkas, each happy visit I had shared with them. Theakston's Library, when I went to fetch books and journals for Francis, was full of visitors wanting the latest novels. And every Thursday the *Scarborough Gazette* list of Visitors grew longer.

The drawing lessons continued. There was much social activity in both the Griffith and Mitton households. Friends whom they saw only on their annual visit to Scarborough. Small musical evenings, expeditions, some afternoon gatherings of the ladies. I was invited out at least twice a week.

Miss Hope's excitement grew as the date of her brother's arrival drew nearer. She had all the arrangements made for their tour of the Highlands – Mrs Butler had found a temporary nurse. Now, looking round the medicine room, she sighed at its present untidiness and said she must do some cleaning up and clearing out.

'Och, I must see have I every bottle labelled – and this drinking cup has a wee crack . . . I shall get everything nice.'

The first days of September were full of sunshine and warmth. Brown-sailed fishing cobles on a gentle sea. In the harbour the Cornish luggers landed their first herring catches.

Dr Timpson went to the Lakes for a walking holiday. A Dr Lumb took his place. He was dour and unlike Dr Timpson spoke little. Miss Hope complained: 'Never a word of cheer for The Reverend . . . With a sickness such as that, it's very important to keep his spirits up. Och, it's not Dr Lumb, but Dr Glum.'

Her own spirits were very high. Only a week and Jamie would be in Scarborough.

The weather changed. It was the equinox. The skies grew grey and then black. A violent thunderstorm was followed by days of wind, churning up the grey seas. It became too bad for the fishing boats to go out.

Kept indoors by the weather, and listening to the howling of the wind, I felt oppressed. I had a sense of doom – as if bad news awaited me.

Which it did. I had a letter from Polly. Her little Charles Edmund, not quite six months old, 'had fits for perhaps a week, each day growing worse – I could not *bear* to see him suffer, dearest . . . and then he went to God. William and I – such sadness . . . Louisa and Benjamin weep to see me weep . . .'

I too wept, for Polly. I did not want Polly ever to be anything but a happy person.

Miss Hope was a happy person. Jamie was in England, and on his way up to see her. He came straight to the Cliff from the station. They were to go together to his lodgings. She brought him in at once to where I sat with Francis. He was a big man, tanned, weather-beaten, with heavy jowls and his sister's downslanted eyes. Resplendent in the blue and red and gold of his uniform. Miss Hope could scarcely take her eyes off him.

He was to be in Scarborough a week before they left for Scotland. Each afternoon or evening Miss Hope would go out with him for an hour or two. He was often up at the house. If Francis objected to these visits, he said nothing.

Day after day now of chill wind and rain. Two days before Jamie and Miss Hope were to leave, and the day before the temporary nurse arrived, I had a letter from Aunt Martha. There was a disquieting passage about Papa. 'He wanders,' she wrote, 'and I do not mean about Halifax, for he's not good now with his legs. It's with his mind he wanders – he fancies himself a bairn again, and calls for our Dad. He's puzzled at my grey hairs . . . And he talks to your mother, but I can make no sense of that for he's so full of fanciful notions. So strange – I would never tell you of them, child – that I wonder how they've come to his head . . . The surgeon was here this noon, and he says we are not to worry for it's not *drink* that makes him this way – for of course while he is in his bed I have given him none, no matter how much he calls for it. He complains too of pain, but that is from the same cause. I have sad, broken nights . . .'

How it disturbed me that letter . . . Not only did I worry for Papa – should I not go at once to his side? Should I not relieve and help Aunt Martha? And – but I scarcely wished to think of this, must I worry too that as he raved he spoke of my parentage? I wondered in that case, if my presence might not exacerbate his illness. That seeing before him his child, *who was not his child*, might only make his sufferings and confusion worse.

Oh, what to do? I looked from the window to where the rain lashed against the glass, and a sea mist obscured the view I so loved. I wondered if perhaps Papa was *dying*? It seemed to me that the storm-laden air smelled of death. I thought yet again of Polly's loss (had not my mother said, of Josh, 'no other child is *that* child'? Was not that how Polly must feel?), and the waste of it all. The waste of the fine man that Papa had been . . .

316

I hoped as I prepared the morning reading for Francis that my distress did not show. I think that it did not, for he said nothing. And he himself was not so well, complaining of acute neuralgia. I put on some of the embrocation and he thanked me so humbly as to make me ashamed.

Yes, ashamed, for in my anger and despair I had had the fleeting thought – why Charles Edmund? Why Papa? Why not this sick man, wasting away in such misery? *Why not him?*

And for a few seconds there came over me some of the old hate, the old anger, that I thought pity had finally consumed.

It passed. How could it stay in the face of such evident suffering? The more so as I saw that he suffered still in spite of the embrocation. I urged him to take some laudanum and to rest.

'No . . . Like head clear, keep head clear . . . Read me now, read me again letter from Minott . . .'

Jamie came to the midday meal. He and his sister talked together incessantly, she more animated than I had ever seen her. All of their jokes were private.

The rain had eased and the mist cleared, although a strong wind had got up. They planned a cliff walk. Miss Hope had been watching the weather anxiously. Now she was impatient to be off. Francis's neuralgia. She hurried in with the embrocation.

'Poor dear, och, the poor dear, aren't you a poor dear, Reverend? There . . . let me hold the cloth against your face . . . Is that better now, Reverend dear?'

'Stings . . . stinging . . .'

'He always says that, does he not, Miss Woodward? Och, I can see it doing you good . . . There, has that not eased it?'

She stood a moment, unnaturally impatient. Then was off again. Francis said only:

'Good woman, good . . . Nurse coming . . . hope good, take good care . . .'

'You will be all right,' I said. 'Mrs Butler would not choose anyone who was not of the best. And I too shall take especial care of you while Miss Hope is away in Scotland.'

'Timpson,' he said. 'Want Timpson back . . . *Good* doctor . . . Lumb, difficult . . . don't know, Lumb.'

'He too is good,' I said reassuringly, 'it is only his manner. He is not a happy person.'

But using that phrase I was reminded of Polly, and of how she was, just now, not such a happy person either. All my distresses came back in the gloom of that autumn afternoon.

317

The time passed slowly. Francis slept a little, fitfully. He seemed when he awoke not to be rested at all, although the neuralgia he said had eased. But he trembled, as he did when even a little tired. Yet he was eager I should continue reading.

I read from the *Edinburgh Review*. I looked at the clock. I saw that Miss Hope should have been back by now. Outside the wind was as strong as ever, but it had begun to rain again. I had a vision suddenly – shocking in its vividness – of Miss Hope and her brother, falling, falling from the cliffs into the boiling sea beneath.

The clock struck the quarter. Francis asked the time. When I told him:

'Miss Hope, late . . . Trust all right, all right?'

'She will soon be with you –'

'Medicine,' he said, 'need medicine . . .'

I saw from the trembling that I would need to give it him immediately and not wait for Miss Hope's return, for it was now the usual time for it.

The small ill-fitting window of the medicine room rattled in the wind. The wind howled. As I opened the cupboard and took out the bottle, I thought of Miss Hope and Jamie and how drenched they must have become. Though surely they had taken shelter somewhere? And that of course was why they were late . . .

I measured two teaspoonfuls and topped it up with a wineglassful of water. Francis took it as always like a lamb, and as always murmured:

'Bitter . . . So bitter . . .'

After a while the trembling seemed to ease a little. I read to him. Mr Thackeray's *Pendennis*. We were on the second volume now.

'Christabel . . . Christabel, please, thirsty . . .'

I filled his drinking cup. He took it all, and asked for more. The herring dish at midday had been highly seasoned. I had felt thirsty earlier. But I was surprised when a few moments later, he asked again for his drinking cup.

'Your meal is coming soon,' I said, 'perhaps you should not drink so much just before.'

When his meal was brought in, since there was still no Miss Hope, I had to feed him. But after one spoonful of coddled egg, he shook his head. I asked him if he was all right. If the neuralgia had returned?

'Not . . . not hungry at all . . . think *bilious*,' he said.

'It is what I said, with all that water. Perhaps if we wait a little?'

So instead of feeding him, I continued reading. I thought at one point that he had dropped into sleep. But that was quite usual. The food was left, to grow cold.

We were sitting like this, when the door burst open. Miss Hope, her wrap dripping water, rushed into the room.

'Oh Reverend!' she cried. 'Such a time as we have had, sheltering from the storm. And then in the end braving it. I am quite overcome . . . And all the while I grew so anxious. Miss Woodward, has The Reverend been all right? Are you all right, Reverend? And your medicine – the time quite gone past for your medicine –'

'I have given it to him,' I said. 'He asked, and I gave it perhaps an hour ago . . . You see, I think he sleeps.'

'Then I shan't worry, but will change from these wet garments – och, you have no idea. The wind and the rain – it might be November –'

She had been gone only five minutes when Francis woke.

'Sick,' he murmured suddenly, 'sick . . . Feel sick.'

I rushed for a cloth, and held it beneath him. He retched. Leaving him for a second, I rang the bell. When little Fanny came, I said, 'Miss Hope, please get Miss Hope.'

'Och, what is this, what is this?' cried Miss Hope, fastening her apron as she came through the door. She took charge, holding him and saying: 'The only way for this – to bring off the bile – you see he is very weak and inefficient with his retching . . . Get Mary to mix some salt and water.'

The emetic worked. Too well perhaps. He was vomiting now continuously: much white phlegm and then a quantity of yellow matter. At first Miss Hope was pleased:

'Well, *that's* better. Nesty stuff that needed away . . .'

But when the vomiting continued, pathetically between bouts Francis complained of pain below the ribs. 'It's the retching,' she said, 'you are sore, Reverend. Sore about the chest.'

'Should we not call the doctor?' I said.

'Och, yes, then, call Dr Timpson.'

But it was of course Dr Lumb who came. In the half hour that it took to send for him, Francis grew rapidly worse. Although no longer vomiting, he seemed limp and barely conscious. Miss

Hope assisted him to bed, while I waited in the sitting-room. Then she came through to me.

'I think he sleeps,' she said. She looked about the room. The uneaten meal had been cleared away. She saw the medicine glass on the mantel. 'They have forgotten to take that now.' She picked it up. She sniffed it for a second. 'Och now,' she said, 'bitter stuff, is it not?' She went towards the door. 'I'll take it away – and you, Miss Woodward, watch The Reverend . . .'

He lay very still. Eyes closed. Occasionally a flicker, of pain? or a dream? twisted his features momentarily. As I waited with him, his eyes opened. He muttered something:

'What is it? What is it?' I asked leaning close.

'*Pain*,' he said, with difficulty. '*Pain* . . . Jesus have mercy . . . Christ . . . have . . . mercy . . . on me . . .'

I ran out into the sitting-room. Dr Lumb was just being shown in.

Miss Hope, coming back into the room a few seconds after him, said:

'Och, wild weather we are having, Doctor, is it not?'

He did not answer, but went through at once to examine the invalid. I was not sure whether I should stay, but assumed that I might. Francis's eyes were closed again. He did not respond to Dr Lumb's few questions.

His hand still on Francis's pulse, the doctor said in a low tone: 'A concise account, please, of the course of this attack. Its onset . . .'

'It is for Miss Woodward to say – *I* was not there. *She* will tell you how it has all begun.'

He was still examining Francis when he said to me: 'Your account, please.'

I tried to give it as simply as possible. Beginning with the thirst, and then the vomiting.

He turned suddenly from the bedside:

'*What has this man had? He has taken something. What?*'

'Only his medicine,' Miss Hope said. Her voice was at its most shrill. She brought through the glass. 'His medicine – that Miss Woodward has given him.'

Dr Lumb dipped a finger in the glass and touched it to his lips. His mouth tightened.

'Bring me the bottle from which this was taken.'

'No, I shall go,' Miss Hope said, pushing me aside as I walked to the door.

She came back with a dark glass bottle from the cupboard. He opened it, sniffed, and closed it again.

'He has not taken this. It is not this mixture he has taken . . .'

'It must be!' cried Miss Hope.

'The diet today – you will describe what he has eaten.'

In an agitated voice, Miss Hope described the herring dish, the duchesse potatoes, the marmalade pudding.

'And what else has he had today, medicinal – *in any form?*'

'Only liniment, on a cloth, for his neuralgia,' I said. 'That is all, and –'

But even as I spoke, I felt as if ice ran through me.

'Yes, Miss Woodward. Yes?'

'Yes, the embrocation . . . It could be . . . Do you think?'

'But I am asking *you* –'

His manner was stern. I felt sick and faint. I fought the woolly feeling in my head, the swirling blackness.

'It is possible. Yes –'

Miss Hope gave a little scream, 'The wicked girl, the careless girl!'

'Fetch me that bottle also, please.'

I wondered afterwards if he gave her the errand to calm her down. She seemed about to burst into a full-blown hysterical attack. Whereas I was calm. Always calm. Too calm. Battening down the terror which had risen now to my gullet. Blocking speech.

Dr Lumb examined the bottle, sniffing. Tasting again . . . But I knew already. *I knew what I had done* . . .

But not how . . . I tried to remember standing at the cupboard, taking out the bottle. Measuring, adding water. But it was all a blur. My head would not clear . . .

Miss Hope was screaming. And screaming. I remember Dr Lumb slapping her face. Asking me to ring for help.

I kept saying, 'What is to be done? What have I done? *Will he live?*'

He looked at me directly. His face was stern. I thought of him afterwards as God the Judge.

'No,' he said. 'If that is what he has taken, I do not think he can possibly survive.'

Francis died an hour later. Miss Hope was by this time under sedation. Her screaming gradually hushed. When, later it was suggested I went to bed, I refused anything for myself. I floated all night it seemed, in and out of consciousness. I was at once numbed by horror and yet would have sudden crystal clear thoughts.

Over and over again: exactly what had I done? *What had I done?* I saw the bottle in its place on the shelf. No. *Yes.* On the crowded shelf. Why had it seemed so crowded? All those blue bottles, and yes, surely *two* dark glass bottles? I knew now, there had been two. Two dark glass bottles. The embrocation which should have been, was *always kept on the bottom shelf*, and the made-up calming draught. In her hurry to be out, Miss Hope had put the embrocation back on the top shelf . . .

But it was still *my* mistake. *It was I had killed Francis.* Round and round and round, the horror went. That everything was unreal was no solace. Tomorrow I knew would be all too real.

I wept and bit the pillow. I thought of getting up and going to sit by Francis's bedside. To keep a vigil over his corpse.

I opened my eyes. Miss Hope was standing at the end of the bed. She was wearing a dark wrap, and her hair hung about her.

It must have been about six o'clock in the morning, or thereabouts, for the light was just coming up.

'Murderess,' she said loudly. '*Murderess!*'

'Oh, but –' I began, struggling to sit up. Feeling my head not with me. I said, 'It is terrible, terrible, I have been so foolish, but you cannot – what are you saying?' I cried. '*What are you saying?*'

The raucous note was still in her voice, although she seemed no longer hysterical.

'Don't think *I* was deceived! Och, haven't you wanted that money from the moment you came? Scheming, disgusting, playing on a sick man's affections and then when –'

'Stop it!' I cried. 'You don't know what you are saying!'

'I know fine. I know fine what I'm saying –'

'You must leave me – go away, please. And stop saying these terrible things . . . Yes, I made a mistake, a *terrible* mistake . . .'

'*Mistake* indeed! That was no mistake, I know fine that was no mistake. Doctor – he may believe a nonsense like that, but then he *does not know, does he?* He does not know that a wee *mistake* as you call it has made you already a rich woman . . . Are you not ashamed, you wicked, you . . .'

Her hysteria was returning. I only wanted her out of the room.

I wanted her out of the house. Anywhere where she would not do damage . . .

'. . . And wait till I tell, for I shall speak up . . . There will be many interested to hear – that you can go to a cupboard and take . . . Can you not read a label? They will want to know I am certain *why you cannot read a label?* I daresay you will tell some story of bad light . . . but I can assure you –'

'What label?' I said, suddenly sharp. '*What label?* Neither bottle was labelled –'

'Oh, I beg your pardon, I beg your pardon Miss High and Mighty Woodward, I do beg your pardon, but *those bottles were labelled.*' She said triumphantly, 'Did you not hear Dr Lumb *read* from the label?'

'If he did, he will know – but . . . those bottles, you have said many times . . . that you . . .'

'Och, what a fairy story, to suit your evil self! As if – am I not a trained nurse? Do you think now I would have such a bottle, such medicines without directions . . . It is not good to pretend you cannot read, Miss Woodward. It will not serve to help you when –'

'Go, you must go, leave me in peace, you don't know what you are saying. *Go!*'

'Murderess!' she was screaming again now.

'Isn't it enough that he's dead, isn't that sorrow enough without these accusations? My mistake, *that* is bad enough – without this – it is all so terrible. Can you not go? *Please go!*'

She came over, nearer to the bed. She took hold of my shoulders and shook them. Shaking, shaking, as a terrier might shake a rat. She hissed and spat, her face close to mine. Over and over, 'Greedy, greedy *murderess!*'

Her actions were so violent, I became so terrified, that I must have blacked out.

When I came round, perhaps only a few moments later, she had gone.

15

'She's very small.' They were saying that again. It was like an echo. Childhood memories, school memories, what I wanted to forget and what I wanted to remember. Two of the wardresses – they were jangling keys as they spoke, it was the only sound, their voices and the jangling of the keys (and the smell, that terrible smell of prison, seeping into my clothes, hair, skin, underneath, in all the orifices, *inside* my body). The two of them talking, low voices, imagining I couldn't hear. 'She's very small – she'll maybe be lost in the dock. Like a child, she's so small.'

And then the other one, a hissing voice, meant perhaps to be a whisper, but something else in it, 'Not too small though to kill a man . . .'

'Poison,' the first one said, 'you have to be crafty for that, you have to be sly . . .'

Fortunately there were those there who were kind to me. And how I needed it.

In after years I thought the most terrible aspect of those first weeks after Francis's death was the notoriety. That I should have become notorious. Which I did. *How* notorious I became. And yet was that notoriety really the worst? Was it not really only part of the whole dreadful nightmare, from which I thought I might never awaken?

The days between the death and the inquest are a blur – stretched out sometimes into months, at other times running into each other, day indistinguishable from night, such were the nightmares.

I barely spoke to Miss Hope again. Had I wanted to eat any breakfast that first morning, I could not have gone in to sit with her. By the time I felt able to leave my room, there was no sign of her. I was never – thank God – to be alone with her again.

That first day was a fog of questions, of arrangements and callers. Incessant rapping of the front door knocker. Outside, the high wind had returned, now with rain. I looked out of the dining-room window, and there was the unreality of the Grand

Hotel. Its scaffolding appearing to sway in the wind. There would be no work done today.

Ah, that dreadful morning, changing gradually into a worse and darkening afternoon. Everyone wanted to speak to me. Questions, questions, questions. Much as I needed it, I was not to be alone a minute of that first day. Except for a short walk over the high Cliff Bridge, cold autumn mist all about me (and why not cast myself down? I thought bitterly), the sea shrouded.

Mr Russell, Francis's solicitor came. Dr Lumb came. I had of course to speak to Mr Russell. I had to go through yet again every single action.

I must say, 'Yes, yes – I gave the medicine because he needed it and Miss Hope was delayed. Yes, I am accustomed to go to the medicine cupboard, to fetch the embrocation, sometimes the calming draught. I have done it a number of times. The embrocation is kept on the bottom shelf, the calming draught on the top . . . Yesterday evening –'

But then exactly what had happened yesterday evening? I had relived the scene so many times, would have to relive it probably even more, that now I could no longer distinguish reality from my fears. Then suddenly the blur would clear (never while I was speaking, but always afterwards). I would see, as if there once again, that cupboard. Although I had not noticed it then, *I would see it now*. And there for certain were *both* bottles on the top shelf. *Without labels*.

But then if I shook my head, the image would go again. So that it might almost be a fancy. A wishful fancy. *I knew it to be true*.

How did they behave towards me: Mr Russell, Dr Lumb – and others? I cannot judge. How they were later has coloured everything. Perhaps they were kind, perhaps not. I was beyond kindness. But not yet ready for hate.

Jamie had come to join his sister. They walked around the house together – and out of it together. When by accident I passed them both in the hall, she gathered her skirts up as if meeting something unclean, and hurried towards the door. 'Come, Jamie.' She seemed not broken, but buoyant in her grief. And purposeful. How purposeful, I was soon to learn.

I wrote to Aunt Martha that first afternoon. I had thought of telegraphing her, imagining her fright if she should read something in the *Intelligencer*. I wrote to Polly. I should have written to Agnes. The paper was smudged with tears. Francis lay dead in the house. And it was all my doing.

There were practicalities. A *post mortem* was arranged. There would be an inquest, of course. Something for me to dread indeed. Meanwhile life must go on. The staff that first day were not sure how to act. They were embarrassed. Apart from an 'Are you all right, Miss?' from Fanny, no one quite knew how to speak to me.

And upstairs lay the body of Francis, his coffin lined in white satin. Hothouse lilies rested between his folded hands. I dreaded visiting him.

On the second day, in the late afternoon, the locum nurse arrived. No one had remembered to telegraph her. She left at once, after showing concern mixed with indignation that we should have been so careless. She said crisply, 'If a patient of mine dies, I would expect to be informed.'

By this time Miss Hope had moved out. She and Jamie were staying in his lodgings. Their holiday in the Highlands was of course out of the question. Miss Hope must stay in Scarborough.

I did not write yet, to Halliwell. At this stage, I could not even imagine telling George. I knew that I must, since in the fullness of time, news would filter through, in either national or provincial newspapers.

At first, for a day or two it was only Scarborough knew. First by word of mouth, then in the *Gazette*:

Under the heading, 'TRAGIC ERROR . . .' there was a short account of what had happened, together with the date and time of the inquest. I could not bear to think of and did not wish to see my friends Mrs Mitton and Mrs Griffith. Even then, before the worst happened, I did not want to embarrass them. But Mrs Butler, I could have wished to speak to her. She appeared in my mind as a haven, a comfort. But unattainable: a cab had been sent for her early on, only to find that she had gone to France for the month of September.

I moved into lodgings myself after two days. I could not tolerate the travesty of normal life, the keeping up of appearances. Miss Hope had gone. Should not I? There were relations of Francis's due to arrive. Two cousins, a father and son. Strangely, I had never thought of Francis's family. The relations I believe were on his wife's side.

Miss Hope had begun her work already, ahead of their arrival. I could not have remained in the house. I remembered sadly, in contrast, the Topham Abbey affair. How we all sat in the kitchen, united in horror. Waiting. Sympathy flowing all around me from those who had once despised me. Now, at the Cliff – how different! The staff who had once been so friendly. Mrs Green whose cooking I had praised. Now, black waves of suspicion washed over me . . .

How soon after the arrival of the Withycombes, Francis's relatives, did I overhear those words, which were to send me in fear and dread up to my chill bedroom?

'They've put the detectives on – have The Reverend's folk.'

So it was no surprise, being visited, being sent for one afternoon. That recollection is not a blur. I shall remember all my life the look of that dingy parlour in the lodging house. The bobbled, fringed tassel of the cloth which I held between finger and thumb. Then twisted and turned so that finally it was almost off.

The man opposite me was an inspector. No less a rank. A dour precise man, with a mouth buttoned tight when not speaking, his mind was made up. It was my task to confirm his suspicions. It became impossible not to do so . . .

A long exchange in which I went, with him, over and over yet again, what happened that night. In which I did not bother, care, try to protest my innocence, for after all I was guilty. Carelessness. It was only necessary to be careless the once . . .

'Tell me now how your family lost their money? A mill, I heard. A big mill . . . You won't be used to this life of work, service? Always had a servant or two yourself to order around? You'll be glad to get back to the comfortable life.'

And me saying, for I had to say something, the silences were unbearable: 'Under happier circumstances, of course. Yes. But *this*, no . . . never . . . I did not want . . .'

Prompted to answer what I *did* want, I fell silent and confused. As I sat there, the fringed tassel between my fingers, I felt the blood run from my face, then seem to leave my heart. *I shall not faint.* I determined that it would not be as Topham Abbey. I would not take refuge now in illness . . . I should be there to defend myself.

Yes, to defend myself. For it had come to that. Here were those very accusations that Miss Hope had made in the night, in the small hours – unreal, terrifying. In daylight now, in a matter-of-fact, precise voice.

But spoken without passion, spoken coldly, were they not

worse? If such a man believed that I . . . It could not be. And yet it was.

'A long and frank talk with the nurse of Mr Hume . . . a most devoted woman, in a unique position to . . . Certain remarks of yours – *Do you deny you said* . . .'

A suspicious man. He admitted it:

'I am a suspicious man. But never, or never yet, without cause. I have a nose for these things. My nose tells me . . .'

I denied nothing. I said nothing. I explained nothing. I was struck dumb. I knew from that moment on that the inquest would go very wrong.

The bad weather continued. When occasionally I walked out, going once down on the sands, the chill mist made it difficult to see how far out the tide was. It cleared for a little, only to reveal a grey choppy sea. The cold from the mist lingered. Up at the Cliff, at the Grand Hotel, between the bouts of misty rain the workmen hammered. Hammer, hammer, hammer, the sound that had once been so friendly.

Aunt Martha wrote. She could not leave Papa. Reading between the lines (more lines than I had ever had from her), I guessed that he was going downhill fast. That soon there would be another death.

About my plight I had told her only the outline. That was bad enough. I had not told her of the suspicions, the accusations . . .

Too many people. The hotel used for the inquest was packed and had to turn them away. It was said that a hall, or assembly rooms should have been used.

And it was all over in a day – that felt like a week. A short time afterwards, I was remanded in custody, on a charge of murder.

I was in prison for about ten days. An inquiry was to be held into the charge, which was expected to lead to a committal. I had never felt so alone . . . Aunt Martha could not come. Polly left her family and travelled up . . . She held my hands and wept. Both in their ways were certain that justice would be done . . . Polly was able to be of practical help. A cousin on her mother's side, a Liddington, was a barrister. She had met him only a few times, at family reunions, but she implored me, I must allow her to telegraph him *at once*.

'He is a very clever person, dearest . . . I think too that he is a *gentle* person. You must have only the best . . . No, we shall not speak of money now, and how he shall be paid. When he hears from me – *if he is free*, he will be with you, soon, soon.'

Dear Polly. And dear Betty and Mercy, who dictated a letter to Mary Ann, saying that they believed nothing of me but the best. Agnes's letter came on my fourth day in prison. I did not want to think that she had written it. It spoke of family shame. '. . . that now you should do *this* to us, as if we had not suffered enough, our family. Now the disgrace is absolute, thanks to you. The name of Woodward – it is on everyone's lips. Septimus says . . .' I tore it up. I did not wish to know what Septimus said, thought or did.

And yet she had touched on a nerve. Truly I felt I had brought not only the Woodwards and Armstrongs into disrepute, but also my real family. As if I were dragging my secret Brontë connections through the mud . . .

The nightmares. I was certain that I was going to hang. I could see no other end to this business. Assurances from such as Polly that outside there were people who had read the newspapers and wished only for my discharge, people who believed it all a nonsense, such assurances did not last long. It was hard enough to believe in daylight. At night time, impossible.

Night was for lying awake, in terror. Or worse perhaps, dreaming. I had this nightmare, a nightmare so dreadful that when I woke . . . No, it was a wardress woke me. It was one of the kind ones. She said, 'The noise, what a noise, you're scaring the others.' I just stared at her, as she held the lantern to my face. Stared and stared. She must have thought me rude, for she reprimanded me. Sharply: 'Don't look at me like that, Miss Woodward!'

But I was shaking all over, I had my hand to my neck, pulling at the skin. The pain was intense. My dream, the rope round my neck. I was not . . . They had not hanged me properly. The blackening of my face – I could not breathe, I had not been able to breathe . . . Now I gulped air, fought for it.

'Don't Miss Woodward,' she said, more gently. Then she called out, 'The little one, she's going to have a turn . . .'

All day I fancied this red mark round my neck. Of course I never saw a glass (thank God, thank God, I would have been mortally frightened to see myself . . . The sheer terror of seeing myself).

*

Frederick Liddington was a very gentle person, just as Polly had said. I needed someone gentle. I should say also, speaking Polly's language, that he was a *good* person. (She had written already twice since her visit. In her last she had said, 'There is to be no talk of money, not when there is a life to be saved. He will save yours . . .')

He had very beautiful hands, which I watched continually, as if by doing so, by concentrating, I could begin to feel safe. I who had not felt safe for so long now.

I felt his gaze on me, and did not mind. Even though I knew – through all the prison misery and smell, my dejected appearance, my unclean feeling – that it was the same gaze of the Talbots' curate, of George. The gaze I feared. And yet it was so gentle. It did not challenge.

'I promise you – Christabel, I should like to call you Christabel, I promise to do my best for you – and my best is very good – if you are honest with me . . . And now –' he paused. I watched his hands. 'You must tell me everything.'

Tall, with an awkward shambling body. A pale face with full lips. Heavy lidded eyes. And a very quiet voice. I thought I heard in its timbre, a reminder of Henry's voice. An echo only. For Frederick Liddington was not rushing about in a great hurry putting the world to rights.

'Tell me everything.'

I did. But as I told it, I went back and back. It seemed that I began with the events of that terrible evening. And then further and further back. Everything it seemed, needed its own particular explanation. Did I tell because he asked, or because he did not? I remember only that it seemed natural, and right.

Back and back – till I shivered as I spoke of St Mary's Luddenden and Francis. I thought of the shame that I should ever relate such things. And to a man . . .

I had begun to receive crackpot letters. Some were even threatening. When I showed them to Frederick Liddington, for I trusted him, he told me to destroy them all, at once.

'Tell me everything.'

'Oh, but I have . . .'

And yet there was always more. I talked and wept. And wept and talked.

'I killed a man. After all, I killed him. Accident or not. And it was an accident. *I killed him* . . .' Then at last painfully, the terrible admission: that fleeting second, the thought only, *I wish Francis were dead* . . .

But now we were speaking of Miss Hope.

Ah, Miss Hope. How she haunted me. How often she featured in my nightmares. Even now she would be preparing to tell, yet again, her story, which at the inquest had sounded so convincing.

'I want you to talk about Miss Hope. Everything she said or did. All you remember. I want to feel that I too lunched and dined with Miss Hope. That it was in my ears she chattered, and complained . . . And then her medicine room, her cupboard. Every detail, please.'

I grew to look forward to his visits. It felt somehow as if Polly came to see me. Although we spoke of her little. He could recall only one meeting. His sister's wedding, when Polly had been one of the ten child bridesmaids.

On my way to the court, I was able to look out of the cab. It was not a coach with blinds drawn as I had feared. Outside the sun shone. It was a day of Indian summer. When the cab was held up – some altercation with a dray, a delivery of beer, we had to wait. In those few moments I watched a sparrow, hopping onto the branch of a poplar. I fancied myself free like that. Free to trip from the high branch to the low, free to search for my food. Free to *fly* – away, anywhere, nowhere. I would have given everything in those few moments to be metamorphosed. Myself a bird. And free.

And then the cab moved off again. The swaying motion, going faster now because time lost must be made up. I felt sick. Sick with fear, apprehension. (And sick with *that* smell, of prison, always in my nostrils.)

Six magistrates on the bench, one of whom was the chairman. I was told there were others amongst the audience. The room was crowded. People had been turned away.

My seat in the dock. A high seat. The prison supterintendent who had travelled with me in the cab sat beside me now. I wore black, with a heavy crape veil.

I had not thought how I would be, how I would behave outwardly. I walked as if through a dark forest. I had such a tight hold of myself that anyone looking at me (and all did, all did, I felt the heat of so many eyes), anyone gazing would see only my composure, my steadiness, my lack of any facial expression.

At first, I listened. I heard when I did not wish to.

Now here was Frederick Liddington: saying he appeared on behalf of Miss Woodward.

'And I would therefore be much obliged if I might see the information on which the warrant was granted?'

And Mr Frobisher, for the Withycombe family, 'It is not necessary in the case of felony to have a written information . . .'

Then Mr Liddington, requesting that the witnesses might be out of court during the examination.

And so it went on, back and forth. I did not hear the warrant read out. I shut my ears – I rang the bells of St John Baptist in my head. They drowned, with their *Daughter of the northern fields*, the words I did not wish to hear.

The submission by prosecution. Mr Frobisher, prosecutor, opening the case. A grinding voice. Harsh, eager.

'I appear to prefer and to bring home, as I trust I shall, the charge against the prisoner at the bar . . . I will not dilate on the abhorrent nature of the offence . . . If you are of opinion as I believe you will be, that I have established facts to justify in committing the prisoner for trial . . .'

I did not want to hear yet again the tale of that night . . . Words came through to me. It was a story of someone else. I travelled. In space. In time . . .

I absented myself. I left everybody, everything. I was a child again at Kit's uncle's farm. I read books to Kit. I remembered a happy time – my happiest? – teaching Kit to read. (Forget those other happy times, learning Latin with Francis.) I kept myself busy, so that I was scarcely listening. I stood watcher at the gate. Memory. One memory so perilously near another. Happy days with Betty in the nursery (ah, but then did we not gather prim-roses with Josh?).

And all the while the voices went on round me.

Now the *post mortem* findings:

'. . . The duodenum presented appearances of very active inflammation of its lining membrane, which was softened and, in patches, dissolved. Some spots were so dark that if life had endured sufficiently long they would have ended in mortification, so great was the inflammation . . .'

For much of the talking I was simply not there. Kit and Ellen, I sent them happiness. The child they expected: I saw it in the cradle. I willed happiness for the three of them . . .

It all happened around me. Now it was Jamie Hope in the witness box. Why Jamie? Jamie was too much. Yet perhaps things went wrong (or should one say right?) with the inquiry from that moment on . . .

Jamie. I felt him alien, hating me. For the little that he had to do with it all, I wonder he should have been called. His testimony was a paean of praise for his sister. Her nursing qualities, talents, devotion, how she kept her medicines. The orderly way – he could not but marvel.

Cross-examining, Mr Liddington was led to ask:

'Forgive me if I am wrong, but I do not think the warrant is in the name of Miss Janet Hope? Do you by chance think it is your sister there in the dock?'

Then a moment later, 'You have not told us – you were not exactly asked – have you ever seen inside the medicine cupboard at No. 15, St Nicholas Cliff?'

'Och, now, my sister took me there. She showed me always where she was working – I wanted to know what like the place was. And if they were good to her –'

'Quite so, quite so. But this cupboard. You were in the room. Were you ever in the cupboard? Any day. Ever?'

'There was a cupboard there, yes. She had her cupboard there . . .'

'Did she open it for you? Did you open it?'

'Not exactly – open. I wouldna say, *open*.'

'What *would* you say?'

'I know fine that anything my sister – och, she's a good wee nurse, very caring.'

'I think the court knows that by now, Sergeant Hope . . . I really would like an answer to my question. It is very simple. Did you, at any time, see the inside of the cupboard at No. 15, St Nicholas Cliff?'

'No, sir. I didna. But . . .'

'Thank you, Sergeant Hope . . . No further questions.'

Indian summer. Summer had returned for a day or two. The atmosphere grew close. Too many people packed into a small space. High windows difficult to open.

I closed my eyes. I was a long time with them shut. Sounds blurred, now far, now near. If the audience there wished for someone alert, protesting, forever sending down little notes to the solicitors for passing on . . . Once or twice a hand on my arm brought me back. A whispered, 'Are you all right?'

Mrs Butler. In a plaid dress and Empire bonnet. Her comfortable, comforting voice and manner sounding a warm friendly note in this atmosphere. She is speaking of my devotion to Francis (we have heard much of Miss Hope's). I hear her tell of how she had chosen me – she is praising me . . .

And then it is the medicine room again.

'I must say on the occasions that I visited that room – and I was there several times in Miss Hope's last absence from The Reverend Hume . . . Yes, that would be February of this year . . . I was several times there, for I had keys, and helped myself to sarsaparilla . . . I noted then the disorder in which the cupboard was kept. A number of bottles were not labelled at all . . . I had it in mind then to speak to Miss Hope on her return. I am very much at fault that I did not do so . . . I had also supposed, I think, that only *she* would dispense the medicines, that she would not encourage others to do so . . .'

If I could have managed never to see Miss Hope again. If only that gathering up of her skirts, as if to avoid contagion, had been our last meeting. But here she was, where I could not escape her. I did not look at her then. I looked at Frederick Liddington. I watched his hands as he arranged his papers. (As once I had watched Francis.)

He showed little interest in her deposition, appearing not to listen. Twice though, he made an objection. Mr Frobisher was 'leading' the witness.

There she stood. Slant-eyed. Righteous in her grief, allowed to tell her story again. Yet another account of her good steward-ship.

'. . . and then she says, Miss Woodward says, "It will be a mercy when he goes, it's no good to prolong his life, he has nothing to live for –" She was always on so . . . Wishing him out of this life . . .

'. . . And I really do not recollect that I ever wished her to do the medicines for me, and och the more so when we see she cannot read a label . . .' But she was stopped there. I saw that she might not speak as she wished.

I did not look about me to see what others might be thinking. I could think only that she had not heard, since she had not been there, what Mrs Butler had said of her.

When I glanced at her, she wore a tight little smile such as I had so often seen. So often avoided. I looked away.

Mr Liddington rose clumsily to his feet.

Ah, that gentle voice. He took her so quietly and courteously through point after point . . .

'Mr Hume was a suffering man, yes? Did you wish his life prolonged?'

'I wished for the Lord to take him *when it was time*.'

'And when speaking to Miss Woodward, you never yourself used the words, "Do you not think it will be a mercy when he goes?"'

'And if I did, what so?'

'Yes, and might not Miss Woodward have said something like, "Since his life is one of such suffering, one would not wish it prolonged" . . .?'

Again, Francis's will. Once again, Francis's money, that I had not asked for. That *I did not want. I did not want Francis's money.* And once more, anger and fear and resentment, I could feel it rise, bursting my head, just as in the nightmare the noose had compressed my neck. Then the blood ran to my cheeks, my hands, legs, whole body, running fast and furious to my fingertips, my *fists*.

Mr Liddington to Miss Hope:

'It is about the labelling. I am not quite sure I understand – I must ask you to help me. The bottle containing aconite and morphine – the embrocation – that was a labelled bottle?'

'Och, of course it was a labelled bottle. Is it not there among the exhibits, did they not show it to you? Look at that crimson label. *Poison*, it says. And –'

'Forgive me. Of course, I see it labelled. Tell me, has anyone yet asked you *when* it was labelled?'

'Och, I don't keep a note now of when I place a label on.'

'But you agree every such bottle should be clearly labelled? To ensure against just such an occurrence happening accidentally?'

'Och yes. Yes, yes. That is the practice.'

'But with this bottle, you have no clear recollection of labelling it at any particular time? You only suppose you must have done it?'

'Not a clear recollection. No. But then . . .'

'Perhaps you do not recall that because you do have another recollection – a clear one this time?'

'I don't know what you speak of . . . I don't understand.'

'I suggest that in your haste to leave that afternoon you wrongly placed the embrocation on the top shelf. That it was not labelled, and that as a consequence, this tragic error occurred . . . No malice. Only carelessness – and not all of it Miss Woodward's.'

She licked dry lips. 'Och, not at all. That is not what you

should be saying. Not at all. Och – if there wasn't murder in that girl's heart. If she –'

'Please remember you are on oath. You would not wish to perjure yourself. That is a very serious matter. I put it to you now, that you did in fact label the bottle *after* the accident?'

'It is possible, och well, perhaps I forgot. Maybe I've been a wee bit confused. The distress, och you can imagine –'

'In effect, Miss Hope, the bottle was not labelled when taken that last time from the cupboard? Remember your oath . . .'

'Well then . . . it was not. I made a wee mistake . . .'

I did not dare to look about me. I saw only a grim-faced Miss Hope leave the box.

Mr Frobisher was summing up now, for the prosecution. A long day was drawing to a close. I remembered Frederick Liddington's promise. Mr Frobisher's voice ground on. And I was filled once more with fear. Fear – and despair.

The person he spoke of I did not recognize:

'. . . And yet this ageing and ailing gentleman, who had over the years been nothing less than a father to Miss Woodward. Who had been her teacher, her mentor . . . After a family disaster and loss of fortune, he not only takes her into his home, gives her employ, but also *makes her his heir*. Alone with him so much of the day, it is not difficult for her to sway the mind of a sick man, often in pain . . . He *tells* her he has made her his heir. You may well think that was his error, his folly, that he did not realize to what sort of person he spoke . . . someone so corrupt, so grasping, so evil, that seeing this money within her grasp, she could not wait, *but must hurry the day on* . . . And in order to accomplish this, what does she do, to this man, a *father* to her?'

Stop! I could not bear it. I could not bear it. Blood rushing to my head. I wanted to stand up, to shout:

'*No!* Never a father to me, *never* a father. Something else. Something else. I forgave, I forgave, but . . .'

I felt faint, with the great effort to be silent, a wave of nausea. I could scarcely listen to my friend. To Mr Liddington.

'. . . I say fearful step, for this is not an ordinary case. It is a case where committal must doom this young woman to a term of imprisonment, whether long or short. The Judges will not admit to bail in a capital felony. It is a case not only that entails upon the prisoner an unjust punishment – for who is the enthusiast mad enough to believe that any jury would convict this young woman of murder? One of the consequences of your committal must be that you stamp her with ignominy for the remainder of her life. There is no getting out of it, no use disguising it – if once committed by the magistrates for trial, even though she be afterwards acquitted, the stigma is left upon her that there was even a prima-facie case which warranted gentlemen of honour and independence in sending her before another tribunal . . .'

I heard the applause for his speech, as if from afar, through water. This applause was suppressed. But a little while later and there was more. For the magistrates' discussion had been very short. The Chairman made his announcement – and I was free.

I felt nothing. No relief, no joy. Sick fatigue only.

And gratitude. Much gratitude.

Frederick Liddington took my hands in his large, beautiful ones. He said that he had been only too glad to help, that I must put all, but all, out of mind at once. I must begin again. He asked me, had I somewhere to go?

He looked into my eyes as I thanked him. He hoped one day we would meet again . . . I wanted only to leave and be finished with it all.

Aunt Martha came for me. I went straight back to Halifax with her. Papa was dying.

In a way I was dead too. I had a head full of horrors that I must take somewhere, would take wherever I went.

And where should I go now?

PART FIVE

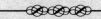

Home

16

The last time I had been in a foreign country, had been at The Beeches. Now, sitting in the train, looking out on to the slow moving canal, the wide flat fields beneath low massed clouds, the green of spring barely evident, I remembered how strange had been the landscape there. How far from home I had felt. How foreign everything.

But the view from the train window today was Belgium. Now I was really abroad. I had crossed the sea, for the first time. Everything different. Sounds, sights, smells.

Smells. As I walked slowly my first day in Brussels down from my new home in the Rue de la Régence – freshly roasted coffee wafted from a doorway. From another, an eating house, aromatic roasting meat. Tobacco. But not the tobacco smell of Papa's snug . . . It was not unpleasant, but different. Strange. Reminding me of nothing I knew.

Which was what I wanted, did I not?

After my name had been cleared, I sought nothing so much as peace. I needed time also to mourn. For death was very much with us again. By the time of my arrival in Halifax, Papa had lapsed into a coma. He was never conscious again.

I sat by his bedside, hoping that even for a few minutes I might yet be his darling again. That I might give him that happiness. But it was not to be. He knew no one. By the time Agnes arrived, he had already slipped out of life. In death he looked calm, at peace perhaps – only past ravages showing in the cavernous face. Now I had no father, real or otherwise. I wept that night for another wasted life (as if that first one had not been enough). I wept again for Mama. And for Branwell.

Agnes and I were polite to each other. And a little cold. She embarrassed and ashamed, I think. I, bitter. For a second as she was leaving, she kissed and clung to me in the old manner.

At first it was enough to hide at Aunt Martha's – so often for me a place of refuge. Hide is what I did, for I could not have borne people in Halifax to know I was there. Rightly or wrongly

341

I imagined gossip all around me, wagging tongues not silenced by the verdict. The general feeling that I had done no good to the name of Woodward. Only the continued kindness of such as Kit and Ellen, Mercy and Betty, the Christian spirit of Mr Everett, gave me faith and hope.

And always and every time, Polly. Polly who urged me to go there to live in Essex with them, and to *worry about nothing*: '. . . We shall take care of you, dearest. You may hold your head up with us . . .'

But I did not want to hold my head up. I wished only to hide it. Darkness. If I could have made myself invisible . . . More than that, I wanted passionately no longer to exist. I, who had been spared the noose of my nightmares, now wished *not to exist*.

Aunt Martha protected me. It was possible to hide in the house, only to go out after dark, and then protected always by a head shawl, dressed simply, often with clogs. I could not help her at the Mechanics' Institute, could not teach there, nor anywhere else. I could not attend St John Baptist on Sunday. When the bells rang, singing for me their familiar tune, how ironic their peal. '*Daughter of the northern fields, daughter of the northern fields* . . .' The one occasion I was out, seven o'clock of a winter's evening, I stopped up my ears. It was all I could do not to run from the sound.

Since there was so little I was able to do outside the home, I did what I could inside. I sewed. I, who so hated sewing, stitched by the hour for the missionary basket, and for paupers. I made several simple layettes – clothing for the child that I would never have. Sometimes as I sat and sewed, the tears fell gently.

Certainly I would never have a child . . .

Yet all the while I might have been a married woman. If marriage had been what I sought. I had no less than seven proposals after the inquiry. After my discharge. I asked myself then what sort of persons, what sort of men, would wish to wed themselves to the notorious, to a woman who in spite of the verdict, might yet be a murderess? How to sleep at night, wondering, fearing what potion might be dropped in their ears? How sit calmly to a meal, when that dish of braised tongue, that baked custard, those gritty greens might conceal poison? *Why did they not feel fear?*

But surely they did. And it was exactly *that* they desired. That fear, that excitement. And I was to supply it.

Dear Miss Woodward [one letter ran],
Some two years ago, Our Creator saw fit to take from me my
betrothed – dead within eighteen hours of a fever. I know now
that mourn as I might, she was taken from me only that I might
be Chosen for another. When I read the account of how you
conducted yourself at the inquiry . . . (of your innocence I had
no doubt), I knew that in you I would find a spouse worthy of
my waiting . . .

And then another:

Dear Madam,
Have you ever woken in the night and cried to your Maker to
give you another chance? I am that chance. Here waiting,
eager to show you how, as helpmeet in a loving household you
may redeem yourself in God's eyes for your sins. With me at
your side, a new name, you can face not only the world, but
also your Maker. The enclosed *carte de visite* will show you
that although of late middle age . . .

But perhaps worst of all . . .

. . . I alone know. I was in court and saw the truth in your
eyes. Do you wish your secret to be safe? With me it would
be. Joined to me for the rest of your natural life, you would
be protected for ever and ever against those who seek to
devour you . . .

Money. I was of course about to be a rich woman. And that was
surely my attraction to at least some of my suitors. I had become
a catch. Who would believe me when I said I had not wanted
Francis's money? And that I did not want it now. Associated as
it was, and always would be, with guilt over Francis's death.

All those pounds, shillings and pence. Before, I had been
penniless except for what I earned first as a governess then later
as a companion. Hardly riches. But at least I had not been
dependent on Aunt Martha. Now, my inheritance had altered
everything, and weighed on me. Often when I woke in my small
room at Aunt Martha's, I would feel it – a weight, an albatross,
about my neck.

Hateful money indeed. Except that I could do good with it. I
wanted none of it for myself. Suggestions that I might live abroad
in comfortable, even luxurious exile – since I was obviously
unhappy in England – did not attract me. By March when I had

inherited, I was able with the help of the family lawyer to place much of it in a trust. The remainder was invested, and accessible, should I change my mind. Aunt Martha would accept nothing. A small sum for my keep, but no *charity*, as she called it. I would have liked to give some to Kit – for had not he and Ellen affirmed their loyalty to me? I planned ways in which I might do it, anonymously. Mercy and Betty, also. Polly and William, I persuaded, no forced them to accept for their children what they would not accept for themselves.

Then there was Halliwell – in India still. I was able to buy him his captaincy. *Captain Halliwell Woodward, the Green Howards.* Later I would be able to help with his majority. Halliwell at least was happy, and fulfilled.

With Agnes, it was still difficult. She would have liked now perhaps to make amends. But by this time I truly did not care. It was so difficult to see her – having to wait always until Septimus should be absent – that I did nothing about it. I sensed in myself a certain coldness towards her. (And yet, I must remember, she was weaker than I. I remembered now how she had been after Mama's death, and the fire. Only by marrying – and to Septimus of all people – had she been able to face the future.)

And I would not have wished to visit Luddenden. It was not just that I would have felt it necessary to go in disguise, and after dark. Since Francis's death, followed so soon by Papa's, it had become a place of too many memories. I did not think there was any part of it that did not hold either a past unhappiness, or else a memory of some joy forever gone.

Added now were all the associations with my real father – associations that had meant so little to me as a child, but now . . . the Lord Nelson, the station at Luddenden Foot which Kit and I had visited. Even Agnes's home, Buckley House – where Mama had seen Branwell for the first time.

Certainly I did not plan another visit to Haworth. My memories of that last time, before Scarborough, were now for me unbearably sad. My revelation, my vision, my call to sacrifice. Ah, dear God, how that had ended . . .

It was not a sacrifice I planned now – when I at last felt able to imagine a future. No, not a sacrifice, but an escape.

It was Aunt Martha who brought everything to a head. She had been strangely patient, never offering advice, even less criticism – instead providing as always her own robust form of support. I owed and owe her a debt I can never repay.

She said suddenly, watching me sewing, and weeping yet again, 'Look at that seam – it's a disgrace, child. You never were one for the needle. And likely worse than ever now.'

It made no odds that I wept, for Papa, and continued to weep. She went on:

'I hope you don't reckon to spend the remainder of your life sat like that? There's other work than bad sewing to be done in this world –'

'And I mean to do it,' I told her, as stoutly as I was able. Feeling myself once again the small child she had dragged past the Roman Catholic church – in those days bold and impudent enough for anybody. Scourge of governesses. Aunt Martha had known what to do with me.

Now, it was I did not know what to do with myself.

But she had shaken me by her remark, so unlike her previous kindness. That very same day I made a decision – that within a week I would do something about my future.

Over the next few days I read carefully both *The Times* and the *Morning Post*. But every situation advertised that week was in England. Where could I go in England?

A Lady (Protestant), 24 years of age, of good education, is desirous of meeting with an engagement as Companion to English lady. Paris or Brussels. If advertisement meets with a comfortable home, salary would not be an object.

My own advertisement. I placed it in both French and Belgian papers. I vowed to accept the first reasonable reply. Once in either of those countries, if not suited I would not find it too difficult to change. And when my (very poor) French improved, I might be companion instead to a French or Belgian person.

I did not plan further ahead than a year or at the most two. Aunt Martha reminded me – after refusing, yet again, any of my money – that I was rich and that one day I would acknowledge it.

'The day'll come when you've a mind to enjoy it . . . Whatever would your Dad have said –' She checked herself, as we both remembered what Papa had done with the Woodward fortunes.

My employer was to be a Madame Martin, in Brussels. Her reply was amongst the first to arrive, and certainly the most likely. Some were distinctly odd. One woman in Paris wanted me almost solely for walking out a pair of pug dogs twice daily. She spoke little or no English – her letter was written for her – and hoped that I would not speak at all, in any language. Several others also had taken no note of my request for an Englishwoman.

Since I feared that Madame Martin or her friends might have read the English newspapers, I decided to change my name. I did not need a man's hand in marriage in order to do that. I took my mother's maiden name and became Christabel Armstrong. I had thought of changing to Charlotte, after my aunt – a feeling of kinship, since I would be in Belgium. But I went no further with that idea.

Madame Martin was the English widow of a Belgian lawyer. He had left her very well off, with a spacious and comfortable home in the Rue de la Régence. She had come originally from Shropshire, but it was over forty years now since she had left. I was to be the latest of many companions, for although she had plenty of servants, since her husband's death she had liked always to have an English person with her.

Her children had long since left home. Two daughters: one, to her great disgust, a nun, now in a convent in Liège. The other was married with children. There was a son too, a professor teaching in Africa. It was him of whom she was the most proud and, I suspected, the most fond. His name was mentioned three times as often as that of his sisters.

She was a moody woman. A moody woman who detested her own company. She loved to talk about herself. My task was only to listen. I was not required to comment, so my listening did not need to be whole-hearted. I could think, I could dream. Occasionally, a question would bring me back suddenly, reminding me that I had been too far away.

In appearance she was immensely plump, with tiny hands and feet. In crinoline and huge shawl or loose three-quarter cloak, she seemed to fill any doorway (and they were large doorways) that she passed through. I wondered sometimes that the feet could bear the weight. Indeed she often complained of fatigue by half-way through the day. Her afternoons, before going out to pay calls, were spent in deep sleep in a darkened room.

She loved to talk, to grumble, about her husband, her family. Her small eyes grew smaller still, hardly visible in their folds of fat, as she told me: 'Monsieur Martin, he was typical of course, of a certain type of Belgian. Money is their god. Far more so than the Romish God they worship (I have had no truck ever with my husband's religion, it was a subject we *never* discussed. I allowed him his way of course with the children . . .).'

Monsieur Martin's closeness with money was a favourite topic. (She never reflected how much it must have contributed to her present comfort.)

'Yes, Monsieur was *extremely* careful. Now if I can give you a little instance . . . We had taken this house at Ostend for a month and were at the door, departing, when he learned that the rent would be cheaper if we arrived two weeks later. We did not go . . . You can imagine how humiliated I was – the luggage already loaded and the neighbours thinking us gone . . . But did *he* care? Not so long as the money was saved. And then on another occasion, a picnic in the . . .'

The instances jumbled in my memory, half-heard. I did not always recognize them when they returned for a second airing.

Talk, talk, talk, as we sat at meals (oh, those meals), or went out calling in the carriage. In the draughty salon, sometimes even in her bedroom when she had persuaded me to keep her company 'while I soak my poor little feet. Ring for Klimt, would you, to bring more salt water . . .'

Madame's friends. She did not have many, and certainly none suitable for me. With a few exceptions they were all English. The widow of the former chaplain to the Anglican church, the wife of the present one, an English doctor, a colonel's widow from Surrey, and (which could have been exciting but was not) an elderly couple of whom the husband was supposed to have fled England nearly fifty years before. Madame hinted that it had been to do with cards. I could have believed anything, or nothing, of the tiny shrunken figure who sat hunched up in his chair while his chatty wife exchanged complaints and criticisms of the 1860s world with Madame.

Her son, Claude – she was inordinately proud of him. He wrote to her in English – one of the languages, together with German, that he taught. A letter from Algeria was always a great excitement.

'He has been such a good son, Claude. Always good to his mother. His father and he, they did not always see eye to eye. But there was never anything like that with me. A good son – but a bad boy that he does not try to come home more often. It is already *seventeen* months since he was here – and you see, no mention yet of a visit . . .'

I asked once if she expected him to marry. She grew quite fierce.

'No, I do not. Unless some scheming woman . . . He is quite the monk – he has never shown any interest in young women. If God allows me to live long enough I should like him to retire from his work and live here – with his old mother . . .'

His picture, which hung in her bedroom, was of a long-faced, narrow-lipped, balding man, with a disapproving expression.

The letters were not interesting. They told me nothing of Algeria and could have come from any provincial Belgian or French town – with their accounts of petty squabbles amongst the staff of the school, and delinquencies of the students. 'What he has to put up with . . .' his mother sighed.

Her married daughter, Hortense, visited always on Sundays. She was tall and horse-faced, with her mother's colouring and a thickening waist. They did not get on together. Neither could wait for the other to finish speaking.

Who would be married to Hortense? Her husband, Jacques, a gentle, timid man, tried his English on me – embarrassing me greatly since I could not make out one word. Because of my poor French, after the first encounter we sat always in silence, occasionally smiling at each other.

Their children, three girls and a boy, came accompanied by their *bonne d'enfants*, a pretty Flemish girl. It was hard to believe they belonged to the same family as Madame. The youngest girl, Sophie, as they were about to leave, rushed across the room and threw her arms about me.

'*Je vous aime, ma'm'selle,*' she cried, '*je vous aime, aime, aime!*'

Her father only smiled, but her mother was angry with her, pulling her away from me roughly, while Madame Martin tut-tutted.

'You don't discipline them, Hortense. You never could. They are perfect examples of the *badly brought-up* and spoilt continental child . . .'

The older girl, Marie, offered to teach me French. Her own English was quite good (her grandmother had insisted on that).

'We begin *immédiatement*,' she said, sitting on a low stool beside me. 'You will say after me, "*Pierre qui roule n'amasse pas mousse*". That is what we are writing in our copybooks. Say it, please. It means that *mousse* didn't grow when a stone rolls . . . After me then, "*Pierre qui roule . . .*"'

Hortense, halting a second in her flow, heard Marie and pounced. I could not make out what she said. Marie, crestfallen, left my side.

'Really, Maman,' Hortense said, before I could protest in either language, 'she grows so bossy and impudent . . .'

'It is your doing, of course,' her mother said. 'It is all in the manner of rearing . . .'

I thought to say something, but by now Marie was on her father's knee, her head buried in his chest. He was stroking her hair.

'And while we are speaking English,' Madame said, 'is it any wonder? Look how foolish a certain person is with them . . .'

But I was determined to learn French – for I had only what little I remembered from The Beeches.

'Whatever is all this?' Madame asked in surprise. 'It will take you away from the house – I don't want you too long and too often away. You don't need French to speak with me . . .'

She was rude anyway about the French spoken in Belgium. 'You waste your time,' she said, 'since it will not be correct.' But I was careful in my teacher – finding, with the help of the Anglican chaplain's widow, an elderly professor, Monsieur Avisseau, who was excellent. My few hours a week in his apartment, plied with coffee and cakes by his wife, who had not a word of English, were the highlight of my week.

If Madame was rude about the French Belgians, she was even more so about the Flemish. I felt sorry for her servants, several of whom were Flemish.

'Just to hear them,' she grumbled. 'I stop my ears sometimes. And I advise you to do the same . . . Monsieur Martin always said, "Dutch is bad German, and Flemish is bad Dutch, so . . ."' and she shrugged her shoulders.

The most serious loss perhaps was that of free time. She liked me with her for much of the day. Unfortunately she did not retire early at night. Often I would be yawning (with boredom) and longing to leave, while she chattered on. If I pleaded tiredness, she exploded into irritable pity.

'What a poor little thing, you are, to be sure,' she said. 'You *look* strong enough in all conscience, but the young these days wear out their nerves before twenty-five.' She added once un-kindly, 'You ought to be married. That is your trouble of course.

That you are not married . . .' Then she returned to her favourite subject, Madame Martin. I do not think she ever once asked me about myself. When occasionally we were out, and her friends did so, she would look mildly surprised.

And that suited me, for the less I talked of my past the better. Was I not by my own choice Christabel Armstrong, that hybrid, fictitious person? Nor did I think that I myself was a very interesting person. It was my past, what had happened to me, that was dramatic – and horrible.

Madame was very fond of her food. A large meal was eaten at one and again at seven. Nothing particularly appetizing: some dishes made from dried fish, a savoury beef stew that was not too bad, and occasionally some good pastry. In the late afternoon she would often eat mouth-watering *pâtisseries* which she had sent out for. And again last thing at night. There was not normally any for me on the tray. 'You don't care for these, do you?' she would say, wiping the cream from her fingers with an embroidered linen square. 'I am sure they are not to your taste at all.'

She would have sudden cravings for English food. Speaking with feeling of great glistening puddings, steamed or boiled, studded with currants or covered in treacle. Pork pies, Welsh rarebit. She would order these from the kitchen, and then when they were not right – for she was quite unable to provide any recipes – she would push aside petulantly the pork pie made not with a hot water crust but a flaky pastry. 'As I thought – I knew it, I knew it – they cannot cook!' Childishly disappointed, she made as much fuss as if something momentous had happened. An emotional mishap, a bereavement . . .

Summertime. At first the air was clear. Radiant days of sunshine in late May, lilac after rain. A freshness about everything, even though it was the city. I thought of going out to see the Château Koekleberg, where Polly had been to school. A little way out of Brussels.

Why not go further afield? Several times on bright June mornings, I thought – I could perhaps travel. Why stay in Brussels, why stay even in Belgium? I could send for some money and . . . But even thinking like that – it was too soon perhaps – would send me spiralling downwards, back into the depths. That money – and *how I came by it*.

I woke one morning to blazing sun. A blue sky. When I went out to fetch a newsaper for Madame, the workmen on the new Palais de Justice looked bemused by the heat, seemed to be moving slower than usual. My mind was absolutely clear, and made up. I had had enough of Madame.

Well, I shall go, I thought. I imagined it would be easy enough to find work teaching English. Monsieur Avisseau would help me with that. And then, in the meantime there were many small places where I could rent rooms. I had, after all, some money. I could send for more. I was not without means – even without touching my capital.

Yes, I found energy that day. Or rather, that evening. We were in the salon – so cold in early spring, now pleasantly warm. Madame sat, a small ivory fan beside her, which she would wave at intervals. 'This gives me all the fresh air I need. The night air outside. Not a good idea . . .'

I read to her from the *London Illustrated News*. She liked to hear of the Prince and Princess of Wales. Today there were some drawings of Alexandra. 'What a delightful girl! If I could have had someone like *her* as a daughter . . . But then, of course – if you were to meet the family of Monsieur Martin. It explains itself . . .'

'Madame,' I said, laying the *News* aside, 'I have been thinking . . .' And I told her of my plans.

'So you see,' I said, 'if perhaps in a fortnight or so, a month perhaps, I could be released –'

I got no further. Leaning forward, she rapped my fingers with the fan.

Her face was very fierce. I feared one of her moods. I wondered if I could leave in defiance of her anger. *Yes, I shall,* I thought, and waited then for the onslaught.

But something quite different happened . . .

Her fat face, with its angry folds, collapsed, crumpled. Leaning forward, she grabbed my arm, urgently.

'No!' she cried, pushing her face close to mine. 'Don't go! You shall not go!' And all the while her eyes, squeezed together, oozed tears.

'But surely –' I began.

Now she was weeping in earnest. She had hold of me with both hands. Clutching at me. Her widow's cap awry.

'You shan't! I must not be left alone . . . How could you, can you? Don't tell me you could be so cruel! An old lonely woman. With not many years left – I *hope* I have not many years left . . . You promised!'

I tried to calm her, to shake her off. 'I don't know what this is about. I am not –'

'Don't leave me,' she wailed, 'promise you won't leave me alone . . . You promised!'

'I promised nothing,' I said.

'*Don't leave me!*'

'Yes, yes,' I said soothingly, 'there, there,' as to a child. I was disgusted and embarrassed too. Trying now to detach myself from her fat clinging arms.

'You know –' she hiccuped, 'no, of course you do not. But the doctor said, Monsieur Martin's own special physician, quite the best in Brussels – he said, when I was sent to him, he said I –'

Another fearful fit of weeping overcame her.

'What did he say?' I asked wearily.

'That my heart . . . if I am crossed unnecessarily, if people don't understand – you see, I *must not be alone!*' She had stirred up her emotions afresh.

Like a child, she continued to sob even when the matter was at an end, and I had agreed that no, I would not leave. I would stay. I would continue to be her companion.

Yes, I agreed. Without time limit. I did not set one, although of course I should have done so. I don't know what mistaken notions of duty and compassion and sacrifice befogged my decision. I had thought Scarborough and Francis's death had cured me of all that. But they lingered, how they lingered. No longer a fine glow now, these days, but a dreary knocking of conscience. Madame was elderly, she was widowed, afraid of the dark, of her own company, in some sort of terror and distress that *I* could alleviate. She was weak. I was strong. (Or was it the other way?) I would stay.

Now it was high summer. The hot weather, the days growing more stifling, seemed to have crept up on us. A change came over the city – but not alas, over Madame. She did not change, I suspected. Winter or summer, the routine would not vary.

More and more of Madame's acquaintances began to leave for the country or the seaside. I had not thought of this. Life in Luddenden had not been like that. Holidays such as I had had with Polly in Scarborough had been the exception – Mama and Papa had not seen the need to depart for some other home. Now, the number of carriages diminished daily. A gradual heavy sleepy uncaring feeling came over the city.

At first I did not bother to wonder why Madame was not part of the exodus. All the same she told me:

'It is all such a nonsense. Look at them – they do it every year! Leave all the comforts of their home, where everything runs on oiled wheels and the beds are comfortable. Off they go, risking bugs and prickly heat and perhaps drowning in the sea or a fall from the cliffs. They are never the better for it, although they may say so. Of course they are bound to justify all the expense . . . Let Hortense and the others, let them be as foolish as they will . . .'

Not only Hortense. But many others were foolish, as she would have it. Not only her own friends, but also Monsieur Avisseau. He warned me well in advance. But he and his wife – they spent six weeks always with their son and his family, at their house in the Ardennes.

Hortense left. All Madame's friends had gone. She did not seem too bothered. She slept longer in the afternoons and did not go calling. Often she said, 'Why bother? It is cooler in the house . . .' She ate as much *pâtisserie* as in the coldest days of winter.

She appeared to have quite forgotten the scene she had made with me. But as I looked at her, I had no difficulty in remembering how she had looked, and sounded, in collapse.

The loneliness. It was terrible. I felt it like a searing pain. Now icy, now hot. It accompanied me everywhere. I was homesick, and longed and longed, not just for England but for Yorkshire – Yorkshire faces and Yorkshire *voices*. And above all for Luddenden. I blotted out the church, the churchyard – I remembered Kit. His uncle's farm, his mother's fireside. When I had been Papa's darling.

The most trivial sights and sounds brought tears to my eyes, a wave of homesickness. Life lived differently. The sight of the everyday, mundane task, done well, yes – but done *differently*. Thus, catching sight of the servant sweeping the hall, I could not bear it that she should use not scattered piles of tea leaves as at home, but coffee grounds. It reminded me – I was not amongst my own people . . .

I walked. I walked whenever I was free. The circle of the boulevards, which marked the boundary of old Brussels. I would walk and walk, in the hope of sleeping soundly that night. Once or twice I made arrangements with Klimt, the maid, that I should have a key and the door be left unbolted, so that I might go out at night. The chances of Madame waking and calling for me were not great.

Letters did not come often. Aunt Martha wrote, and Polly wrote, but that was all. She told me that Frederick Liddington had enquired after me. George I had heard from only once since I arrived. His letters (like mine) had been long but infrequent.

I was surprised to hear from Halliwell. He was not one for putting pen to paper. We had not been properly in touch directly since the Topham Abbey visit. He had sent messages always through George.

But it was about George that he wrote. A bout of typhoid fever, a week's illness, and he was dead. Halliwell had lost a good friend, his best friend.

'I know he liked writing to you, he always saved up everything that happened at all interesting, and he knew you wanted to hear because you said so, and he could tell you about his family too, he was fond of you I think. I am not going to be able to take his place, I do not write many letters as you know . . .'

I did not believe it at first. Did not want to. I too had lost a good friend. Perhaps, who knows, more than a good friend? For had there not been, very occasionally, the thought at the back of my mind that when, in two years or so, he and Halliwell returned from India . . . No, I was not for marriage. And yet – something had been growing, was being nurtured, which now had been violently uprooted.

Loneliness, and now bereavement. I was not alone as my aunt had been, as Charlotte had been that summer of 1843 – alone in the deserted Pensionnat Heger, Monsieur and Madame Heger and their children on holiday in Blankenberghe, the pupils all gone home. When, driven nearly demented with homesickness and loneliness, in despair, she . . . But you know the rest. She wove it some ten years later into her novel *Villette*. Her heroine, Lucy Snowe, alone in the days of the equinox: ill, hallucinating. The coronal above each white dormitory bed becomes a death's head, a sun-bleached white skull. She is 'crushed by the roof, as by the slab of a tomb'. Leaving her sick bed, donning a warm cloak, she intends to walk to a quiet hill, but she hears on the way . . .

No, of course I was not alone as Lucy had been (with only Goton, the cook, in her far distant attic), in an empty school. I was, on the contrary, far too much part of a household – at the beck and call of (note that word beck, reminding me of Madame Beck, villainess of *Villette* . . .) Madame Martin.

Alone in the empty school, my aunt's heroine tries to pray,

but she can utter only these biblical words, '*From my youth up Thy terrors have I suffered with a troubled mind . . .*'

For me, here in Brussels, no ghosts, no visions of nuns, only the overwhelming sadness of George's death. And the loneliness.

It was a heavy evening, that day I received the letter, the early evening of an airless, humid day. The sky seemed ready to press down upon the chimney tops. I longed for fresh air. Fresh fresh fresh, I longed to be high up – above, above the sea. I thought that surely I must detest low-lying countries. I thought as I walked, of the moors, how they must be now in mid-August. If I shut my eyes (as once I had done in court), I could imagine a summer breeze blowing off the moors, rustling through the bracken – still green, ready soon to turn. I thought I caught for a second the smell of damp peat, newly dug.

There was the sound of a bell tolling. A church bell. St Mary's? St John Baptist's? No, this was real. This low note, was Ste Gudule. I found myself, yes, just as had done Lucy Snowe, walking into Ste Gudule. Walking into the darkness from the light.

I thought of those lines, '*Mon père, je suis protestante.*' But I could not say them. What led me to tell a lie instead? Or if not to tell one, to deceive. I knew the formula. I had heard it one Sunday, talking with little Marie who in May had made her first confession.

The flickering of the votive candles round the Virgin: I thought of my mother, of God's mother. I stepped into the box. There was a small door. It clicked behind me. There was no going back. I knelt still. I was afraid to speak. I could make out a figure sitting sideways to me, his head against the grille, *waiting for me*.

And then I said it, in French, I said what Catholics say, 'Bless me father, for I have sinned . . .'

I must have forgotten what should follow, for he asked: 'And how long since your last confession, my child?'

How long since? How long is never?

'A long time, Father.'

He asked me then, had I forgotten my Easter duties? No, no, I told him. (I did not know what they were, so how could I?)

And then, but then, what to tell him? (Lucy Snowe had been asked, 'Was it a sin, a crime?') Stumbling, haltingly, I told him . . . of the inquiry. And when he said, 'But you were innocent, there was no sin . . .' then in my despair I told him, 'That is not so. I *wished him dead*, I wished Francis dead . . .' And when he asked me about that, I told him.

There was silence the other side. Just laboured breathing. He seemed an elderly man. He stopped to cough, to clear his chest. For me the tears had begun to flow. I felt such a heavy pounding, as if inside my chest a bird struggled to beat its wings. I thought then that if only . . . It was now. Now there was something I could say – or do – that would save me.

Why oh why, did he not speak? Perhaps it was only a minute. A few seconds even. To me, hours. Then:

'God understands, Jesus Christ understands. You must believe that Christ understands. It is a terrible tale you have told me. But if *his* was a sin crying out to heaven for vengeance, remember also "Vengeance is *mine* saith the Lord, *I* will repay." Can you not leave it to Him? For you, the lesson Christ gave is to forgive. To turn the other cheek. To forgive, as Christ forgave His tormentors. Can you do that?'

Yes, yes. Had I not long ago forgiven Francis? I almost said, 'I want to be a Catholic, I could wish to be a Catholic, Father . . .' But I had already passed myself off as one of the Faith, with my easy 'Bless me Father, for I have sinned.' Of course I should have said, '*Je suis protestante.*' Then I would have received as did my aunt, as did Lucy Snowe, an invitation to instruction – and how gladly, not frightened like her, I would have taken it up (and I thought then, I still can. I have only to ask. Anyone may become a Romanist who wishes . . .). A child on the brink of death, had I not been saved by the blessing of a Catholic priest?

It was then he became fatherly, asking me: had I someone to help me? Was I much alone? An Englishwoman in a foreign country . . . He offered then to find me friends, introductions . . . Fellow Catholics amongst the English community, perhaps? Sympathetic persons . . . My French was so good. Surely . . .

And then it was over. My penance, two decades of the rosary. I had no rosary. I did not know the act of contrition I was asked to make out loud. He thought me too overcome to pray. The grille slid shut, then opened on the other side. I left the box, my head bowed. I went back to where I had knelt before. I buried my face in my gloved hands. The tears fell scaldingly. Inside my chest the bird beat its heavy wings still.

There is nothing, I thought. I am nothing. Nobody. The curious smell, scent of the stone, the snuffed candles, the dark fusty fur cape of the woman who knelt beside me. The sound of the confessional box opening and shutting.

Heaving, a convulsion of sobs. I knew I must compose myself. If I could light a candle . . . I believed, of course I believed. I walked over to where the candles burned, by the statue of the Virgin, my head a little bowed so that no one should see my face.

I lit a candle, and prayed as I did so. It was easy to pray. God rest George's soul. God rest the souls of James Woodward and Francis Hume. And then, God rest the soul of Caroline Woodward, née Armstrong, dead at thirty-eight. My mother. God rest the soul of Patrick Branwell Brontë, dead at thirty-one. My father.

The second candle, my father's, would not light. The wick was perhaps damp. I took another. It was then I felt a tap on my shoulder. A low sweet voice said, in French:

'Excuse me, mademoiselle, but are you in distress?'

I have often wondered who it was that sent Louise de Saint Lambert to find me that day. I feel certain now that it was the hand of God. Prompt answer to the prayer scarcely formed. My cry, 'Help me!', not voiced, but so loud inside me that surely her kind heart, she of the kind heart, always looking to help, heard it.

Perhaps I do not need to thank God, but only Louise de Saint Lambert. For she was one of those persons, like Polly, whom just to have known is cause for gratitude. Beacon, refuge, shining light – any absurd name you wish. And all those things, yes, but most of all, possessing that rare quality of happiness, within and without.

'Usually, I am a happy person,' the weeping Polly had said at our first meeting, that afternoon at The Beeches. Louise was just such another.

Certainly also something led me to answer her – not with a quick gruff dissembling ('It is nothing, I am all right') – but rather:

'Yes. Yes, I am in great distress, Madame.'

Her gloved hand rested now on my arm. Below the Empire bonnet, a gentle face, with large dark eyes, looked at me.

'Come outside,' she said, her voice still low, taking me now by the elbow, and leading me down the aisle to the main door.

My head throbbed still. Once outside, I felt absurdly cold. I began to shiver.

'Our carriage,' she said, as we stood on the cathedral steps. 'We can take you anywhere –'

She spoke to the coachman, then when we were inside and the doors shut, she said, 'Perhaps we should go to our apartment. We are almost there. It is no distance – and there we can talk. And you can rest. Calm yourself. And then if you wish to speak. If I can, if we can help at all –'

I must have been a little mad. A nervous prostration, collapse, a fever – I do not know. Any and all of those. But I remember only the frightening shivers – of my whole body, the chattering of my teeth – the strange feeling that my head had separated from my body – that I saw it there, floating above. Away . . .

Her voice. She was speaking to me: 'I am Louise de Saint Lambert . . . please tell me your name. Or if you would rather, would rather . . . would rather, rather, rather . . .'

My head had quite left my body, had gone away. A great wave of blackness engulfed me.

First sight. Whiteness. White sheet, white counterpane. Cool white light filtering in, through white muslin, lace. Oh where am I, *where am I?*

A woman sat by the bed. White-capped, elderly. Hands folded.

The heat, the heat . . . My body burned the white sheets. The old woman touched my forehead.

'Where am I?' I spoke in English, through thick, dry lips. 'Where am I?'

She made soothing noises, muttering something, words I could not catch. She spoke with a Flemish accent . . .

I drifted back again. Was gone.

I returned. I recognized the face which bent over me now. Louise. Ste Gudule. The carriage . . .

'You must not worry about anything. You are here and safe. In our home in the Hôtel Cluysenaar. In the Rue Royale . . . Do you wish me to speak English? I know a little – no, do not try to talk. Just nod or signal . . .'

Then:

'You are not well at all. Yesterday . . . I think you don't remember. We put you at once to bed. But Madame Martin has been told. There was an envelope with your address amongst your things, in the bag you carried – you will forgive us for looking. We sent round at once . . .'

I said absurdly, 'I must go back. I must leave now –'

But the words were hardly out of my mouth before the darkness returned.

I saw that some of my clothes hung in the open wardrobe. A number of my things – a writing case, some books and drawings – had been spread on the table near my bed. For when I should feel able, Louise said.

I was not sure for how long I had been ill . . . Weeks perhaps. But now that I was able to be up and to sit at the window, September was half gone.

The whole room was airy, white, flowery. So many flowers. Late summer roses massed with their sweet scent. I sat by the hour, watching from the window, an unopened book in my lap. Sounds drifted around me. My mind wandered pleasantly. Below me in the Rue Royale, carriages rattled by on the flinty pavement.

My illness had been waiting for me a long while. It had not been just the lonely August days which had brought it on, but so much else. Perhaps most immediately, the news of George's death. But before that – prison, fear of the hangman, the death of Francis – and beyond, beyond . . . Topham Abbey and the child. A blazing mill, the morning of my mother's death. All, all seemed to be burned out in that fever. Sitting there, I felt weak and cleansed.

The doctor who came to see me every other day was gently plump, courteous. On a small table near me were all the strengthening medicines, the tonics prescribed by him. I was to drink good Burgundy each day, two glasses, with my meals. He told me:

'Look in your wineglass before you drink – *that* is how your blood should look. And that is how it shall, if you follow my prescription.'

And the food. Prepared to tempt an invalid. The sweetbreads, creamed, nestling in a purée of carrots. The fluffy egg dishes, the soufflés.

Like Madame Martin, Louise was also a widow – but how different, how different. Where Madame, to close the void, had turned inwards, grasping, clutching, Louise had filled the emptiness to overflowing . . . Her family, who adored her, her servants who could not do enough for her. Friends, and more friends. The poor, the sewing women in the Marolles for whom she did so much.

In her home, the atmosphere was one of light and peace,

repose, yet at the same time it was alive with activity. Such comings and goings, such excitements. Good news, bad news. Problems, solutions. Arrivals and departures. Happiness and sorrow.

Her family: Gilbert, the eldest son, and his wife, Célestine. Their children – two little flaxen-haired girls so alike as to appear twins, a roly-poly younger brother. A daughter, Françoise, also with children – four lively boys. Living further away, she visited only once or twice a month. The remaining six were scattered about Belgium and France. Letters arrived daily. Letters were dispatched daily.

In my memory, the apartment was filled with music. Gilbert played daily. No sooner arrived, than he would sit down and flood the room with sound. Two of the grandchildren played duets. Merry jigging tunes. Early Mozart, Scarlatti. There were friends who came regularly to practise trios or quartets. Sometimes to perform. What must it have cost them all, I wondered later, to remain silent as they did when I was first ill? In those first fevered days, the piano and all instruments, forbidden.

As I convalesced, Louise would sit and talk with me. I wondered she had the time. If she had not, she made it. She never asked questions. Although I think I would have told her anything, everything. Or almost.

She was concerned always not to tire me, since I had to speak in French (her English was not sufficient). And although I might have supposed it would tire me to express myself in another language, it was not so. To sit with a sympathetic listener, to take my time, to tell my tale.

Oh, Louise of the fashionable shot-silk pannier dress, the glacé linen princess dress, the tall-crowned, forward-tilted hat. Louise of the low, gentle voice. My friend.

More and more I was reminded of Polly. As Louise spoke, as she told me of her joy in her family – of the love they gave her (no mention of the abundant love she gave them), I saw in her how Polly might be.

'You see then,' she was saying, 'how I was led to find you. I had come in to the cathedral only on an impulse. A few moments' prayer, a candle to be lit – ten years since my mother's death. And it was just at that moment that I saw you . . . God guided me.'

She wanted, the family wanted me to stay. For as long as I wished. I must feel that the Hôtel Cluysenaar was my home (and after all, what other one did I have?), I would, could give such great happiness.

I wanted to pay them. For I had had several weeks with nursing attendance at first, a doctor, medicines, every luxury. But they would not hear of it. 'We are very rich,' she said, 'one should not speak of these matters perhaps, but I have been left more money than . . . and no, you must not think or feel that this is charity you have received – it is friendship. And you will give friendship in return. So now we are quite equal . . .'

She said yet again, wistfully, 'You don't, won't live with us then?'

Why did I not? Why not stay? Madame expected me back. I had promised. She suffered. I told Louise all this.

'Of course – ah, the poor woman. Afraid to be alone. And you, so kind. But are you sure you are not too kind?'

No, I was not too kind. Only foolish. Driven by some heady mixture of duty and sacrifice and remorse and I do not know what else. But back to Madame I went. And, within a few hours regretted it.

She spoke with horror of the weeks I had been ill.

'If you only knew how it's been for me! Hortense was amazed, and anxious, to see the way I was. "Maman, you have been left in the lurch," she said. And "What can you expect these days?" *I* said. "A companion so-called who goes out for a walk and does not return for nearly four weeks . . ." "You can trust no one," Hortense said. She found someone to sleep with me. Do not concern yourself, or become agitated about my suffering. There has been someone here with me, almost from the day you left . . . It has all been a great inconvenience. Besides, what does a healthy little girl like you do with a high fever, debility, or whatever they call it?'

No, it was not good, back with Madame. Life soon resumed its normal pattern. But now it was autumn: I was having lessons again with Monsieur Avisseau. I felt well and strong.

And I had the Saint Lamberts. That was the big difference. All the difference. When I left I did not lose them. Seldom a week went by but there was an invitation – perhaps a concert in the Zoological Gardens, a visit to the hot houses of the Botanical Gardens, or to the Palais Arenberg.

Through days of golden autumn, the weather turning cold, the carriages rattling now along icy roads . . . Braziers appeared on the streets. Because it was the whole family who had adopted me, it would vary whom I went out with. If Louise was busy, as so often she was with her work down in the Marolles, then it might be Célestine . . . To the children I was Tante Christie . . .

Usually I went there at times when Madame Martin had with her either Hortense and family, or a bevy of chaplain's wives and widows. This was acceptable. But not an evening at the Théâtre Royal, when I might be sitting with *her* . . .

'You have grown very thoughtless, since you met your grand friends.'

Christmas drew near. The Saint Lambert children danced with excitement as we walked together in the glass-domed Galeries Saint Hubert. The long windows sparkled with jewellery and gemstones, toys of every sort, cream-filled chocolates. 'I want, I want . . . What would *you* like, Tante Christie?'

Madame heard that at last her son was to pay her a visit. He was coming home in January for a month at least. Another teacher would do his work. 'He will stay here, with me,' she announced proudly.

She spoke of his visit a great deal. 'When my son comes, when Claude comes . . . All the women will be after him, of course. I hope he has not come home to find a wife . . .'

I wished I had not been reminded, with a wave of sick memory, of Miss Hope and her brother. Waiting for the arrival of Jamie. And what had followed after.

But I soon shook off that foreboding. I had little foreboding of anything that Christmas. Time passed and I marked it, not too unhappily.

We were a large party that evening, at a house in the Rue d'Or. A pianist was to give a recital, mainly Schubert but also some of his own compositions. The Saint Lambert circle were not amongst those who chatter and whisper throughout a performance. They sat always rapt, attentive.

Célestine and Gilbert were there already, and sitting down. With them were a few other persons I knew. Célestine had invited her cousin, Amélie, from Bruges. Amélie in her turn had invited a cousin from her side of the family. He had not arrived yet. He lived in Bruges also but was in Brussels for some weeks in connection with his work – he was an artist of some kind.

As we waited, Amélie, whose seat was the other side near the window, stood beside Célestine and me, talking animatedly.

'My cousin will be late,' she said, 'he is *always* late. It's no good to be so clever with his hands, when he cannot manage the hand of the clock. That is what his mother says . . .' She added, 'But then he is Gérard. And that is how he is. Bad, very bad.'

I watched her as she chattered on. She was small and plump with little white hands which she used a lot for emphasis. Her mouth was pleased with itself, her black eyes flashed with excitement, whether there was any about or not. I envied her a little – that assurance (although I did not wish it for myself), the way that two young men pushed to try and obtain a seat near her. She ended up with one either side.

Célestine said, 'She does it to tease her cousin, I think. They are to marry later this year, when Amélie is seventeen. It is a family thing, they have always been intended for each other.'

The first movement of a sonata was well under way when Amélie's cousin arrived. There was of course no place beside her. She waved a small white handkerchief at him – glancing, I thought, to see if either of the young men was watching.

There were two seats near Célestine and me. He took the one furthest from me.

I did not think much of his looks. Even less of his expression. He scowled. He was small, with very black hair, prominent ears, pale almost sallow skin, a luxuriant moustache. And the scowl . . . It might have been bad temper. It might have been concentration or abstraction, but it did not look well. He muttered as he sat down. Then a moment later brought out of his pockets some papers, which he leaned forward to see better. I thought him, with his rustling papers, quite the equal of those who chattered during the music.

A screwed-up ball of paper fell to the floor. I gave an exasperated glance sideways at it. As I looked up, I caught his eye.

He smiled.

I would wish for other, better words to describe what happened. But I can say only that, he smiled. Yet what a transformation! A dark window opening. It was a smile of such generosity, such light. I knew the light came from within.

The ball of paper rested where it was. He went back to scrutinizing the papers he held. I glimpsed shapes and designs, some sketched in colour. He took out a pencil now and added to one. Then, at last, he put all away. And listened to the music.

What to say of the rest of the evening? I waited only to see that smile again. And thankfully it was not long in coming. Amélie received it.

He received a scolding.

'You do this every time!' she cried, wagging her finger. 'Late, again!' She said to me, and to Célestine:

'You know, the first thing I remember of Gérard – this bad cousin of mine – is when I am seven. He is seventeen, and he is drawing something, one of his designs, on the tablecloth. Can you believe it? On the *tablecloth* . . . My mother and his mother had something to say, I can tell you . . .'

We stayed together in a small group for most of the evening. There was a supper. We sat at small tables. I sat with Amélie, Célestine and Gilbert, two others – and Gérard.

Someone asked him, 'How long is your visit this time?'

Amélie answered for him. He appeared to be far away as he ate his food. The beginnings of, or the memory of, a scowl, while he thought . . .

'Two weeks only,' she said. 'He has a commission – I don't know what it's about. But of course it is *furniture* . . .'

'Yes, yes,' he said, looking up, 'of course it is furniture. But that work is all finished. I have something new now. Some more ideas. But above your head, Ma'm'selle Amélie –'

'Such as, such as?' But she was not really interested. 'Silly old furniture!'

He turned suddenly to me. 'Now surely with your English name – Armesterong – you are not yet another of the great Saint Lambert family?' And when I shook my head: 'Then tell me instead which family you are from. And all about them. You see these two ears?' and he lifted his two hands, fingers to them, 'They are already turned out a little, ready to hear. God has done that for me. So please –'

But I had great difficulty in answering. I, so seldom shy, stammered, stuttered, and forgot my French.

He threw his hands up in mock dismay. And then once again – the smile. I wondered that all the others at our table were not dazzled by its radiance . . .

'So I am not going to learn anything about you? And just now you were telling Célestine a tale so prettily . . .'

But at that moment Amélie, who sat the other side of him, tweaked the sleeve of his jacket. He turned slowly towards her.

She spoke to him. He was hers. I wanted to speak. I wanted to be the one spoken to.

For Amélie was not appreciative of him. Running off soon, to be with others. 'Oh look, there is Yves Cammaerts! I desert you at once, Gérard. Yves is too charming, and droll . . .'

Knowing him from childhood, she could take him for granted. I tried, and failed – to imagine such a thing.

I passed the next hour in a dream. Head, heart, both throbbed – with excitement, with happiness.

Of course after a while, he spoke to me again. We formed a merry group. Laughing, teasing – I was happy that evening. I thought if I might have stayed there for ever, I would never be unhappy again.

I irritated Madame next day. My smile of sheer happiness was intolerable to her. She had a headache, and servant trouble. It was a time of petty annoyances for her. They floated over my head. As did her behaviour.

Of course it could not last. I came down to earth – and the realization that I loved a man who was not free and who had noticed me only out of politeness. Yet the happiness did not desert me. Some, a little, stayed with me. For was it not wonderful, after all the horrors, the nightmares of the last years, the hates and the despairs – was it not wonderful just to love?

The arrival of Claude drew nearer. And as it did so, Madame's impatience with Hortense increased. One Sunday, they flung words at each other. Every aspect of the children's upbringing was criticized. In turn, Hortense blamed her mother for the way *she* had been brought up. ('As if you ever cared . . . the day I cut my ankle to the bone, and you never noticed, so busy with some stupid digestive upset of Claude's.') Jacques sat quietly keeping his counsel. The children stared, and then began to bicker amongst themselves.

Claude arrived. He was cold, that was my first thought. In manner, in appearance. Of course, he was in himself chilled. He was miserable with Brussels in January, which was not at all like Algeria. He had become used to Algeria.

He was thin and cold, with a smile that came infrequently. When it did, his mouth would stay shut, and his eyes would change hardly at all. His nose gave the impression that it had a bad smell beneath it.

No, I did not like him.

I think he realized it. I could see that I both irritated and interested him. In reality I wished to do neither. I would wish him not to have noticed me at all. But that was impossible given the arrangements of the household. I was forced more often than I wished into his company. He was there at all meals. Between times he would disappear either out, or into his bedroom. Sometimes he went out late at night. Sleepless perhaps, I would hear him return, creeping along the corridor.

Madame was tormented. She had him and yet she had not. He paid her very little attention, scarcely listening when she recited what the chaplain's wife had said, and what she had replied . . .

'Perhaps we can make little plans for the summer?' she said hopefully one dinner time. 'When you are settled –'

He cut in, fork speared into bleeding steak.

'As the poet, as Horace said, "*Vitae summa brevis spem nos vetat entrare longam –*"'

'And what does that mean?' she asked. 'He is so learned,' she said to me in an aside. And then to him: 'I wish you would not talk in riddles!'

'Translated – "The short span of life forbids us to entertain far-reaching hopes . . ."' he said.

I said to him: 'But ought it not be *incohare*? *Incohare longam*, not *entrare longam*?'

I should not have spoken. He stared at me icily. The more so because I was right and he knew it. (Those months, those years with Francis – they were not for nothing. How many aphorisms could I not rattle off? And all of them correct . . .)

That we did not like each other should have been obvious. So that I was surprised at what happened. Yet should I not have guessed that Madame's disappointment at his visit would need some outlet? Already Hortense had mocked her. The Sunday before, she had said,

'Perhaps Claude is planning to settle down at last. It is not before time. He needs a home of his own, a hearth of his own. Look how good he is with the children.' (He was not. He was as cold with them as with everyone else.)

And then one afternoon, suddenly, on our way back from visiting the chaplain's wife and other friends, Madame turned to me. She had been mulling something over. Preoccupied. Several times she had muttered to herself. Now she broke out:

'I know what you are up to!'

I was amazed. 'Up to? I have no idea what you mean.'

'Your cap set. That is what we used to call it, that was the phrase we used. You *have set your cap at my Claude –*'

'But . . . What *nonsense*! Madame –'

'You plan to have him for your own, you plan to marry him, and take him from his mother. Is that not the truth?'

'It is *not*. Oh, how it is not!' I cried indignantly.

'The more you protest . . . It only proves that you are determined. And he is so innocent. *He* will not notice . . . The girls were always after him. I have told you that.'

I became silent then, through stupefaction. But her distress and anger mounted. She worked herself into a fine passion and as we turned the corner into the Place du Grand Sablon, she said (she who had once pleaded, clung to me, imploring me to stay):

'Go, get out! The moment we return I wish you to pack your trunk.' She seemed to be urging the carriage to move faster. I thought she would put me out on the street. 'Yes, go! Go to your fine friends. Let them find someone for you. But go, *go*!'

By evening I was in the Hôtel Cluysenaar with the Saint Lamberts. I did not feel upset. I had stayed with Madame only from a foolish, I now thought, sense of obligation. In response to her absurd pleas. I had stayed out of pity. Now I had been set free.

Here I was back in the room where I had been so happy, where once I had woken from a fever and thought myself in paradise.

And too, here with this family, I could, when I allowed myself, think of Gérard. Think myself somehow nearer him. My feelings now – they were still not unhappy. I had so wanted to love, had wanted without realizing it to hunger after someone, as once long ago I had hungered after Francis.

The rest of the winter passed delightfully. I scarcely thought of Madame at all. Once I met Hortense with the children walking in the Galeries Saint Hubert, and another time saw Madame getting out of her carriage. She did not see me.

I asked for news of Amélie. Célestine said, 'We have not seen her now since Christmas. She marries her cousin, you know, in June. But you met him? Gérard de Pret Rogier.'

You met him, met him, met him . . . It was enough just to hear his name again. To speak it myself. *Gérard de Pret Rogier.*

Now I had begun to help Louise with her work for the old. Three days a week that spring, I was down in the Marolles. I saw the good she did – and how I might be of service. I felt as quietly contented those days as I had ever felt. Without thinking too much about it, I did not see why life should not go on exactly as it did.

And so it might have gone along, if I had not had a letter from Aunt Martha, about Halliwell.

Wounded in a skirmish on the North Western Frontier. Aunt Martha enclosed the letter from his colonel. The wound was to the left temple, and shoulder. A blow, catching him just below his helmet had opened the temple, then glanced down onto the shoulder. The severed nerves from that wound had been sewn up, but were causing him much pain and weakness of his arm. He had also a cut across his back, and altogether had lost a lot of blood. Up and about now, he must be invalided home. Everyone hoped his absence would be only temporary, but recovery must be total if he was to return to his regiment . . .

I knew then what I must do. What I wished to do. He would be sailing in a week's time. I must arrange, soon, to go back to England. I would meet him, take him away – and look after him until he was fit again. And back in the army.

I had found a use for Francis's money.

'I must return to England,' I told Louise. 'My brother has been badly wounded and needs me.'

My departure would not be for a few weeks. According to the letter, Halliwell's boat would be leaving about now. I planned to meet it, and then to take him to Yorkshire for a while, after which we would make plans. In the autumn and through the winter, we would travel to a warmer climate. I had thought of it all. How I would save Halliwell, and make him better, and a soldier again – with Francis's money. My money.

I had already sent for some a month or two earlier. Although Louise would accept nothing for my keep – I was an honoured guest, a friend, a support and I do not know what else – she would accept money for her charity. So I was able to give alms as well as time. Louise valued both.

During those last few weeks, I decided also to be frivolous. I gave way to Louise's entreaties – she who was always so beautifully dressed – and allowed her dressmaker to make me some outfits. For when travelling about with Halliwell I should need to appear, if not too fashionable, at least not unfashionable.

Brussels had never looked lovelier to me than in those last days. As I smelled the lilac, just out, scented after rain, I forgot that I had been so miserable, so despairing in the humid airless days of last August. Before I met Louise. *Before I met Gérard.*

And now, I must leave it all.

Two nights before my departure, I went with Louise, Célestine,

Gilbert and others to a soirée. It was a little way out of Brussels. A house I had never visited before, not far from the Château Koekleberg, where Polly had gone to school. The invitation was through Célestine's family.

The house was in its own grounds. It was a warm evening, and doors opened into a large garden, patterned into alleys, a lawn, a copse or two. Indoors, everything sparkled. Great chandeliers swung. Statuary, both inside and out, for the owner was a great collector. Enormous works of art lined the walls. Scenes from the Bible and from mythology – Greek gods imploring mercy, bearded patriarchs in deep conversation. I had heard of none of the artists but was assured by a fellow guest that every work was 'the finest art in Brussels today'.

A soprano with a bell-like voice sang to us Mozart arias. There was music for dancing. Some waltzes, galops, polkas . . .

It was then I saw them. Late arrivals. Amélie, Gérard. And Amélie's family.

I wished suddenly so much, I wished to be beautiful – as my dress that evening was beautiful. I wished to be able to walk up to him boldly (some of the bold Caroline Armstrong was in me surely?). But I could not. I would have to wait until I was noticed.

It happened before very long. I cannot remember if it was Amélie waving to Célestine, who stood near me – or what? But suddenly both of them were there.

I stared. When Gérard was, accidentally, re-introduced, I was struck dumb again.

'It is all too much,' Amélie was saying on one side of me. 'If anyone speaks to me again of brides, and weddings . . . I suppose it must be lived through, I suppose it must.' As she spoke her black eyes darted about the high-ceilinged room.

'And when is the day?' asked Célestine. 'I know we are to be there. But I forget –'

'I cannot. Three weeks only – *if* he is on time, if he remembers to attend and to dress properly, and does not draw designs all over my bridal dress.' And once again, giving Gérard her attention momentarily, she wagged her finger at him.

He said easily, 'Oh I shall do as I am told.' But he too spoke absent-mindedly. His face wore its original scowl, the scowl I remembered. I waited for the smile. For the sun to come out.

And then he noticed me.

'Mademoiselle Armesterong – are we not going to hear the

French you forgot and then remembered so well, last time we met? Remind me what we spoke of?'

I did not talk of myself. I told no lies, then. Afterwards I was to think that perhaps, if I had said more, everything might have been different. Who knows?

Instead I spoke about furniture. The furniture in that house. 'Terrible,' Gérard said, 'that style. It is known as "the style of all the Louis". He is such a collector, our host. But I fear it is collecting for collecting's sake . . .'

Amélie joined in with her opinion, as did two friends of Gilbert. And then in no time, it was supper . . .

It was a fine warm night. The moon came from behind clouds and then remained, clear and unwavering over the whole garden.

Several of us were walking in the alley. On either side grew fruit trees – apple, pear. Large, twisted trees. The pears still heavy with blossom. The moon threw a haze over it all. Silvered the tree trunks. We walked. Perhaps four or five of us.

I wandered off. I walked away from the alley, over a small lawn, already glistening with dew. There was a small garden beyond that, with exotic and weirdly shaped plants, fleshy leaved, sinister in the moonlight. At one side was a small open arcade. And inside it I saw – but I had to approach nearer, to make it out . . .

Both the walls and ceiling, covered. Stars, crosses, circles, half-moons – all formed by sparrows. Thousands of tiny bodies, their corpses nailed up. Desiccated, fragile.

A hand touched my elbow. A voice said:

'Come away. I don't think you like it. You cannot like it.'

I turned to see Gérard.

'This place is not for you. You agree, Mademoiselle, that it is quite horrible . . .'

He walked me away from it at once. He said:

'You see the mania of the collector. Our host is not very discriminating. Now statues, now battle scenes – and here, innocent birds. He is up, you see, every morning early – the nets are set all along this gravel walk. He sits there, string in hand . . . A collection like that, it's the result of many mornings' work. And quite frightful.'

As we walked along, he said, 'He asked me once – he wished to commission me for some great side piece. I refused. I don't wish my work to be in that house. It would be as if a part of me would live there . . .'

370

As we strolled, we had moved away from the poor little birds – so eerie in the moonlight. Voices reached us now, carried over from the other end of the gravel walk. Two couples, laughing and talking, could be glimpsed.

We came to a small lawn, with a coppice just beyond – dense with lilac bushes and acacia. Gérard stopped at a stone bench on the edge of the lawn. 'Please. Let us sit.'

The skirts of my dress, my slippers tipped with dew from the grass. I was in a strange state. The person most in my thoughts, suddenly here in the flesh. Appearing before my eyes – as if I had called and he had answered. For I had never ceased to think of him as I danced, as I ate, drank, listened to music.

Of what did we speak that evening? I have tried to remember, thinking that surely every word, every exchange must be etched in memory. I think I must have spoken of life in England, of my childhood – I remember questions carefully asked, and that I spoke of Luddenden and was it the Irish? And then school and exile.

It was not like talking to Frederick Liddington, to whom I had told *all*, at whose request I had gone back to everything shameful. Reciting it all – that he might the better understand my feelings about Francis.

Now I spoke, from the heart, only of how it had been when Mama was beautiful but unhappy, when I had been Papa's darling, of when Josh had been *my* darling.

How long were we there? Fifteen minutes, half an hour? I have no idea. No one disturbed us. A threesome strolled past, admired the view and turned back. Once, I remember, I said,

'And Amélie? Where is Amélie?'

'Ah, Amélie! Anywhere, everywhere. You can tell from her eyes. They dart everywhere, and she too. Now you see her, now you don't . . . We have known each other so long – really it does not matter. It is not important.'

I think we spoke a little then of arranged marriages – my mother, I said. Two mill-owning families.

'It is life,' he said, in a curiously resigned voice. 'The way of the world.'

And the scowl? He wore that still – I realized then that it meant only concentration. That he wore it when in his mind he thought just how he might give shape to his designs. And he wore it when listening – if he was *particularly attentive to that person.*

Conversation on art topics . . . Our two voices blending, murmuring. We stood up and by common consent, without discussion, walked on, not turning back to the house. Strolling instead towards the copse. Yes, there were the lilacs, differently scented at night, a little bitter perhaps. The acacia, some tall bushes.

Pressure of his arm on mine. Ungloved hand on my wrist. And then he was pulling me towards him. So suddenly, that I could not have (would I ever have?) refused.

When I felt his lips on mine, I began to tremble. But still I did not move or resist. And after a little I knew it was not fear, this trembling, but happiness. And I grew thirsty. I thought my thirst would never be slaked. Oh, what a thirst. What longing. What love.

It ended. And then I stood, my head lying on his shoulder – for he was not so very much taller than me.

He said, 'And I am to be married in three weeks –'

But at that moment, I broke away. Seeing coming round the corner, already in sight – Célestine, Gilbert, and six seven eight others.

Already they were calling out to us.

What possessed me then? Frightened as I was by my happiness, my freedom, my *lack of fear* (I had wanted only more and more. I knew that I need never have stopped).

'And I too,' I cried, 'I am to be married next month, in England. I was shy to speak of it. The others do not know. But it is what I return for.'

17

Everywhere we went that summer Halliwell attracted sympathy. The scar on his temple from his head wound gave a sort of glamour to his dark good looks. When I had first seen him I had been shocked. The pallor, from loss of blood surely, the drawn face – result of much pain. He had not written himself. There had been only a short dictated note which had arrived a week before him.

He was my brother. Aunt Martha apart, he was all the family I had. I did not really count Agnes now, although Halliwell saw her during the few days that we stayed with Aunt Martha. She came over. It was an awkward meeting – she and I never referring to Scarborough. She talked only of Brussels, in a polite fashion, filling in any gaps with praise of her children, their sayings, the little prayer that Edwin had made up, the cleverness of them all, the fullness of her life . . .

Although it was July, Yorkshire and especially Halifax was not the best place for Halliwell. There were cold days which would have passed for autumn. He needed warmth. While there, he showed no interest in visiting Luddenden. But he went to York to see his regiment. He tortured himself with his exile:

'Tell me I'll get back again,' he said. 'Tell me Christabel.'

And every day I told him. Sometimes twice or more a day.

So many places, we went to. We were at Malvern a month, to see what hydropathy could do. We took lodgings in Torquay. Sea air. I counted all money well spent. We made friends wherever we went. Pale, handsome Captain Woodward.

What did we talk about all those long months? Certainly about the army, and soldiering, and how if he could not go back, he did not wish to live. And we spoke of George, who had not had the choice. Who had died.

'I reckoned it meant a lot to him, your letters. I'd the notion, from something he said, that when we came back, he meant to ask you to marry him. I think he'd his majority in his sights, and would have liked to take you wherever we went. A threesome, that's how he saw it. He said once, of someone else, who wed his dearest friend's sister, "They make one big family." He'd no family . . .'

Poor George.

'And right then – what would you have answered him, Christabel? Would you have had him?'

'Who knows?' I said. 'Who knows?'

'But you mean to wed, some time? You never speak of anyone –'

'I'm not sure I'm one who'll marry. Some do, some don't.'

'You must. It can't be all Agnes and that terrible Septimus.'

I did not ask him about himself. For all that his looks attracted and his wounds drew sympathy, he was awkward with women. Not even perhaps very interested, as yet. He said once or twice that one day, perhaps, 'When I've been around a little more – fought in a few wars. The returning, conquering hero, eh?'

When the cold weather came we went to the South of France. And from there to Egypt in the New Year. We rubbed along well enough together. There were army people staying at our Cairo hotel. He gravitated always towards them. A major and his wife, another time an elderly general.

Sightseeing tired him. He had not yet the strength for it. And the pain of his shoulder made concentration impossible. But to me, it was all novelty and excitement. I wrote several times a week to Polly, giving her long accounts. Most especially from Egypt. She wrote to me, notes scribbled hastily amidst the ever-growing multiplicity of her duties. William had become more and more burdened. Their family, growing still. Another small daughter in the autumn. She told me too, that Frederick Liddington had written to her, asking for news of me. And that she had obliged him with a full account.

'I know, dearest, that you do not want to be reminded of such a dreadful time in your life, but all the same you should know that he is very concerned as to what has become of you.'

It was not until around Easter that we returned to England. To London this time.

Halliwell was not making the progress we had hoped. The rest and the warmth, the passage of time – they had not been enough. Now, once again, it was Polly to the rescue. In London, she arranged for him to be seen by a surgeon whom Edmund recommended. (The price to pay was an evening spent at Edmund's home. He had changed little. I remembered him as elderly when young. Now only in his early thirties, he seemed more like fifty.)

We stayed at an hotel first, without making plans. But after we had seen the surgeon, we learned that he recommended galvanism as Halliwell's best hope of recovering full use of his arm. I trusted this man. He made no promises but inspired confidence and hope. Which we needed.

I thanked God yet again, and Francis, for the money. I took a small house in Chelsea. I wanted to be near the river, and also not to be too urban – Chelsea felt still somewhat of a village.

The Thames was an endless source of enchantment to me. The weather when we first arrived was one of cold sunlight, and strong winds, ruffling the surface of the water. There was a window at which I could sit and watch the tugs go up the river, and when it was flood tide, see the barges, weighed down with coal, come in to moor. And other sights. Eel pots being set . . .

Creeper grew up the face of the house. In it, sooty sparrows hopped and twittered. Reminding me suddenly of the crucified little birds that last evening in Brussels. Oh, Gérard, where are you now?

Spring had come. Near the house, there were elm trees in pink bud. Seagulls screamed those first sunny days, swooped down on the river. A low brick wall ran along beside the Thames, with greasy worn steps down to the ferry stage. From my bedroom I could see the old wooden Battersea Bridge rise out of the morning mist.

To occupy myself, I began now to paint what I saw. Also what I did not see. I tried to paint Gérard. I knew that I should not, and was punished by my complete failure. It was the struggle to capture Josh all over again.

I tried too to write about him. But that was worse. At the same time, it gave me the idea that although my own art was nothing, I might nevertheless write about the work of others. And that I might find that a welcome discipline.

My paintings were all in watercolour. The Thames in all its moods. Old Battersea Bridge, gaslit. The contrasting views from my window, morning and evening. Halliwell admired all of them. And insisted that they be laid out on tables for anyone visiting to look at.

Not long after those first real spring days, one afternoon in April, Frederick Liddington came back into my life.

'I have often worried about you . . .'

That shambling, clumsy, concerned figure from my past. The past I so much wished buried.

How often had I wished *not* to think of him, because of the memories, terrible memories, that even his name brought back. I could see our first interview, catch again that prison smell, I could see the courtroom, feel the close packed atmosphere (those vain endeavours with a hook to open the windows). And Janet Hope. Janet Hope. It was almost as if I could not separate the two.

He was not as large as I remembered. Or perhaps I was not quite so small? I felt I had grown at least a little in other ways. Experienced with it a true increase in stature. I was a different person surely from the frightened young woman of three years ago. I had after all lived through my time in Brussels. I had met in friendship the Saint Lamberts. I had mixed with their friends. Wide social contacts, albeit continental. Above all, I had known – still knew – what it was to fall in love and *not be afraid*. That it should have been someone who was not free – was that not the chance of life? The ache I had taken to the South of France, to Egypt, and now experienced back in London – it would not last for ever. It must not last for ever. And in the meantime, was I not used to loneliness?

Frederick was sensitive to how I felt. I should have known that. His first remark, as he took my hand in his (last time it had been both hands in his. Relief, congratulations, gratitude: 'I hope we shall meet again').

'I thought very hard before making this call. It is Polly of course who has given me news of you. I would not wish – it was a very terrible time. You would not wish to live it again – through me.'

'Oh,' I exclaimed, 'through you, indeed. If it had not been for you . . .'

Standing there in the small drawing-room, with the sash window half-open, letting in the cries and shouts from the coal barges, I tried to express my gratitude.

He shook his head. 'Please. That was well enough said at the time. You did so exactly as I asked. Were so frank and open . . . I am going to tell you again what to do. Am going to ask you to be as co-operative as *then*. I would like us henceforth to speak only of the present – and those parts of the immediate past you would wish to tell me of. Will you, can you do that?'

I smiled. How could I not? 'Yes, Mr Liddington.'

'Once it was Christabel – I know I speak wrongly, I am already in the wrong because I speak of the past. But I should like it if it might be Christabel again. With your permission. And I am Frederick . . .'

We sat together, and it was all right. I harked back to the Scarborough days only to think: He seemed, he *was* a friend then. He is and will be a friend now.

Almost at once, he remarked on my watercolours. I forced him to agree with me that although they might be good, they were not good enough. I told him that I had thought of doing as well, art criticism.

We spoke of Brussels. He had spent time there, although he knew Antwerp better. I told him how it had been with Madame Martin. Of her family. Of Claude. Of how I had met the Saint Lamberts. I was not ashamed or shy to tell him of my collapse. Of the illness. I was not ashamed of that, or of going to confession. Did he not know *all* about Francis and me?

'It was not surprising,' he said, 'such a collapse. Nature works as she will. In her own time. But I expect too, you saw the hand of God in this good person. This family. That Madame Saint Lambert should have been there.'

The time came for him to go.

'. . . And so if I can help with your brother . . . The medical attention he is receiving, I do assure you, that man is the best. But if I can help in other ways?'

How long had we been talking? I had not noticed the time. Now I heard the chimes of midday.

And there was a cab at the door, and Halliwell getting out. Back from his treatment.

'May I introduce my brother, Halliwell. Captain Woodward . . . Halliwell, Mr Liddington. Frederick Liddington.'

Halliwell had electrical treatment several times a week. At first there was little sign of improvement. The pain from the severed nerves was still intense. He grew discouraged. It would be difficult to find ways of occupying him, once the novelty of living in London had worn off.

Frederick was true to his word. He found occupation for him. He himself had more than a passing interest in military history. His library – on that and other subjects – was extensive. Halliwell, never one for reading, became enthused and would talk to Frederick by the hour. Planning, reconstructing, mapping, arguing, discussing. He even spoke of perhaps one day becoming himself a military historian. 'When I'm a sixty-year-old crusty general. Covered in campaign medals.'

377

He was optimistic once more. Gone the days of despair that a soldier's life was no longer for him, that it was all over.

And he was right. For it seemed by the early summer that the nerves were at last beginning to heal. The pain was so much less, the use of his arm so much better. Passage of time, or galvanism – what matter? He spoke of rejoining his regiment perhaps by the end of the summer. He chaffed to be with them, now that they were back from India.

Halliwell was not the only one Frederick helped. Those first remarks about my paintings. He followed that up.

'I am not good,' I told him again. 'You see, it is amateur. A little better than the usual young lady's accomplishment. But only a little. Here and there – a view, a memory. It has meaning, for me. There is a little inspiration. But you know there is no fire.'

'Where is the fire?'

'Oh, it is there,' I said, cagily. Not wishing to say more. Oh Gérard, if I could have painted you! So clear in the mind's eye. True in the mind's ear. (And touch, what of touch? That might have been yesterday. I burn, I am thirsty in memory.)

'I assure you it is there. But it is not needed, I am not required to call on it just now . . .'

And as soon, tactfully, he was on to practical matters.

'An introduction to Mr Ruskin? That would be an easy matter . . . And in the meanwhile, there is a Mr Oswald Green. Mr Green is the brother of a great friend who was in chambers with me. He begins a journal next month, which will be purely of the arts. He . . .'

Yes, Frederick was very much part of our lives that summer of 1869.

I continued to paint. I had great satisfaction from it. The views from my window. The changing lights. The elm trees, now unfurled. The clouds above the river. The water in sunshine, by moonlight.

I never tried now to paint Gérard. I buried my poor efforts, together with the words I had written about him. I saw myself as someone lame, a little crippled, who has learned to live with their disability – and all its losses. As Halliwell might have had to, but now certainly would not.

As good as the painting, and richer in social contacts, was the art criticism at which I had tried my hand. And succeeded, a little. I had submitted here and there some small unsolicited pieces. Essays really. Two had been accepted. But more importantly, through Frederick, I began to write regularly for the new small journal of which he had spoken. I was not trusted with the larger exhibitions, but I went often to smaller galleries and halls.

I had not kept up with Louise and her family as I should have done. I meant to give poste restante addresses whilst abroad, but had not done so. All those fine promises. I had fully intended that I should return to see them. But part of the effort, the resolution to forget Gérard, was surely also to forget the Saint Lamberts?

And all the time, I saw much of Frederick. The day Halliwell returned with his good news, he was at the house.

Halliwell was to rejoin his regiment in three weeks' time. Once again to be resplendent in his blue cloth spiked helmet, with its gilt and its silver plate. The soldier again. He had begun to speak already of his majority.

Frederick that day also spoke of something. He spoke of marriage.

Surely I should have guessed? As I listened to him now, it seemed at once, right, probable – and not perhaps too frightening. And yet . . .

He told me that he found me beautiful. (I, Christabel Woodward, *beautiful* . . .) He had wanted from the first meeting to take care of me. To be with me. His life – so rich in work and excitement, yet lacking in that one thing. So far – no one. I was that someone.

And of how I would bring lustre, warmth to his life. A home, and children.

'I should have asked earlier. I had wished to. I almost did. And then it seemed – to wait until Halliwell was safely a soldier again, which I never doubted. I had faith always.'

'Which you gave to me. Just as . . .'

'Just as –'

What reason was there to refuse? What reason ever? Not fear. I did not feel afraid. But rather safe. And yet there lingered. As once I had thought: Marriage is not for me, and I am not for marriage.

No, I could not simply say, Yes.

'If you should wish to think it over? Of course you must think it over.'

Time. I must have a little time. A fortnight. Was that too long

379

for him? No. He would wait. And besides, for at least a week if not more, he was engaged on a case which would take him out of London.

His hand on mine. My hands in his. 'And then you will tell me?'

'I will tell you . . .'

Halliwell's last week was one of September heat. Only in the mornings, did I catch a sudden smell of autumn. The day before he was to leave – and the day before I must give my answer to Frederick, I was asked to review a craft exhibition. The hall in which it was held was not far from the house. So near that I did not take a cab.

Once in the hall, I walked about with my notebook. I stopped at a cast-iron umbrella stand, decorated with pheasants. It was strangely graceful, yet so nearly ugly, that I thought I would write of it. Then after reading the card to see whose work it was, I moved on to some scent bottles and decanters of cased glass.

At the far end of the hall was an enormous sideboard of ebonized wood. The fittings were silverplate, and it had panels covered with Japanese embossed leather paper. I thought that it was a little preposterous, yet exciting. I liked it. I looked at the card beside it.

Gérard de Pret Rogier.

Ah, dear God. And now what? I stared harder at the card, to see if there was any address, or any information at all. But it told me only that the sideboard had been commissioned by a Mr E. Watts Thompson.

A voice behind me said, 'You know that de Pret Rogier is over for the exhibition? It seemed to me you might have some comment. He likes to hear what people think.'

The voice belonged to the organizer of the exhibition. I stammered out some foolish question.

No, he told me, Mr Rogier was not expected in today. Tomorrow perhaps? Yes, of course, it was known where he was staying. At Brown's Hotel. Meanwhile, if I cared to leave a letter here?

But I could not wait. I scribbled a few lines and sent them round to Brown's. I asked if Amélie was with him, and if I could entertain them at my house.

He came that evening. Alone. Halliwell had gone early to bed. The servant was just about to lock up.

He was hardly through the door, before I saw him glance at my hand.

'I am not married,' I said. My heart beat wildly. I felt sick.

He stood still, half-way across the room: 'Miss Armesterong? No – what is this *Woodward* then?'

The scowl again. Beloved scowl.

I told him then. Not everything, but enough. Why I had played with my name.

'And you,' I said, for I was upset just with recounting the past. 'You have not brought your wife with you? No Amélie?'

'I am not married, either,' he said. And he smiled. *That smile.*

Oh, such a rush of happiness. My hand to my heart.

'But – *how*?'

'Amélie. Anywhere, everywhere . . . Three days before the wedding she ran off with a young man she had known only a month. I lost only my pride – of which I have too much. I thought it best to be from the scene a little. I went to the East. I have been in Japan up until this June . . .'

I was silent. My hand remained on my heart.

'That marriage,' he was saying. 'It was family, of course, the arrangement. Such matters . . . So foolishly, so easily accepted. But then afterwards – afterwards, I was *certain* I had lost you . . . I never thought. I never dared to hope. Someone so beautiful – of course you were to be married! Already *were* married –'

'Beautiful.' It did not seem strange to me, that word (although it had sounded strange when spoken by Frederick). But how I trembled now, shook with longing, for I knew it to be true.

I spoke hurriedly, 'If you had only made enquiries! If you had only bent those ears out a little further –'

'Now you are angry! Are you angry? I should wish you to be. That I did not come at once in search of you –'

Still we remained there, not touching. Not even a handshake of greeting. And yet it was as if already we were one.

'You see, you see!' he said. He spoke so urgently. 'You thought you could live without me? You really thought that?'

Such arrogance. Yes, yes, I had learned to. I had even been at peace. But I would not tell him so.

'*You really thought that?*'

This was not peace now. Quite different this. This was happiness.

'And you,' I cried, 'and you? What of *you*? How could –'

But we were in each other's arms.

*

I would not want to write of the rest of that evening. Of the kissing. Of the joy. Of the plans for the future.

And the regrets about Frederick. Frederick, who now had lost me. I thought sadly of Frederick, and his friendship. His goodness. I prayed that soon it would be someone else – someone worthier perhaps – who would know that loyalty, that warmth.

And I? I had everything. I married Gérard. The wedding was at Christmas, in Brussels.

But before that we paid a visit to Yorkshire.

We went to Haworth. I showed him to Betty and Mercy. Then we walked through the village. To the Parsonage first. Then to the church. No ghosts, that joyful day. (And with Gérard by my side, of whom would I be afraid?) In the church, we prayed for my father.

We visited Aunt Martha. And yes, we walked about the streets, unrecognized. He was not horrified because it was dirty and smoky and malodorous . . . It was part of my childhood, part of me.

As we came down Kirkgate, the bells of St John Baptist were pealing. Such a peal of bells calling out on the autumn air. That day I did not stop up my ears.

'*Daughter of the northern fields, daughter of the northern fields,*' they sang. Over and over. And I was happy.

I told him my secret. I told him of Branwell and Caroline, my mother. As I am telling *you*, my dearest son – for whom I write this story. Once, my mother left me her story. A story I read only after her death. I now write this for you, my son. My secret is yours – to keep or to divulge.

Yes, I married Gérard. We have had a son. I write this today in happiness and sunlight, in sunlight and happiness. To live happily ever after, it is possible. It may yet be. It shall be.